The Black Spaniel: Lut friends, and assumes they Deeming is a successful L man interested in the arts. But for some reason, Vernon, an animal lover, takes an immediate dislike to the pragmatically cruel Deeming. When Vernon discovers that Deeming owns a black spaniel, the dog becomes a focal point in the enmity between the two men.

The Hindu: John Latimer is a practical man. But when he suspects his wife with having an affair with a Hindu gentleman—now deceased—he agrees to a séance. He calls the Hindu to him to exact revenge. But his plan has an unfortunate result, for now the spirit of the Hindu follows him everywhere, its evil casting a pall over his life.

Sea Change: The Reverend Uniacke welcomes painter Sir Graham into his island home. The older man is not well. He is being consumed by melancholy at having caused his young London model to run away. The painter had filled the city boy's head full of the sea in order to create his art, and in the end, the romance of the sea had consumed him. But the lad's fate is known all too well to the reverend…

Enter the mysterious realm of Robert Hichens. These stories and four more tales of unease await you…

The Black Spaniel
& Other
Strange Stories

....

ROBERT HICHENS

Introduction by S.T. Joshi

STARK
HOUSE

Stark House Press • Eureka California

THE BLACK SPANIEL AND OTHER STRANGE STORIES

Published by Stark House Press
1315 H Street
Eureka, CA 95501, USA
griffinskye3@sbcglobal.net
www.starkhousepress.com

"The Black Spaniel" from *The Black Spaniel and Other Stories* (originally
published by Methuen & Company, London, 1905, and Frederick A.
Stokes, New York, 1905; copyright © 1905 by Robert Hichens).

"The Face of the Monk" and "The Silent Guardian" from *Bye-Ways*
(originally published and copyright © 1897 by D. Appleton, New York).

"The Hindu" and "The Lighted Candles" from *Snake-Bite and Other
Stories* (originally published and copyright © 1919 by Cassell and
Company, London).

"Sea Change" from *Tongues of Conscience* (originally published and
copyright © 1900 by Methuen & Company, London, and Frederick A.
Stokes, New York).

"Demetriadi's Dream" from *The Afterglow and Other Stories* (originally
published and copyright © 1935 by Cassell and Company, London). First
published in *Pall Mall Magazine* #438, November 1929).

"Introduction" copyright 2023 © by S. T. Joshi

ISBN: 979-8-88601-056-5

Book design by Mark Shepard, shepgraphics.com
Proofreading by Bill Kelly
Cover art by C. B. Williams

First Stark House Press Edition: November 2023

Contents

Introduction
by S.T. Joshi

A number of authors, chiefly known for their mainstream fiction, have found the weird or supernatural so compelling that they continually return to it over the course of their careers, even if it is only in isolated stories or novels. English writer Robert Hichens (1863–1950) is unquestionably one of these. He published twelve short story collections over the course of his long life, and almost every one of them contains at least one story that we can consider weird. It is true that the bulk of his weird work was written early in his career, but even his later work is tinged with horror. In this volume, we find tales dating to as early as 1897 to as late as 1929.

Hichens was a master of the novella—a form that a number of weird writers, ranging from J. Sheridan Le Fanu to H. P. Lovecraft to Ramsey Campbell to T. E. D. Klein, have found particularly felicitous for the expression of weird ideas. The novella allows for detailed character development not possible in a short story; it also facilitates the slow accumulation of horrific details that creates a grimly powerful climax at the conclusion of the tale.

No better example of the efficacy of the novella for the exposition of terror can be found than in "Sea Change," in *Tongues of Conscience* (1900), a volume that is perhaps Hichens's most concentrated gathering of weird tales. This brooding account of an elderly cleric, Peter Uniacke, on a remote island "set lonely in a harsh and dangerous northern sea," and his acquaintance with the young painter Sir Graham Hamilton, underscores the "conscience" of both characters as they become enmeshed in spite of themselves in horror and tragedy. Hamilton is a renowned painter of sea life; he seizes upon a working-class boy, Jack Pringle, and infuses in him a passionate love of the sea so that he can paint the ecstatic expression on the boy's face as he contemplates the ocean. But this selfish and self-aggrandizing act turns horrific when Uniacke learns that a grave of a teenage boy who was drowned after a shipwreck is that of Jack Pringle. Is it appropriate for a cleric (of all people) to deceive Hamilton so that he does not realize that his actions have unwittingly led to the boy's death? Uniacke's wrestling with his conscience would be terrifying enough; but Hichens adds a further turn of the screw when the story veers into the supernatural at the end. It is evident that Hichens required the space of a novella to convey the complex swirl of emotions that course through all the characters, leading to an ending that is both appalling and tragically inevitable.

"The Black Spaniel" (in the 1905 collection of that title) is another expansive novella. Here a sharper conflict between characters is depicted, as Peter Deeming believes that animals should be "the servants of humanity, to minister to our comfort, our pleasure, our necessities," while Vernon Kersteven is even more ardent in his belief that animals and human beings should be "friends": "I love all animals," he bluntly declares. He goes on to indict the human race for cruelty to animals, going so far as to think that, if someone has exhibited such cruelty, "at death his soul passes into a similar animal, which endures the fate he once meted out when he was a man." This passage may telegraph the overall thrust of the narrative, but the story remains hypnotic in the working out of its inexorable plot. Can it really be that the soul of Deeming, who was found to have mistreated a black spaniel he owned as a pet, has entered the body of a new-born black spaniel—whom Kersteven then adopts and mistreats in his turn? It should be noted that at this period of Anglo-American history kindness to animals was still regarded as a somewhat eccentric human trait; a secondary character, the anti-vivisectionist Arthur Gernham, is portrayed as something of a wild-eyed fanatic. It is vital that the entire narrative be told from the point of view of another character, Luttrell, who is acquainted with both Deeming and Kersteven; and it is Luttrell who delivers a pungent, single-word verdict on the latter's revenge against the former.

"The Hindu" (in *Snake-Bite and Other Stories*, 1919) is a work that proposes the possibility of revenants, or those who return from the dead. John Latimer, a wealthy newspaper owner, feels that the affections of his wife have been alienated: she has fallen for an Indian, Nischya Varman, and has lost her love for her husband. What can be done—especially when Latimer learns that Varman has recently died? Is it really the Indian whom Latimer now sees at every turn, just out of sight? And isn't Latimer himself to blame for Varman's reappearance, since he consulted a medium and, when Varman's spirit was apparently summoned, demanded that Varman return in the flesh so that Latimer can punish him for seducing his wife? Once again, the gradualness with which Latimer, after apparently repeated glimpses of the Indian, descends into paranoia is handled with paramount skill. It should not be assumed that there is any racism in Hichens's depiction of the Indian; it may amuse us to note that in 1919, according to the story, there was apparently only a single Indian restaurant in the whole of London (named, appropriately enough, "the Indian Restaurant"); and it may be true that Varman is a kind of "other" whose exoticism and cultural differentiation from Anglo-Saxon values render him (in Latimer's eyes, at any rate) vaguely sinister; but Varman is not portrayed in a hostile manner. It is Latimer's physician who finds that the resolution of the matter is very different from what his patient believed.

Even the shorter tales in this volume are powerful in their own right. Two stories from *Bye-Ways* (1897), "A Silent Guardian" and "The Face of the Monk," are studies of domestic conflict with a supernatural twist. In the former, we see a recently married young sculptor, Reginald Brune, succumb to an illness after fashioning an exquisite sculpture of a male nude entitled "A Silent Guardian." When Brune's physician attempts to seduce Brune's widow, that statue appears to have something to say on the matter. The latter story is the narrative of a doppelgänger. A popular writer, Hubert Blair ("one of the cleverest young writers in London"), falling into depression, consults a clairvoyant who sees the face of a monk lurking behind him—"he is your spirit in some former state." The tale evolves into an account of fractured consciousness and the pangs of conscience.

"The Lighted Candles" (in *Snake-Bite*) seems to be another tale of a ghost or a revenant, but evolves into something more complex. Why did the Princess Andrakov—whose cruelty when she lived in Russia became notorious—die in an apartment in Rome? What does the Russian student—encountered by the narrator, who is staying in the princess's apartment—fear spending a night in the back bedroom where she died? Hichens weaves an intricate story of revenge and betrayal—and the various implausible naturalistic explanations for the phenomena in the tale are perhaps meant to emphasize that something supernatural has actually occurred.

"Demetriadi's Dream" is the latest tale in the book—it appeared in *Pall Mall Magazine* for November 1929 and was collected in *The Afterglow and Other Stories* (1935)—but it shows that Hichens's literary skills were undiminished. We are now in Switzerland, where Adrian Syke, a kind of amateur detective, meets an elderly Greek man, Demetriadi, who had a horrible dream of traversing a hotel and seeing something dreadful happening in every room: in one, "a married couple were having a desperate quarrel"; in another, "a child was dying in convulsions while its nurse, seated in an armchair, was smiling slyly over a love letter"; and so on. Is there some significance in the fact that Demetriadi looked into fourteen rooms—and the fact that he himself is staying in room 14 of the Swiss hotel? Sykes, who believes he has the "curious faculty of gathering secret information about certain people with whom I am brought into contact," thinks so—and Hichens so arranges the narrative that the supernatural climax is sprung on the reader in the final paragraph.

The world of Robert Hichens may perhaps be considered a masculine one. None of the stories in this volume features a significant female character; in some stories no women appear at all. It may also be said that Hichens feels most comfortable depicting upper-class (male) characters who have no problem gallivanting all around Europe, hiring cooks and butlers wherever they are staying, and so on. This was clearly the kind of world Hichens knew, and there is no reason why he should not write about it. But beyond or beneath this refined social milieu Hichens always sensed the presence of the weird; as a character states in "The Black Spaniel," "there is a spirit hidden in one which does sigh plaintively for the strange." In prose of impeccable refinement and elegance, Hichens generated tales that achieved the acme of terror and weirdness. But the weird was never used merely to send a shudder up one's spine; there was always a moral concern underlying it—the "tongues of conscience" that every civilized person must feel when faced with the grisly tragedies of human existence.

—June 2023

S. T. Joshi is a freelance writer and editor. He has prepared comprehensive editions of H. P. Lovecraft's collected fiction, essays, poetry, and letters, including an annotated edition of *The Case of Charles Dexter Ward* (2010). He is the author of *The Weird Tale* (1990), *The Modern Weird Tale* (2001), *I Am Providence: The Life and Times of H. P. Lovecraft* (2010), and *Unutterable Horror: A History of Supernatural Fiction* (2012), and has edited the anthology *American Supernatural Tales* (2007).

The Black Spaniel & Other Strange Stories

....

ROBERT HICHENS

The Black Spaniel

Part I—The Death

I

In the big hall of the Grand Hotel at Rome I introduced Peter Deeming to Vernon Kersteven.

The two men were friends of mine, and I wanted them to like each other; and, perhaps because they were both fond of me, I thought that they would get on well together, and that we should form a happy and a lively trio at dinner. Was this the fancy of an egoist? I have sometimes wondered since.

At the time I speak of I had known Deeming for over two years, having met him first in London at a friend's house. Vernon was a comparatively recent acquaintance whom I had encountered when I was travelling in Algeria; but already in my heart I gave him the dearer title, for I had come to like him greatly, and I knew that my sympathy was returned.

The two men were very different—in their appearance, their natures, their ways of life—but differences sometimes seem to make for pleasant intercourse, and even for intimacy. We often love ourselves; but do we generally love those who markedly resemble us?

Vernon usually spent his winters in Rome, where he had a delightful house on the Trinita dei Monti. Deeming had come from England to take a long holiday, as his health had partially broken down from overwork. He was a very successful London doctor, devoted to his profession. Vernon was a rich man, passionately interested in the arts and in travel. How well I remember that first evening we spent together, that—I had almost written fatal evening! We were dining in the restaurant, and directly I had made my friends known to each other we went in and sat down at our table, which was in the middle of the room.

Deeming was a very thin man, nearly forty, clean shaven, with iron-grey thick hair, narrow clear-cut features, and a tremendously decisive mouth and chin, betokening power and resolution. His face was pale, and bore traces of his recent illness. In his long, rather colourless grey eyes, penetrating and usually calm, one could see the slightly anxious and irritable expression of a man whose nerves had been, and still were, overwrought. His hands were delicate, with thin fingers curving backward perceptibly at the tips. He leaned forward as he sat in his chair, glancing over the crowd of English, Americans, and foreigners who were busily eating and talking round us.

Vernon was tall and fair, younger than Deeming by some five or six years, with meditative, almost gentle, and very kind brown eyes, a sensitive, though not handsome, face, with a clear boyish colour in it, a voice that was generally low unless he got much interested in the subject he was discussing, and an extremely fascinating manner, whose fascination sprang from his great courtesy, combined with a perfectly natural self-possession, as of a man who seldom thought about himself, and who was desirous of making things go easily and pleasantly for those with whom he was brought into contact.

I saw Deeming look at him steadily, rather as a doctor looks at a new patient, more than once as we drank our soup, and I knew that with his invariable acuteness he was taking stock of his new acquaintance. Vernon, on the other hand, showed at first no special interest in Deeming, did not regard him earnestly, but was gracefully agreeable to him as he was to everyone. He was far more what is generally called a man of the world than Deeming, whose devotion to, and great success in, his profession had kept him bound to the wheel of work in London, and had prevented him from having the opportunity of knowing the nations and mixing perpetually with society which Vernon had enjoyed.

At first we talked quietly, almost languidly, of Rome, of its changes and its tourists, of the influence of America upon its society, of its climate, of the differences between life in England and life abroad, and so forth. It was not till the middle of dinner that anything occurred to wake us up into great animation. Then a stout, dark, and very vivacious little lady, with a commanding air, came into the restaurant followed by two men, and sat down at a table near us. She and her companions were obviously Italians, and almost directly she screwed up her eyes at Vernon and nodded to him. He returned her salute with *empressement*.

"Would you mind telling me who that lady is?" said Deeming.

"Margherita Terrascalchi," replied Vernon.

"What—the famous authoress?" I said. "The writer of *Pieta*?"

"Yes."

Deeming stared hard at the little lady, who was beginning to eat with extraordinary, almost comical, gusto.

"I have read that book," he said. "In a translation."

"What do you think of it?" asked Vernon.

"No doubt it is well done and calculated to move the ordinary reader."

"Only the ordinary reader?" said Vernon, with a slight upward movement of his eyebrows.

"I think it wrongheaded and sentimental," said Deeming, with more energy than he had yet shown. "She appears to wish to elevate the animals above humanity, to take them out of their proper place."

"What would you say is their proper place?"

"They are in the world, in my opinion, to be the servants of humanity, to minister to our comfort, our pleasure, our necessities, to help to increase our knowledge and satisfy our appetites, to give us ease and to gain us money. Don't you think so?"

"No doubt many scientists, many sportsmen, and most, if not all, butchers do."

I laughed.

"But you, Vernon," I said, "are neither scientist, sportsman, nor butcher, and Deeming asks you what you think."

Vernon was looking less tranquil, less gentle than usual at this moment. His face was lit up by a fire I had never seen burning in his eyes before.

"My sympathies march with Madame Terrascalchi's," he answered, "though perhaps she expresses them with a feminine enthusiasm that may seem to some almost hysterical, and is carried away by her passion of pity into an excess of animosity against men and women, who often err against the animal world more from lack of imagination than from any definite bias towards cruelty."

"The question is, are we to be the servants of the animals or they to be our servants?" Deeming said rather drily. "I notice that Madame Terrascalchi is eating something that looks remarkably like a veal cutlet at this very moment."

"Oh," said Vernon, with his pleasant smile. "I hold no brief for her. I believe her, in fact, to be very—shall I say human? But as to what you were saying. Is it wholly a matter of whether we are to be masters or slaves? Cannot we and the animals—we are not, of course, discussing dangerous wild beasts—be friends, or, let us say, could we not be friends, good and close friends, they serving us in their way, we serving them in ours?"

"How are we to serve the animals?" asked Deeming, still drily.

"By considering them far more than we generally do, by studying them, their natures, habits, desires, likes and dislikes far more closely, by encouraging their affection for us, and giving them more of ours."

"I think that would be a great waste of time."

"Deeming is a terribly busy man, Vernon," I said.

"I know my London well enough to know it," Vernon remarked politely. "Still, I think we might find time for that; even that we ought to find time for it. I am rather what you might call a 'crank' on the subject of the animal world."

"I didn't know it," I said.

"Oh, yes, I am."

The almost fierce light again shone in his eyes.

"I love all animals. Ouida speaks of their 'mysterious lives,' spent side by side with ours, and comparatively little noticed, little sympathised with by us. I know that many animal lovers would raise a cry of protest against this. 'Look,' they would say, 'how dogs are worshipped and petted, how horses are loved by their owners, how cats are stroked and fondled!' and so forth. Yes, it is true. Out of the great world of the animals, we—those of us who are fond of animals—select a few who, we think, can minister to our pleasure, and we give them, or think we give them, a good time. But these pet animals who enjoy life are few in number compared with the many who are made to suffer by man; the dogs that are kept everlastingly tied up, or are half-starved, or are perpetually cuffed and kicked and beaten; the cats that are abandoned to die when their thoughtless owners change home; the horses that are overdriven, tortured by tight bearing-reins, lashed with the whip, made to draw loads that are too heavy for them; the birds—let me include them—that are forced to spend their lives in tiny cages in dark places. To any real, observant lover of animals, even of the so-called pet animals—excluding the beasts of burden, donkeys, mules, oxen, and the beasts that form part of our food supply, and the dumb creatures that are given over to the tender mercies of the sportsman: the hares that are coursed, the foxes and stags and deer that are hunted, the pigeons that are let out of traps (their eyes pierced to make them fly in a given direction) to be shot and are often left maimed to die, the seabirds that the Cockney 'wings' and abandons to starve and rot, floating helpless on the waves of the sea, the pheasants that, wounded in a battue, are crushed one on the top of the other into bags to perish of suffocation; excluding all these—to any real and observant lover of animals the lack of sympathy, or the actual cruelty of man, is a perpetual source of disturbance, of anxiety, even of lively distress and misery."

I was quite amazed at the energy with which Vernon had spoken, at the vigour and force of his manner. He paused for a moment, then he added—

"My love of animals has given me very many horrible moments in my life, moments in which I confess that my heart has been turned to bitterness and I have longed to make men suffer as they were making animals suffer. Yes, I have longed to see the cursed Cockney sportsman drifting face to face with a lingering death upon the sea, the callous game-preserver wounded in one of his traps and alone in the darkness of night in the forest, the careless hunter at bay with hounds rushing in upon him. But especially have I known the longing to turn one whom I have seen being cruel to a pet animal into that animal, and to be his master for a little while. You know some hold that theory."

"What theory?" said Deeming.

"That what we do is eventually done to us in another life; for instance, that if a man has been brutal to an animal, at death his soul passes into a similar animal, which endures the fate he once meted out when he was a man."

"Good heavens!" exclaimed Deeming. "You surely can't believe such unscientific nonsense!"

"I did not say I believed it, but I should not be sorry to."

He sipped his champagne. Then, more lightly, he said—

"I told you I was a bit of a crank. I am even hand-in-glove with Arthur Gernham."

At the mention of this name, Deeming moved, and I saw his eyes flash.

"The prominent anti-vivisectionist?" he said.

"Yes."

"And you share his views?"

"To a considerable extent, though I don't always approve of what he writes or of what he says."

"I'm glad of that. We doctors, you know, ab—well, we don't love that eager gentleman. If he had his way humanity would undoubtedly suffer far more in the future than it will. For I don't think his sentimentalities and wild exaggerations will ever gain over our legislators to his views."

"Perhaps not. But I sometimes wonder whether anyone has the right, whether anyone was intended by the Creator to have the right, to avoid suffering at the cost of inflicting it, even to save life by causing death. However, the vivisection question is hardly a pleasant one for the dinner table, eh!"

There was a moment's silence. Then Deeming said:

"Of course you never shoot or hunt?"

"Never."

"I do," I said. "But I am not such a contemptible hypocrite as to deny that cruelty, and often very gross cruelty, enters into sport."

Deeming slightly smiled.

"Do you keep any pets?" said Vernon to him, rather sharply.

"Yes. I have a dog at home, a black spaniel; and you?"

"No. For years I have kept no animals. I shall never keep one again."

"That surprises me. You would give them a remarkably good time, I feel sure."

"I have a reason."

"May I ask what it is?"

"Certainly. I once had a dog that I—that I cared about. She was out with me one day in London and disappeared. I made every possible inquiry, offered a reward, went to the Dogs' Home, but I couldn't find her. Eventually, through an odd chain of circumstances that I needn't trouble you with, I learnt her fate."

"What was it?" I asked.

"She had been picked up by a dog-stealer and sold to the proprietor of an establishment called 'Lilac Hall,' near London."

"An establishment?" I said, struck by the tone in which he had uttered the words.

"Where a large number—stock, I'll say—of animals of all kinds, horses, cats, rabbits, guinea-pigs, dogs, was kept on hand for scientific purposes. My companion and friend died under the knife of the vivisector. What do you think of the food here? They've got a new *chef*."

"I—I—oh, it's very good, I think; it's excellent."

Deeming seemed startled by the sudden change of topic, and when we went into the hall to smoke he tried to return to the discussion. But Vernon did not rise to the bait he threw out, and at last frankly said:

"You'd much better not get me on to the subject of animals. I am really a bore when I let myself loose, as I did at dinner. And I am quite sure you"—and he met Deeming's eyes—"don't agree with my views. Are you staying long in Rome?"

"Till I feel quite set up again and ready for work."

"Then I'll hope you'll come and see me."

He gave his card to Deeming, and soon after went away.

I felt sure he had asked Deeming to call in order to please me. My two friends, I feared, had not taken a fancy to each other. One curious thing struck me as I watched Vernon's tall figure going out through the doorway to the street. It was this—that I knew a side of Vernon's, and a side of Deeming's character that had been hitherto completely concealed from me. Each had elicited a frankness from the other that I, of whom they were fond, had not been able to bring forth.

Their two enmities—so I thought of it—had clashed together and struck out sparks of truth.

By the way, Vernon's last remark to me in the outer hall of the hotel, whither I had accompanied him, leaving Deeming in the winter-garden, was this—

"I shouldn't care to be Deeming's black spaniel."

II

A day or two afterwards Deeming said to me, "I'm going to call on your friend Vernon this afternoon. When is he likely to be in?"

"He's generally at home between six and seven," I said. After a moment I added, "You want to find him then?"

"Why—yes. He's a very agreeable fellow. Did you think I disliked him?"

"Disliked him—no, hardly that. But, somehow, I scarcely fancied you two were quite in sympathy the other night."

"Oh, you mean that animal-versus-human-being discussion. Now it is just because of that I want to meet him again."

"To win him over to your views? "

"Well, I confess that I should like to get him to see how harmful such a man as his friend Gernham is or may become to the world—of men understood. He's probably got all kinds of absurd notions as to how vivisection is carried on. I should like to have a quiet, reasonable talk with him."

"Go to-day, then, at six. You're almost sure to find him."

"I will."

And Deeming set his lips together with determination.

I was, I confess, a little curious as to the result of the interview. I heard something about it the same evening from Vernon, who sent round a note asking me to dine with him alone.

"Your friend Deeming has been here," he said, almost directly I was in the house.

"I know. Did you have a pleasant time?"

"He's extremely intelligent—got a great deal of character, real force. That ruthless mouth and chin of his tell the truth."

At this moment the servant said that dinner was ready. We continued our conversation in the dining room, which was hung with sacred pictures, gentle-eyed Madonnas—one by Luini—Saints, an Agony in the Garden by an unnamed painter, the little children coming to Christ, the Magi offering their gifts, watched by calm-eyed beasts in a dim stable.

"Yes," I said. "Deeming is very decisive."

"To me there's something very strange in the thought that he is a healer."

"Why?"

"Well—do you mind my speaking frankly about a friend of yours?"

"Not a bit."

"I shall startle you, perhaps. You know one reads sometimes in the papers of people who are afflicted with what is called the mania to persecute. There was a trial of a woman not long ago—a Mrs. Denby."

"I know. But—"

"And there have been various instances in distant Colonial possessions of France and Belgium—and, perhaps, of other countries—various instances of men placed practically in the position of tyrants who have indulged in orgies of persecution of natives."

"But, my dear Vernon, you surely don't mean that you think Deeming has the bloodlust because he believes good can come of vivisection. Upon my word, if you don't take care, I shall begin to think you really are a crank."

"It isn't that. It isn't what the man says. I can quite understand that as a doctor he wishes by every means to advance the spread of medical knowledge. No, no; it's the man himself. Do you know him well?"

"I have seen a good deal of him in London. Not a great deal, because he's such a busy man. But I have often been with him."

"Often in his house?"

"More often at his club, and in my own house and at restaurants. Being a bachelor, when he entertains he nearly always does so at Claridge's, or the Savoy, or one of those places. But, of course, I have been in his house."

"Have you ever seen his dog, that black spaniel he spoke of?"

"No, I can't remember that I have."

For a moment Vernon spoke of a certain dish that had just been brought in, a special *plat* for which his cook was famous. Then he said:

"That dog I spoke of the other night—the dog I lost—you remember?"

"Yes."

"She was a black spaniel."

His tone in saying this was so peculiar that I was misled and exclaimed: "But you told us the poor beast was killed in that house—in Lilac Hall!"

"So she was."

"I thought—really, by the way you spoke, you led me to imagine that perhaps you fancied Deeming had got possession of your dog."

"Oh, dear no! Whisper is dead, years ago. I seldom speak of her."

"I never heard you mention her till the other night."

"The other night I showed you a side of me that you had never suspected the existence of, didn't I?"

"You did indeed."

"Well, having broken through my reserve, I feel that I don't mind being frank with you."

His eyes began to shine as they had shone in the restaurant when he spoke of man's cruelty to animals.

"My dog was the greatest solace in my life," he said. "I am not a sentimental fool. There is nothing either sentimental or foolish in loving that which, with a whole heart and perfectly, loves you. And a dog's devotion really is one of the most perfect, one of the most touching, and one of the most complete sentiments that can be manifested by one living creature to another. Not to respond to it would be absolutely devilish. But one can't help oneself if one isn't made of stone. I won't bore you with a long account of Whisper's devotion and fidelity. Why should I? It's enough to say that she loved me as much as a dog can love, and in a dog's way, with absolute unselfishness, with entire singleheartedness. I never felt lonely when she was with me, scarcely ever even dull. When I had been out without her, and, on my return, she met me at the door, almost hysterically eager to show her rapture, I—well, I was glad to be alive, and felt that life was worthwhile so long as I could evoke such a tempest of delight in any living creature. A faithful dog, believe me, is the best bulwark against the coming of cynicism. You can't be a cynic when a dog's cold nose is pushed into your hand, or a dog's paw is placed gently and solemnly upon your knee. When I lost Whisper, when I found out what had been her fate, I felt something that was more than grief"—he leaned over the table and laid his hand on my arm—"I felt hatred, burning hatred, against those who had snared and murdered her, against all who use animals cruelly for the purposes of men."

His face was transformed. I seemed to see before me a man whom I had never seen before. This man, I felt, could be not only gentle, but vindictive, and would be quite capable of expressing himself not only in words, but also through actions.

"I can understand your bitterness," I said. "But does not this recalling of a painful event only stir up recollections that—?"

He interrupted me almost roughly.

"That doesn't matter at all. I want to tell you now. I prefer to."

"Go on, then," I said.

He took his hand from my arm, and continued

"The fate of my companion altered me. It either stirred from sleep, or actually woke into life, a fierceness that till then I had not known existed, or could exist, in me. It made me understand that, in certain circumstances and to certain people, I could be implacable, almost ferocious; that I could deny the sole right of Providence—you know the text: why quote it? —to administer that gorgeous justice we name vengeance; that I could stand up and exclaim, 'I will repay,' and repay without fear, without flinching, and even to the uttermost farthing. But that was not all it did to me. With this awakening, or this creation of fierceness in me, there came a deepening of pity, of tenderness for the slaves of man. Yet I was selfish, and I have remained selfish."

"How?" I asked, wondering.

"It was, and is, in my power to make at least some animals happy, as I had made my dead dog happy. I could not, and cannot, bring myself to do that. I feared and I fear too much to suffer again as I suffered when I lost Whisper, and when I learnt the truth about her end. That end has been a nightmare to me ever since. I cannot think of it even now without torture."

"My dear fellow," I said. "Don't dwell upon it. To do so is really morbid."

"I don't dwell upon it, as a rule. Have I ever even mentioned this subject to you before?"

"No, no. But—"

"That man, your friend Deeming, has roused me up. I—I tell you that I hate—that it is almost unbearable to me to think of his having a dog—a black spaniel, like Whisper—in his power."

He said the last words with extraordinary vehemence.

"That was what you meant then!" I exclaimed.

"When you mistook me just now? Yes, that!"

He relapsed into silence, but kept his still glowing eyes fixed upon me. I seemed to read in them that he had more to tell me, to see that there was some project, some intention of action, blazing in his mind.

"Look here, Vernon," I said, determined to be quite frank with him at whatever cost, "Deeming is a friend of mine."

"I know."

"That being so, I don't think you can expect me to be ready to harbour foul suspicions of him without any reason for them being adduced. If he were to be suspicious of you, and told me so, I should speak to him as I speak to you now. What on earth has the man done or said to make you so violent—yes, my dear friend, that is the word—against him?"

He did not look angry at my energy, but, on the other hand, he did not look doubtful or disposed towards modification. He only said, "How well do you know Deeming? "

"Not very intimately, but well enough to feel sure that he is a humane man. Patients of his have spoken to me of him, of his skill, his care, and devotion in the highest terms."

"I don't doubt it. I don't doubt that he is humane as a doctor. Anyone can see that he is devoted to his profession, and his profession is to heal human suffering. Ambition alone would cause him to be humane—as a doctor."

"You said yourself you were a bit of a crank. Aren't you ever afraid that your crankiness may lead you—now do forgive me! —into something approaching malice?"

I thought he might be angry, but he wasn't.

"My intuition—apart from anything else," he said—"my intuition tells me that Deeming is a cruel man."

"I don't believe it. Vivisection—"

"I'm not thinking of that now. What I am thinking is that I should like to see Deeming's dog."

"That wouldn't be difficult, I imagine."

"You don't mean that she is with him here, in Rome?"

"Oh no. A dog in a hotel is apt to be a nuisance."

"I don't agree with you."

"Well, well; but you always come to London in the late summer. I suppose you'll do so this year? "

"Probably."

"Call on Deeming. He's a hospitable man, and if you entertain him here in Rome, he is sure to ask you out in London. There you can see for yourself whether his dog isn't properly treated, as I'll swear she is, and as happy as dog can be."

I spoke lightly, even with a deliberately jocose and chaffing air. He listened to me gravely.

"I will invite Deeming here," he said. "Indeed, I intended to in any case, as he is a friend of yours."

"Thank you."

"But you say he usually entertains in restaurants when he is in London. I have no reason to think I shall ever set my foot inside his house."

The extreme gravity of his manner, the earnestness of the eyes that were fixed upon me, made me realise how strong was his strange desire, and therefore, how strong was his—as I thought then—absurd and unreasonable suspicion. I might have continued to laugh at it, and chaff him about it, but I did not. Something in his face and manner made me unable to do so, made me suddenly conscious that, however much I laughed, I could never laugh him out of his curious, and surely morbid, anxiety to verify, or lull to rest, his fears. And I must confess—so easily are we influenced by certain convinced people whom we care for—that I, too, was becoming, at that moment, oddly interested in this matter of Deeming and his black spaniel. Why had I never seen the dog, never heard Deeming mention it till the other night?

"If Deeming doesn't invite you to his house," I said, changing my tone, "there's a very easy method of getting into it."

"What method?" said Vernon eagerly.

"Go to him as a patient."

I had scarcely said the words before I felt uncomfortable, almost traitorous. Here was I entering into something that was like a plot with one friend to get at a knowledge of another which that other had never voluntarily tendered to me. I was angry with myself.

"Upon my word, Vernon," I exclaimed, "I'm ashamed of myself! Don't let us discuss this matter any longer. Deeming and you are both my friends, and I wish to act always fairly and squarely by you both."

"What unfairness is there in enabling me to prove the folly and falseness of my suspicions?" he rejoined quickly.

"I know—I know; but—oh, the whole thing is really absurd. It is madness to think such things of a man with no evidence to go upon."

"How do you know that I have no evidence?"

"How can you have any?"

"Are a man's words no evidence? Is his face while he says them no evidence?"

"Did you talk about his dog when he was here this afternoon?" I asked abruptly, moved by a sudden impression that he was keeping something from me.

"He wouldn't talk about her. I am quite certain of one thing."

"What is that?"

"That Deeming wishes now that he had never mentioned to us that he had a dog."

I suppose I looked incredulous, for he added, without giving me time to speak—

"When you see him again, try to turn the conversation upon the black spaniel, and see how he takes it. And now let us talk of something else."

During the rest of the evening Deeming and his dog were not mentioned. Vernon resumed, almost like a garment, his old self, the self I had always known, cultured, gentle in manner, full of interest in every topic that lent itself to quiet discussion and amiable debate. The evil spirit—I thought of it as almost that—had departed out of him, and when I got up to go I could hardly believe that I had ever been the recipient of his vehemence, or seen his eyes blazing with the light of scarcely controlled passion. He came with me to the hall door and let me out into the quiet night.

"Good-bye," he said, pressing my hand.

"Good-bye," I answered.

I hesitated. Then I said:

"Doesn't this calm of the night embracing Rome make you—make you feel that in your suspicions of Deeming you have been unreasonable; that, after all, it is unlikely he should be what you have fancied him to be?"

In an instant all the calmness, all the gentleness went out of his face. But he only answered:

"When you get back to the hotel talk to him about his black spaniel, and see how he takes it. Good-night."

Before I could say anything more he had drawn back into his house and shut the door quickly behind him.

III

As I walked back to the Grand Hotel I thought over Vernon's last words and the way in which he had said them. Should I obey his injunctions? I confessed to myself with reluctance that my conversation with him that evening had made me suspicious of a friend. Yet I had Vernon's own word for it that he was a crank on the subject of animals, and my recent experience of him almost forced me to the conclusion that in his nature, usually so gentle, there must be an odd strain of fanaticism. My mind was troubled, and I reached the hotel without coming to a decision as to whether I would speak to Deeming about his dog or not. As I came into the outer hall I saw him through the glass door sitting alone in the winter garden, smoking, with a paper, which he was not reading, lying on his knee. He did not see me, and, for a moment, I watched him with a furtive curiosity of which I was secretly half-ashamed. Perhaps stirred by my gaze, he suddenly looked up, caught sight of me, smiled, and made a slight gesture, as if beckoning me to come in and have a talk. I took off my overcoat and joined him.

"I've just come from Vernon," I said, sitting down and lighting a cigar.

"Ah!" said Deeming.

He uncrossed his legs, crossed them again, and added:

"He's got a beautiful house."

"Yes, one of the most beautiful in Rome. He wants you to dine with him one night, I believe. Probably he'll ask you in a day or two."

"Very good of him." His voice was scarcely cordial. "He's a curious fellow," he continued. "Easy in his manner, but difficult really to know, I fancy."

"If you dine with him you may find him less reserved," I said, rather perfunctorily.

"I don't suppose he'll ask me alone."

"Oh, I shouldn't wonder."

"I don't think he cares much about me," Deeming continued abruptly. "Do you?"

"My dear fellow, he hardly knows you," I exclaimed. "You haven't been quarrelling over the animal world this afternoon, have you?"

And I laughed, but without much cordiality, I fear.

"Did he say we had?"

"Good heavens, no! But you differ on the dog question, and so—"

Deeming frowned.

"The dog question!" he said. "Why on earth should you call it that?"

"Well, I mean that he's very sensitive since he lost his dog, and that perhaps makes him a little unreasonable at times, though I must say that till the other night when he dined here I never heard him mention the subject of animals and their relation with man. And, by the way, you've been equally silent. Till the other night I never knew you possessed a dog."

"Is it such an important matter that I should go about proclaiming it?"

His tone was suddenly hard and impatient.

"No, of course not."

"I hate people who bother their friends about their pets. It's almost as bad as the women who are always talking about the marvellous beauty and genius of their squalling babies."

He set his lips together as if he never meant to open them again, and I saw a look as of acute nervous irritation in his eyes. It warned me not to persevere in the conversation, and made me vexed with myself for having given way to Vernon's desire.

"Let's have a nightcap," I said. "What do you think of doing to-morrow? What do you say to getting a carriage and driving over to lunch at Tivoli?"

He looked more easy.

"If it is fine I should enjoy it immensely," he said in a calmer voice.

And we talked of old gardens and the beauty of rushing water.

We spent the following day together at Tivoli. When we came back towards evening, the hall porter handed to Deeming a note. It was from Vernon, inviting him to dine two days later.

"You see how he hates you!" I said chaffingly when he told me. "Do you mean to go?"

"Oh, yes. Why not?"

He spoke lightly, holding the note open in his hand.

He did not go, however, and for this reason. On the morning of the day he was to dine with Vernon, he left Rome for England. An urgent summons from a patient, he told me, made it necessary for him to go to London without a moment's delay.

I remonstrated with him, but in vain.

"I've had quite enough rest," he said. "I'm all right. And this is an important matter. It means a very large sum of money."

"Health's more than money."

"Certainly, but I feel quite my own man again."

He did not look it, but I said no more.

I knew that argument would be useless. He sent a note to Vernon, and, when I bade him good-bye, begged me to express his regret at being obliged to cancel the dinner.

"But I hope someday he'll come to dine with me in London. Do tell him so," he said, as he stepped into the omnibus to go to the station. "I should like to meet him again."

Those were his last words. I repeated them to Vernon.

"I shall not forget that invitation, I assure you," he said quietly. "And I may be able to enjoy Deeming's hospitality sooner than he, perhaps, expects."

"Why? You're surely not going to London yet awhile? I thought you loved your June in Rome better than any other month of the year."

"But I've had so many Junes in Rome that I think I shall make a change. By the way, when will you be in London?"

"Oh, certainly by the last week in April."

"If I asked to travel back with you, would you object to my company?"

"My dear fellow! Of course I should be delighted."

"Let us consider it a bargain, then."

He spoke decisively, and shook me by the hand as if to clinch the bargain. Nor did he forget it.

The third week in April found us in Paris, and on the twenty-second of that month we stepped into the *rapide* at the Gare du Nord, bound for England.

We sat opposite to one another in the compartment, with, at first, ramparts of London papers between us; but, as we drew near to Boulogne, first Vernon's rampart fell, and then mine. The thought of the nearness of England had got hold of us both. London ideas were taking possession of us, and, as the train rushed on towards the sea, we became restless, as if the roar of the great city were already in our ears.

"Do you know," I said, breaking our mutual silence, "that, familiar as I am with London, I can never return to it after an absence without a feeling of apprehension. It always seems to me that in its black and smoky arms it must hold some disaster which it is waiting to give to me."

"I've had that sensation, too," said Vernon. "Among the cities of the world London is the monster, not merely by right of size but by other, and more mysterious rights. It affects my imagination more than any of the European capitals, but rather frightfully than agreeably. I feel that it is the city of adventure, but that every adventure there must have a fearsome ending."

"No doubt we are affected by its climate and its atmosphere."

"I dare say. Still, if anything very strange, very uncommon, should ever happen to me, I am quite sure that it will be in London."

I smiled.

"My experience," I said, "has been that in London I am perpetually expectant of gloomy and mysterious events, but that my life there is remarkably unromantic and commonplace."

"You speak almost regretfully. Do you wish for gloomy and mysterious events in your life?"

"I suppose not. Yet there is a spirit hidden in one which does sigh plaintively for the strange."

"Perhaps this time it will be gratified."

Something in the tone of his voice moved me to say—

"Do you expect it to be gratified?"

"I! Why should I?"

"I don't know. Something in your voice made me fancy that you did."

He laughed.

"The London atmosphere is, perhaps, affecting me already," he said. "The London influence is taking hold of me. I told you it always stirred my imagination."

"At Boulogne-sur-mer!" I said, as the train ran into the station. "The monster's arms are longer than Goliath's!"

The stoppage of the train interrupted our conversation. We got out to stretch our legs for a moment, and as we did so I found myself wondering why Vernon, generally a very frank man, at any rate with me, should have met my plain question with an attempt at laughing subterfuge. It was a very slight matter, of course. In another man I should, perhaps, scarcely have noticed it. But it was not Vernon's way, and therefore it struck me. I felt that he wished to prevent me from getting at the truth of his mind at this moment. Usually, his desire certainly was that the truth of his mind should be known to me.

We travelled to Calais in silence. Then came the bustle of going aboard the steamer and fortifying ourselves against the painful attentions of a sharp north-easterly wind. When we were established in our deck chairs, and closely wrapped in rugs, we glanced round to see whether we had any acquaintances among our fellow passengers. The steamer was just casting off, and some, like ourselves, were already settled down for the voyage, while others were tramping up and down briskly, with an air of determination, as if bent upon making their blood circulate, and getting the maximum of benefit out of the crossing. Among the latter was an elderly man, with pepper-and-salt hair and a thin, aristocratic face.

"Hullo," I said, "there's Lord Elyn. I wonder where he's come from."

Turning in his walk, he was in front of us almost as I said the words, and, seeing me, stopped, and, bending down, shook my hand.

"Where do you hail from?" he asked.

"Paris," I answered. "I've been in Rome. And you?"

"Calais."

"You've been staying at Calais?"

"No. I'm here for my medicine. I live on the Channel at present, or nearly. My doctor, Peter Deeming—he'll be Sir Peter before long, I suppose—has prescribed the double voyage, from Dover and back, every day of the week for a month. I sleep at the Burlington and eat boeuf-à-la-mode" at the Calais buffet every midday of my life just now."

"Deeming's a friend of mine—of ours," I said. May I introduce Mr. Kersteven—Lord Elyn."

The two men bowed.

"It's a pity he doesn't take his own medicine," said Lord Elyn. "I've tried to persuade him, but in vain so far. However, I've got his promise to come down to-night—Saturday, you know—and stay till Monday, and make the voyage with me to-morrow. I expect to find him at the Burlington when I get back."

I saw a sharp look of eagerness come into Vernon's face.

"Is Deeming looking ill, Lord Elyn?" he asked. "You say it is a pity he doesn't take the medicine he prescribes for you."

"I think him looking very ill-pale and worried and played out. He is too great a success and pays the penalty—works too hard, like most successful men. He ought to have prolonged his holiday in Rome. I can't imagine why he hurried back to town so unexpectedly."

"Oh," I said, "I can explain that. He was summoned to town by an important patient."

"Really!" said Lord Elyn. "I never heard of it."

He sounded slightly incredulous.

"I saw him almost directly he arrived," he added; "and when I inquired why he had shortened his trip to Italy, he merely told me that he was all right and had got sick of doing nothing."

"Well," I answered, "he left Rome at a moment's notice, and gave me the reason I told you."

"Oh! Well, then, of course, it was so. A pity for him—though not for us, eh? He's a wonderful doctor. No one like him. And now, if you'll excuse me, I must take exercise. I keep walking the whole time, by command."

He nodded, and went off up the deck at a brisk pace.

"I'm sorry to hear that about Deeming," I said to Vernon.

"Yes. It's a pity he was called away from Rome."

His voice, too, sounded incredulous.

"Why d'you say it like that?" I asked. "You don't think he told us a lie?"

"Why put it so cruelly? He may have made an excuse. When one receives a boring dinner invitation, one has sometimes a previous engagement."

"A dinner invitation! Surely you don't—?"

"Well, he was to have dined with me the night of the day he left. But, of course, it may have been a pure coincidence."

Lord Elyn passed us again, and repassed.

"I say, Luttrell," Vernon added, "what do you say to one more night out of London? What do you say to a night at the Burlington?"

"At Dover?"

"Yes."

"But the luggage! It's all registered through."

"We've got our dressing-cases, and my man has a bag with my pyjamas. Evening dress doesn't matter for a night. I'm sure the Burlington will forgive us, especially if we engage a sitting room."

"Oh, yes, that doesn't matter."

"What do you say, then?"

"I don't know that I mind, but—what's made you think of it all of a sudden? Have you taken a violent fancy to Lord Elyn?"

My voice was challenging. He only smiled quietly.

"A very violent fancy. I like obedient men."

Lord Elyn passed once more with a serious, determined air. He did not look at us. He was intent on his medicine.

"You're joking."

"So were you." I laughed.

"Of course. You don't choose to tell me your reason for wishing to stop at Dover?"

"I think you've guessed it."

He unrolled the rug from his legs and got up.

"I'm going to take some medicine, too. Think over the Burlington and tell me presently."

In a moment I saw him join Lord Elyn, and they walked up and down together, talking busily.

Of course, I had "guessed it." He wanted to meet Deeming again, to meet him directly we landed in England. My previous suspicion—it had been almost more than a suspicion—was confirmed. I felt positive now that Vernon had cut short his stay in Rome, given up his June there, in order to follow Deeming to London and try to see more of him. The obsession of the black spaniel—I called it that now in my mind for the first time—was still upon him, had been upon him ever since the night when I had made my two friends acquainted with each other in the winter garden of the Grand Hotel. And Deeming? Had he really invented an imaginary patient in order to have a good excuse for leaving Rome and so avoiding Vernon's dinner? If that were so, then I was assisting at a sort of manhunt, in which two of my friends were pursued and pursuer. I began to feel as if I were going to be involved in something extraordinary. And yet how vague, how fantastic it all was! And my own position? I tried to review it. If I assisted Vernon in any way, could I be called—or rather, should I be, that was the only thing that mattered—disloyal to Deeming? I felt rather uncomfortable, and yet— and this was strange—rather excited. I thought of my conversation with Vernon about London. I had been absent from it for some time, yet already, and on the sea, I felt affected by its powerful and dreadful influence, felt that curious sense of apprehension which I had mentioned to Vernon in the train. Suddenly I resolved to fall in with my friend's wish to stay the night at Dover. After all, what did it matter? He and Deeming would certainly meet in London. Why strive to postpone the meeting? It seemed to me—I was thinking somewhat absurdly, I acknowledge it—that it would be better, safer, that the encounter should take place at Dover, under the white cliffs, with the sea wind coming in, perhaps, through open windows. London was mephitic, and turned one to gloomy and morbid imaginations. The sea wind might blow away Vernon's extraordinary suspicions of Deeming, and lay to rest the obsession of the black spaniel.

Moved by this idea, when Vernon presently stopped before me with Lord Elyn, I said—

"I give my vote for a night at the Burlington."

"Capital!" said Vernon. "I've been telling Lord Elyn we thought of staying, and he is sure our tweeds and coloured ties will be forgiven us."

IV

At the Burlington in the hall we found Deeming. I saw him before he was aware of us, and was startled by the change in his face. There was the stamp of nervous exhaustion upon it. The complexion was grey, the mouth was drawn, the eyes were anxious, almost feverish. When he turned and faced us fully he made an abrupt movement which was certainly not caused by pleasure, and I saw the fingers of his two hands clench themselves violently in the palms. Then he recovered himself, came forward, and greeted us with self-possession.

"I never expected to see you in England so soon," he said to Vernon. "I thought you usually spent part of the summer in Rome."

"I often do. But this year something has called me to London."

"Oh. Well, all the better. We shall see something of you. I hope we shall bring off our dinner together in town. Only you must let me be the host."

"Thank you. I shall be delighted."

The note of cordiality was, I thought, forced by both men. Few more words were spoken, for it was getting late, and the hour of dinner was approaching. As we went upstairs I said to Vernon:

"Deeming does certainly want medicine of one sort or another. Don't you think he looks horribly ill?"

"He has a strung-up expression. I should say he's overworking. Did you notice how he started when he saw us?"

"Did he?" I answered, disingenuously I confess. "Naturally he was surprised. He had no idea we were in England."

"Exactly. Here are our rooms. *Au re*voir at dinner."

The dinner I need not chronicle at length. It took place downstairs, although we had engaged the sitting room to appease a management shocked at our lack of evening clothes. The talk ran easily enough, helped by Lord Elyn's unconsciousness of the obsession of the black spaniel, which sometimes seemed to me to be hovering about our table, creeping beneath our chairs, a shadow importunate, servile, yet menacing. I felt that the thoughts of Deeming and Vernon, interlacing and inimical, were on this whining, whimpering, uneasy shadow, that had called the latter from his home in Italy, that had stopped him here by the grey sea. I knew it as if those thoughts were spread before me by my plate. And all the time we chatted, glancing from subject to subject without great earnestness, laughing lightly at the last London absurdity, or discussing with apparent animation the chances of politics and the trend of art, I felt that our conversation was but a thin veil spread over a depth in which were other voices than ours, murmuring, in which the pale forms of future events glided, like spectres, to and fro.

Directly after dinner Lord Elyn excused himself.

"The eyes of the nurse are upon me," he said, jocosely. "I see them saying: 'Master Elyn, it's time for you to go to bed!' Eh, Deeming?"

"Quite right, Lord Elyn," answered Deeming, smiling.

"Well, good-night. You'd much better come too, Deeming."

"Oh, I couldn't sleep yet. I haven't been on the sea. I think I shall go out and take a breath of air on the front."

"Perhaps it may do you good. I feel full of sleep."

And he went off, leaving us in the hall.

"Will you come out?" asked Deeming.

The invitation seemed addressed to both of us. I expected Vernon to accept it with alacrity, but, to my surprise, he took up the *Westminster Gazette.*

"I'm a bit tired," he answered. "I think I'll stay here."

"I'll come with you," I said.

"Right. I want a turn or two to summon slumber."

There was something almost pathetic in his voice. It moved me to ask, as we went down the steps, and along the row of houses to the sea-front:

"Have you been sleeping badly, then?"

"Pretty badly. I say, what's brought Vernon over so soon?"

The question was sharply suspicious.

"He didn't tell me," I answered.

"Then you don't know?"

We turned to the left and walked along the parade towards the cliff. No one was about in the cold and gusty night. Now and then a light flashed out across the sea, swept it in a half circle, and vanished in the darkness.

"Oh, I'm not in all Vernon's secrets," I said.

Directly I had spoken I regretted my choice of words.

"Secrets!" he said.

"I only mean that Vernon's not specially given to making confidences. If he has any particular reason for coming to England at this time of year, he hasn't told it to me. But why should he have any special reason?"

Deeming shrugged his shoulders.

"Where is he going to stay in town?" he asked.

"At Claridge's, I believe; at any rate, for a time."

"Then he means to make a long stay?"

His voice still sounded intensely suspicious. Suddenly I felt as if I could not stand all this subterfuge, as if I must brush away from me the spider's web of mutual distrust in which my two friends were entangling me with each other.

"My dear fellow!" I exclaimed. "You really make me feel as if I were under cross-examination. I begin to wish I had never introduced you and Vernon to each other."

Deeming stopped dead, and looked at me.

"Perhaps it would have been better," he said.

"Much better."

"You think so, too? Why?"

"Can't you see that Vernon hates me?" he said, with violence.

"What earthly reason can he have for hating you?"

"Some men don't ask for reasons. There is something about me which is antipathetic to Vernon, and he's a strange fellow. You think him gentle, I know. But I—well, I believe that underneath his apparent gentleness hides the soul of a fanatic, a black fanatic."

We were still standing face to face. Now I looked into his eyes and said:

"I'm going to be very rude to you."

"Go on. I'll bear it."

"I am perfectly certain you are suffering from nervous exhaustion. You have all the symptoms. You are horribly pale and full of irritability and suspicion, ready to entertain any dark idea that may present itself to you, unable to see things in a clear light of reason."

"And you, Luttrell; do you know what you are?"

"I!"

"Yes. I'm going to be rude to you. You are either a self-deceiver or a— well, something one doesn't care to call a man. You know quite well, in your heart, that Vernon has come over so soon because because—"

Suddenly he hesitated, faltered, broke off.

I seemed to hear the whimper of a dog near us in the night.

"I've had enough of the wind," he said. "I'm going in."

And we went back to the hotel without another word.

Next morning, Vernon and I went up to town by an early train, leaving Lord Elyn and Deeming to take their Channel trip. At Charing Cross, as we were parting, Vernon to go to Claridge's and I to my flat in Albemarle Street, Vernon said, "By the way, what is Deeming's address?"

"Three hundred, Wimpole Street," I said.

He took out a card and a pencil.

"Three hundred, Wimpole Street," he repeated slowly, as he wrote it down.

"Goodbye. Let's meet to-morrow. Come and lunch with me."

He got into a hansom and drove away. I followed in a moment. As my cab came out of the station yard and crossed Trafalgar Square I was enveloped in what I called to myself "the London feeling." The day was warm, but dull and grey. The tall buildings, the statue of Gordon, the Nelson column, the lions, looked sad and phantom-like to my eyes, for many months accustomed to the pellucid clearness of African landscapes, to the brilliant blue of Italian skies. And the well-known depression which always settles down upon me like a fog when I first return to London came to me once more, bathing me in a gloom which

I strove in vain to shake off. In this gloom I seemed to see, like shadows passing in a fog, the forms of Vernon, of Deeming, and another form, small, black, and cringing, the form of a dog.

"P'f!" I said to myself. "Am I going to be the slave of a too sensitive imagination?"

And I resolutely began to think of pleasant things, of the friends, of the amusements, of the occupations that would solace me. Yet, when I reached Albemarle Street, I was heavy-hearted, and all that day and the next my depression persisted. Even a cheerful lunch with Vernon at Claridge's and the renewal of many old acquaintanceships failed to restore me to my normal temper.

A week passed by, and I had not seen Deeming. I was beginning to wonder what had become of him, when I received from him a note asking me to dine with him at the Carlton on the following evening to meet Vernon. I was, unfortunately, already engaged to dine with some American friends and go to the play; so I wrote to excuse myself, and added this postscript:

"May your dinner banish your mutual misunderstanding. Remember that it will always be a grief to me if my two friends are at cross-purposes."

The day after the dinner, when I had just come in from the club at seven o'clock in the evening, my servant announced "Doctor Deeming," and Deeming walked into the room. I saw at once that he was in a condition of unusual excitement. We shook hands, and directly my man had gone out and the door was shut, Deeming, who was still standing and who did not seem to see the chair I offered to him, exclaimed:

"Of course, you have heard about Number 301?"

"Number 301? What the deuce do you mean?" I asked.

"Number 301, Wimpole Street, the house next door to mine."

"What about it? Has it been burgled, or burnt down, or what?"

"Burnt down! Nonsense! It's been to let for the last three months. Yesterday morning I found the board was down, and last night Vernon told me that he has taken it. He's taken it as it is, furnished, and is going in at once."

I was surprised, and, I suppose, showed that I was in my face, for he continued:

"Oh, then you didn't know! He hadn't told you!"

"He has told me nothing."

"It's a strange business. I—I—"

He began to walk to and fro.

"Why should he come to live next door to me? Why should he—?"

He stopped in front of me.

"Did you tell him where I lived?" he said, almost menacingly.

I resented his tone.

"Look here, Deeming," I said, quietly. "If we are to continue friends, there must really be an end of all this mystery and suspicion about nothing. Why shouldn't I tell Vernon where you live?"

"Did you tell him?"

"Certainly. He asked me, and of course I answered. Are you a criminal hiding from justice, and is Vernon a detective? Upon my word—"

I felt I was getting hot, and was silent. He stood quite still, staring at me for a moment with eyes that were almost fierce. Then he sat down on a sofa a little way from me, and said in a calmer voice:

"Yes, of course there was no reason. Still, it's very odd. You must see that."

"What is there odd in it? If it's a good house, why shouldn't Vernon take it as well as anyone else?"

"It's a fairly good house."

He moved, and leaned towards me.

"Originally," he said, speaking slowly, "originally it was one with mine. The two houses were thrown into one. That was when Renold, the author, lived there. Afterwards, it was as it is now. But it's still almost like one house."

"How can that be?"

"Well, the alteration was very flimsily carried out, I suppose; for in the one house one can—I hope to goodness Vernon isn't much of a musician."

"You're afraid of being disturbed?"

"If he plays the piano—by Jove!"

He burst into a laugh.

"Look out in the papers very soon," he said. "I shall probably be bringing a case against him for annoyance. I can't stand a hullabaloo next door after I've finished my day's work. I want rest and peace. It's no joke being a successful physician, I can tell you."

I laughed too, almost as unnaturally as he had.

"Oh," I said, "you needn't be afraid. Vernon does play, but I'm sure, if you ask him, he'll put his piano against the wall of the other house, and keep the windows shut when he is practising. Why didn't you speak about it last night?"

"I'll ask no favours of Vernon," he said sternly.

Then he got up.

"I thought I'd just tell you," he said. "Now I can't stop. I've got a patient to see."

He gave me a feverish hand, and went quickly out of the room.

While he was with me, I had endeavoured to make light of his news, to deceive him into the belief that I thought Vernon's action a chance one, but directly I was alone I felt, though less agitated, nearly as angry at this affair as he did. It was a strange business—this pursuit. Deeming had said to me at Dover that Vernon was a "black fanatic"; what if it were so? What if my friend, so kind, so calm, even so unusually gentle in ordinary life, well balanced and eminently sane in his outlook upon men and affairs, really had a "screw loose"—to use the current phrase? What if the fate of his dog had actually affected his mind? I knew that there are men in the world who are sound on all subjects except one. Touch upon that subject, and they show an eccentricity that is akin to madness. It might be so with Vernon. I began to feel as if it must be so, and a great restlessness, a great uneasiness, beset me. Driven by it, I caught up my hat, hurried downstairs, hailed a hansom, and went to Claridge's.

The hall porter informed me that Mr. Kersteven was out.

"Do you happen to know where he has gone?" I asked.

"No, sir; he didn't leave any word."

My cab was waiting. I jumped into it again and called to the man:

"Go to 301, Wimpole Street."

My instinct told me that I should find Vernon there.

Night was now falling. It was the hour when, to me, London presents its dreariest aspect. The streets are not yet thronged with those who, having worked during the day, are beginning to seek their nocturnal pleasures. The just-lit lamps are waging a feeble combat with the last fading rays of the flickering twilight. There is a sense of something closing in, like a furtive enemy, upon the great city. As I neared Wimpole Street I noticed that a fine rain was beginning to fall. The air was damp, without freshness, oppressive. In the gloom the cabman mistook the number and stopped at Deeming's door. I got out quickly, paid and dismissed him, and was about to move on to Number 301, when it seemed to me that I heard the shrill, short whine of a dog. It startled me, and I remained where I was, listening in the rain. The sound was not repeated. I looked down the dismal street, but I saw no animal. I had not been able to locate the noise. I glanced at Deeming's house. It was dark. Only from a window in the area shone a pale gleam of light. After two or three minutes' hesitation I moved away, ascended the step of Number 301, and pressed the electric bell. There was no response.

I pressed it again and kept my finger upon it for at least a minute. This time my summons was answered, though in a rather unorthodox fashion. A window on the first floor was pushed up, and I saw a vague face looking out at me from above.

"Vernon," I said, "is it you?"

No voice replied, but the window was shut down, and almost directly, through some glass above the hall door, I saw a bright light start up, and I heard a faint movement within. Then the door was opened and Vernon stood before me. He looked greatly surprised.

"You?" he said. "How on earth did you know I was here?"

"I didn't know it. Can I come in?"

"Yes. Why not?"

But he still stood in the doorway, blocking up the entrance.

"You're alone?" he asked, rather suspiciously.

"Quite alone."

"Come in."

I stepped into a hideous passage, and he at once shut the door.

"Well?" he said.

Not only his voice, but his attitude questioned me.

"I went to Claridge's. They told me you were out, so I came on here on the chance that you might be looking over your new abode."

"So Deeming's been with you!"

"Yes, he came in for a minute, and mentioned casually that you had taken this house."

"Oh! he mentioned it casually, did he? Well, come and have a look at it, won't you?"

"If you don't mind."

He spoke with constraint, and so did I. Indeed, I had never before felt so uncomfortable with Vernon as I did at this moment. I did not know exactly what I had expected of him if I found him at the house; but it certainly was not this cold reserve, as of one who scarcely knew me, and to whom my appearance was unwelcome.

"It's not a bad house," he said, as we went towards the stairs. "It will do very well for me for the season."

"You're in luck, then."

The words faltered on my lips even while I strove to speak carelessly, for, in truth, knowing Vernon as I did, knowing his house in Rome, it was almost impossible not to express my amazement at his choice—or, no, perhaps not that, for I could no longer be in any doubt as to why he had rented Number 301—but it was almost impossible to keep up the ridiculous pretence, forced upon me by his words and manner, that I thought he had rented Number 301 because it had seemed to him a suitable London home.

A more dreadful house I have seldom seen. The stamp of bad taste, of pretentious middle-class vulgarity, was upon it, showing in every detail, in the colouring of walls, in the patterns of carpets, in the shapes of the furniture, in the tiles of the hearths, in the very balusters and fire-irons. The mirrors were painted with bulrushes, poppies, tulips. Cushions of brown and sulphur-coloured plush lay upon settees that imitated shells. Chocolate-hued portières hung across double doors, upon which were views of Swiss lakes and Alpine heights. There were ceilings that represented the starry firmament, and there were floors that suggested the vegetable-monger's shop. In cosy corners, thick with dusty draperies, nestled imitation beetles and frogs, among Japanese fans and squads of photographs of possibly well-known actresses, roofed in by open umbrellas of paper, from whose spokes hung gilded balls.

And there were yellow spotted palms in pots, wrapped, like a face distraught with toothache, in smothering cloths of bilious yellow and of shrieking green.

"Not a bad house, is it?" said Vernon once more, when we had partially explored it. By the words, by his manner, I was made at once to realise that from this moment he intended to keep me out of his confidence. Why this was so I could only try to surmise. As to action, all I could do was to accept the situation and follow him in travesty with as good a grace as possible. It was evident that Vernon's suspicions of my good faith had been aroused by my unexpected visit, following so immediately upon Deeming's announcement of the taking of the house, and that he had resolved to show me that he would not permit any criticism, even any discussion of his doings, however strange, however hostile to Deeming they must seem to me in the light of recent events.

"Not at all bad," I answered. We were standing at the moment in the terrible double drawing room. I carefully abstained from looking round. There was an instant of, to me, rather embarrassing silence. Then Vernon said:

"Well, shall we go out together? It's getting rather late. You hadn't anything special to say to me, I suppose?"

"No, nothing I just called at the hotel, and thought, as you were out, I might find you examining your new abode."

Even as I spoke I involuntarily shuddered; I thought at the idea of Vernon living in this house, this inmost sanctuary of Philistinism.

"Why did you do that?" he said sharply.

"What?"

"Shiver like that. Did you—did you hear anything?"

His eyes searched mine; and once more I saw the fierce light in them.

"Hear? No. What should I hear?"

He did not answer; but continued to stare at me as if he doubted my words. Then he said abruptly:

"Let us be off, then."

We descended the stairs and let ourselves out into the darkness and the rain. As we passed Deeming's house I seemed once more to hear the shrill whimper of a dog. I wondered if Vernon had heard it too, for he hesitated by the step of the door, almost as if he thought of mounting it, and glanced swiftly down to the area, from which still shone the ray of light. But he said nothing, and we walked on, and were soon in the bustle of Oxford Street.

V

After seeing Vernon that evening in No. 301, Wimpole Street, I knew two things for certain. One was that he had taken the house in order to be next door to Deeming; the other, that whatever project he might have formed, whatever intention or desire was driving him on into a strange path, he did not mean me to know of it through him. I was to be shut out from his confidence.

This fact, while it irritated me, also relieved me. It rendered my position as the friend of both men more tenable than it could have been had Vernon confided in me. Now, if at any time Deeming were suspicious of me, I should be able to confront him with the complacency of a complete innocence, whereas hitherto I had more than once experienced the discomfort of—I hope I may say it without offence—an honourable man who is forced by circumstance to practise a mild deceit. This was a relief.

Nevertheless, I did feel both irritation and surprise at Vernon's attitude towards me. It seemed to throw a chill over our friendship. If he had never spoken to me of Deeming and his black spaniel, the matter would not have troubled me, but a confidence begun and then abruptly discontinued surely implies that one's friendship is doubted. I could no longer feel quite at ease when I was with Vernon. A dark and cringing shadow separated us.

Vernon moved into his dreadful house two days after I had first seen it. I naturally expected that, being a rich man, he would immediately begin to tear down draperies, to get in new furniture, to lay down carpets that did not recall the vegetable-monger's, to turn out the frogs and the beetles, and to do away with the paper umbrellas. I was mistaken. He left things much as they were.

"I don't suppose I shall be here long," he said.

"I thought you had the house on a year's lease?" I rejoined.

"The owner wouldn't let it for a shorter time. But I don't expect to be here for twelve months, or anything like it. I may be out of it in a month. Who knows?"

He glanced at me as if he expected me to find some hidden meaning in his words, some meaning which he did not choose to put before me.

"I'm not even going to be bothered with a staff of servants," he continued. "I shall only have my man, Cragg, and one woman who can do all that is necessary for me."

"Really! What does Cragg think of it?" I ventured.

"Oh, Cragg has been with me for years and thoroughly understands me."

I knew that; I knew, too, that Cragg was a rare being, a confidential servant who was absolutely faithful. But, still, Cragg was unaccustomed to such a peculiar kind of "roughing it" as was now in prospect.

"I hope you'll be comfortable," I said, rather lamely.

"Oh, yes. Of course, I don't intend to entertain here. I shall imitate Deeming. I shall exercise all my hospitality in restaurants. The Englishman's house is more than ever his castle since the restaurant came into fashion."

And he laughed.

"But perhaps, now I'm next door, Deeming may ask me in sometimes in the evening," he said. "We ought to be neighbourly."

Something in his voice, as he said the last words, turned me cold. I felt quite sure, for the first time, that hatred was blazing in his heart, hatred against Deeming. Of course, I could not speak of my new certainty now that I was confronted by his reserve, but a sudden idea sprang up within my brain. There was one way, and one way only, of brushing aside this spider's web of suspicion and intrigue, which was being woven day by day, and it was this. If I could only ascertain for myself, and prove to Vernon, that the mysterious black spaniel was happy as had been his "Whisper," well-cared-for, well-loved, these two men who were at secret enmity would doubtless at once be reconciled, and I should no longer have to endure the vexation of being on uneasy terms with both. Vernon knew me well enough to know that if I made a solemn statement he could absolutely rely upon it. Deeming disliked him, as men generally and naturally dislike those who, without good reason, are suspicious of them. But though he was now cold and distant with me, I could not think that he disliked me. Where Vernon would probably fail, I might surely succeed. It was such a simple matter after all. I merely wanted to see a dog with his master, Deeming with his black spaniel. That could surely be managed without much difficulty and before many days had elapsed. I said nothing to Vernon of my project.

Indeed, I resolved not to seek a meeting with him until I had accomplished it. Our present intercourse was too restrained to be particularly agreeable. The London season was setting in and there was much to be got through. I could easily avoid Vernon for a few days and, when I had the news I wanted, go to him and put an end to a condition of things at once painful and—so I called it resolutely to myself—ridiculous.

Having made up my mind, I had only to act. I must see Deeming's black spaniel, and see him with his master.

I began my campaign by calling one evening at Deeming's house at an hour when I thought it probable that the last sufferer would have gone.

But I had miscalculated his popularity as a doctor. His extremely thin and sympathetic butler informed me in a whispering voice that the waiting room was still thronged with anxious patients.

"When is he free?" I inquired.

"He is engaged all day, Sir, at this season of the year."

"Does he never get out for a breath of air?"

"Oh, yes, Sir, when he drives out to the hospital."

"And on a Sunday, I suppose. No doubt"—I tried to make my voice very natural and careless at this point—"he goes out on a Sunday if it's fine, to give the dog a run, eh?"

It seemed to me that the butler's pale face slightly twisted as I said the last words, as if he made a sudden effort not to show in it some expression which would have betrayed a feeling; as if he suppressed, perhaps, a smile, or concealed a knowing leer.

"The Doctor's generally shut up on a Sunday, writing, Sir," he murmured, "or pursuing his researches."

"Oh!"

There seemed nothing more to be done just then, and as I saw a patient coming out and looking for his hat in the hall, I went away.

That evening I wrote to Deeming, telling him I had called to see if I could persuade him to take a stroll, as I was sure his health needed some rest, air, and relaxation.

"Will you come for a walk in Regent's Park some Sunday morning?" I ended, regardless of the butler's information.

He answered, by return, that he would come, if I liked, on the following Sunday. I replied, fixing the hour, and saying I would call for him. This done, I went out and—bought a dog.

It was a gay fox-terrier, young, full of abounding life, and quite ready to attach itself to anyone who was kind to it. When Sunday arrived, it was already devoted to me, and gleefully accompanied me to Wimpole Street to fetch Deeming for the promised walk. While I rang the bell it squatted on the step, wagging its short tail, and looking eagerly expectant. The butler opened the door.

"The Doctor is quite ready, Sir," he said, when he saw me. "Will you step in?"

Suddenly he caught sight of the dog, who had jumped up when the door was opened, and was evidently preparing for exploration. "Is that your dog, Sir?"

"Yes," I said.

"I don't think the Doctor— Get back, you little beast!"

The last exclamation came in a voice so different from the whispering one I was accustomed to that I could hardly believe it was the butler who had spoken. At the same moment my dog dodged his outstretched foot and vanished, pattering, into the house.

"Call him back, Sir; call him back, for the Lord's sake, or there'll be trouble!" exclaimed the butler, turning sharply with the evident intention of trying to catch the little culprit. But he had no time to act nor I to call. Almost as he spoke there came from within the house the piercing cry of a dog in pain, and the fox-terrier darted out of the hall, down the street, and disappeared, yelping shrilly as he went, with his ears set flat against his head, and his tail tucked down in his back. As he vanished, Deeming appeared at the hall door.

"How dare you let stray dogs into my house?" he said to the butler in a savage voice.

"I beg pardon, Sir," stammered the butler; "but it was this gentleman's dog, and—"

"It was your dog, was it?" said Deeming, turning to me. "I did not know you had a dog."

I was feeling so angry that I could hardly trust myself to speak.

"Certainly it's mine," I said curtly. "I must go and find it."

And without another word I walked away down the street. I could not discover the dog. Its terror had evidently been so great that it had fled blindly and far. From that day to this I have never seen it or heard anything of it. When it rushed out of Deeming's house it rushed out of my life. Having failed to find it, after walking some distance, I gave up the search and stood still. The natural thing, I suppose, would have been to retrace my steps to Wimpole Street, where Deeming was waiting for me. But this I did not do. I felt that I could not do it. An invincible repulsion against Deeming's society had come into my heart. When I thought of him I saw the fox-terrier fleeing, with his ears set back against his head; I heard the yelping of a dog.

I stood, therefore, for a moment, and then walked home to Albemarle Street.

I had bought the dog in order to find out, if possible, how Deeming was with animals, how they comported themselves towards him. Secondarily I had thought of using the dog as a pretext for introducing the subject of the black spaniel. I had meant, when Deeming came out, to point to my dog and suggest that, as I had mine with me for the walk, he should bring out his.

Well, my curiosity had surely been satisfied. I had not, it is true, seen the mysterious black spaniel; but I could hardly remain in doubt as to Deeming's attitude towards pet animals. The expression upon his face as he came out from the hall had been ferocious. Vernon was right. Deeming was a cruel man. As I realised that, I began to wonder more about the black spaniel. Why should such a man keep a pet—a man, too, who was so incessantly occupied that he had no time for amusement, for almost any relaxations? And why had the butler—for I now felt sure that I had seen his face contorted for an instant on the evening when I had spoken to him of the black spaniel—why had the butler felt such amazement, or bitter contempt, or sardonic amusement, when I had alluded to the possibility of Deeming giving the black spaniel a run?

It almost began to seem to me just then as if the black spaniel were a baleful chimera, like the creation of a madman's brain, a nothingness that yet can govern, can terrify, can cause tragic events and lead to bitterness and crime. Who had ever seen this creature? Where was it, in what place of concealment? Did it ever come forth into the light of day? I longed to know something of it, of its existence in that house, of its relations with its master.

Perhaps Vernon knew or would know. He lived next door. He had gone there to discover; of that I was sure. He watched at his window to see the spaniel let out. He listened at his wall at night, perhaps, to hear its whining.

Perhaps Vernon knew or would know.

And when he knew, would he tell me?

In the afternoon of that day I received a note from Deeming:

> I waited for you to come back for an age. What was the
> matter? I am very sorry about your dog. The fact is I am not
> very well and in a nervous condition, and it startled me to
> come suddenly upon it in the dimly lighted hall. Let me
> know when we can meet.
>
>   P. D.

That was the note. I read it several times before I threw it into the wastepaper basket. But I did not answer it. I felt that I did not want to meet Deeming again for some time.

I felt that. Fate willed it that I should never look upon him again as mortal man. Within two days from that time I was called to the North of England by the serious illness of my dear mother, who lived in Cumberland. And there I remained until she died. Her death took place on the twenty-seventh of June. Her funeral was three days later. After it was over I returned to the house where I had been born, where I was now quite alone with the servants. I had to wind up many affairs, to put many things in order, to sort and examine papers and pay off some of the household. Despite my grief I was obliged to be busy, to be practical. For several days I was so much occupied that I did not look at a newspaper. I even set aside the letters that came by the post-letters of condolence, I felt sure they were, most of them—wishing to read them and answer them all together when I had leisure, and felt less miserable and deserted, and more able to take an interest in such affairs as were not actually forced upon me.

At last one evening I had got through everything. I had dined, and was sitting alone in the drawing room, where my mother had always sat, feeling really almost as if I dwelt in a world unpeopled, or peopled only by the spectres of those who once had lived, when a servant came in with the last post. There were no letters, only two or three papers from London. Without interest, merely to do something, I tore the paper covering from one and unfolded it. My eyes fell at once upon the following paragraph:

> As so many rumours have been put into circulation with regard to the lamented decease of Dr. Peter Deeming, which took place on the 30th of June, we are glad to be able to state authoritatively that the actual cause of death was blood poisoning, which was, it seems, set up by the bite of a dog. Doctor Deeming, like many other eminent medical men, while solicitous for the health of others, was singularly careless about his own. The bite was severe, but he took little heed of it, although he had the dog, which was a pet, destroyed. He has now paid the penalty of his regrettable carelessness, and society is the poorer. For no West End physician was more trusted and esteemed by his patients than Dr. Deeming.

The paper dropped from my hand.

So Deeming and the black spaniel were dead! And each had destroyed the other!

Part II—The Resurrection

VI

Peter Deeming died on the thirtieth of June, in the year 1900. In June of the following year, as I was walking past the Knightsbridge Barracks, I met Vernon strolling along in the sunshine, with a cigarette in his mouth. When he saw me, he stopped, took my hand, and clasped it warmly.

"Back at last!" he said.

"Yes. I only arrived yesterday. Did you winter in Rome, as usual?"

"No. I've not been out of England."

"Good Heavens!" I exclaimed. "You don't mean to say you've been facing the London fogs while I've been in Africa and Sicily?"

He nodded.

"What can have been your reason?"

He put his arm through mine.

"Let's go into the Park," he said. "We'll take a stroll, and I'll tell you."

We turned into the Park by the nearest gate, and walked gently along under the trees. It was a strangely radiant day for London—a day that seemed full of hope and gaiety. Many children were about laughing, playing, calling to each other. Poor people basked in the sunshine, stretched upon the short grass. Carriages rolled by, drawn by fine horses. In the trees the birds were singing, as innocently as they sing in retired country places. And I felt glad and at ease. It was pleasant to be with Vernon once more, pleasant to be once more in my own land among my own people.

"Well, Vernon?" I said.

"First," he answered, "you must tell me something. You must tell me why you left England after the death of your mother, without coming to say good-bye to me."

"I felt upset, broken down, as if I didn't want to see anyone, as if I wanted to get away and be alone among new scenes and people who were strangers."

"That was it?"

I heard the doubt in his voice, and added:

"There was another reason, too, an under-reason."

"Yes?"

"That sudden death of poor Deeming, coming just after my mother's, upset my nerves, I think. It made me feel as if—as if I had been cruel.

It filled me with regret."

"Cruel! I don't understand."

"No. How could you? But when a man's dead, one thinks very differently about him often. And I had been suspicious of Deeming. At the end, indeed, I had been unfriendly."

"I am quite in the dark," he said, rather coldly, I thought.

I explained to him what I meant. I told him of my last meeting with Deeming, of the incident of the fox-terrier, of Deeming's note to me, of how I had left it unanswered. He listened with a profound attention.

"When I read of his death in the paper I wished I had answered his note," I concluded. "I wished it more than I can tell you. And I regretted bitterly that the last weeks of our intercourse had been clouded by suspicion, by misunderstanding."

"Ah!"

His voice still sounded cold. After a moment he said: "And you didn't come to see me because—"

"Well, you had been mixed up with my suspicion of Deeming, and—"

"Now I understand. You felt a very natural longing to be away from all that recalled sadness to you, that might deepen your grief or serve to irritate your nerves."

"I suppose that was it. I went right away. I wanted to forget, to escape out of a dark cloud into a clear atmosphere. But you? Why have you been in London all this time?"

"I've been working."

"Working! You?"

"Even I—idler, dilettante."

"Music?"

"I've been working with Arthur Gernham."

"For the animals?"

"Exactly. For our brothers and sisters who do not speak our language. I've been writing pamphlets, I've been gathering subscriptions, I've been stirring people up, and by doing so I've been stirring myself up, my slothful, sluggish, unpractical self."

"Wonderful!"

"Isn't it? Do you know that I've toured the United Kingdom giving lectures on the subject of man's duty to the animals, that I've helped to form a league of kindness? Luttrell, I'm a busy man now, and I am an enthusiastic man."

While he spoke his animation had been growing, and as he ended his voice was full of energy.

"And when did the impulse come to you to begin this new life?" I asked.

"I can tell you the very day," he said. "It was on June the 30th of last year."

"June the 30th!" I said. "Why, that was the day that Deeming died!"

"Well, it was on that day."

I looked at him sharply. I had never yet heard any details connected with the accident that had brought about Deeming's illness and so caused his death. I wondered if Vernon knew any. He had lived next door. I longed to ask him, but something, some inner voice of my nature, advised me not to.

"Is Gernham a good fellow?" I said carelessly.

"A splendid fellow. You must know him."

"As you have changed so much," I continued, "have you altered that resolution of yours?"

"What resolution?"

"Never to make another animal happy as you made your spaniel, Whisper, happy?"

"Ah, that—no! I could never have another pet. I suffered too much from my affection, Luttrell. I am resolved not to suffer again in that way. The mountains may fall, but I shall never keep another dog."

He spoke with a decision that carried conviction. At that moment I should have been ready to stake my entire fortune on his sticking to his assertion and backing it up by his acts. If anyone had come to me that night and said, "Your friend Vernon has just bought a dog and taken it home to live with him," I should have laughed, and answered in polite terms, "You're a liar." But one cannot deny the evidence of one's own eyes.

Now this is exactly what occurred.

While we walked along beneath the trees, not very far from the Statue of Achilles, I saw in the distance a man approaching us, leading a number of dogs by strings and carrying a couple of puppies under his arms. He wore a fur cap and earrings, a short, loud-patterned coat with tails, and a pair of very tight trousers. As he drew near I saw that among the dogs who accompanied him there was a fine black spaniel.

"Here comes a choice assortment of dumb friends," I said to Vernon. "Yes."

I saw him looking at the dogs, which were sniffing the air, and pulling at their leads in the endeavour to investigate delicious smells. Suddenly he stopped short, just as the man was passing us. At the same moment I saw the black spaniel shrink back and cower down against the ground, pressing his broad, flapping ears against his head.

"What is it, Vernon?" I said. He did not reply. He was staring at the spaniel. The owner of the dogs saw a possible purchaser, and at once, in a soft and very disagreeable voice, began to enumerate their merits.

"H'sh!" Vernon hissed at him.

The man stopped in astonishment.

"That dog there," said Vernon, pointing to the black spaniel, which was still shrinking down, and pulling back from his lead in an effort to get away. "How long have you had him?"

"Ever since he was baun, gen'leman," replied the man. "'E's the gentlenist, the bestmannered dawg as hiver—"

"How old is he? What's his age?"

"Just upon a year, Sir, a year 'e'll be this very selfsame month. 'E was one of as fine a litter o' pups as—"

"You bred him?"

"Yes, Sir."

"A year old, is he?"

"Just upon, Sir. The thirtieth's the day, Sir—the thirtieth of this selfsame month. Law bless you, I knows the birthdays of hivery dawg as hiver—"

"What's his price?"

The man licked his lips, and I saw a gleam in his small eyes.

"Well, Sir, I dunno as I'm dispoged to part with 'im. You see, I gets to love—"

"How much?"

The tone was sharp. The words came almost like a pistol shot.

"Ten puns, Sir," said the man. "I should say, fifteen puns, Sir."

"I'll give you twelve."

"I reely couldn't tike it, Sir. The dawg's the very happle of—"

"There's my address—301, Wimpole Street." He gave the man his card. "Bring the dog there at six o'clock this evening, and you shall have twelve pounds, not a penny more. Good-day."

"I'll be there, Sir. You can trust me, you can—"

We walked on. As we did so, the spaniel whimpered, ran to his master, and fawned about his legs as if demanding protection.

For several minutes neither Vernon nor I said a word. I was in amazement. What had just happened may seem to some a very small matter. To me it seemed extraordinary, mysterious, even—I could not tell why—horrible. There had been something peculiar in Vernon's attitude, in his face, while he stood looking at the spaniel, something fatal that had affected my nerves. Then my wonder was naturally great that such a man should thus abruptly go back from his word. And the spaniel's cringing attitude of terror when Vernon had gazed at him, had spoken to his master, was disagreeable to me, acutely disagreeable in the remembrance of it! It seemed to me very strange and unnatural that such an ardent lover of animals as Vernon was should inspire an animal with fear. Animals have an instinct that always tells them who loves them. This spaniel was apparently without this instinct.

Perhaps it was this lack in him that made me now think of him with a faint dislike, even a faint disgust, such as the healthy-minded feel when brought into contact with anything unnatural.

I broke the silence first.

"I did not know you were a changeable man," I said.

"You mean that I have changed my mind about keeping a dog."

"Yes, and with such extraordinary suddenness."

"I suppose it does seem odd," he remarked. "But who knows what he will do?"

"But what was your reason?"

He looked at me, very strangely, I thought.

"A sudden impulse," he answered. "A memory, perhaps, moved me."

"The memory of Whisper?"

"Of Whisper—of course."

His voice seemed to me just then as strange as his face. Perhaps seeing that I still wondered, he added:

"That spaniel appeared to be nervous, terrified. Perhaps that man is cruel to it."

"Oh, but—" I began, and stopped. "What is it?"

"You didn't think it seemed to me that it was you who inspired the dog with fear."

"I!" He laughed. "My dear fellow, a dog-lover like myself cannot inspire a dog with fear. You must be mistaken. Animals always know who loves them."

"Yes. It's very strange," I murmured.

"What is strange?" he asked, in rather a hard voice.

"Oh, I don't know—nothing," I answered evasively. "Here we are at the gate."

"Yes. Well, you are coming to see me?"

"Of course. You are still in that house?"

"Oh, yes. It suits me. When will you come?"

"Whenever you like."

He stood for a moment, making patterns with his stick on the pavement and looking down. Then he glanced up at me.

"Come and have a cup of tea this afternoon at half-past five, will you?" he said.

I immediately thought of the man with the earrings and the fur cap. Then I was to see the transfer of the black spaniel.

"I'll come," I answered.

"Right!"

Vernon nodded and walked away slowly in the direction of Hamilton Place.

VII

At a quarter past five that day I started for Wimpole Street, filled with a sensation of strong curiosity, for which, in mental debate with myself, I could not quite satisfactorily account. It was a very ordinary matter, surely, this selling and buying of a dog. Why, then, did it seem to me an affair of importance? I asked myself that question while I waited. The only answer I could find was that the dog was a black spaniel, and that before the sad death of my friend Deeming a black spaniel, the creature that had caused the tragedy, had mysteriously complicated, and indeed altered, my pleasant relations both with him and with Vernon. But all that was a year ago. The past does not return, and therefore it was absurd to be—to be—what? What was really the exact nature of the emotion that now beset me? Had I been strictly truthful with myself I should, perhaps, have called it apprehension. But we are not always strictly truthful even with ourselves. I think that day I named it nervousness. I was nervous, out of sorts, a little bit depressed. Vernon's *volte-face* had surprised me. The dog's cringing fear had made an unpleasant impression upon me. And so, now, as I drew near to Wimpole Street I was slightly strung up. That was the long and short of it.

In some such fashion I think I spoke to myself, explanatorily, falsely.

When I turned into Wimpole Street the image of poor Deeming was very present in my mind, and I could scarcely believe that he did not still inhabit the house to which I had come that Sunday morning. I wondered who lived there now, who was Vernon's neighbour; and when I reached the house I looked towards it with a sad curiosity, which quickly changed to surprise. The house was transformed. Where once had been a doorstep there was now an area railing. The front door had vanished. In its place was a window, with a box in which roses and geraniums were blooming. In a moment I realised what had happened. Formerly the two houses—Nos. 300 and 301—had been one house. Since I had been there they had once more been thrown together. Vernon, then, was living now in the house that had been Deeming's. As I grasped this fact, Vernon appeared at a window of what had been the second house. Seeing me, he smiled and waved his hand. Before I could ring, the door was opened by Cragg, his faithful man.

"Glad to see you again, Sir," said Cragg, with a respectful bow which he had learnt, I think, in Italy. He had several little foreign ways, but was extremely English in appearance—calm, solid, neat, and closely shaven. I returned his greeting and stepped in.

"Ah," I said, looking round. "So it's all changed."

"Yes, Sir. After Doctor Deeming's death we got rid of the old stuff, and Mr. Kersteven bought the Doctor's house and threw the two houses into one. It's more suitable now."

"It was awful before."

"Well, Sir, it was scarcely to Mr. Kersteven's taste. We rather roughed it for a time, Sir."

He took my hat and stick and showed me upstairs into a charming drawing room, in which I at once recognised many beautiful things from Vernon's house in Rome. Here Vernon met me with an outstretched hand.

"By Jove, what a transformation!" I exclaimed.

"To be sure, you haven't seen it since—"

"Since the frogs and the beetles and the Japanese umbrellas were turned out. No. And so now you've got Deeming's house too?"

"Yes. I have joined the two together, but I use his chiefly for my work in connection with our dumb friends."

"Oh!"

His voice was significant in that last sentence, and I realised that in him imagination was often the guide, leading him strangely, dominating him powerfully.

Tea was ready, and we sat down. Giving expression to my thought, I said, "Strange that you should be living in Deeming's house."

"Why so?"

"Oh, well, you were antagonists, weren't you?"

"Could the difference between us be called antagonism?" he asked, pouring out the tea.

"Wasn't it? Once Deeming told me that he knew—"

I hesitated.

"Knew what?"

"Knew that you hated him."

"Really. Did he say that?"

"Was it true?"

"Why discuss it?"

"You're right. It's all over now. And he, poor chap, has gone beyond the reach of earthly love or hate."

He made no rejoinder, and I had an odd feeling as if he were silent because I had said something with which he did not agree; yet that was not possible.

"Do you think," I said, to change the subject, "do you think that fellow will come?'

"The dog fancier? Oh, I suppose so. He won't let slip a chance of making twelve pounds. His dog isn't worth more than six."

"Then why do you give double?"

"A caprice."

"I begin to think you are a capricious man," I said.

"The dilettante generally is."

He drew out his watch.

"It's close upon six. That chap ought to be here in a moment. Ah, there's the bell! He's come, no doubt."

I was conscious of a certain discomfort, but scarcely knew its cause. Putting down my cup, I sat listening intently. Vernon, too, was listening. There was in his face an expression of strained attention. When the door opened gently, I started and looked hastily round.

"Lord Elyn!" said Vernon, getting up from his chair.

"Yes. Glad to find you at home. Hulloa, Luttrell! So you're back at last! I haven't seen you since the death of our poor friend Deeming."

He shook my hand.

"That was a sad business. No one to take his place. No one like him, is there?"

He sat down and stretched his legs. I said something suitable, but with rather an uncertain voice. This unexpected arrival irritated me. And yet I thoroughly liked Lord Elyn. Vernon, too I felt sure of it—was vexed by his arrival, but he was charmingly courteous, though, in the trifling conversation that followed, he showed traces of absent-mindedness. I knew he was listening for the sound of the bell. I knew he was eagerly awaiting the arrival of the black spaniel. Six o'clock struck. The hand of a clock on the mantelpiece pointed to five minutes, then to ten minutes past six. Vernon began to betray a certain restlessness, a certain uneasiness. He twice changed his place in the room. Finally, he got up and remained standing.

"You are expecting someone?" said Lord Elyn, looking at him in some surprise.

"Yes. The fact is I've bought a dog—or named my price for one—and he ought to be brought here this evening."

"Oh, I'm very fond of dogs. Kept them all my life. What sort of animal is this one?"

"A black—there's the bell!"

He broke off, went swiftly over to the window and looked out. As he stood with his back turned to us I heard him utter a low exclamation.

"What did you say, Vernon?" I asked sharply.

I had not heard a word, but there was a thrilling sound in his voice which startled me. I got up also from my chair, possessed, gnawed by an inexplicable restlessness. Vernon turned round from the window. I saw the strange light in his eyes which I had sometimes noticed there when he talked about the animals and their relation with man.

"It's the spaniel," he said.

The words were simple enough, but the way in which he said them was not simple. It sounded cruel and triumphant.

Lord Elyn looked more surprised. He also got up.

"The arrival of this dog seems quite an event," he said.

"Yes, quite an event," repeated Vernon, looking towards the door. "It's years since I've had a—pet."

"If you please, Sir, there's a person here with a dog."

"I know. I expected him."

"Indeed, Sir. Am I to admit him?"

"Certainly."

"And the dog, Sir? Is he to come in too?"

"Of course. It's the dog I want, not the man."

Cragg remained in the doorway, looking at his master.

"What is it, Cragg?" asked Vernon. "What the deuce is the matter?"

"Well, Sir, I don't see—I don't, really— how we are ever going to get that dog into the house."

"What do you mean?" said Vernon.

On his lips there was playing a slight smile.

"I never see an animal in such a state, Sir; I really never did. Hark, Sir!"

He lifted his hand. From below there came to us the sound of a long-drawn howling. Again I felt a cold chill go over me. Lord Elyn, too, was unpleasantly affected. He shook his shoulders, and said:

"Good God, what a dreadful noise! It sounds like something being tortured."

Vernon was still smiling.

"Oh!" he said; "it's only the natural nervousness of a dog brought to a strange house to change one master for another. Go along, Cragg. Show the man into my study. I'll come down in a moment."

Still looking very doubtful, Cragg disappeared, shutting the door. We three remained silent for a moment. Then Vernon said:

"I'm afraid you're having a very fussy visit, Lord Elyn. Do sit down. I'll go and pay the man, and be back in a minute."

It was evident to me that he wanted—wanted ungovernably—to see the dog brought into the house. As he stopped speaking he was gone. He had almost darted out of the room.

"Dear me!" said Lord Elyn. "Dear me."

He was a delicate, naturally nervous man, and highly sensitive. I could see plainly that he was upset, mystified by this affair of the arrival of the dog. He looked at me as if inquiring of me what it all meant.

"I wonder—" he began. Then he broke off. After a pause he said:

"If the dog often howls as he did just now, Vernon won't have much peace. I never in my life heard a more distressing noise, eh?"

"It was very distressing," I assented.

Lord Elyn did not sit down, but went to and fro in the room like one disturbed.

"A most distressing noise!" he repeated, uncomfortably. "Most distressing. It really almost sounded like a human being in agony, didn't it?"

"Yes, it did."

"What sort of dog is it?" he asked presently, standing before me. "Do you know?"

"A black spaniel."

"A spaniel? They're the most sensitive breed of dog I know, intensely nervous and easily frightened, but very affectionate. They attach themselves in an extraordinary manner to those who are kind to them."

"Hulloa!" he exclaimed. The door had reopened, and Vernon came in.

"Well," he said, "it's all right. I've got the dog for twelve pounds."

"Where is it?" said Lord Elyn.

"Downstairs in my study. I've had to tie him up for the moment. Poor fellow, he's nervous at getting into a strange house."

"Let's have a look at him," said Lord Elyn.

I saw that Vernon hesitated, and thought he was going to refuse the request, natural though it was. But if he had intended to do so, he quickly changed his mind.

"Certainly," he said. "Come downstairs. My study is in the part of the house that once belonged to Deeming."

Lord Elyn went out of the room, I followed, and Vernon came last.

"To the right!" he said, when we reached the bottom of the staircase. "This corridor unites the two houses."

We followed the direction indicated.

"Here's the study," said Vernon. "It's a real workroom, dedicated to the cause of our dumb friends."

"The animals?" said Lord Elyn. "It seems to me, after this evening, that dumb is scarcely the appropriate adjective to apply to them."

Vernon laughed. He had his hand on the door of his study, and was still laughing as he opened it.

VIII

Lord Elyn went in first. I followed. The study was, as Vernon had said, a real workroom. There was little furniture in it, and what there was was plain and serviceable. Near the one window, which looked out at the back on to the backs of other houses, was a large writing table covered with documents, pamphlets, magazines, address books, gum bottles, elastic bands, balls of string, a Remington typewriter, piles of paper bands for fastening newspapers and manuscripts, etc. In the midst of this ordered rummage stood a cabinet photograph of a man.

I did not examine it then, but I knew later that it was Arthur Gernham, the notorious anti-vivisectionist. A few chairs, a thick Turkey carpet, and two revolving bookcases completed the furniture. The walls were tinted a dull red, and there were red curtains at the window. There were no pictures or ornaments. On the mantelpiece stood a clock which struck the quarter after six as we came in.

"Where's the—oh, there he is!" said Lord Elyn.

The black spaniel was lying crouched upon the floor in a corner near the window, a dark patch against the red of the curtain which touched him. He had been tied by a piece of cord to the writing table, but had shrunk back, as if in an effort to escape, until he could go no farther. Now he lay with his face turned towards the door, motionless, staring. When we saw him he did not move. He only looked at us.

He only looked at us, I have said. Then why did Lord Elyn stop short just inside the door, as if startled? Why did I feel an almost invincible desire to get out of this room, even out of this house of my friend? It must have been the violence of terror in the dog's eyes contrasted with the absolute stillness, the stillness as of death, of his body. Yes, I think it must have been that which affected us. For in violence there is always contained the suggestion of intense activity, the suggestion of movement, and the dog's eyes conveyed to me the feeling that his soul was rushing from us, while his body lay there before us against the red curtain like a carven thing.

"There he is!" Lord Elyn repeated in a low voice.

He looked at me and then at Vernon. I thought he was going out of the room, and I am sure he wanted to do so; but he stood where he was in silence and again looked towards the spaniel.

"Well, what do you think of him?" asked Vernon.

The sound of his voice perhaps made Lord Elyn conscious that we were behaving somewhat absurdly, that we were almost huddling together, he and I, beside the door. For he took a step—but only a step—forward, and answered, with an evident effort to speak more naturally:

"Oh, he looks a good specimen. He's well bred; I should say, well bred—yes."

Again he glanced at me as if questioning me. All this time the spaniel did not move, but lay staring at us with eyes full of horror. His stillness appalled me.

"And what do you think, Luttrell?" said Vernon.

It was with a difficulty that was extraordinary to me that I answered him.

"You'll have a lot of trouble with him," I said.

"Why?" said Vernon quickly.

"Why? Why, he's evidently a very nervous dog. I should think it'll take time to reconcile him with his new home and his new master."

"Good God!" said Lord Elyn.

As I finished speaking the dog had suddenly howled again. Involuntarily I stepped back.

Vernon laughed once more.

"Why, anybody would think you were afraid of him," he said. "What's the matter?"

I tried to laugh too—to laugh at myself.

"He gave tongue so very unexpectedly," I said. "Poor fellow! Poor fellow!"

I was speaking to the dog, but I did not go towards him. The faint disgust with which he had already inspired me in the Park was stronger now that I was with him in a room. I was conscious of an almost invincible desire to go straight out of the house, to get into the open air, quickly, without delay. But with this feeling blended another, more subtle, one that surprised me by its force.

I longed, before I went, to untie that crouching dog, to let him escape from the room, the house, to set him free. With the disgust of him mingled a curious pity for him that was inexplicable to me then.

I think Lord Elyn shared my feelings, but he acted differently from me. For, whereas I now moved away to go, he suddenly, with determination, walked forward towards the spaniel. Seeing this, I stopped just outside the door in the corridor. From there I witnessed a sight that increased my sensation of pity, and at the same time deepened my sensation of disgust.

Lord Elyn, when he was near the spaniel, bent down a little, snapping his fingers and saying, "Poor beast! Poor beast!" whereupon the dog suddenly sprang up from the floor against his breast, in an obvious attempt to nestle into his arms as if for protection against some danger.

Lord Elyn, surprised, tried to hold him, but failed, and let him drop heavily to the floor.

Vernon interposed. Going forward quickly he said, "I'm awfully sorry, Lord Elyn. He's muddied you. Come out and Cragg shall brush it off."

The dog shrank back against the curtain.

"Oh, it doesn't matter," Lord Elyn began.

But Vernon took his arm and drew him with a sort of gentle inflexibility towards the door and into the corridor where I was standing.

"Cragg," Vernon called, "Cragg."

"Sir," said the man coming from the hall.

Vernon shut the door of the study sharply.

"Just get a brush, will you? The dog has put his dirty paws on Lord Elyn's coat."

"Certainly, Sir."

He turned on the electric light. Lord Elyn stood under it to be brushed. I noticed that his face looked very white, but thought it might be the effect of the light upon it. When Cragg had finished, Lord Elyn said:

"Good-night, Vernon," and walked hastily towards the hall door.

"May I come with you?" I said.

"Do."

I bade Vernon good-bye with a word and a hand-grasp, and in a moment Lord Elyn and I were out in the street.

"Ouf!" said Lord Elyn, blowing out his breath.

He stood still, looking towards that part of the house which had been Deeming's.

"By Jove!" he said, as if speaking to himself.

Then, suddenly conscious that he was not alone, he exclaimed:

"Pray forgive me, Luttrell, but the fact is I—well, I don't know why, but that dog has made a very disagreeable impression on me, very disagreeable. D'you know, when he sprang upon me just now I felt a sensation—by Jove, it was a sensation of horror, of abject horror."

He walked on slowly.

"I noticed you were looking very pale in the hall," I said.

"Pale? I should think so! The whole business— I say, what did you think of it, eh?"

"How do you mean?" I asked evasively.

"What d'you think of the dog?"

"Poor beast! It seemed very nervous."

"Nervous! It was half-mad with terror. I never saw a dog in such a state before. And Vernon such a lover of animals, too! That's the strange part of it."

"You think it was Vernon it was afraid of?"

"To be sure. Didn't you see it spring upon me for protection, and directly he approached it shrank away like a thing demented? Now, I've been with animals all my life—brought up among 'em—and never before have I seen an animal's instinct betray it. Animals know in a second the men that are fond of 'em and the men who hate 'em. But this dog's all at sea. It thinks Vernon's a regular devil—a dog torturer. It's half-crazed with fear of him. That is as plain as a pikestaff. The thing's unnatural, Luttrell—it's d—d unnatural!"

He spoke with a vehemence that showed how greatly his nerves were upset. I could not contradict, because I absolutely agreed with him.

"That dog," he added, "gives me the shudders."

"Poor wretch!" I said.

"You pity him too?" he asked.

"Yes. But when he gets to know Vernon it will be all right. Vernon has a positive passion for animals."

I strove to speak with conviction, for I was trying to convince myself.

"I know he has. And yet—"

He hesitated.

"What, Lord Elyn."

"Well, didn't it strike you that he looked at the dog very queerly?"

"Queerly?"

"Yes, not as if he had a great fancy for it."

I said nothing

"What made him buy it?" said Lord Elyn.

"I've no idea," I answered.

And indeed at that moment I was wondering, wondering almost passionately.

"I'll swear he doesn't like the dog," said Lord Elyn, still with vehemence. "He may be as fond of animals as you like, but he isn't fond of this one."

"If he hadn't taken a liking to it why should he buy it?"

"That's more than I can say. It's a queer business. I had an idea that— that you perhaps, had some inkling what was up."

And again his look questioned me.

"I haven't indeed," I said.

And I spoke the truth. I was in the dark, in blackness.

A hansom passed us slowly at this moment. Lord Elyn hailed it.

"I must get home," he said. "I'm dining out. Shall I give you a lift?"

"No, thank you. I'll walk. I like the exercise."

"Good-bye, then."

He stepped into the cab and drove off, while I walked slowly back to Albemarle Street.

Lord Elyn had made my thoughts clearer to me by his blunt expressions. He had asked me if I had any inkling of what was up, and, when he said that, I knew quite certainly that, to use that slangy phrase, I thought something was up. Vernon had been moved by some strange impulse to buy the black spaniel, had some strange purpose in connection with it. I felt sure of this. My instinct told me that it was so. What had caused this impulse? What was this purpose?

I wondered, but could not tell.

I reviewed Vernon's character as I knew it carefully, considered all that I had heard of him from others, trying to find a clue that would guide me to comprehension. But I remained perplexed. I knew good of him. I had always heard praise of him, except from one person, the man who was dead and in whose house he now lived. Deeming had said to me once that Vernon was a black fanatic; the phrase was strong, brutal even. It recurred to my mind as I walked, and stayed there. Then I thought of the terror in the spaniel's eyes as it lay motionless against the red curtain of the workroom. And I was troubled, I was strangely ill at ease. It seemed to me that in my friend, hidden away like a thing hidden in a cave, was something mysterious, something even terrible, and that the black spaniel was connected with it. But how could that be? Vernon loved all animals. He was at this very moment devoting his life to the advancement of their welfare. For them he had thrown off his long idleness of the lounging traveller, the luxurious art lover, who wandered from country to country buying to please his whim. For them he stayed in England and lived laborious days. Why, then, when I thought of the spaniel shut up in his study, should I be chilled with fear? I reasoned with myself, but in vain. The sense of fear, of mystery, remained with me. It was deepened by an incident which occurred six days later.

During those days I had not seen Vernon; I had heard nothing of him or of the black spaniel.

The incident to which I alluded was my meeting for the first time with Arthur Gernham.

At a man's dinner, given by a famous throat specialist renowned not only as a surgeon but as a host, I found myself sitting opposite to a very remarkable looking man of about forty years of age. I had not been introduced to him, and had no idea who he was, but he at once attracted my attention by his air of fiery vitality and his unconventional attire. Instead of the ordinary evening dress, he wore a pair of black trousers, a loose silk shirt with a turned-down collar and very small black tie, and a double-breasted smoking coat which concealed his waistcoat, if he had one. His powerful, sinewy wrists were unfettered by cuffs, and his powerful throat was free from the stiff linen ramparts over which the average Englishman faces the world in the evening. He was evidently a man who hated restraint. His face was pale, of the hatchet type, with a long hooked nose, the bridge of which was unusually marked; a large mouth, unsmiling but not unkind; a narrow, very high forehead, and gleaming hazel eyes. His head was sparsely covered with odd tufts of light-brown hair.

During dinner Gernham talked a great deal in a rasping voice. His conversation was interesting, for he was not only intelligent, but obviously an enthusiast, and one who was entirely fearless of the opinion of others. I wondered much who he was, and as we were getting up from the table I found an opportunity to ask my host.

"Arthur Gernham," he said. "Very down on us doctors, but an interesting fellow. In another age he'd have courted persecution for the faith that is in him. Let me introduce you."

And he did so.

Gernham shook me warmly by the hand.

"My dear colleague Kersteven has often spoken of you," he said. "You sympathise with our efforts, don't you?"

He jerked his head upwards and looked at me keenly. I said something—I've forgotten what—and he continued abruptly:

"Come along. Let's have a good talk. Have a cigar."

He gave me a very large one, flung himself down in an armchair, and talked enthusiastically of Vernon.

"I've been almost living in his house this last week," he said. "We're preparing a fresh campaign on behalf of the blessed beasts, our brothers. We've got together some statistics that'll startle the comfortable elbow-chair Englishmen, I can tell you. I'll never rest till I've roused the country to the horrors that are being perpetrated every day, every hour, every minute, upon the defenceless animals God has committed to us to be good to. And Vernon—what a splendid chap he is! What a colleague! All pity! The man's made of pity, made of tenderness. Ah, but you know that!"

"Yes!" I said.

I thought of the black spaniel. Here was an opportunity to find out how Vernon and his pet were getting on together.

"You've been in the house with Vernon a great deal lately?" I began.

"Every day and all day," he said, "this last week."

"How's that new pet of his?" I asked. "Reconciled and happy in his new home?"

"Pet?" said Gernham.

"Yes, the dog."

"He hasn't got one. Don't you know the hideous story? He once had a spaniel called—"

"I know," I interrupted. "And he's got another."

"Not he!" rejoined Gernham, with sledgehammer certainty. "He'll never have another. I understand the poor chap's feelings. At the same time—"

But here I interrupted again, and told Gernham the story of Vernon's acquisition of the spaniel. He heard me with an amazement he did not try to conceal.

"And you mean to say the dog's in the house now?" he cried, when I had finished.

"I suppose so, unless he's got rid of it already."

Gernham sat quite still with his thin hands spread out on his knees staring at me hard.

"This is extraordinary," he said at last, with a sort of biting decision. "You mean that he didn't mention the fact that he had a dog?"

"I mean more than that. I mean that he concealed it from me."

"Concealed it?"

Certainly. I've got any amount of animals—dogs, cats, the whole show—and I'm always urging Kersteven to set up a happy family. We preach kindness, he and I. We ought to practise it actively as much as we can. But his feelings about his dead dog have always stood in the way. I'm perpetually trying to convert him to my view. I've been at it this week."

"And he said he hadn't a dog?"

"No. But he never said he had one. It's much the same thing under the circumstances. I should never have thought Kersteven could be deceitful. I don't like it. I—I hate it!"

At this moment we were interrupted. Two of the other men came up and we had no more private talk that evening. When I was going away Gernham said—

"Come and see me—will you? Here's my card."

He gave it to me, shook my hand, and as I turned to go said:

"You've spoilt my evening, I can tell you that."

I thought, "And you've spoilt mine," but I did not say it.

IX

I went home that night wondering whether Vernon had got rid of the black spaniel. Perhaps he had found it impossible to reconcile it to its new quarters, and had sold it or given it back to the man with the fur cap. Or perhaps it was still in the house. If that were so, it was very strange, very unlike Vernon to have concealed the fact from Arthur Gernham. But, in either case, he had been deceitful, deliberately deceitful, with a friend, and a friend whom he greatly admired and respected.

This incident of my meeting with Gernham deepened my sense of fear, of mystery. My instinct—I now felt sure of it—was right. Some strange under side of Vernon's character was active at this moment. I knew him only in part; much of him I did not know. A stranger now seemed to confront me in the night, a stranger by whose feet crouched something black and terrified. What was this stranger's purpose? What could it be?

I reviewed carefully my whole acquaintance with Vernon, but especially the latter part of my acquaintance with him, when Deeming was in relation with us both. It was then, when Deeming came into his life, and only then, that Vernon had shown me for the first time a man in him whose presence I had not suspected, whose exact nature I did not know. This man was roused by Deeming. I should have let him sleep. But, having been roused, he had surely been sleepless ever since. Yes, that was so. Thus far, things were clear to me. Something—the strange man in Vernon—had been wakeful, ardent ever since, was wakeful, ardent now. This man it was who worked shoulder to shoulder with Gernham. This man it was who had bought the black spaniel.

So far, light. But now came the darkness. What had been Vernon's purpose in buying the black spaniel? When he saw it he had looked at it fatally. At that moment, while he looked at it, his purpose had sprung up full-grown in his mind, full-grown and fierce. I was not to know that purpose. Arthur Gernham was not to know it. He now had some purpose in connection with an animal that Arthur Gernham, his close friend and colleague, his leader in a campaign of kindness, of pity, to which he was dedicating all his activities and giving all his enthusiasm, was not to know or even suspect. That purpose, since it was in connection with an animal, must surely be one of kindness, of pity.

But here my instinct rebelled violently against my knowledge of Vernon. My instinct said that it was not so; that Vernon's purpose in buying the black spaniel had been sad, even perhaps terrible. Yet how could that be?

The dog's eyes haunted me. They seemed to me to know what I did not know, to know what Vernon's purpose was.

Deeming—again I thought of him, of Vernon's short and strange connection with him. Once Vernon had said to me that he believed Deeming was a man haunted by a mania for persecution. He had spoken without knowledge then. Later, he had travelled to England to gain knowledge. He had taken the house in Wimpole Street to gain knowledge. Had he gained it? I did not know. Vernon had never told me. Was that why I was in the dark now? It began to seem to me that, perhaps, if I could find out what Vernon knew of Deeming I should understand something of his present purpose, of his purpose in buying the black spaniel.

At this stage in my mental debate I reached the Piccadilly corner of Albemarle Street, and was just going to turn towards my house, when a familiar face, a face respectable, close-shaven, English, looked upon me in the lamplight, and a bowler hat was deferentially lifted.

"Cragg!" I said.

"Good-night, Sir," said Cragg. "A fine night, Sir."

"Yes—wait a minute, Cragg."

"Certainly, Sir."

Vernon's man stood still.

"Just walk with me to my door, will you?"

"With pleasure, Sir."

We turned side by side into the comparative quiet of Albemarle Street.

"How is Mr. Kersteven, Cragg?"

"Well, Sir—" The man slightly hesitated. "Oh, Sir, he's in his usual health, I think."

"Working hard, isn't he?"

"Very hard, Sir."

"With Mr. Gernham."

"Yes, Sir, with Mr. Gernham."

"And—and how's the dog, Cragg?"

I looked at him as I spoke, and saw his forehead contract.

"The dog, Sir? —oh, the dog is getting on all right so far as I am aware."

"How do you mean—so far as you are aware?"

"Well, Sir, I don't see much of it. That's a fact."

"Really. How's that?"

I was pumping the man, I acknowledge it. I can make no excuse for it. I was driven by something that seemed to me then more than an ignoble curiosity.

"Well, Sir, Mr. Kersteven keeps the dog shut up mostly. I suppose he thinks that till it gets accustomed to the place and to us it's better."

"But if it's always shut up, how can it get accustomed to you?"

"That's more than I can say, Sir."

I could see that the man was constrained, was not telling me something of which his mind was full. We had now reached my door, and I had no further excuse for keeping him with me.

"Well, Cragg," I said. "Good-night."

"Good-night, Sir."

"I hope the dog will settle down and be friendly with you."

"Friendly with me, Sir! That dog! The Lord forbid!" cried Cragg.

He seemed startled by the sound of his own lamentable exclamation, looked at me as if asking pardon, lifted his hat, and walked quickly away into the darkness. I stood staring after him. I longed to follow him, to question him, to find out what he meant. But how could I?

That night it was late before I went to sleep. The black spaniel seemed to be crouching at the foot of the bed. I seemed to see its yellow eyes fixed upon me, trying to tell me what I longed to know.

Late in the afternoon of the next day I received a very unexpected visit from Arthur Gernham. When I saw him come into my room, dressed in a suit of homespun, with a flannel shirt and a red tie, and holding a soft brown wideawake in his hand, I jumped up from my chair eagerly. I guessed at once that he had something to say with reference to our conversation of the previous night.

"How are you?" he said, in his rasping, energetic voice. "I got your address from the Red Book."

He sat down and stretched out his long legs.

"I'm delighted to see you," I said. "You've been at work with Vernon?"

"I've been with him."

He ran one hand over his tufts of scanty hair.

"I'm disappointed in Kersteven," he said. "I never should have thought he was a shifty fellow."

The word shifty, applied to Vernon, roused my sense of friendship.

"Oh, you're mistaken," I exclaimed. "Vernon's not a shifty man."

"I beg your pardon—he is."

I waited in silence for him to explain himself. I saw plainly that he was going to. There was a sledge hammer honesty about Gernham that was startling but rather refreshing. He now proceeded to give me a specimen of it.

"I can't stomach a friend who isn't perfectly straight with me," he said, "and what's more, I'm bound to tell him so. I can't keep anything in. Whatever I feel I have to out with it. That's my nature. It's got me into plenty of trouble, and it will get me into plenty more. Fights were my lot at Eton, and fights have been my lot, more or less, ever since."

He unbuttoned one of the cuffs of his flannel shirt, pushed the flannel higher up his arm, and went on:

"With Kersteven I got on magnificently until to-day."

"Have you had a wordy fight with Vernon to-day, then?" I asked.

"I went straight to him this morning and told him I'd met you last night. He asked me how I liked you, and I told him, 'Very much.' Then I said, plump out, 'You've been tricky with me, Kersteven.'"

"Oh!" I exclaimed.

He took no notice of my interruption, and went on:

"'You've let me make a fool of myself with you. That's nothing. One makes a fool of oneself most days one way or another.' 'What do you mean?' he asked. 'That you've allowed me to think that you would never keep a dog or animal of any kind in your house, that you've sat here and listened to me trying to persuade you to keep one, while all the time there is—or was—one perhaps within a few feet of me. You've let me think what wasn't true, you've made me think what wasn't true. I don't know what your reason is, but I know that I hate your action, and that I never thought you were capable of doing such a low thing to a friend.'"

"Pretty strong," I said. "How did he take it?"

"That's the nastiest part of all. He took it lying down."

"Lying down?"

"Yes. Merely said the matter of the dog was such a trifle he hadn't thought it would interest me to know of it, that he wasn't sure of keeping it for any time, that he'd been so busy with me that—etc., etc. The lamest excuses man ever offered to man. I was disgusted, and showed it. It's my way to show things—can't help doing it. 'Let's get to work,' he said, trying to change the subject. 'No,' I said. 'I can't work with you to-day. That's certain.' And I took up my hat and went."

"And you—you didn't see the dog?"

"Oh, dear no. But it wasn't that I cared about."

"I wish you had seen it. I wish you would see it."

I was speaking almost involuntarily, as if the words were forced from me, words scarcely prompted by any thought in me, words that were uttered for me.

"Why?" he asked. "Why? What do you mean?"

His face and manner were always alert, but now they had suddenly become intense with a sort of quivering vivacity.

"What's wrong about the dog?"

"I don't know that anything is wrong."

"Know! Do you suspect anything is wrong?"

I waited a minute. I was repeating to myself Gernham's question.

"Yes," I said at last, "I do. But I don't know why I suspect, and I don't know what I suspect. That's the honest truth and vague enough. But I can't help it."

He looked me straight in the eyes for a full minute, I should think. Then he said—

"I want you to be less vague, Luttrell; and I think you can. A man doesn't say such a thing as you've said without more meaning than you've acknowledged."

"I assure you—" I began.

But he stopped me.

"Now look here," he said. "One often has a thought behind one's thought, like a body behind its shadow. You've found the shadow; now look for the body, and I'll bet you'll find that too."

His words seemed to clear away some mystery from my mind, but I shrank from what was now revealed—the body behind the shadow.

"I see you know now what you suspect," he said, still looking into my eyes with intensity. "What is it?"

"I do know now," I answered. "But it's monstrous, and upon my word I'm ashamed to say it. For you must know that I've a great regard for Vernon."

"And so have—or had—I. His tenderness for the suffering of the animal world drew me to him. I can't forget that even now, after this beastly affair of the dog."

"His tenderness for the animal world," I repeated. "It's just that just my knowledge of that, which makes my suspicion so monstrous."

"Let's have it, I must have it!" he said. "You're no backbiter, you're an honest fellow. I can see that. Go ahead. I shan't mistake your motives."

There was a compelling frankness about him. I yielded to it.

"My suspicion is that perhaps Vernon is being cruel to that dog," I said.

Gernham sat quite still. I saw that my words had deeply astonished him. But he did not burst forth, as many another man would have done, in a denial of the possibility of my suspicion being roused by a horrid fact, being well founded. He was a very quick man, and full of finesse despite his bluntness.

"What are your reasons?" he said slowly.

"I can scarcely say I have any. Let me think, though."

After a minute I described to him minutely how Vernon had regarded the spaniel in the Park, the dog's fear there, its much greater terror on being brought into the house in Wimpole Street, Vernon's strange excitement on its arrival, and excitement in which there seemed to be an admixture of triumph, his laughter as he opened the door of the room in which the spaniel was confined; the dog's rush for safety to Lord Elyn, and shrinking away when Vernon approached it. When I had finished, I added:

"There's one thing more."

"What is it?"

Then I related to him my meeting with Cragg on the previous night, and what the man had told me about Vernon's keeping the spaniel perpetually shut up.

"That's all," I ended. "Not much, is it?"

"D'you know," he said, "what's far the most striking fact in all that you've told me?"

"What?" I asked.

"The dog's horror of Kersteven. The rest may be nothing—fancy of yours or oddity of manner on Kersteven's part. But the dog's horror of Kersteven is very strange, and—unless your suspicion is correct, which God forbid—very unnatural."

"Unnatural—that's just what Lord Elyn called it."

"Ah!"

"And his trying to keep the fact of the dog being in the house from you. Isn't that very strange?"

"Certainly it is. But—by Jove! —the strangest thing of all would be that Kersteven should be cruel to an animal."

"Yes, that's true. I can't—no, I can't believe it possible."

"What could be his motive?"

"I can't conceive."

"I know the man. He has a passion of pity in him for the sufferings of the animals, a real passion. Only one thing could account for his being cruel, deliberately and persistently cruel, to a dog."

"What?"

"If he were mad."

"Oh, that—impossible!"

"It would be the only thing," he repeated. "I know something of insanity. A chief feature of it is this, that it often creates in a man the reverse of what he was before it took possession of him. Thus the kind, sane man becomes the cruel madman; the lively, mercurial sane man the bitter, melancholy madman—and so on. You take me?"

"Vernon isn't mad," I said with conviction.

"Then he isn't being cruel to his dog," he said with equal conviction.

"I can't understand it," I said dubiously. "The whole thing's a mystery. Why should he buy the dog after swearing he would never have another? A whim, he said it was, a caprice. But I don't believe that. No, there was some deeper, stranger reason. What could it be?"

I was asking myself, not him.

Gernham got up to go.

"One thing I promise you," he said. "I'll set at rest your doubts in a very short time. I'll find out for certain that Kersteven is treating that dog properly. I devote my life to our dumb friends, as you know. Well, they shan't find me wanting now, though a man who has been my chum and my colleague is concerned in this matter."

"What are you going to do?"

"To-morrow I ought to be working with Kersteven. After to-day I didn't mean to go, I didn't feel as if I could go. But now I will, and I'll see the spaniel and see him with Kersteven. Never fear!"

He spoke with biting decision. I looked at him and felt that he would do what he said.

"Brush my suspicions away," I said, "and I'll be only too thankful. Good-bye."

He went off quickly.

When the door was shut behind him I thought how strange it was that Gernham's purpose in connection with Vernon was exactly the same as had been Vernon's in connection with Deeming when he left Rome for London.

He had wanted to see a black spaniel with Deeming. Gernham wanted to see a black spaniel with him.

X

Just before lunch the next day Gernham was announced.

"Good morning," he said, coming into the room close upon the heels of my man. "Can I lunch with you?"

"Certainly. Lunch for two, Bates."

"Yes, Sir."

The man went out and shut the door. Then I turned to Gernham.

"You've been to Wimpole Street?" I asked.

"Yes. Do you remember I told you yesterday that Kersteven had taken my punishment lying down?"

"Of course I do."

"Well, since then he's thought it over, and got up."

"What do you mean?"

"Yesterday I declined to work with him. To-day, he's declined to work with me. He's refused me admittance to his house. See that!"

He put a note down on the table beside me. I took it and read as follows:

DEAR GERNHAM—I don't know whether you will come to-day; but should you do so, I've told Cragg to give you this. I did not care to quarrel with a man in my own house; and so yesterday, when you were impertinent to me, I did not appear to resent it. As you know, I admire your character and respect your enthusiasm, and it has been a great pleasure to me to be associated with you in a work which I love with my whole heart and soul. But I allow no man to criticise my conduct as you have chosen to criticise it. I am sorry, therefore, that unless you feel inclined to apologise, I cannot admit you to my house. —Believe me, faithfully,

VERNON KERSTEVEN.

"What do you think of that, eh?" asked Gernham, when I finished reading the note. "Pretty blunt, isn't it?"

"Vernon has decidedly got up," I said. I looked again at the note.

"Tell me just what you think," Gernham said.

"Well," I answered, with some hesitation, "it's an abrupt change of front after his behaviour yesterday."

"Too abrupt," he said. "I don't like it; I don't like it at all. You were right, Luttrell; there is a mystery here—a mystery connected with that dog. But I haven't got your opinion yet!"

He was a persistent man, and did not readily lose sight of his object.

"You want to know how I explain Vernon's change of front."

"Exactly."

"It seems to me that he has thought things over since yesterday, and resolved to avail himself of this pretext to keep you out of his house."

"That's it!" exclaimed Gernham. "I've given him his opportunity like a fool, and he's taken it, like a clever man. But where an animal is concerned I'm not so easily dished. A good many people who've appeared in the London police courts know that."

"When you got this note, what did you do?"

"I tried to question Cragg."

"And the result?"

"Nil. Directly I mentioned the dog, he looked as grim as death, and became monosyllabic. There's something up, and Cragg has an inkling of it. But he'll never tell it to me. You've got to go into this, Luttrell."

At this moment lunch was announced, and the rest of the conversation took place in the dining room. Directly after lunch Gernham hurried away, leaving me pledged to act where he could not act, pledged to probe to the bottom, and without delay, the mystery of the black spaniel.

My relation with Vernon was now almost exactly similar to his former relation with Deeming, and Gernham was to be the inactive watcher, the waiter on events engineered by others, that I had formerly been. But there was a difference in this new situation which had followed so strangely upon the death of Deeming. Vernon had never been Deeming's friend. From the first moment when they met the two men had been instinctively hostile to one another. But I was Vernon's friend. I cared for him. Till now I had believed in him. This fact complicated matters painfully. And yet I did not hesitate, did not feel that in my understanding with Gernham I was being treacherous, disloyal.

For the eyes of the black spaniel haunted me, summoned me, seemed to force me to go on, to investigate this mystery. By them I was driven to do as I did. By them I was told that in my friend a new man, a stranger, had arisen, and that in attacking this stranger—if attack were necessary—I should not be false to my friendship with the man who had lived in Rome, the quiet lover of pictures, the gentle, idle, cultivated Vernon of the Trinita dei Monti.

Vernon was generally at home after six in the evening. I resolved to seek him at that hour on the same day, and carried my resolution into effect. Cragg opened the door to me.

"Mr. Kersteven at home, Cragg?"

"Yes, Sir."

"Can I see him?"

"If you'll wait a moment, Sir, I'll ask."

He paused, then added in explanation—

"I don't think Mr. Kersteven is very well to-day, Sir. Perhaps he may not wish to be disturbed, even by you. You'll excuse me, Sir."

"Of course. Go and see. I'll stay here."

"Pray take a seat, Sir."

He placed a chair for me in the little hall, and went discreetly away up the stairs.

I sat down and waited.

The hall was quiet and dim. Somewhere a large clock was ticking. Now and then I heard a carriage roll by outside. As I sat there I fell into deep thought. What was I going to do? I had come to the house without making any plan. I could not make any plan till I had seen Vernon. His demeanour, his action, must guide me. Would he see me? I thought it probable. There was evidently no one with him. Had there been, Cragg would have told me; and, if I saw him, should I find the black spaniel with him? I glanced round me. On the opposite side of the hall, close to where I was sitting, opened the short corridor, or passage, which linked the two houses in one. I could see the darkness of what had been Deeming's house where the passage stretched away beyond the door of Vernon's workroom. Poor Deeming! Gone, with all his fine abilities, his energy, his persistence, his ambition his cruelty, perhaps! Had he been cruel? Possibly Vernon knew. If he had, he was perhaps now being punished in that other mysterious world of which we know nothing, of which we seldom think in health, but which seems to loom near us when we are ill, or weary, or in trouble of mind—to loom as a great vault before whose entrance we stand, gazing but seeing naught. As I stared down the corridor into the dimness of the other house, the thought of Deeming haunted me, came to me vividly, till I almost fancied that something of him, some thrown-out essence of his personality, of his strong soul, still remained in the dwelling that had been his, still knew what went on there, still watched the coming and going of the man who governed where he had governed once.

I fancied, did I say? It was more than that. I felt as if he were near me, as if he were even intent upon me.

Then from the thought of him, and still with that sensation of his nearness, of his attention, upon me, my mind travelled to the black spaniel. His dog, that mysterious creature never seen by me, had pattered in the dimness towards which I was gazing. And now, as Deeming's place was taken by Vernon, its place was taken by the black spaniel Vernon had first seen in the Park cowering down against the earth, its ears laid back, its body trembling, its eyes full of a message of voiceless fear. Perhaps it was close to me now, this successor of Deeming's pet or victim. Perhaps it was shut up in the room in which I had seen it lying against the red curtain. I could see the door of the room. It was shut. A few steps would bring me to it. I glanced towards the staircase. Cragg was not coming down. I got up. Again I had the sensation that Deeming was near me, was intent upon me, wanted something of me, and with this sensation was mysteriously linked my consciousness of the nearness of the black spaniel, till—till the two sensations seemed to merge the one into the other, to become one, in some indefinable, fantastic way. I can hardly explain exactly what I felt at this moment, but my feeling was connected with Vernon's workroom. It was as if—as if I almost knew that, did I but take those few steps to the shut door, did I but open that door, I should find awaiting me within the room not only the black spaniel, but the dead man, Deeming, with it. It was as if—as if—

I moved across the hall, walking softly, reached the corridor, gained the door, stood by it, listening for the uneasy movement, for the whimper of a dog, for the stir, for the murmur of a dead man. But there was no sound within. There was no sound, and yet I felt positive that the spaniel was inside the room, separated from me only by a piece of wood. Once, twice, I put my fingers upon the handle of the door, yet refrained from turning it. I felt a strong desire to open the door, yet at the critical moment I was held back from doing so by an imperious reluctance which seemed to me to be physical, as if my body sickened and protested against what my mind told it to do.

How long I stood thus uncertainly before the door I do not know. It seemed to me a very long time. At last—in the struggle between mind and body, if it were that—the body conquered. I turned to move away without opening the door. I even took a step towards the hall. But I was arrested by a sound that startled me, that sent—I could not tell why—a chill through me.

I heard the scratching of a dog against the inside of the door.

I stood still, held my breath, and listened. The scratching was repeated, prolonged. It was gentle, surreptitious almost, yet insistent, a summons to me to return.

Again my body sickened. I was physically afflicted. Nausea seized me. But now my mind rose up and protested against the condition, against the domination of my body, like a thing angry and ashamed. Suddenly I took a resolution. I would open the door without delay in answer to the appeal of the black spaniel. Swiftly I went back to the door, grasped the handle, turned it, pushed. The door resisted me. It was locked. As I realised this I heard from within the desolate whining of a dog imprisoned.

"Luttrell! Luttrell!"

Vernon's voice called to me from above, and at the same time I heard a footstep. Cragg was coming down. I moved swiftly back into the hall and met him. He glanced at me inquiringly, looked down the passage, then at me again. His face for an instant was eloquent with inquiry—with—was it sympathy? Then he was once more the discreet servant, saying in a formal voice

"Please come up, Sir; Mr. Kersteven will be very glad to see you."

Vernon met me on the landing by the drawing room door. I saw at once that he was not well. His face was very pale, and had a peculiar look, as if the skin were drawn upward towards the wrinkled forehead, which I had sometimes noticed in people suffering from prolonged insomnia. It gave a horribly strained appearance to his countenance, in which the eyes looked unnaturally eager and full of curious observation.

"Were you in the hall?" he said, taking my hand for the fraction of an instant, and then dropping it as if with relief.

"I waited in the hall," I replied evasively.

"You were there then while Cragg was up here?"

"He asked me to wait there," I said. "While he went to see if you were well enough to receive me. I'm sorry to hear you're seedy."

"Oh, it's of no consequence. Come in."

We went into the drawing room.

"What's been the matter?" I asked, as we sat down.

"Oh, I don't know. I've been overworking, I suppose."

"With Gernham?" I said.

"Gernham!" he looked at me narrowly. "You—have you seen Gernham to-day?"

"Yes."

"Oh."

He sat silent for a moment. I could see that he was hesitating whether to tell me about his breach with Gernham or not.

"How d'you like Gernham?" he said at length. "He likes you. He told me so."

"I know him very slightly, but one can't help respecting such a genuine fellow," I replied.

"Genuine—yes, he's that."

"If he undertook a thing, nothing would stop him from going through with it."

"You think so?"

He slightly smiled.

"But suppose he were to encounter an opposition as thorough as his own attack? What then?"

I knew at once that he was thinking of Gernham and himself.

"Then," I said, "there would be a battle royal."

"A battle royal, would there? Yes, no doubt."

With the last words his interest seemed to fail suddenly. He slightly drooped his head, and sat like one listening for some distant sound. I watched him closely. Gernham's declaration that if Vernon were maltreating the spaniel he must be mentally diseased was present in my mind. I was looking for symptoms that would guide me to a conclusion one way or the other. I saw a great change in Vernon—a painful change. He looked like a man suffering under some terrible distress, which had altered, for the time, his whole outlook upon life. But I felt that I was with a perfectly sane man. As I regarded him he seemed to recover his consciousness of my presence, glanced up, and met my scrutiny.

"What is it?" he said. "Why do you look at me like that?"

I felt embarrassed.

"What's Gernham been saying to you?" he added sharply.

"Gernham—oh, you know him," I answered. "You know where his heart is, with the animals. What an enthusiast he is!"

"He's been talking to you about his work then. Well, did he tell you that we've had a quarrel, he and I?"

"He said your work together had come to a stop, for the moment. Why should it?"

"Why? Oh, well, sometimes Gernham is too blunt, says more than he, than any man ought to say to another. There is a limit to frankness; occasionally he oversteps it. He overstepped it with me, and I resented it. Don't you think I was right?"

I felt that he was being strangely insincere with me as he had been insincere with Gernham, trying to raise a cloud which would obscure the reality of his mind, the true scope of his intentions.

"I see no reason why two such men as you should quarrel," I answered. "Especially if it interrupts, and perhaps, to some extent, cripples a splendid work. You should sink your little differences, and go on together, hand in hand, to further the noble cause you love."

He had been trying to play me. I was now trying to play him. Yet, as I finished, a genuine warmth came, I think, into my voice. It moved him. I could see that, for he looked up at me as if demanding my sympathy. Suddenly I felt a profound pity for him, a profound desire to help him. But how? Against what?

"Perhaps we shall be friends again," he said. "But he misunderstands me, and you, Luttrell, perhaps you misunderstand me too."

"I!"

"Yes—you. Are you sure that, in these last days, you have never had any cruel suspicions of me? Are you sure you have not any cruel suspicions of me now?"

"If I had, if I have, you could easily clear them up," I answered. "By the way, how's the dog getting on? All right?"

His face changed at once, hardened.

"Oh, yes!" he said.

"I should like to have another look at him," I said. "Where is he?"

"He's downstairs in the study. Didn't you know it?"

"I–I did think I heard something scratching and whining. Why do you keep him shut up?"

"He hasn't got accustomed to being with me yet. If I let him out he might bolt."

"Oh!"

"I don't want to have spent my twelve pounds for nothing," he added. His face had hardened. Now his voice was hard too hard and fatal.

"May I have a look at him?" I said.

The sense of mystery was returning upon me. I tried to combat it by speaking bluntly, expressing my desire plainly. At least, I would no longer deal in subterfuge. Instead of answering my question he said, throwing a curious, wavering glance upon me, "Are you engaged to-night?"

I was, but I said at once, "I'm entirely at your service, Vernon."

"Dine with me, then."

"Here?"

"Yes, here."

"Certainly."

"That's right. And now let's have some music. I've got a new piano since last year."

We spent the next hour with Richard Strauss and Saint-Saëns.

XI

Night had closed in. Vernon and I were seated opposite to one another at the oval dining table. Cragg waited upon us.

Now and then, as he moved softly to and fro, I glanced at him, and I thought I detected in his well-trained face a flicker of anxiety as his eyes rested upon his master, a flicker of appeal as they rested upon me. It seemed to me at such times that he wanted me to do something to help Vernon, that he was longing to have a word with me alone.

The dinner was excellent, but Vernon ate scarcely anything. He talked, however, a good deal, though hardly with his usual nerve and relish. When dessert was on the table, he said:

"Bring us our coffee here, Cragg; at least, one black coffee."

"Yes, Sir."

"I won't take it," Vernon said to me. "I've been sleeping wretchedly lately. Morphia would be more the thing for me than coffee."

"I knew you had been suffering from insomnia."

He laughed drearily.

"I don't look up to much, do I?"

Cragg brought my coffee and cigars.

"You can leave us now, Cragg; go and have your supper; go downstairs."

The man looked slightly surprised, but said nothing and went away.

When he had gone Vernon lit a cigar, puffed out some rings of smoke, watched them curling up towards the ceiling, then said:

"You wanted to have a look at the spaniel, didn't you?"

"Yes," I said.

"Well, if I bring him in, be careful with him, will you?"

"Careful with him! Why? Is he dangerous?"

"I don't say that. But he's got an odd temper. I keep him muzzled."

"In the house?"

"Yes, always. I don't want to be bitten. You remember how Deeming died? Well, I don't want to die like that."

His mention of Deeming gave me an opportunity of which I at once availed myself.

"That was a sad business," I said. "Did you see much of him before he died, as you were living next door?"

"Oh," he interrupted, "Deeming was not a friendly neighbour. Do you know that I took your advice?"

"What advice?"

"To get into his house as a patient."

"You really did that!"

"Yes. One morning, as he never invited me in as a friend, I went in as a patient."

"How did he take it?"

"Well, he could hardly decline to treat me. It happened that I was really unwell at the time, so I had a good excuse."

"And—and—your strange suspicions"—I was almost stammering, conscious, painfully conscious of my own—"your strange suspicions— did you ever find out whether they were justified?"

"They were justified, fully justified. But the dog took its own part in the end and killed its persecutor."

I felt a sensation of horror take hold upon me.

"Do you really mean that Deeming was treating his spaniel cruelly?" I asked.

"I do. He had the mania for persecution that I suspected. He was venting it upon his dog. The servants had some inkling of the truth, especially his butler. He knew, I believe, all that was going on. But he was well paid, very well paid."

I remembered my Sunday morning call, and the butler's exclamation when the fox-terrier ran into the house.

"This is horrible, Vernon," I said. "Are you sure of what you say?"

"Quite sure. I heard—well, I heard things at night, and at last I saw the dog."

"How?"

"I got into the house when Deeming was out. I bribed his butler, paid him more than Deeming did, I suppose. Anyhow, I got in. I think the man was sympathetic; was anxious really that an end should be put to the disgusting business. I burst open the door of the room in which the spaniel was confined, and then I saw—no matter what. It was quite enough. While I was there Deeming came back unexpectedly."

"Good God!" I exclaimed. "What a ghastly situation!"

"It was not exactly pleasant. I saw the man's soul naked that night— stark naked. It was on that occasion the dog bit him."

"Ouf!" I said.

Again nausea seized me.

Vernon looked at me steadily.

"Don't you think Deeming deserved anything he got?" he asked. "Anything he could ever get?"

"But he was mad—he must have been mad!"

"I suppose that sort of thing is what might be called a form of madness. Unfortunately a good many sane people have it—people as sane as you or I in all other respects."

When he said the words "or I" a flush, I think, came to my cheek. It seemed to me that he spoke with significance—as if he knew what Gernham and I had spoken of the day before.

"As sane as you or I," he repeated. "This work I've been doing with Gernham has opened my eyes to a good deal in human nature that they were shut to before. I once said to you in Rome, to you and Deeming, that man's cruelty sprang often from a lack of imagination. Sometimes it springs from just the opposite, from a diseased imagination that lusts for gratification in ways we won't discuss."

"But Deeming—that he should be such a man, he whose profession it was to make whole!"

"Yes, that made the thing more strange and, to him, more enticing."

"Enticing!" I exclaimed.

My voice was full of the bitterness of disgust mingled with incredulity that I was feeling.

"Just that," he said. "He healed, as it were, with one hand, and destroyed with the other. Deeming was one of the human devils who have an insatiable craze for contrast. They revel in virtue because it is so different from vice. They revel in vice because it is so different from virtue. Deeming quivered with happiness when the last patient was gone and he could steal to the room where the spaniel—"

"Enough! Enough!" I exclaimed. "I won't hear any more! Thank God he's dead! Thank God it's all over now! Why did you do that?" Vernon had suddenly laughed.

"Why did you do that?" I repeated. "What is there to laugh at?"

"I was laughing at your certainty, Luttrell, at the calm assurance with which we—poor, ignorant beings that we are—assert this or that regarding the fate of a soul, without knowing anything of the purposes of the Creator."

"I don't understand."

"And yet you say—'Thank God, it's all over now!'"

He looked at me so strangely that I was struck to silence. I opened my lips to speak, but, while his eyes were upon me, I could say nothing. He made me feel as if, indeed, I were plunged in a profound gulf of ignorance, as if he watched me there from some height of understanding, of knowledge.

"Now I'll go and fetch the spaniel," he said.

And he got up and quietly left the room.

I turned in my chair and sat facing the door. The room was softly lit by wax candles, and on the walls were the pictures of gentleness, of mercy, of goodness and adoration which had hung upon the walls of Vernon's dining room in Rome. My glance ran over them, while my mind dwelt upon the horrors of Vernon's narrative—horrors that seemed all the greater because he had told me so little, had left my imagination so unfettered. Then I looked again towards the door, and listened intently. Presently I heard a door shut, the sound of a step. Vernon was coming with the spaniel. I had asked to see the dog; I had wished to see it. Yet now my wish was about to be gratified I felt an extreme repugnance invade me. I longed to escape from the fulfilment of my wish. I was seized with—was it fear? It was something cold, something that lay upon my nerves like ice, that surely turned the blood in my veins to water. But, I could do nothing now, nothing to escape. Something within me seemed to make a furious effort to take up some weapon and attack the cold heavy thing that was striving to paralyse me. I was conscious of battle. In the midst of the battle the door opened and Vernon came in.

He was carrying the black spaniel in his arms.

He walked in slowly, kicked the door backwards with his heel to shut it, came to the table and sat down, still keeping the dog in his arms.

The dog was muzzled, and had on a collar to which a steel chain was attached; but, for the first moment, the only thing that struck me was his thinness. He was excessively thin—almost emaciated. He sat on his master's knee, with his chin on the edge of the table and his yellow eyes gazing at me. A long trembling ran through his body, ceased, and was renewed with a regularity that reminded me of the ticking of a clock. Vernon kept his two hands upon the spaniel. They shuddered on the dog's back when he shuddered.

"Well," Vernon said. "What do you think of him?"

"He's horribly thin," I said. "Horribly."

I turned my eyes from the spaniel to Vernon's face.

"Do you think—" I began and hesitated.

"What?" he asked calmly.

"Do you think you give him enough to eat?" I said.

"Oh, it's very bad for dogs to overfeed," he answered. "Nothing ruins their health like overeating, and spaniels are like pugs, inclined to be greedy."

I noticed that he had not answered my question.

He lifted one hand, laid it on the spaniel's head, and smoothed the black hair, moving his hand backwards to the neck. The dog turned its head back towards him and showed his white teeth, as if his master's hand drew him but to a demonstration of hatred, not of affection. Vernon smiled, lifted his hand, and repeated the action. The dog gave a low growl ending in a whine.

"Now you haven't told me what you think of him," Vernon continued, "and I want to know. I want very much to know."

I looked into the spaniel's eyes, and again something cold lay upon my nerves like ice.

"Why?" I said. "What does it matter what I think?"

"Do answer my question!" Vernon said with unwonted irritation.

"There's something about the dog," I said, "that's—that's—"

"Yes?" he said sharply.

"That's uncanny."

"Ah!" The word was a long-drawn sigh. "You think that!"

"Yes, I shouldn't care to have him about me. I shouldn't care to sleep with him in my room."

"Sleep! Heaven forbid!"

His exclamation was almost shrill. It startled me.

"Where does the dog sleep?" I asked. "Where do you put him at night?"

"There's a dressing room opening out of my bedroom. He's shut in there."

"And you—you say you've been sleeping badly lately?"

"I haven't been sleeping at all."

"Does he whine? Does he disturb you?"

"He never makes a sound at night. I think he's afraid that if he did I should punish him. He's evidently had an unkind master, poor fellow."

There was something so hideously insincere in Vernon's voice as he said the last words that I could not help expressing the thought, the suspicion that had been, that was haunting me.

"Has he got a kind master now?" I said.

I fixed my eyes on Vernon's.

"Has he?" I repeated.

At that moment I wanted to force things. The entrance of the dog had deepened my sense of moving in mystery until it became absolutely intolerable. A hard determination took hold upon me to compel Vernon to explain—what? I did not know. But that there was something to be explained, some strange undercurrent of motive, of desire, of intention, deep and furtive, I seemed to be aware.

"What do you mean?" Vernon said. "Surely you know my feeling for animals."

"I do."

"Then what do you mean?"

"I mean that as regards this animal, this spaniel, I don't—I can't trust you," I said. "I don't know why it is, I don't understand, I don't understand anything. But I don't trust you, Vernon. That's the truth. It's best to speak it."

To my great surprise, he did not indignantly resent my words, nor did he look guilty or ashamed. Indeed, it seemed to me that an expression of something like relief flitted across his face as I finished speaking.

"I knew it," he said. "I knew quite well you didn't trust me. And Gernham? Have you spoken to him of your mistrust?"

"He knows I don't understand why you bought this dog, and what you're going to do to him. He knows I'm—I'm afraid of—of what you may be going to do."

He was silent, and again drew his hand across the spaniel's soft black coat. The dog struggled. He struck his open hand down on the dog's head, and the dog lay still, cowering upon his master's knees.

"Gernham doesn't enter into this," he said inflexibly.

"And I?"

"You! That's different. You introduced me to Deeming."

Again the dog began to struggle upon his knees, but this time more violently.

Vernon lifted his hand again.

"Put him down!" I said. "For God's sake put him down! Don't strike him!"

"Very well."

He dropped the spaniel to the floor. The spaniel ran under the dining table. I sprang up from my seat.

"Don't, don't!" I began.

"It's all right," said Vernon. "I've got him by the chain." He dragged the spaniel out, and fastened him up to the sideboard at the far end of the room.

"Why, you're trembling!" he said, as he came back to his chair.

"Am I?" I said, ashamed. "I'm not a coward, but—but this dog–I can't stand him near me, close to me, when I can't see what he's doing."

I cleared my throat, went to the window, threw it open, leaned out, and spat. Leaving the window open, I came back to the table. The spaniel was now lying down on the floor, close to the sideboard.

"What is it?" I said, almost fiercely, I think, in my inexplicable physical distress, "what is it that's wrong with the dog? What is it that's unnatural about him?"

"You have no idea?" said Vernon.

"Not the slightest. The poor beast seems harmless enough, though he's terrified. One can see that."

"Exactly. He is terrified."

"And the strange thing is that his terror terrifies me."

"Now you're getting to it," Vernon said. "Why should the spaniel be terrified?"

"Why? How should I know? Isn't that for you to say?"

"Sit down again," he said. "The dog can't get to you now."

As he spoke, he sat down. I glanced towards the dog, saw that what Vernon had said was true, and followed his example.

"The dog's terror," he said. "Think of that, Luttrell! Seek for an explanation in that."

"I have, but I haven't found one."

"Whom is it terrified of?"

"Of you," I answered. "The first time we saw him, I noticed that he was abjectly, terrified of you."

"Perfectly true. Why should that be? Is it natural?"

"Utterly unnatural," I said. "Unless he's been badly, brutally treated, and is afraid of everybody."

"He is not afraid of everybody. He is only afraid of me. Was he afraid of Lord Elyn?"

"No."

"He is only afraid of me."

"Are you certain?"

"Would you like to test it?"

"How?" I asked.

"I will leave the room for a moment—leave you alone with the dog."

"No!" I exclaimed.

"You are afraid?"

"I'm not a coward, but there's something about this spaniel which horrifies my imagination as a spectre might horrify it."

"Nevertheless, you must summon your courage. I wish it. I wish to know how the spaniel will be with you when you are alone together. Come, make the experiment."

He got up and went towards the door. I did not try to keep him.

"I'll be back in a moment," he said.

And he went softly out of the room and shut the door behind him.

When he had gone, I sat where I was, looking at the black blot on the floor by the sideboard. A strong curiosity was awake in me fighting my strange physical repulsion. I longed to put the thing to the test, yet I feared to approach the spaniel. How long I sat there I do not know, how long I might have sat there I cannot tell had nothing occurred to bias me towards action. But something did occur. The spaniel suddenly whimpered softly, as if to attract my attention, whimpered again and struck his feathery tail upon the floor. Those natural sounds of an anxious dog reassured me.

I got up quickly and went over to the sideboard. Instantly, with a sort of strangled wail, the spaniel sprang up, put his forepaws on my legs, and thrust his hot nose into my hand, pushing, pushing hard, as if he sought to hide himself in a friendly shelter. I felt a wetness on my hand, the wetness of an animal's tears. Then all my horror vanished and only pity remained. I knelt down on the carpet. I put my arms round the dog. I felt his trembling body with my hands. He was thin, hideously thin. His piteous eyes begged something of me. Still holding him with one arm, I stretched out the other, and opened a door in the sideboard. Within I saw a basket with some cut bread in it. I took out the bread. The spaniel sprang upon it passionately, tore it out of my hand, and devoured it ravenously. Then a wave of hot indignation went over me. At that moment I hated Vernon with all my soul. I hated him so much that I lost all sense of everything except my fury against him. I held the dog tightly as I knelt on the floor, and, turning my head towards the door, I called out:

"Vernon! Vernon!"

Instantly the door opened and Vernon appeared. The dog looked as he had looked when he was being brought into the house.

"Vernon," I said, " you're a d—d blackguard!"

"Why?" he said.

"This dog is starving. You're starving him! D'you hear? You're starving him!"

"I know I am," he answered.

I got up. The spaniel rushed against my legs and leaned against them as I stood.

"Then Gernham was right," I said. "You are a madman."

"Is it madness to see what is when others are blind to it?"

"To see—to see?" I exclaimed. "What is there to see but this dog, this spaniel that you are torturing?"

"There is this spaniel—yes. Look at him. Look into his eyes. Look at the soul in them."

There was something compelling, something almost mystical, in his voice. I looked down into the yellow eyes of the spaniel. They met mine, then looked away from mine as if unable to bear my gaze.

"What is it?" I said, in a whisper. "What is it?"

Again I was assailed by the sensation which had come to me when I waited in the hall to know if Vernon would receive me, a sensation that, with the black spaniel, linked with it, mysteriously mingled with it, was something of the man who was dead—something of Deeming.

"Deeming!" I stammered. "Deeming!"

I did not know what I meant, but I was compelled to pronounce the name of my friend.

"Deeming?" I said once more, looking towards Vernon.

"Don't you feel that he is here?" said Vernon.

"But he is dead."

"Don't you feel that he is here?"

"Yes," I said. "But it can't be. He is dead."

"His body is dead—yes. But his soul, is that dead?"

When he said that, I understood what he meant, and I recoiled from the black spaniel as from a nameless horror.

"Vernon!" I said. "Vernon!"

"Do you understand now?" he asked. "Do you understand why I bought the spaniel, why I have kept the spaniel here in the house where he tortured his dog? It was to punish him as he punished it, to torture him as he tortured it. Directly I saw the spaniel crouching down in the Park, directly I looked into his eyes, I knew. Deeming died on the 30th of June, the spaniel was born on that very day. The soul of the dog torturer passed at the death of the body of the man into the body of the dog. I am not mad—no. I am only just. I am the instrument of the justice of Providence. Deeming's soul has been sent back into the world to pay its penalty. And I am here to see that the penalty is paid."

There was blazing in his eyes the light which I had seen in them for the first time in the restaurant in Rome, the light which had made Deeming say that in Vernon there was the spirit of a black fanatic.

"It's not true!" I said. "It can't be true!"

"But Lord Elyn has felt it, Cragg has felt it, you have felt it—the strangeness of the spaniel. You know now, you know that what I say is true. Deny that you know it is true! Deny it then!"

I opened my lips to deny it, but they refused to speak. I was filled with a horror of the imagination, but I was resolved not to succumb to it. I seized the steel chain that was attached to the collar of the spaniel, and untied it from the sideboard.

"What are you doing?" said Vernon sharply.

"Good-night, Vernon," I said, trying to keep my voice calm; "I am going to take the spaniel with me."

As I spoke I moved towards the door. The spaniel slunk along beside me, with its belly close to the floor, trying to press itself against my legs.

"What!" said Vernon, "to happiness—to affection!"

I was close to the door. I had my fingers upon the handle.

"That!" he cried with violence. "No! Rather than that, let it end now and here!"

He made a rapid movement; the spaniel howled and cowered against the door. I heard the crack of a pistol shot. I felt the chain leap in my hand as the spaniel sprang upwards and fell on the floor.

I bent down, touched him, turned him over.

He was dead.

Then I faced Vernon.

"Murderer!" I said. "Murderer!"

"But—he was only a black spaniel!" Vernon said, laying the revolver down on the table.

"Murderer!" I repeated.

Then I lifted up the corpse of the spaniel, and went out into the night carrying it in my arms.

The Face of the Monk

I

"No, it will not hurt him to see you," the doctor said to me; "and I have no doubt he will recognise you. He is the quietest patient I have ever had under my care—gentle, kind, agreeable, perfect in conduct, and yet quite mad. You know him well?"

"He was my dearest friend," I said. "Before I went out to America three years ago we were inseparable. Doctor, I cannot believe that he is mad, he—Hubert Blair—one of the cleverest young writers in London, so brilliant, so acute! Wild, if you like, a libertine perhaps, a strange mixture of the intellectual and the sensual—but mad! I can't believe it!"

"Not when I tell you that he was brought to me suffering from acute religious mania?"

"Religious! Hubert Blair!"

"Yes. He tried to destroy himself, declaring that he was unfit to live, that he was a curse to some person unknown. He protested that each deed of his affected this unknown person, that his sins were counted as the sins of another, and that this other had haunted him—would haunt him forever."

The doctor's words troubled me.

"Take me to him," I said at last. "Leave us together."

It was a strange, sad moment when I entered the room in which Hubert was sitting. I was painfully agitated. He knew me, and greeted me warmly. I sat down opposite to him.

There was a long silence. Hubert looked away into the fire. He saw, I think, traced in scarlet flames, the scenes he was going to describe to me; and I, gazing at him, wondered of what nature the change in my friend might be. That he had changed since we were together three years ago was evident, yet he did not look mad. His dark, clean-shaven young face was still passionate. The brown eyes were still lit with a certain devouring eagerness. The mouth had not lost its mingled sweetness and sensuality. But Hubert was curiously transformed. There was a dignity, almost an elevation, in his manner. His former gaiety had vanished. I knew, without words, that my friend was another man—very far away from me now. Yet once we had lived together as chums, and had no secrets the one from the other.

At last Hubert looked up and spoke.

"I see you are wondering about me," he said.

"Yes."

"I have altered, of course—completely altered."

"Yes," I said, awkwardly enough. "Why is that?"

I longed to probe this madness of his that I might convince myself of it, otherwise Hubert's situation must forever appal me.

He answered quietly, "I will tell you—nobody else knows—and even you may—"

He hesitated, then he said:

"No, you will believe it."

"Yes, if you tell me it is true."

"It is absolutely true."

"Bernard, you know what I was when you left England for America—gay, frivolous in my pleasures, although earnest when I was working. You know how I lived to sound the depths of sensation, how I loved to stretch all my mental and physical capacities to the snapping-point, how I shrank from no sin that could add one jot or tittle to my knowledge of the mind of any man or woman who interested me. My life seemed a full life then. I moved in the midst of a thousand intrigues. I strung beads of all emotions upon my rosary, and told them until at times my health gave way. You remember my recurring periods of extraordinary and horrible mental depression—when life was a demon to me, and all my success in literature less than nothing; when I fancied myself hated, and could believe I heard phantom voices abusing me. Then those fits passed away, and once more I lived as ardently as ever, the most persistent worker, and the most persistent excitement seeker in London.

"Well, after you went away I continued my career. As you know, my success increased. Through many sins I had succeeded in diving very deep into human hearts of men and women. Often I led people deliberately away from innocence in order that I might observe the gradual transformation of their natures. Often I spurred them on to follies that I might see the effect our deeds have upon our faces—the seal our actions set upon our souls. I was utterly unscrupulous, and yet I thought myself good-hearted. You remember that my servants always loved me, that I attracted people. I can say this to you. For some time my usual course was not stayed. Then—I recollect it was in the middle of the London season—one of my horrible fits of unreasonable melancholy swept over me. It stunned my soul like a heavy blow. It numbed me. I could not go about. I could not bear to see anybody. I could only shut myself up and try to reason myself back into my usual gaiety and excitement. My writing was put aside. My piano was locked. I tried to read, but even that solace was denied to me. My attention was utterly self-centred, riveted upon my own condition.

"Why, I said to myself, am I the victim of this despair, this despair without a cause? What is this oppression which weighs me down without reason? It attacks me abruptly, as if it were sent to me by some power, shot at me like an arrow by an enemy hidden in the dark. I am well—I am gay. Life is beautiful and wonderful to me. All that I do interests me. My soul is full of vitality. I know that I have troops of friends, that I am loved and thought of by many people. And then suddenly the arrow strikes me. My soul is wounded and sickens to death. Night falls over me, night so sinister that I shudder when its twilight comes. All my senses faint within me. Life is at once a hag, weary, degraded, with tears on her cheeks and despair in her hollow eyes. I feel that I am deserted, that my friends despise me, that the world hates me, that I am less than all other men—less in powers, less in attraction—that I am the most crawling, the most grovelling of all the human species, and that there is no one who does not know it. Yet the doctors say I am not physically ill, and I know that I am not mad. Whence does this awful misery, this unmeaning, causeless horror of life and of myself come? Why am I thus afflicted?

"Of course I could find no answer to all these old questions, which I had asked many times before. But this time, Bernard, my depression was more lasting, more overwhelming than usual. I grew terribly afraid of it. I thought I might be driven to suicide. One day a crisis seemed to come. I dared no longer remain alone, so I put on my hat and coat, took my stick, and hurried out, without any definite intention. I walked along Piccadilly, avoiding the glances of those whom I met. I fancied they could all read the agony, the degradation of my soul. I turned into Bond Street, and suddenly I felt a strong inclination to stop before a certain door. I obeyed the impulse, and my eyes fell on a brass plate, upon which was engraved these words:

VANE.
Clairvoyant.
11 till 4 daily.

"I remember I read them several times over, and even repeated them in a whisper to myself. Why? I don't know. Then I turned away, and was about to resume my walk. But I could not. Again I stopped and read the legend on the brass plate. On the right-hand side of the door was an electric bell. I put my finger on it and pressed the button inwards. The door opened, and I walked, like a man in a dream, I think, up a flight of narrow stairs. At the top of them was a second door, at which a maidservant was standing.

"'You want to see Mr. Vane, sir?'

"'Yes. Can I?'

"'If you will come in, sir, I will see.'

"She showed me into a commonplace, barely-furnished little room, and, after a short period of waiting, summoned me to another, in which stood a tall, dark youth, dressed in a gown rather like a college gown. He bowed to me, and I silently returned the salutation. The servant left us. Then he said:

"'You wish me to exert my powers for you?'

"'Yes.'

"'Will you sit here?'

"He motioned me to a seat beside a small round table, sat down opposite to me, and took my hand. After examining it through a glass, and telling my character fairly correctly by the lines in it, he laid the glass down and regarded me narrowly.

"'You suffer terribly from depression,' he said.

"'That is true.'

"He continued to gaze upon me more and more fixedly. At length he said:

"'Do you know that everybody has a companion?'

"'How—a companion?'

"'Somebody incessantly with them, somebody they cannot see.'

"'You believe in the theory of guardian angels?'

"'I do not say these companions are always guardian angels. I see your companion now, as I look at you. His face is by your shoulder.'

"I started, and glanced hastily round; but, of course, could see nothing.

"'Shall I describe him?'

"'Yes,' I said.

"'His face is dark, like yours; shaven, like yours. He has brown eyes, just as brown as yours are. His mouth and his chin are firm and small, as firm and small as yours.'

"'He must be very like me.'

"'He is. But there is a difference between you.'

"'What is it?'

"'His hair is cut more closely than yours, and part of it is shaved off.'

"'He is a priest, then?'

"'He wears a cowl. He is a monk.'

"'A monk! But why does he come to me?'

"'I should say that he cannot help it, that he is your spirit in some former state. Yes'—and he stared at me till his eyes almost mesmerised me—'you must have been a monk once.'

"'I—a monk! Impossible! Even if I have lived on earth before, it could never have been as a monk.'

"'How do you know that?'

"'Because I am utterly without superstitions, utterly free from any lingering desire for an ascetic life. That existence of silence, of ignorance, of perpetual prayer, can never have been mine.'

"'You cannot tell,' was all his answer.

II

"When I left Bond Street that afternoon I was full of disbelief. However, I had paid my half-guinea and escaped from my own core of misery for a quarter of an hour. That was something. I didn't regret my visit to this man Vane, whom I regarded as an agreeable charlatan. For a moment he had interested me. For a moment he had helped me to forget my useless wretchedness. I ought to have been grateful to him. And, as always, my soul regained its composure at last. One morning I awoke and said to myself that I was happy. Why? I did not know. But I got up. I was able to write once more. I was able to play. I felt that I had friends who loved me and a career before me. I could again look people in the face without fear. I could even feel a certain delightful conceit of mind and body. Bernard, I was myself. So I thought, so I knew. And yet, as days went by, I caught myself often thinking of this invisible, tonsured, and cowled companion of mine, whom Vane had seen, whom I did not see. Was he indeed with me? And, if so, had he thoughts, had he the holy thoughts of a spirit that has renounced the world and all fleshly things? Did he still keep that cloistered nature which is at home with silence, which aspires, and prays, and lives for possible eternity, instead of for certain time? Did he still hold desolate vigils? Did he still scourge himself along the thorny paths of faith? And, if he did, how must he regard me?

"I remember one night especially how this last thought was with me in a dreary house, where I sinned, and where I dissected a heart.

"And I trembled as if an eye was upon me. And I went home.

"You will say that my imagination is keen, and that I gave way to it. But wait and hear the end.

"This definite act of mine—this, my first conscious renunciation—did not tend, as you might suppose, to the peace of my mind. On the contrary, I found myself angry, perturbed, as I analysed the cause of my warfare with self. I have naturally a supreme hatred of all control.

Liberty is my fetish. And now I had offered a sacrifice to a prisoning unselfishness, to a false god that binds and gags its devotees. I was angry, and I violently resumed my former course. But now I began to be ceaselessly companioned by uneasiness, by a furtive cowardice that was desolating. I felt that I was watched, and by someone who suffered when I sinned, who shrank and shuddered when I followed where my desires led.

"It was the monk.

"Soon I gave to him a most definite personality. I endowed him with a mind and with moods. I imagined not only a heart for him, but a voice, deep with a certain ecclesiastical beauty, austere, with a note more apt for denunciation than for praise. His face was my own face, but with an expression not mine, elevated, almost fanatical, yet nobly beautiful; praying eyes—and mine were only observant; praying lips—and mine were but sensitively sensual. And he was haggard with abstinence, while I—was I not often haggard with indulgence? Yes, his face was mine, and not mine. It seemed the face of a great saint who might have been a great sinner. Bernard, that is the most attractive face in all the world. Accustoming myself thus to a thought-companion, I at length— for we men are so inevitably materialistic—embodied him, gave to him hands, feet, a figure, all—as before, mine, yet not mine, a sort of saintly replica of my sinfulness. For do not hands, feet, figure cry our deeds as the watchman cries the hour in the night?

"So, I had the man. There he stood in my vision as you are now.

"Yes, he was there; but only when I sinned.

"When I worked and yielded myself up to the clear assertion of my intellect, when I fought to give out the thoughts that lingered like reluctant fish far down in the deep pools of my mind, when I wrestled for beauty of diction and for nameless graces of expression, when I was the author, I could not see him.

"But when I was the man, and lived the fables that I was afterwards to write, then he was with me. And his face was as the face of one who is wasted with grey grief.

"He came to me when I sinned, as if by my sins I did him grave injury. And, allowing my imagination to range wildly, as you will say, I grew gradually to feel as if each sin did indeed strike a grievous blow upon his holy nature.

"This troubled me at last. I found myself continually brooding over the strange idea. I was aware that if my friends could know I entertained it, they would think me mad. And yet I often fancied that thought moved me in the direction of a sanity more perfect, more desirable than my sanity of self-indulgence. Sometimes even I said to myself that I would

THE BLACK SPANIEL & OTHER STRANGE STORIES

reorganise my life, that I would be different from what I had been. And then, again, I laughed at my folly of the imagination, and cursed that clairvoyant of Bond Street, who made a living by trading upon the latent imbecility of human nature. Yet, the desire of change, of soul-transformation, came and lingered, and the vision of the monk's worn young face was often with me. And whenever, in my waking dreams, I looked upon it, I felt that a time might come when I could pray and weep for the wild catalogue of my many sins.

"Bernard, at last the day came when I left England. I had long wished to travel. I had grown tired of the hum of literary cliques, and the jargon of that deadly parasite called 'modernity.' Praise fainted, and lay like a corpse before my mind. I was sick of gaiety. It seemed to me that London was stifling my powers, narrowing my outlook, barring out real life from me with its moods and its fashions, and its idols of the hour, and its heroes of a day, who are the traitors of the day's night.

"So I went away.

"And now I come to the part of my story that you may find it hard to believe. Yet it is true.

"One day, in my wanderings, I came to a monastery. I remember the day well. It was an afternoon of early winter, and I was *en route* to a warm climate. But to gain my climate, and snatch a vivid contrast such as I love, I toiled over a gaunt and dreary pass, presided over by heavy, beetling-browed mountains. I rode upon a mule, attended only by my manservant and by a taciturn guide who led a baggage mule. Slowly we wound, by thin paths, among the desolate crags, which sprang to sight in crowds at each turn of the way, pressing upon us, like dead faces of Nature, the corpses of things we call inanimate, but which had surely once lived. For the earth is alive, and gives life. But these mountains were now utterly dead. These grey, petrified countenances of the hills subdued my soul. The pattering shuffle of the mules woke an occasional echo, and even an echo I hated. For the environing silence was immense, and I wished to steep myself in it. As we still ascended, in the waste winter afternoon, towards the hour of twilight, snow—the first snow of the season—began to fall. I watched the white vision of the flakes against the grey vision of the crags, and I thought that this path, which I had chosen as my road to Summer, was like the path by which holy men slowly gain Paradise, treading difficult ways through life that they may attain at last those eternal roses which bloom beyond the granite and the snows. Up and up I rode, into the clouds and the night, into the veil of the world, into the icy winds of the heights. An eagle screamed above my head, poised like a black shadow in the opaque gloom. That flying life was the only life in this waste.

"And then my mule, edging ever to the precipice as a man to his fate, sidled round a promontory of rock and set its feet in snow. For we had passed the snowline. And upon the snow lay thin spears of yellow light. They streamed from the lattices of the monastery which crowns the very summit of the pass.

III

"At this monastery I was to spend the night. The good monks entertain all travellers, and in summertime their hospitalities are lavishly exercised. But in winter, wanderers are few, and these holy men are left almost undisturbed in their meditative solitudes. My mule paused upon a rocky plateau before the door of the narrow grey building. The guide struck upon the heavy wood. After a while we were admitted by a robed figure, who greeted us kindly and made us welcome. Within, the place was bare and poor enough, but scrupulously clean. I was led through long, broad, and bitterly cold corridors to a big chamber in which I was to pass the night. Here were ranged in a row four large beds with white curtains. I occupied one bed, my servant another. The rest were untenanted. The walls were lined with light wood. The wooden floor was uncarpeted. I threw open the narrow window. Dimly I could see a mountain of rocks, on which snow lay in patches, towering up into the clouds in front of me. And to the left there was a glimmer of water. On the morrow, by that water, I should ride down into the land of flowers to which I was bound. Till then I would allow my imagination to luxuriate in the bleak romance of this wild home of prayer. The pathos of the night, shivering in the snow, and of this brotherhood of aspiring souls, detached from the excitement of the world forever, seeking restlessly their final salvation day by day, night by night, in clouds of mountain vapour and sanctified incense, entered into my soul. And I thought of that imagined companion of mine. If he were with me now, surely he would feel that he had led me to his home at length. Surely he would secretly long to remain here.

"I smiled, as I said to myself—'Monk, to-morrow, if, indeed, you are fated to be my eternal attendant, you must come with me from this cold station of the cross down into the sunshine, where the blood of men is hot, where passions sing among the vineyards, where the battle is not of souls but of flowers. To-morrow you must come with me. But to-night be at peace!'

"And I smiled to myself again as I fancied that my visionary companion was glad.

"Then I went down into the refectory.

"That night, before I retired to my room of the four beds, I asked if I might go into the chapel of the monastery. My request was granted. I shall never forget the curious sensation which overtook me as my guide led me down some steps past a dim, little, old, painted window set in the wall, to the chapel. That there should be a church here, that the deep tones of an organ should ever sound among these rocks and clouds, that the Host should be elevated and the censer swung, and litanies and masses be chanted amid these everlasting snows, all this was wonderful and quickening to me. When we reached the chapel, I begged my kind guide to leave me for a while. I longed to meditate alone. He left me, and instinctively I sank down upon my knees.

"I could just hear the keening of the wind outside. A dim light glimmered near the altar, and in one of the oaken stalls I saw a bent form praying. I knelt a long time. I did not pray. At first I scarcely thought definitely. Only, I received into my heart the strange, indelible impression of this wonderful place; and, as I knelt, my eyes were ever upon that dark praying figure near to me. By degrees I imagined that a wave of sympathy flowed from it to me, that in this monk's devotions my name was not forgotten.

"'What absurd tricks our imaginations can play us!' you will say.

"I grew to believe that he prayed for me, there, under the dim light from the tall tapers.

"What blessing did he ask on me? I could not tell; but I longed that his prayer might be granted.

"And then, Bernard, at last he rose. He lifted his face from his hands and stood up. Something in his figure seemed so strangely familiar to me, so strangely that, on a sudden, I longed, I craved to see his face.

"He seemed about to retreat through a side door near to the altar; then he paused, appeared to hesitate, then came down the chapel towards me. As he drew near to me—I scarcely knew why—but I hid my face deep in my hands, with a dreadful sense of overwhelming guilt which dyed my cheeks with blood. I shrank—I cowered. I trembled and was afraid. Then I felt a gentle touch on my shoulder. I looked up into the face of the monk.

"Bernard, it was the face of my invisible companion—it was my own face.

"The monk looked down into my eyes searchingly. He recoiled.

"'*Mon démon!*' he whispered in French. '*Mon démon!*'

"For a moment he stood still, like one appalled. Then he turned and abruptly quitted the chapel.

"I started up to follow him, but something held me back. I let him go, and I listened to hear if his tread sounded upon the chapel floor as a human footstep, if his robe rustled as he went.

"Yes. Then he was, indeed, a living man, and it was a human voice which had reached my ears, not a voice of imagination. He was a living man, this double of my body, this antagonist of my soul, this being who called me demon, who fled from me, who, doubtless, hated me. He was a living man.

"I could not sleep that night. This encounter troubled me. I felt that it had a meaning for me which I must discover, that it was not chance which had led me to take this cold road to the sunshine. Something had bound me with an invisible thread, and led me up here into the clouds, where already I—or the likeness of me—dwelt, perhaps had been dwelling for many years. I had looked upon my living wraith, and my living wraith had called me demon.

"How could I sleep?

"Very early I got up. The dawn was bitterly cold, but the snow had ceased, though a coating of ice covered the little lake. How delicate was the dawn here! The gathering, growing light fell upon the rocks, upon the snow, upon the ice of the lake, upon the slate walls of the monastery. And upon each it lay with a pretty purity, a thin refinement, an austerity such as I had never seen before. So, even Nature, it seemed, was purged by the continual prayers of these holy men. She, too, like men, has her lusts, and her hot passions, and her wrath of warfare. She, too, like men, can be edified and tended into grace. Nature among these heights was a virgin, not a wanton, a fit companion for those who are dedicated to virginity.

"I dressed by the window, and went out to see the entrance of the morning. There was nobody about. I had to find my own way. But when I had gained the refectory, I saw a monk standing by the door.

"It was my wraith waiting for me.

"Silently he went before me to the great door of the building. He opened it, and we stepped out upon the rocky plateau on which the snow lay thickly. He closed the door behind us, and motioned me to attend him among the rocks till we were out of sight of the monastery. Then he stopped, and we faced one another, still without a word, the grey light of the wintry dawn clothing us so wearily, so plaintively.

"We gazed at each other, dark face to dark face, brown eyes to brown eyes. The monk's pale hands, my hands, were clenched. The monk's strong lips, my lips, were set. The two souls looked upon each other, there, in the dawn.

"And then at last he spoke in French, and with the beautiful voice I knew.

"'Whence have you come?' he said.

"'From England, father.'

"'From England? Then you live! you live. You are a man, as I am! And I have believed you to be a spirit, some strange spirit of myself, lost to my control, interrupting my prayers with your cries, interrupting my sleep with your desires. You are a man like myself?'

"He stretched out his hand and touched mine.

"'Yes; it is indeed so,' he murmured.

"'And you,' I said in my turn, 'are no spirit. Yet, I, too, believed you to be a wraith of myself, interrupting my sins with your sorrow, interrupting my desires with your prayers. I have seen you. I have imagined you. And now I find you live. What does it mean? For we are as one and yet not as one.'

"'We are as two halves of a strangely mingled whole,' he answered. 'Do you know what you have done to me?'

"'No, father.'

"'Listen,' he said. 'When a boy I dedicated myself to God. Early, early I dedicated myself, so that I might never know sin. For I had heard that the charm of sin is so great and so terrible that, once it is known, once it is felt, it can never be forgotten. And so it can make the holiest life hideous with its memories. It can intrude into the very sanctuary like a ghost, and murmur its music with the midnight mass. Even at the elevation of the Host will it be present, and stir the heart of the officiator to longing so keen that it is like the Agony of the Garden, the Agony of Christ. There are monks here who weep because they dare not sin, who rage secretly like beasts—because they will not sin.'

"He paused. The grey light grew over the mountains.

"'Knowing this, I resolved that I would never know sin, lest I, too, should suffer so horribly. I threw myself at once into the arms of God. Yet I have suffered—how I have suffered!'

"His face was contorted, and his lips worked. I stood as if under a spell, my eyes upon his face. I had only the desire to hear him. He went on, speaking now in a voice roughened by emotion:

"'For I became like these monks. You'—and he pointed at me with outstretched fingers—'you, my wraith, made in my very likeness, were surely born when I was born, to torment me. For, while I have prayed, I have been conscious of your neglect of prayer as if it were my own. When I have believed, I have been conscious of your unbelief as if it were my own. Whatever I have feebly tried to do for God, has been marred and defaced by all that you have left undone. I have wrestled with you; I have tried to hold you back; I have tried to lead you with me where I want to go, where I must go. All these years I have tried, all these years I have striven. But it has seemed as if God did not choose it. When you have been sinning, I have been agonising. I have lain upon the floor of my cell in the night, and I have torn at my evil heart. For—sometimes— I have longed—how I have longed! —to sin your sin.'

"He crossed himself. Sudden tears sprang into his eyes.

"'I have called you my demon,' he cried. 'But you are my cross. Oh, brother, will you not be my crown?'

"His eyes, shadowed with tears, gazed down into mine. Bernard, in that moment, I understood all—my depression, my unreasoning despair, the fancied hatred of others, even my few good impulses, all came from him, from this living holy wraith of my evil self.

"'Will you not be my crown?' he said.

"Bernard, there, in the snow, I fell at his feet. I confessed to him. I received his absolution.

"And, as the light of the dawn grew strong upon the mountains, he, my other self, my wraith, blessed me."

There was a long silence between us. Then I said:

"And now?"

"And now you know why I have changed. That day, as I went down into the land of the sunshine, I made a vow."

"A vow?"

"Yes; to be his crown, not his cross. I soon returned to England. At first I was happy, and then one day my old evil nature came upon me like a giant. I fell again into sin, and, even as I sinned, I saw his face looking into mine, Bernard, pale, pale to the lips, and with eyes—such sad eyes of reproach! Then I thought I was not fit to live, and I tried to kill myself. They saved me, and brought me here."

"Yes; and now, Hubert?"

"Now," he said, "I am so happy. God surely placed me here where I cannot sin. The days pass and the nights, and they are stainless. And he—he comes by night and blesses me. I live for him now, and see always the grey walls of his monastery, his face which shall, at last, be completely mine."

"Good-bye," the doctor said to me as I got into the carriage to drive back to the station. "Yes, he is perfectly happy, happier in his mania, I believe, than you or I in our sanity."

I drove away from that huge home of madness, set in the midst of lovely gardens in a smiling landscape, and I pondered those last words of the doctor's:

"You and I—in our sanity."

And, thinking of the peace that lay on Hubert's face, I compared the so-called mad of the world with the so-called sane—and wondered.

A Silent Guardian

I

The door of the long, dreary room, with its mahogany chairs, its littered table, its motley crew of pale, silent people, opened noiselessly. A dreary, lean footman appeared in the aperture, bowing towards a corner where, in a recess near a forlorn, lofty window, sat a tall, athletic-looking man of about forty-five years of age, with a strong yet refined face, clean shaven, and short, crisp, dark hair. The tall man rose immediately, laying down an old number of *Punch*, and made his way out, watched rather wolfishly by the other occupants of the room. The door closed upon him, and there was a slight rustle and a hiss of whispering.

Two well-dressed women leaned to one another, the feathers in their hats almost mingling as they murmured: "Not much the matter with him, I should fancy."

"He looks as strong as a horse; but modern men are always imagining themselves ill. He has lived too much, probably."

They laughed in a suppressed ripple.

At the end of the room near the door, under the big picture of a grave man in a frock coat, holding a double eye-glass tentatively in his right hand as if to emphasise an argument—a young girl bent towards her father, who said to her in a low voice:

"That man who has just left the room is Brune, the great sculptor."

"Is he ill?" the girl asked.

"It seems so, since he is here."

Then a silence fell again, broken only by the rustle of turned pages and the occasional uneasy shifting of feet.

Meanwhile, in a small room across the hall, by a window through which the autumn sun streamed with a tepid brightness, Reginald Brune lay on a narrow sofa. His coat and waistcoat were thrown open; his chest was bared. Gerard Fane, the great discoverer of hidden diseases, raised himself from a bent posture, and spoke some words in a clear, even voice.

Brune lifted himself half up on his elbow, and began mechanically to button the collar of his shirt. His long fingers did not tremble, though his face was very pale.

He fastened the collar, arranged his loose tie, and then sat up slowly.

A boy, clanking two shining milk cans, passed along the pavement, whistling a music hall song. The shrill melody died down the street, and Brune listened to it until there was a silence. Then he looked up at the man opposite to him, and said, as one dully protesting, without feeling, without excitement:

"But, doctor, I was only married three weeks ago."

Gerard Fane gave a short upward jerk of the head, and said nothing. His face was calmly grave. His glittering brown eyes were fastened on his patient. His hands were loosely folded together.

Brune repeated, in a slightly raised voice:

"I was married three weeks ago. It cannot be true."

"I am here to tell the truth," the other replied.

"But it is so—so ironic. To allow me to start a new life—a beautiful life—just as the night is coming. Why, it is diabolical; it is not just; the cruelty of it is fiendish."

A spot of gleaming red stained each of the speaker's thin cheeks. He clenched his hands together, riveting his gaze on the doctor, as he went on:

"Can't you see what I mean? I had no idea—I had not the faintest suspicion of what you say. And I have had a very hard struggle. I have been poor and quite friendless. I have had to fight, and I have lost much of the good in my nature by fighting, as we often do. But at last I have won the battle, and I have won more. I have won goodness to give me back some of my illusions. I had begun to trust life again. I had—"

He stopped abruptly. Then he said:

"Doctor, are you married?"

"No," the other answered; and there was a note of pity in his voice.

"Then you can't understand what your verdict means to me. Is it irrevocable?"

Gerard Fane hesitated.

"I wish I could hope not; but—"

"But—?"

"It is."

Brune stood up. His face was quite calm now and his voice, when he spoke again, was firm and vibrating.

"I have some work that I should wish to finish. How long can you give me?"

"Three months."

"One will do if my strength keeps up at all. Good-bye."

There was a thin chink of coins grating one against the other. The specialist said—

"I will call on you to-morrow, between four and five. I have more directions to give you. To-day my time is so much taken up. Good-bye."

The door closed.

In the waiting room, a moment later, Brune was gathering up his coat and hat.

The two ladies eyed him curiously as he took them and passed out.

"He does look a little pale, after all," whispered one of them. A moment later he was in the street.

From the window of his consulting-room, Gerard Fane watched the tall figure striding down the pavement.

"I am sorry that man is going to die," he said to himself.

And then he turned gravely to greet a new patient.

II

Gerard Fane's victoria drew up at the iron gate of No. 5 Ilbury Road, Kensington, at a quarter past four the following afternoon. A narrow strip of garden divided the sculptor's big red house from the road. Ornamental ironwork on a brick foundation closed it in. The great studio, with its huge windows and its fluted pillars, was built out at one end. The failing sunlight glittered on its glass, and the dingy sparrows perched upon the roof to catch the parting radiance as the twilight fell. The doctor glanced round him and thought, "How hard this man must have worked! In London this is a little palace."

"Will you come into the studio, sir, please?" said the footman in answer to his summons. "Mr. Brune is there at present."

"Surely he cannot be working," thought the doctor, as he followed the man down a glass-covered paved passage, and through a high doorway across which a heavy curtain fell. "If so, he must possess resolution almost more than mortal."

He passed beyond the curtain, and looked round him curiously.

The studio was only dimly lit now, for daylight was fast fading. On a great open hearth, with dogs, a log fire was burning; and beside it, on an old-fashioned oaken settle, sat a woman in a loose cream-coloured tea-gown. She was half turning round to speak to Reginald Brune, who stood a little to her left, clad in a long blouse, fastened round his waist with a band. He had evidently recently finished working, for his hands still bore evident traces of labour, and in front of him, on a raised platform, stood a statue that was not far from completion. The doctor's eyes were attracted from the woman by the log fire, from his patient, by the lifeless, white, nude figure that seemed to press forward out of the gathering gloom. The sculptor and his wife had not heard him announced, apparently, for they continued conversing in low tones, and he paused in the doorway, strangely fascinated—he could scarcely tell why—by the marble creation of a dying man.

The statue, which was life size, represented the figure of a beautiful, grave youth, standing with one foot advanced, as if on the point of stepping forward. His muscular arms hung loosely; his head was slightly turned aside as in the attitude of one who listens for a repetition of some vague sound heard at a distance. His whole pose suggested an alert, yet restrained, watchfulness. The triumph of the sculptor lay in the extraordinary suggestion of life he had conveyed into the marble. His creature lived as many mollusc men never live. Its muscles seemed tense, its body quivering with eagerness to accomplish—what? To attack, to repel, to protect, to perform some deed demanding manfulness, energy, free, fearless strength.

"That marble thing could slay if necessary," thought Gerard Fane, with a thrill of the nerves all through him that startled him, and recalled him to himself.

He stepped forward to the hearth quietly, and Brune turned and took him by the hand.

"I did not hear you," the sculptor said. "The man must have opened the door very gently. Sydney, this is Dr. Gerard Fane, who is kindly looking after me."

The woman by the fire had risen, and stood in the firelight and the twilight, which seemed to join hands just where she was. She greeted the specialist in a girl's young voice, and he glanced at her with the furtive thought, "Does she know yet?"

She looked twenty-two, not more.

Her eyes were dark grey, and her hair was bronze. Her figure was thin almost to emaciation; but health glowed in her smooth cheeks, and spoke in her swift movements and easy gestures. Her expression was responsive and devouringly eager. Life ran in her veins with turbulence, never with calm. Her mouth was pathetic and sensitive, but there was an odd suggestion of almost boyish humour in her smile.

Before she smiled, Fane thought, "She knows."

Afterwards, "She cannot know."

"Have you a few moments to spare?" Brune asked him. "Will you have tea with us?"

Fane looked at Mrs. Brune and assented. He felt a strange interest in this man and this woman. The tragedy of their situation appealed to him, although he lived in a measure by foretelling tragedies. Mrs. Brune touched an electric bell let into the oak-panelled wall, and her husband drew a big chair forward to the hearth.

As he was about to sit down in it, Gerard Fane's eyes were again irresistibly drawn towards the statue; and a curious fancy, born, doubtless, of the twilight that invents spectres and of the firelight that evokes imaginations, came to him, and made him for a moment hold his breath.

It seemed to him that the white face menaced him, that the white body had a soul, and that the soul cried out against him.

His hand trembled on the back of the chair. Then he laughed to himself at the absurd fancy, and sat down.

"Your husband has been working?" he said to Mrs. Brune.

"Yes, all the day. I could not tempt him out for even five minutes. But then, he has had a holiday, as he says, although it was only a fortnight. That was not very long for—for a honeymoon."

As she said the last sentence she blushed a little, and shot a swift, half-tender, half-reproachful glance at her husband. But he did not meet it; he only looked into the fire, while his brows slightly contracted.

"I think Art owns more than half his soul," the girl said, with the flash of a smile. "He only gives to me the fortnights and to Art the years."

There was a vague jealousy in her voice; but then the footman brought in tea, and she poured it out, talking gaily.

From her conversation, Fane gathered that she had no idea of her husband's condition. With a curious and fascinating naturalness she spoke of her marriage, of her intentions for the long future.

"If Reginald is really seedy, Dr. Fane," she said, "get him well quickly, that he may complete his commissions. Because, you know, he has promised, when they are finished, to take me to Italy, and to Greece, to the country of Phidias, whose mantle has fallen upon my husband."

"Do not force Dr. Fane into untruth," said Brune, with an attempt at a smile.

"And is that statue a commission?" Fane asked, indicating the marble figure, that seemed to watch them and to listen.

"No; that is an imaginative work on which I have long been engaged. I call it, 'A Silent Guardian.'"

"It is very beautiful," the doctor said. "What is your idea exactly? What is the figure guarding?"

Brune and his wife glanced at one another—he gravely, she with a confident smile.

Then he said, "I leave that to the imagination."

Dr. Fane looked again at the statue, and said slowly, "You have wrought it so finely that in this light my nerves tell me it is alive."

Mrs. Brune looked triumphant.

"All the world would feel so if they could see it," she said; "but it is not to be exhibited. That is our fancy—his and mine. And now I will leave you together for a few minutes. Heal him of his ills, Dr. Fane, won't you?"

She vanished through the door at the end of the studio. The two men stood together by the hearth.

"She does not know?" Fane asked.

The other leaned his head upon his hand, which was pressed against the oak mantelpiece.

"I am too cowardly to tell her," he said in a choked voice. "You must."

"And when?"

"To-day."

There was a silence. Then, in his gravest professional manner, Fane gave some directions, and wrote others down, while the sculptor looked into the dancing fire. When Fane had finished:

"Shall I tell her now?" he asked gently.

Brune nodded without speaking. His face looked drawn and contorted as he moved towards the door. His emotion almost strangled him, and the effort to remain calm put a strain upon him that was terrible.

Gerard Fane was left alone for a moment—alone with the statue whose personality, it seemed to him, pervaded the great studio. In its attitude there was a meaning, in its ghost-like face and blind eyes a resolution of intention, that took possession of his soul. He told himself that it was lifeless, inanimate, pulseless, bloodless marble; that it contained no heart to beat with love or hate, no soul to burn with impulse or with agony; that its feet could never walk, its hands never seize or slay, its lips never utter sounds of joy or menace. Then he looked at it again, and he shuddered.

"I am overworking," he said to himself; "my nerves are beginning to play me tricks. I must be careful."

And he forcibly turned his thoughts from the marble that could never feel to the man and woman so tragically circumstanced, and to his relation towards them.

A doctor is so swiftly plunged into intimacy with strangers. To the sculptor it was as if Fane held the keys of the gates of life and death for him; as if, during that quarter of an hour in the consulting room, the doctor had decided, almost of his own volition, that death should cut short a life of work and of love. And even to Fane himself it seemed as if his fiat had precipitated, even brought about, a tragedy that appealed to his imagination with peculiar force. His position towards this curiously interesting girl was strange. He had seen her for a quarter of an hour only, and now it was his mission to cause her the most weary pain that she might, perhaps, ever know. The opening of the studio door startled him, and his heart, that usually beat so calmly, throbbed almost with violence as Mrs. Brune came up to him.

"What is it?" she asked, facing him, and looking him full in the eyes with a violence of interrogation that was positively startling. "What is it you have to tell me? Reginald says you have ordered him to keep quiet—that you wish me to help you in—in something. Is he ill? May he not finish his commissions?"

"He is ill," said Gerard Fane, with a straightforward frankness that surprised himself.

She kept her eyes on his face.

"Very ill?"

"Sit down," the doctor said, taking her hands and gently putting her into a chair.

With the rapidity of intellect peculiar to women, she heard in those two words the whole truth. Her head drooped forward. She put out her hands as if to implore Fane's silence.

"Don't speak," she murmured. "Don't say it; I know."

He looked away. His eyes rested on the statue that made a silent third in their sad conference. How its attitude suggested that of a stealthy listener, bending to hear the more distinctly! Its expressionless eyes met his, and was there not a light in them? He knew there was not, yet he caught himself saying mentally:

"What does he think of this?" and wondering about the workings of a soul that did not, could not, exist.

Presently the girl moved slightly, and said:

"He only knew this for certain yesterday?"

"Only yesterday."

"Ah! but he must have suspected it long ago,"—she pointed towards the statue—"when he began that."

"I don't understand," Fane said. "What can that marble have to do with his health or illness?"

"When we first began to love each other," she said, "he began to work on that. It was to be his marriage gift to me, my guardian angel. He told me he would put all his soul into it, and that sometimes he fancied, if he died before me, his soul would really enter into that statue and watch over and guard me. 'A Silent Guardian' he has always called it. He must have known."

"I do not think so," Fane said. "It was impossible he should."

The girl stood up. The tears were running over her face now. She turned towards the statue.

"And he will be cold—cold like that!" she cried in a heartbreaking voice. "His eyes will be blind and his hands nerveless, and his voice silent."

She suddenly swayed and fainted into Fane's arms. He held her a moment; and when he laid her down, a reluctance to let the slim form, lifeless though it was, slip out of his grasp, came upon him. He remembered the previous day, the doomed man going down the street—his thought as he looked from the window of his consulting room, "I am sorry that man is going to die."

Now, as he leant over the white girl, he whispered, forming the very words with his lips, "I am not sorry."

And the statue seemed to bend and to listen.

III

Six weeks passed away. Winter was deepening. Through the gloom and fog that shrouded London, Christmas approached, wrapped in seasonable snow. The dying man had finished his work, and a strange peace stole over him. Now, when he suffered, when his body shivered and tried to shrink away, as if it felt the cold hands of death laid upon it, he looked at the completed statue, and found he could still feel joy. There had always been in his highly-strung, sensitive nature an element, so fantastic that he had ever striven to conceal it, of romance; and in his mind, affected by constant pain, by many sleepless nights, grew the curious idea that his life, as it ebbed away from him, entered into his creation. As he became feeble, he imagined that the man he had formed towered above him in more God-like strength, that light flowed into the sightless eyes, that the marble muscles were tense with vigour, that a soul was born in the thing which had been soulless. The theory, held by so many, of reincarnation upon earth, took root in his mind, and he came to believe that, at the moment of death, he would pass into his work and live again, unconscious, it might be, of his former existence. He loved the statue as one might love a breathing man; but he seldom spoke of his fancies, even to Sydney.

Only, he sometimes said to her, pointing to his work:

"You will never be alone, unprotected, while he is there."

And she tried to smile through the tears she could not always keep back.

Gerard Fane was often with them. He sunk the specialist in the friend, and not a day passed without a visit from him to the great studio, in which the sculptor and his wife almost lived.

He was unwearied in his attendance upon the sick man, unwavering in his attempts to soothe his sufferings. But, in reality, and almost against his will, the doctor numbered each breath his patient drew, noted with a furious eagerness each sign of failing vitality, bent his ear to catch every softest note in the prolonged *diminuendo* of this human symphony.

When Fane saw Mrs. Brune leaning over her husband, touching the damp brow with her cool, soft fingers, or the dry, parched lips with her soft, rosy lips, he turned away in a sick fury, and said to himself:

"He is dying, he is dying. It will soon be over."

For with a desperate love had entered into him a desperate jealousy, and even while he ministered to Brune he hated him.

And the statue, with blind eyes, observed the drama enacted by those three people, the two men and the woman, till the curtain fell and one of the actors made his final exit.

Fane's nerves still played him tricks sometimes. He could not look at the statue without a shudder; and while Brune imaginatively read into the marble face love and protection, the doctor saw there menace and hatred. He came to feel almost jealous of the statue, because Sydney loved it and fell in with her husband's fancy that his life was fast ebbing into and vitalising the marble limbs, that his soul would watch her from the eyes that were now without expression and thought.

When Fane entered the studio, he always involuntarily cast a glance at the white figure—at first, a glance of shuddering distaste, then, as he acknowledged to himself his love for Sydney, a glance of defiance, of challenge.

One evening, after a day of many appointments and much mental stress and strain, he drove up to Ilbury Road, was admitted, and shown as usual into the studio. He found it empty. Only the statue greeted him silently in the soft lamplight, that scarcely accomplished more than the defining of the gloom.

"My master is upstairs, sir," said the footman. "I will tell him you are here."

In a moment Sydney entered, with a lagging step and pale cheeks. Without thinking of the usual polite form of greeting, she said to Fane, "He is much worse to-day. There is a change in him, a horrible change. Dr. Fane, just now when I was talking to him it seemed to me that he was a long way off. I caught hold of his hands to reassure myself. I held them. I heard him speaking, but it was as if his words came from a distance. What does it mean? He is not—he is not—"

She looked the word he could not speak.

Fane made her sit down.

"I will go to him immediately," he said. "I may be able to do something."

"Yes, go—do go!" she exclaimed with feverish excitement.

Then suddenly she sprang up, and seizing his hands with hers, she said in a piercing voice: "You are a great doctor. Surely—surely you can keep this one life for me a little longer."

As they stood, Fane was facing the statue, which was at her back, and while she spoke his eyes were drawn from the woman he loved to the marble thing he senselessly hated. It struck him that a ghastly change had stolen over it. A sudden flicker of absolute life surely infused it, quickened it even while she spoke, stole through the limbs one by one, welled up to the eyes as light pierces from a depth, flowed through all the marble. A pulse beat in the dead, cold heart. A mind rippled into the rigid, watching face. There was no absolute movement, and yet there was the sense of stir. Fane, absorbed in horror, seemed to watch an act of creation, to see life poured from some invisible and unknown source into the bodily chamber that had been void and dark.

Motionless he saw the statue dead; motionless he saw the statue live.

He drew his hands from Sydney's. He was too powerfully impressed to speak, but she looked up into his face, turned, and followed his eyes.

She, too, observed the change, for her lips parted, and a wild amazement shone in her eyes. Then she touched Fane's arm, and whispered, rather in awe than in horror, "Go—go to him. See if anything has happened. I will stay and watch here."

With a hushed tread Fane left the studio, passed through the hall, ascended the stairs to the sculptor's room. Outside the door he hesitated for a moment. He was trembling. He heard a clock ticking within. It sounded very loud, like a hammer beating in his ears. He pushed the door open at length, and entered. Brune's tall figure was sitting in an armchair, bowed over a table on which lay an open Art magazine.

His head lay hidden on his arms, which were crossed.

Fane raised the face and turned it up towards him.

It was the face of a dead man.

He looked at it, and smiled.

Then he stole down again to the studio, where Sydney was still standing.

"Yes?" she said interrogatively, as he entered.

"He is dead," Fane answered.

She only bowed her head, as if in assent. She stood a moment, then she turned her tearless eyes to him, and said:

"Why could not you save him?"

"Because I am human," Fane answered.

"And we did not say good-bye," she said.

Fane was strung up. Conflicting feelings found a wild playground in his soul. His nerves were in a state of abnormal excitement, and something seemed to let go in him—the something that holds us back, normally, from mad follies. He suddenly caught Sydney's hand, and in a choked voice said:

"He is dead. Think a little of the living."

She looked at him, wondering.

"Think of the living that love you. He neither hates nor loves anymore. Sydney! Sydney!"

As she understood his meaning she wrung her hand out of his, and said, as one trying to clear the road for reason:

"You love me, and he bought you to keep him alive. Why, then—"

A sick, white change came over her face.

"Sydney! Sydney!" he said.

"Why, then he bought death from you. Ah!"

She put her hand on the bell, and kept it there till the servant hurried in.

"Show Dr. Fane out," she said. "He will not come here again."

And Fane, seeing the uselessness of protest, ready to strike himself for his folly, went without a word. Only, as he went, he cast one look at the statue. Was there not the flicker of a smile in its marble eyes?

IV

People said Dr. Gerard Fane was overworking, that he was not himself. His manner to patients was sometimes very strange, brusque, impatient, intolerant. A brutality stole over him, and impressed the world that went to him for healing very unfavourably. The ills of humanity rendered him now sarcastic instead of pitiful, a fatal attitude of mind for a physician to adopt; and he was even known to pronounce on sufferers sentence of death with a callous indifference that was inhuman as well as impolitic. As the weeks went by, his reception room became less crowded than of old. There were even moments in his day when he had leisure to sit down and think, to give a rein to his mood of impotent misery and despair. Sydney had never consented to receive him again. Woman-like—for she could be extravagantly yet calmly unreasonable—she had clung to the idea that Fane had hastened, if not actually brought about, her husband's death by his treatment. She made no accusation. She simply closed her doors upon him. She had a horror of him, which never left her.

Again and again Fane called. She was always denied to him. Then he met her in the street. She cut him. He spoke to her. She passed on without a reply. At last a dull fury took possession of him. Her treatment of him was flagrantly unjust. He had wished the sculptor to die, but he had allowed nature to accomplish her designs unaided, even to some extent hampered and hindered by his medical skill and care. He loved Sydney with the violence of a man whose emotions had been sedulously repressed through youth, vanquished but not killed by ambition, and the need to work for the realisation of that ambition. The tumults of early manhood, never given fair play, now raged in his breast, from which they should have been long since expelled, and played havoc with every creed of sense, and every built-up theory of wisdom and experience. Fane became by degrees a monomaniac.

He brooded incessantly over his developed but starved passion, over the thought that Sydney chose to believe him a murderer. At first, when he was trying day after day to see her, he clung to his love for her; but when he found her obdurate, set upon wronging him in her thought, his passion, verging towards despair, changed, and was coloured with hatred. By degrees he came to dwell more upon the injury done to him by her suspicion than upon his love of her, and then it was that a certain wildness crept into his manner, and alarmed or puzzled those who consulted him.

That his career was going to the dogs Fane understood, but he did not care. The vision of Sydney was always before him. He was forever plotting and planning to be with her alone—against her will or not, it was nothing to him. And when he was alone with her, what then?

He would know how to act.

It was just in the dawn of the spring season over London that further inaction became insupportable to him. One evening, after a day of listless inactivity spent in waiting for the patients who no longer came in crowds to his door, he put on his hat and walked from Mayfair to Kensington, vaguely, yet with intention. He looked calm, even absent; but he was a desperate man. All fear of what the world thinks or says, all consideration of outward circumstances and their relation to worldly happiness, had died within him. He was entirely abstracted and self-centred.

He reached the broad thoroughfare of Ilbury Road, with its line of artistic red houses, detached and standing in their gardens. The darkness was falling as he turned into it and began to walk up and down opposite the house with the big studio in which he was once a welcome visitor. There was a light in one of the bedroom windows and in the hall, and presently, as Fane watched, a brougham drove up to the door. It waited a few moments before the house, then someone entered the carriage. The door was banged; the horse moved on. Through the windows Fane saw a woman's face, pale, against the pane. It was the face of Sydney. For a moment he thought he would call to the coachman to stop. Then he restrained himself, and again walked up and down, waiting. She must return presently. He would speak to her as she was getting out of the carriage. He would force her to receive him.

Towards nine o'clock his plans were altered by an event which took place. The house door opened, and the footman came out with a handful of letters for the post. The pillar-box was very near, and the man carelessly left the hall door on the jar while he walked down the road. Fane caught a glimpse of the hall that he knew so well. A step, and he could be in the house. He hesitated. He looked down the road. The man had his back turned, and was putting the letters into the box. Fane slipped into the garden, up the steps, through the door. The hall was empty. At his right was the passage leading to the studio. He stole down it, and tried the door. It opened. In the darkness the heavy curtain blew against his face. In another instant he closed the door softly at his back, and stood alone in the wide space and the blackness. Here there was not a glimmer of light. Thick curtains fell over the windows. No fire burned upon the hearth. There was no sound except when a carriage occasionally rolled down the road, and even then the wheels sounded distant.

The silence and darkness had their effect upon Fane. He had done a desperate thing; but, until he found himself alone in the vacant studio, he had not fully realised the madness of his conduct, and how it would appear to the world. After the first moments of solitude had passed he came to himself a little, and half opened the door with the intention of stealing out; but he heard steps in the hall, and shrank back again like a guilty creature. He must wait, at least, until the household retired to rest.

And, waiting, the old, haunting thoughts came back to assail him once more. He began to brood over Sydney's cruel treatment of him, over her vile suspicions. Here, in the atmosphere which he knew so well—for a faint, strange perfume always lingered about the studio, and gave to it the subtle sense of life which certain perfumes can impart—his emotions were gradually quickened to fury. He recalled the days of his intimacy with the sculptor, of his unrestrained converse with Sydney. He recalled his care for the invalid, persevered in, despite his passion, to the end. And then his thought fastened upon the statue, which, strange to say, he had almost forgotten.

The statue!

It must be there, with him, in the darkness, staring with those white eyes in which he had seen a soul flicker.

As the recollection of it came to him, he trembled, leaning against the wall.

He was in one of those states of acute mental tension in which the mind becomes so easily the prey of the wildest fantasies, and slowly, laboriously, he began to frame a connection between the lifeless marble creature and his own dreary trouble.

Because of one moment of folly Sydney treated him as a pariah, as a criminal. Her gentle nature had been transformed suddenly.

By what subtle influence?

Fane remembered the day of his first visit to Ilbury Road, and his curious imagination that the statue recognised and hated him.

Had that hatred prompted action? Was there a devil lurking in the white, cold marble to work his ruin? When Sydney sent him out of her presence forever, the watching face had seemed to smile.

Fane set his teeth in the darkness. He was no longer sane. He was possessed. The tragedy of thought within him invited him to the execution of another tragedy. He stretched out his hand with the rehearsing action of one meditating a blow.

His hand fell upon an oak table that stood against the wall, and hit on something smooth and cold. It was a long Oriental dagger that the dead sculptor had brought from the East. Fane's fingers closed on it mechanically. The frigid steel thrilled his hot palm, and a pulse in his forehead started beating till there was a dull, senseless music in his ears that irritated him.

He wanted to listen for the return of Sydney's carriage.

His soul was ablaze with defiance. He was alone in the darkness with his enemy; the cold, deadly, blind, pulseless thing that yet was alive; the silent thing that had yet whispered malign accusations of him to the woman he loved; the nerveless thing that poisoned a beautiful mind against him, that stole the music from his harp of life and let loose the winds upon his summer.

His fingers closed more tightly, more feverishly upon the slippery steel.

Sydney actually thought, or strove to think, him a criminal. What if he should earn the title? A sound as of the sea beating was in his ears, and flashes of strange light seem to leap to his vision. What would a man worth the name do to his enemy?

And he and his enemy were shut up alone together.

He drew himself up straight and steadied himself against the wall, peering through the blackness in the direction of the statue.

And, as he did so, there seemed to steal into the atmosphere the breath of another living presence. He could fancy he heard the pulse of another heart beating near to his. The sensation increased upon him powerfully until suspicion grew into conviction.

His intention had subtly communicated itself to the thing he could not see.

He knew it was on guard.

There was no actual sound, no movement, but the atmosphere became charged by degrees with a deadly, numbing cold, like the breath of frost in the air. A chill ran through Fane's blood. A sluggish terror began to steal over him, folding him for the moment in a strange inertia of mind and of body. A creeping paralysis crawled upon his senses, like the paralysis of nightmare that envelops the dreamer. He opened his lips to speak, but they chattered soundlessly. Mechanically his hand clutched the thin, sharp steel of the dagger.

His enemy—then Sydney.

He would not be a coward. He struggled against the horror that was upon him.

And still the cold increased, and the personality of Fane's invisible companion seemed to develop in power. There was a sort of silent violence in the hidden room, as if a noiseless combat were taking place. Waves of darkness were stirred into motion; and Fane, as a man is drawn by the retreating tides of the sea out and away, was drawn from the wall where he had been crouching.

He stole along the floor, the dagger held in his right hand, his heart barely beating, his lips white—nearer, nearer to his enemy.

He counted each step, until he was enfolded in the inmost circle of that deadly frost emanating from the blackness before him.

Then, with a hoarse cry, he lifted his arm and sprang forward and upward, dashing the dagger down as one plunging it through a human heart.

The cry died suddenly into silence.

There was the sound of a heavy fall.

It reached the ears of the servants below stairs.

The footman took a light, and, with a scared face, went hesitatingly to the studio door, paused outside and listened while the female servants huddled in the passage.

The heavy silence succeeding the strange sound appalled them, but at length the man thrust the door open and peered in.

The light from the candle flickered merrily upon Fane's bowed figure, huddled face downwards upon the floor.

His neck was broken.

The statue, that was the dead sculptor's last earthly achievement, stood as if watching over him. But it was no longer perfect and complete.

Some splinters of marble had been struck from the left breast, and among them, on the smooth parquet, lay a bent Oriental dagger.

Demetriadi's Dream

Many people are too stupid for the happiness of others. But there are some who are too clever, or who possess gifts which are troubling to those with whom they are brought into contact. Adrian Syke was one of these. He never posed as a Sherlock Holmes. He made no claim to the possession of the faculties which must belong to the supreme detective. He was not perpetually drawing elaborate deductions and explaining to others what they were. But it seemed that he possessed a peculiar power of gathering secret information about people from themselves. And it was often information which they were probably anxious to withhold.

Syke was well off and fond of travel. He wandered about a great deal, and usually alone—he was unmarried—staying here and there as the fancy took him. Wherever he went he got to know people. But he never seemed to care much for them. Many interested him. Few or none touched his heart. But he was a companionable man, a good talker, a very good listener. Men liked him. Yet he had this power of troubling people at times.

One autumn, coming from Italy, he found himself rather taken by a certain town in Switzerland. He meant to stay there for two or three nights. But the Palace Hotel was extraordinarily comfortable, the weather was splendid—mellow delicious autumn weather—the colour of the woods which streamed down the mountain sides to the lake edge was a marvel of copper, reds, orange, bronze, there were some pleasant people, and there was quite a decent club. So Syke stayed on for a while. And he joined the Club. There he often played bridge, generally between the hours of four-thirty and seven in the afternoon. He played with men of various nationalities. Among them was an elderly Greek, pale, melancholy, sardonic, an excellent bridge player. Indeed, he seemed to exist only for bridge.

One evening, when the last rubber had been played, this Greek, Syke, and some other men were gathered in the hall of the Club where there were easy chairs and a species of bar. And in the course of a desultory conversation in a nimbus of smoke the Greek—his name was Demetriadi—remarked that on the previous night he had had a dream which had greatly impressed him. Now as a rule there is perhaps nothing more boring than to have to sit and listen to the relation by a man of his dream. The men gathered about Demetriadi remained silent after he had made his statement. Quite evidently they had no wish to hear anything about his dream. But Adrian Syke, after directing an apparently casual look at Demetriadi, said: "Won't you tell us your dream?"

"With pleasure," said Demetriadi, who obviously wished to share his experience, at second hand as it were. "I dreamed that I was out walking alone in the dead of night in a great city. It seemed to me such a city as modern New York is, a place of enormous buildings, of towers lifted far up into the sky. While I was passing down a broad, deserted thoroughfare I heard steps coming up behind me and was joined by an elderly man. He was tall. He looked very evil but also very sad. There was a bitterness as of satire in his face combined with acute melancholy. I felt that he was certainly wicked, but that he was somehow grieved, perhaps even shocked, at his own wickedness."

"That's very possible!" interjected Syke at this point.

The Greek looked at Syke with his dark, melancholy eyes and continued:

"On joining me this man took me by the arm and whispered in my ear, 'You must come with me.' I felt compelled to do as he wished and I went with him. He led me to the door of a vast modern hotel. As we went into it I heard a clock in a tower strike three. We passed through a deserted hall dimly lighted, and entered an automatic lift which my companion operated. The lift glided up to the third floor of the hotel. We got out and stood at the entrance to a very long corridor thickly carpeted and lit by electricity. On the left of this corridor was a line of shut doors with gilt numbers above them.

"'You think they are all sleeping in those rooms?' whispered my companion. 'Wait a moment!'

"He led me a short distance into the corridor, paused in front of a door with the number one above it, and stamped on the carpet. Directly he did this all the doors in the corridor opened, so that I was able to look into the interior of every room. In the first room I saw a young woman in pyjamas being strangled by a man in a fit of sexual fury. We passed on to the next number. Here a married couple were having a desperate quarrel. Their harsh voices uttering hideous words, the sort of words that can never be forgotten or forgiven, were audible to us. We could see black hatred imprinted on their congested faces. We went to the door of the next room. In this a child was dying in convulsions while its nurse, seated in an armchair, was smiling slyly over a love letter. We went on and on down the interminable corridor, and in every room we were witness to some indignity, some horror, some crime, some display of the desperate evil or misery hidden in humanity. At last I could bear no more and I turned to rush out into the night. But my companion caught my arm and held it firmly. He stamped again on the carpet. All the doors in the corridor shut. Then he looked deep into my eyes, and said with an accent of indescribable bitterness: 'And that's what we are!'

"I heard the clock in the tower strike four. I woke. Directly I woke I looked at my watch. The hands pointed to four o'clock."

When the Greek's thin voice—a voice without any "body" in it, a pessimistic voice—ceased there was a moment of dead silence. And in this silence I seemed to detect—I was among the men round the Greek—a creeping uneasiness.

"And that's what we are!" It wasn't a very pleasant end to the dream. I saw two or three of my companions looking furtive. I saw one—he was the British Chaplain of the place—glance round the circle quickly and look down. Then there was a slight movement, and I had the feeling that somebody was going to get up, that in a moment men would be going away with attempts at a cheery "Well, good night", or "au revoir". But then Adrian Syke spoke, and at once the movement ceased. I think we all felt that there was more to come, and that it was going to be unusual or interesting. Addressing Demetriadi, he said:

"You told us that in your dream this tall elderly man led you down the corridor and that all the doors giving on to it were open," he said.

"Yes," said Demetriadi.

"How many rooms did you look into?"

"A great many."

"You took them consecutively?"

"Consecutively?"

"I mean did you go from number to number consecutively? One, two, three, four—and so on?"

"Ah, I see. Yes, monsieur, we did."

"Did you get as far as number fourteen?"

After a quite definite pause, Demetriadi answered: "Yes."

"And number fourteen was the last room you looked into, wasn't it?"

"What—what can make you suppose that?" said the Greek, leaning forward in his chair, and staring at Syke intently.

"I just thought it might be," Syke said.

"Ah!" said the Greek.

For a moment I thought he was going to drop the subject, was not going to answer Syke's question. But I was wrong. After some hesitation he said, as if with an effort:

"Yes, the last room I looked into was numbered fourteen." We all, I think, had our eyes on Syke at this moment. I suppose all the men were astonished. Certainly I was. The Greek put the question that was probably in most of our minds. "What made you suppose that room was number fourteen?" he said.

"What made me?" said Syke in a careless sort of voice. "Oh, it just came to me. I seemed to see number fourteen and then a lot of doors shutting."

"Very—strange!" said Demetriadi.

His eyes were always fixed on Syke.

"It seems you are a thought reader," he added.

"I get impressions now and then," said Syke. "I don't claim to be a thought reader. I just get impressions occasionally."

And then as Demetriadi said nothing more, and as it was getting late, our little group broke up, separated. Men went off rather gravely that evening. A heaviness of thought seemed to have been laid upon them like a burden by the dream of Demetriadi and by Syke's reception of it.

I was staying at the Palace Hotel—I had been in the place much longer than Adrian Syke had—and that evening I asked Syke whether I should walk home with him as we were going the same way. He assented readily, and we set out together through the gay little town in the autumn evening. All the shops were brilliantly lit. A half circle of coloured lamps gleamed above the gaudy entrance to "Chez la petite Madame", as for some unknown reason the one *boîte de nuit* of our town had been named. Many elderly ladies were going discreetly home from the various tea rooms. Young girls and laughing young men came out of a restaurant where dancing went on every afternoon to the noise of a jazz band. The casino disgorged its habitual crowd. The long street, the street of an idle town, was full of the murmur of voices, the tiptap of footsteps. Above us on the right the mountains leaned, their riot of colours dying away from us in the darkness of night. On the left was the sleeping lake. A bell chimed the hour, and made me think of the Greek's dream-clock chiming three and then four in the tower of his dream. And just as that thought slipped through my brain my companion said:

"You have been here some time?"

"Yes."

"Much longer than I have?"

"Oh yes."

"Does that fellow, that Greek, Demetriadi, live in a hotel?"

"I believe he does. I think he lives in some very second-rate hotel."

"Know the name?"

"I'm not sure. But I think I heard someone say that he lives in the Hôtel des Fleurs. It's a small hotel not ten yards from the Casino and close to the lake."

"I've seen the name. Is he alone here?"

"I really don't know. I barely know him. I've always seen him alone. But then I have scarcely ever seen him except at the Club."

"I too! He seems to live solely for bridge. He plays a very good game."

"A dried-up sort of life that seems to me," I couldn't help saying. "And he looks to me a very arid individual. But I must say that I found his dream exceedingly interesting. And I'm sure I shall never forget it."

"Nor I," said Syke. "And the reason of that is that it was a dream which cut very deep. It made every man who heard it ponder on the things that go on behind the shut doors. They look so bland, those shut doors. And the silence in the great corridors is so profound. And it seems that everyone is sleeping peacefully. But not a bit of it. Life is going on behind those doors, life with its terrible activities. No wonder the silence could be felt once or twice when Demetriadi stopped speaking—the dried-up individual, the arid individual!"

"You don't think he is!" I said, detecting a sound as of sarcasm in the voice of Syke.

"I doubt if a really arid individual would ever have had that dream."

"You think men express character by their dreams?"

"Why not? We are always expressing character."

"And yet it is often difficult to read character."

Syke didn't say anything, and after a slight pause, I added: "I wish you would tell me how you knew that number fourteen was the last room that Demetriadi looked into in his dream."

"As I said in the Club, I saw fourteen and then a lot of doors shutting."

"And that was all?"

Syke gave me a rather queer sideways look. "By no means," he said.

I was silent, hoping that he would add something to his last statement, which had, I confess, greatly roused my curiosity, already excited by what had just happened at the Club. But he made no further remark and we walked on towards the Palace Hotel in silence, I feeling decidedly baffled. Yet how could I question him? I was no great friend of his. I only knew him slightly. If he wished to tell me anything more he would do so of his own accord. If he did not, well, I must put up with it and try to get rid of my curiosity.

We were turning in at the gate of the hotel garden when he at last spoke once more.

"I'm dining in the restaurant at eight-thirty," he said. "If you are alone to-night, perhaps you will dine with me."

I accepted his invitation rather eagerly.

We parted in the hall. As I was about to go to the lift the concierge came up to me and handed me a note. I opened it at once and found that it was from a distant cousin of mine, a Major Custe, and was to tell me that his wife and their daughter had just arrived for a short stay in our town and hoped to meet me. They had seen my name in the hotel list in the local paper. They were staying at the Hôtel des Fleurs near the Casino. Would I come to tea with them on the morrow? The Hôtel des Fleurs! That was the hotel where I fancied—I wasn't sure—that Demetriadi was staying. I wondered why Syke was interested to know where he lived. Syke's question about that had been put in a very casual voice. Nevertheless, I was convinced that his mind, when he put it, had not been at all casual.

And now here was I being asked to visit the Hôtel des Fleurs.

That evening at dinner in the restaurant I told Syke of my cousin's note and added that he and his wife were staying at the Hôtel des Fleurs near the Casino. (I didn't mention the daughter. I had no reason not to, but I just didn't happen to mention her.)

"Isn't that the hotel where you fancied that Demetriadi might be staying?" asked Syke.

I said it was.

"If you go there to-morrow—"

"I *am* going," I interrupted.

"Oh, then if it's not too much trouble you might do something for me there."

"Certainly. What is it?" I asked.

"If Demetriadi is staying in that hotel could you find out the number of his room for me?"

I was much intrigued by this question, which of course I couldn't help connecting with the odd conversation which had taken place between Demetriadi and Syke, after the former had related his dream.

"I see you are wondering why I take such an interest in the number of Demetriadi's room, whatever it is," said Syke.

"I must say I am."

"Well, that has something to do with that dream of his."

"I felt sure it must have."

Syke poured himself out another glass of Château Lafite. (He had told me at the beginning of dinner that he couldn't bear having really first-rate wine poured out for him by a waiter.)

"The whole thing must seem rather peculiar to you," he said, after slowly sipping and savouring his wine. "It doesn't to me, because I have long been accustomed, naturally enough, to a certain—well, suppose I call it a certain faculty which I possess and which seems to be denied to the average man. I don't pretend to be anything extraordinary. In most ways I am a very ordinary individual. But I possess—at least I believe so—a curious faculty of gathering secret information about certain people with whom I am brought into contact."

"Secret information!" I said.

"That is the name I give to it. These people are obliged to inform me of certain things about themselves without wishing or meaning to. Sometimes even against their intention, against their will."

"Am I one of those people?" I inquired abruptly.

Syke smiled.

"No, you are not." he answered.

Again he slowly and carefully sipped his wine. Then he added: "But our friend, Demetriadi, is."

"Were you gathering secret information about Demetriadi this afternoon?"

"I believe I was. That remains to be proved. But when this sort of thing occurs, I mean when it is borne in upon me, as it has been today, that such and such things are, or will be, truth is always at the bottom of it, not error."

"You said 'will be'. Do you claim to be able to read the future?"

"I am really not much given to laying claims," said Syke, rather sardonically. "But as I see you are interested I am giving you a sort of rough idea of what is up."

"Thanks very much. I am tremendously interested."

Syke went on sipping his wine.

"As you have spoken so frankly," I said, after a moment, "may I ask you something?"

"What is it?"

"Why do you want to know the number of the room in which Demetriadi is living here, either in the Hôtel des Fleurs or in some other hotel?"

"I don't think I want to tell you that just yet."

I felt snubbed, and I believe I must have reddened.

"Don't be vexed!" Syke said.

"I'm not vexed. Of course not!" I said, rather insincerely.

"Later on, perhaps, if anything comes of it!" Syke continued, enigmatically. "And now tell me something."

"Yes, if I can."

"Were you specially struck by any one thing which Demetriadi said when he told us his dream?"

I thought for a moment and then said: "I'm not sure that I was. The whole thing impressed me. Oh, wait a moment though! Yes! I think that I was specially struck by something."

"And may I ask what it was?"

"By the words the tall elderly man said at the end of the dream, 'And that's what we are!'"

"Oh that! Yes, that certainly cut down pretty deep. Yes! But no, I wasn't so much struck by that really as by something else."

He paused, but this time I was careful to ask no question. I had just had my lesson, and I hadn't forgotten it.

"You remember, of course, what Demetriadi said he saw in the first three rooms; a girl being strangled by a man, a hideous quarrel between husband and wife, a child dying in convulsions while its nurse sat smiling over a love letter. Not very pretty things, not very pretty! And then, according to his own account, he visited ten other rooms—"

"Eleven!" I corrected him.

"One moment!"

"I beg your pardon!"

"Visited ten other rooms, bringing the number of rooms visited up to thirteen. In each of these thirteen rooms he saw something hideous and frightful, some exhibition of the vileness or misery of human nature. But apparently his dream-curiosity wasn't satiated even then. No! For he went on to room number fourteen, and it was only when he looked into *that* room that he could, in his own words, 'bear no more'. It was that fact which struck me most in his curious narrative, that which riveted my attention, that which still engages my mind."

"And you knew that it was number fourteen!"

"I did know. Well, now, I was struck by this. A man has looked into thirteen rooms and seen a horror in each one of them, the first horror, the very first, which evidently didn't cause any slackening in his dream curiosity, being the strangling of a girl by her lover. But in room number *fourteen* he sees something which makes him suddenly feel that he can't bear any more. That was what struck me—room number fourteen—the effect *that* room had on him."

He said the last words with almost tragic significance.

"But don't you think the dream-horror was simply cumulative?" I said. "That's how I took it. And isn't that natural? A man sees horror after horror, an accumulation of dreadful happenings, until at last his nerve cracks and he can't stand anymore."

"You took it like that?"

"Yes."

"Well, I didn't."

There was something so definite in Syke's voice when he said that, and something so assured in his manner, that I was seized with a conviction which startled me. I looked hard at him and said: "Did you receive secret information about what Demetriadi saw happening in room number fourteen in his dream?"

"Perhaps I did," said Syke, finishing his wine and getting up from the dinner table. "But whether it was correct or not remains to be proved."

On the following day soon after four o'clock I walked to the Hôtel des Fleurs to call on my cousins. I had often seen the hotel when going to the Casino, but I had never been inside it. Although it was in a good position, described by the management in advertisements as "central", it was a second-class hotel, with a flight of steps inside the entrance leading up into a dark and rather dismal hall, where a somewhat moth-eaten hall porter crouched despondently in a shadowy nook among cinema advertisements and picture post-cards. But my cousins, I knew, were not very well off and no doubt the hotel was inexpensive.

They were at home and I was sent into a public sitting room full of plate glass and cane chairs, where I found them waiting for me by a cane tea-table already arranged for our sustenance. After cordial greetings and the usual somewhat unmeaning inquiries, we sat down to tea and opened with bromides. But unusually soon we got to something that wasn't a bromide. I made a banal remark about hotels—something probably to the effect that in most parts of Switzerland one can find a decent hotel at a moderate price—and elicited from Derrick Custe the following piece of information.

"We chose this hotel because a friend of ours is living here."

"Really?" I said.

"Yes, a man we were with for some time in a *pension* at St. Moritz last winter, an awfully good bridge player."

"You're mad on bridge, I know," I said.

"No madder than Susie," said Custe. (Susie is Mrs. Custe.)

"An Englishman?" I asked carelessly.

"No, a Greek. His name is Demetriadi."

As my cousin said this I happened to look across at his daughter, Elise, and I thought I detected a look of self-consciousness, perhaps even of half-disguised distress, on her very pretty face. (Elise is a strikingly good-looking girl of the fair English type, tall, blooming with health and youth, blue-eyed, with bright hair and the sort of complexion that amazes the sallow and swarthy foreigner.)

During the next half-hour I was secretly considering how best to find out what was the number of Demetriadi's room. I didn't want to ask the concierge what it was, and when coming through the hall I had seen no visitors' lists stuck up. It was most unlikely that my cousins would know such a thing. Still, it was possible that they, or that one of them, might happen to know it. I wished, before I went away, to find out for certain whether any of them did know.

I told them of course that I knew Demetriadi, though but slightly, having met him at the Club. My bridge, I said, wasn't up to his. I made no allusion to the subject of his dream. But I mentioned my acquaintance, Adrian Syke, who was a far better player than I was.

On hearing of this Derrick Custe pricked up his ears.

"Hope we shall meet him," he said. "Is he up to Demetriadi?"

"Pretty much on the same level, I believe."

"Perhaps he'll come into our game some evening," said my cousin. "Demetriadi tells me the Club here doesn't open at night."

"No, it doesn't."

"We mean to get a game every night in the hotel. We are three already, but we shall have to look for a good fourth."

He didn't ask me. He knew my game. I said I should be glad to introduce him to Syke.

Tea was over, conversation was rapidly getting back to the bromide level, evening was drawing on, and I hadn't found out the number of Demetriadi's room. I couldn't stay forever. I was getting bored and, worse still, knew I was becoming a bore. Something must be done. I began to talk about bedrooms.

"Hope you've got nice bedrooms," I said. "Which floor are you on?"

"Derrick and I are on the second floor facing towards the lake," said Susie Custe. "We've got two quite different rooms."

"And how are you off?" I asked Elise.

"Oh, I'm in clover, quite glorified in comparison to Mother and Dad."

"How's that?" I said.

"I've got a big room on the first floor that apparently doesn't let easily because people are so absurd."

"Absurd in what way?"

"Idiotically superstitious. It's numbered thirteen—I jumped at it."

Thirteen! Elise was in number thirteen. And where was Demetriadi?

At last even bromides failed and I was forced to get up to go. My cousins kindly went with me to the hall. In the hall I resolved— prompted evidently by my solicitous angel, though I didn't know it—to make a last attempt, in the dark as it were, and I said: "I wish you'd show me your rooms. I should like to feel sure you're quite comfortable here."

My cousins seemed gratified by my interest in them. They said "of course", and we all plunged into the somewhat decrepit lift and ascended asthmatically to the second floor. The bedrooms there examined and approved, we descended on foot to the first floor, and I was shown Elise's bedroom. It was, as she had said, larger and much better than the rooms of her parents. I expressed my satisfaction and commended her lack of superstition. As we left her room the door of the room beyond, number fourteen, opened and Demetriadi came out of it.

That evening before dinner I went into the cocktail bar of the Palace Hotel and having ordered a "sidecar" waited in the hope of presently seeing Adrian Syke. Just before half-past eight he came in. I asked him to join me, and while William was preparing another "sidecar" I told Syke I had some news for him. A sharp look of inquiry came into his eyes.

"You've found out about the number of Demetriadi's room?" he said.

"I have. It is number fourteen."

The look of sharp inquiry in Syke's face gave way to another look— of a satisfaction that was almost, not quite, complacent.

"Thank you," he said. "I wanted to know."

William brought him his cocktail.

"You're not much surprised, I fancy," I ventured.

(After all, hang it, I'd been busy for him!)

His reply was perhaps intended to be non-committal, but I think that a very human feeling of vanity—or shall we say of semi-vanity?—got in the way of his intention.

"Oh, his number might have been anything," he said; and then added, "Still there was no reason why it shouldn't be fourteen."

I was quite positive from that moment that he had expected it to be fourteen.

While he sipped his cocktail I told him about my cousins' passion for bridge and their wish to find a good fourth for their game with Demetriadi in the evenings.

"If you care sometimes to make a fourth I'll gladly get them to know you," I said.

"I should like it," he said, but with no eagerness.

"The hotel's very second rate," I said.

"That doesn't matter. And perhaps now and then they wouldn't mind being my guests here."

"They've got their daughter with them," I said.

"Ah!" said Syke.

And again I noticed the sharp look in his eyes.

"But I dare say she could come too, and I could look after her, she might dance while you're playing bridge."

"A good idea!" said Syke, finishing his cocktail. "Is she a pretty girl?" he added in an uninterested voice.

"Extremely pretty. At least, I think so."

As we went into dinner—we weren't dining together that night—he said: "Wonderful lot of pretty girls there are nowadays. I foresee the time when it will be considered a deadly sin on any girl's part not to be pretty."

When I left him and went to my table, I said to myself: "Why is he interested in my cousin Elise?"

There seemed absolutely no reason why he should feel the faintest interest in her. He had, I felt sure, never heard of her existence until I mentioned that she had arrived with her father and mother. But directly I did so that odd, sharply inquiring look which I was beginning to watch out for had come to his face. Then that question about her looks. Why had that been put? It had not been put idly. I was certain of that. He had really wanted to know whether Elise was pretty or not. And his slightly ironical remark about the almost universal prettiness of the girls of our day had been an attempt to throw me off the scent, as it were, had been made for the purpose of, if possible, cancelling the effect upon me of that sharp look of his, which he must have known I was wondering about.

I was completely puzzled by all this.

In order to force Syke to take the next step in this odd business I said nothing more about my cousins, made no move to make them known to Syke. Three days passed. Then Syke came up to me in the Club and said: "About those cousins of yours!"

"Yes?" I said.

"Have they got a fourth for bridge yet?"

"I believe they've found someone in the hotel," I said.

(They had, "a damned rotten player, but what are we to do?" according to Custe, who had more than once pressed me to get hold of "that friend of yours, Syke." Custe hadn't yet joined the Club, but was going to.)

Syke was silent for a moment. I felt sure he didn't wish to say anything more. But something was too strong for him and at last he said: "I should be very glad to welcome your cousins and Demetriadi here any evening if you think they would care to come and make up a rubber. Say next Friday, for instance. There's a dance in the hotel that night which might amuse the girl. We needn't stand on formalities, need we? Nobody does here."

Having got what I wanted from Syke I was charming. I went straight off to the Hôtel des Fleurs and arranged the party. On the following Friday my cousins and Demetriadi came to the Palace Hotel, and I introduced Syke.

Almost immediately the two Custes, Demetriadi and Syke sat down to bridge, while I took Elise off to find her some partners for the dance which was just beginning. As we were moving away I turned sharply and looked at the bridge players. Demetriadi and Syke were following us with their eyes. Both of them immediately looked away when I turned and became keen bridge players. But I had seen that they were both strongly interested in Elise.

She danced all the evening. I only had a few words with her when the dancing was over. It seemed to me then that she was excited, oddly excited but not happy. I asked her if she had enjoyed herself. She said, "Yes—immensely!" As she joined her parents I noticed that she sent a strange look to Demetriadi. It suggested to me two contending emotions—enticement and fear. I saw that Syke had observed it. And in that moment I realised that this odd interest in Elise, which I had wondered about, was not concentrated on Elise *qua* Elise, but on Elise as a possible object of interest to Demetriadi.

From that moment—I couldn't help it—I connected Elise with Demetriadi's dream.

There was something, there must be something, which caused Syke to find a link between this young girl, my cousin, and that most horrible dream. But what could it possibly be? I searched mind and even imagination in vain for the link. And then, baffled, I remembered that phrase of Syke's, "secret information". Could he possibly during that evening of bridge, while Elise was dancing, have gathered from her secret information of which I knew nothing? It seemed unlikely. Elise was not at all what is usually called an "interesting" girl. She was merely a typical English girl of the healthy, good-looking type. And yet perhaps she had in her some hidden strangeness. I remembered the look she had cast at the Greek which I had surprised. It certainly suggested underthings, suggested that she had some feeling for Demetriadi which she concealed. But how could that be? He was no longer young. He looked weary, "played out", devoid of zest, disenchanted, oh! very much disenchanted with life. Could such a man possibly make any appeal to a vigorous and beautiful girl? Something within me said "Impossible!" But something else replied that with women one never knows.

It was, I remember, just at this time I first became conscious of an uneasy feeling about the situation of Elise's bedroom.

After that evening at the Palace Syke became rapidly intimate with my cousins, that is intimate as a bridge player becomes with other bridge players whose game he exactly suits. Custe was enthusiastic about him and warmly thanked me for getting hold of him.

"A first-rate player, absolutely first-rate!" he said of Syke.

Susie Custe, too, was delighted with him. They met for bridge four evenings a week, twice at the Hôtel des Fleurs, twice at the Palace, and of course Demetriadi was always of the party.

I did not go to the Hôtel des Fleurs. Why should I sit among aspidistras on a cane chair doing nothing? But I was always there when they came to the Palace. And on these occasions I looked after Elise.

She danced energetically with the best of the available men, and even with me when nothing else was doing. She flirted, or seemed to flirt. She seemed to be enjoying herself. And yet I had the feeling that something was worrying her seriously and that she wasn't happy in our gay little town.

One night this feeling was so strong upon me that I spoke of it to her.

We were sitting in the great hall of the Palace Hotel. In the distance, with light nicely concentrated upon them, sat the four bridge players. Demetriadi was facing us. Syke, who was playing with Susie Custe, was in profile to us.

"Is anything bothering you?" I said.

Instantly Elise's face changed and she looked at me, I thought, with suspicion.

"Bothering me! What can you mean? What is there here to bother me?"

"I don't know. I don't see why there should be anything."

"There—isn't anything."

She said it with a touch of defiance which often accompanies a lie.

"Glad to hear it!" I said.

"Why should you think such a thing?"

Quite involuntarily my eyes went to Demetriadi. And Demetriadi was looking, was—it seemed to me—staring across the great room at us. I felt the gaze of his large black eyes just then acutely. For an instant his eyes held mine. In that instant a secret shiver went through me.

"Why? Why?" repeated Elise, with a sort of nervous irritation I had never noticed in her before.

"I have no reason except something in you."

"Something in me?" she said, as if startled.

Then she laughed. Her laugh sounded forced, artificial. "I'm quite happy here except—"

"Ah—except?"

"Except that I don't care for the hotel. It's rather dismal and dull. I hope we shan't stay here forever. But now that Mother and Dad have got such a marvellous four at bridge there seems no chance of our going away for a long time."

But they went away very soon.

Four nights after my little talk with Elise I dined once more with Syke in the restaurant. The Custes and Demetriadi were again coming for bridge and Elise was as usual expected.

That evening Syke seemed preoccupied. He talked, but he seemed decidedly distrait and had sometimes the peculiar look of a man who imagines himself to be alone. Several times during dinner I had the quite definite feeling that he had for the moment forgotten I was there. During these moments I kept silence. Then presently his expression changed and he would begin talking again, but without animation.

Just at the end of dinner when we were about to get up he looked at me in a quite different way, not merely like one very conscious of my presence and personality, but like one about to say something intimate. Everyone surely knows the sort of look I mean. It seems to bring one man very near to another. He was certainly going to say something intimate, confidential to me. I knew that.

"Yes?" I said.

I couldn't somehow help saying it. It was a mistake. It was premature. It must have suggested to Syke an eagerness, perhaps even a curiosity on my part which, striking unpleasantly upon his mood, shut him up. I had sounded the false note. The disharmony was manifest.

"Yes?" he echoed.

And his face had completely changed.

"I thought you were about to say something?"

"Only that I expect the bridge players must be waiting for us."

"Let's go and see," I said, concealing my discomfiture as best I could. And we got up from the table.

The bridge players were just coming in—without Elise. Susie Custe explained that her daughter "didn't feel like coming" that night.

"She's not ill, I hope?" I said.

"Ill!" said her mother. "Elise is never ill."

I looked at Demetriadi. His eyes were on Syke. I thought he was looking horribly pale. But he was always pale; one of your bloodless men—apparently.

They went to their bridge table and I was alone. I felt disappointed. Having of course expected Elise to come with her parents I missed her. My evening was left empty. I didn't know what to do. There was dancing as usual, but I am not one of those elderly persons who have a passion for jazz. There was no one whom I particularly wanted to talk to. I didn't feel in the mood for reading. Finally I went into the hall to look at the cinema programmes.

At the Savoy Cinema, which was close to the Hôtel des Fleurs, they were giving a film with Emil Jannings in it, *Vaudeville*. I decided to go to it, put on hat and coat, took the tram, and was soon at the entrance. People were streaming in, but I didn't join them. Something enticed me away, something led me to the steps leading up into the Hôtel des Fleurs.

I mounted them and came into the dismal entrance hall. The moth-eaten hall porter was crouching among the postcards and programmes.

"Is Miss Custe at home?" I asked.

"Yes, sir," said the man.

"Can I see her? Here's my card."

"If you will wait a moment, sir, I will go and see."

He emerged and shambled away. In a few minutes he came back. "Mademoiselle is very sorry, sir, but she can't see you to-night. She is not dressed."

"She isn't ill, I hope?"

"I don't think so, sir. She dined as usual."

I stood for a moment. I felt within me an impetus pushing me to insist on seeing my cousin. But I didn't give way to it. I said goodnight to the hall porter and left the hotel. But now I had no heart for the cinema, and I walked back to the Palace Hotel, feeling depressed, even downhearted.

When presently I went into the big hall I found the four bridge players intent on their game. I joined them and for a while watched the play. Although I play badly I understand the game thoroughly and I was struck by the play of Demetriadi. He was, I recognised, playing marvellously well, far better than any of the others. He played, in fact, like a man inspired. Even when his cards were bad he did wonders. In his mood of that night he could have saved almost any game.

When the last rubber was finished—it was won by Demetriadi and Susie Custe—Custe said: "Monsieur Demetriadi, you're a bridge genius! But even you, I should think, will never play again as you've played to-night. Wonderful, wasn't he?" he added, turning to Syke.

Syke didn't answer immediately. His eyes were on Demetriadi. At last he said: "It was splendid bridge. Too good for us!"

Demetriadi said nothing, only smiled slightly. When he said goodnight to Syke and myself I thought that he pressed my hand rather strangely, as if he wished to express physically some feeling that he didn't choose to express in words.

But that may have been only my imagination.

When my cousins and he had gone I put a question to Syke. It was abrupt, but I had to put it that night. I said: "I wish you would tell me something."

"What is it?" he asked.

"Is my cousin, Elise, one of the people who gives you secret information?"

He looked rather surprised. But he answered without hesitation.

"Oh no!" he said. "She gives me nothing, absolutely nothing."

I knew he was speaking the truth.

By then I had been living for many weeks in the Palace Hotel and was on friendly terms with the young German-Swiss waiter who brought me my breakfast every morning at half-past eight. When he came in with it on the following day he said at once: "Monsieur, such a dreadful thing has happened!"

"What?" I said. "Wait! Was it at the Hôtel des Fleurs?"

I was out of bed in my dressing gown standing by the breakfast table.

"Why, how did you know, monsieur?" said the waiter, surprise showing in his shallow blue eyes.

"I don't know. Tell me!"

"That poor Greek gentleman who often comes here to play cards—he was here only last night—"

"What about him?"

"He has been found dead in his bedroom—hanging, monsieur, from the curtain rod by the window."

I stood for a minute without speaking. I was horrified. And yet it seemed to me that, without being self-consciously aware of it, I had been expecting something like this.

"Horrible!" I said at last. "What was the reason?"

The young waiter looked rather embarrassed.

"I don't know for certain, monsieur. But they say—" he hesitated.

"Yes—go on!"

"They say he was in love with that young English lady, monsieur, your cousin. There is a letter left—they say."

"Thank you, Fritz. Well, I'll go round to the hotel in a few minutes."

Fritz went away.

As soon as I had dressed I went to the Hôtel des Fleurs. The body of Demetriadi had already been taken away. I didn't see Elise or her mother, but I saw Custe, who was much upset. He told me that what the waiter had said was true. Although neither he nor his wife had suspected it, Demetriadi had been madly in love with Elise ever since they had met at St. Moritz. Apparently the girl had actually been fond of him. But on the previous day, evidently realising how utterly unsuitable a marriage with him would be, and apparently also influenced by some incident which was never made public, and which my cousin refused to disclose to me, she had sent him a letter forbidding him ever to speak of love matters to her again, and threatening that if he did she would make her people take her away at once from our town.

The result of this letter was the tragedy.

Demetriadi's marvellous game of bridge at the Palace Hotel was his last.

I did not see Syke during the day. I don't know where he was. Perhaps—the weather was fine—he had gone out for some expedition. In the evening, however, he was in the restaurant as usual. After dinner I joined him.

"Can you tell me anything now?" I asked.

"Yes," he said. "Now I can! Do you know what it was Demetriadi saw in room number fourteen in his dream?"

"What was it?"

"He saw himself—hanging."

The Hindu

I have a friend whom I will call Sir William Turnbull, although that isn't his name. He is a famous specialist in nervous diseases, lives in Cavendish Square, London, and leads, I should think, a very interesting, though certainly an arduous, life. He is a white-haired man, with a long white moustache, a rather beaky nose, blue eyes, and an inexpressive face. His voice is quiet; his manner is always tranquil, seldom animated and scarcely ever vivid. In general conversation he says but little. But when I am alone with him at night, as I am perhaps once a month, he tells me interesting and sometimes fascinating, stories of the people who consult him. Of course, he never reveals their real names. I have noted down some of these "cases" in a book. Two or three days ago I was looking over it and came upon a strange narrative. It concerns a newspaper proprietor, and I call it "The Hindu."

"John Latimer came to consult me about a year ago" (said the doctor, in his quiet, rather colourless voice). "He owns several big papers, and is an extremely successful man. In person he is a large, rather burly, individual, just over forty, with brown eyes, short brown hair, a firm mouth and chin, and a straightforward but unaffected manner. But when I first saw him he looked very ill. He had a furtive demeanour which was at odds with his dominating appearance; his large hands were terribly restless, and by various other signs I was able to judge of his condition. It was very bad.

"When we had had a little talk I realised that behind Latimer's nervous state there was some prompting tragedy, some haunting fear or misery, and that until I could find out what it was I could do very little for him. I told him this.

"But it will take a long time," he said. "If I'm to go thoroughly into it—"

"Nothing else would be of much use," I interrupted. "But I can only give you half an hour this morning. Could you come again"—I consulted my engagement book—"say, on Thursday afternoon?"

"What!" said he, with a deplorable accent. "Three days ahead?"

"That seems to be my first free hour," I replied.

"Oh, but—" Latimer paused. Then he thrust forward his powerful head and exclaimed:

"I don't want to wait so long. Will you waive etiquette and dine with me at my house, say, tonight?"

"That's very good of you."

"Good!"

His lips twisted, and his big hands shifted on his knees. He clasped them tightly together.

"Good!" said he. "Why, doctor, I'm hanging on to you as my only hope. I've heard that you succeed where everyone else fails. Can you come and will you?"

I said I would, and I went.

The Latimers live—let us say—in Portman Square. I was there by half-past eight the same evening, and found Latimer waiting for me in a very eccentric drawing room, which, I have reason to believe, was a replica with slight variations of an interior his wife had seen when witnessing the Russian ballet. Mrs. Latimer came in almost directly, one of the thinnest women I had ever set eyes on, perhaps thirty-eight, tall, good-looking in a wasted sort of way, with brown hair which framed a low forehead, white cheeks, and pale observant eyes. She wore jade earrings in her rather large white ears and jade bracelets on her sticks of arms. She greeted me quickly in a voice which sounded thoroughly overworked. Almost immediately we went down to dinner.

The dinner was quite super-excellent. During it Mrs. Latimer talked with a sort of anxious pertinacity. Latimer said little. I did my best, which is pretty bad as you know. When dinner was over Mrs. Latimer got up and held out her hand.

"Good night," she said, in her tired voice. "I am going to bed."

"To sleep?" I asked.

"No, to read. I'm not much of a sleeper. Good night, Johnny. "

Her pale eyes travelled quickly over her husband's face and figure. Then she turned and went out of the room, her long earrings swinging gently beneath her white ears, one thin hand holding the jade bracelet on her left arm.

"Will you smoke, doctor?" asked Latimer.

"No, thank you, I never smoke," said I.

"And you don't take coffee. Nor do I—now. Then let us go to my room where we shan't be interrupted."

"With pleasure."

Latimer led the way to a large library on the ground floor behind the dining room. There were no Russian ballet touches in it. All was plain, comfortable, and practical. Books were ranged round the walls. Deep armchairs were set near the fire. Dark green curtains hid the windows. A telephone was handy on a big flat writing table. And the silence in this sanctum seemed of a special brand, heavier, deeper than the silence of the dining room.

Latimer shut the door.

"No one will disturb us here," he said. "Do sit down by the fire."

"Thank you," said I. "Now you can be as long as you like. You'd better tell me everything as far as you can remember, until I interrupt you."

"Oh, as to that, I have an excellent memory."

"Good."

I leaned back in my chair calmly, laid one hand over the other, and gazed into the fire. I took care not to look at all observant. Latimer was glad of that.

"I'll smoke my pipe, if you'll allow me," he said; and he filled and lighted his pipe with deliberation. Then he sat down rather heavily, and began to speak in his steady baritone voice.

"As you know, doctor, I'm a newspaper proprietor, and control *The Daily Echo, The Week, The Evening Journal,* and *The Sunday News.* Lately my control has really been nominal. I've been travelling. I have no children. My papers bring me in a great deal of money. I'm a very successful man."

He sighed deeply, puckered his brows, and let his firm chin drop for a moment, as he looked down on the floor.

"My wife is clever and artistic, and, like many clever women, imaginative and apt to be carried away by whims. I, on the other hand, have always been looked upon as a hard-headed, practical man, good at organisation, the last sort of type, I suppose, likely to be the prey of the imagination. In fact, many of my friends say I haven't got one."

He smiled bitterly.

"If I had, some of them have said, I should be a bigger man than I am. I tell you this lest you should presently be inclined to fancy that my appearance belies me. For I know I look stolid enough. Well, now—" He drew his armchair a little nearer to mine. "It began in this way. Do you remember, about fifteen months ago, there was a great pother about psychical research?"

"Do you mean when Professor Elton launched a violent attack in one of the papers?"

"In my paper, *The Daily Echo.*"

"Was it? On one of the principal investigators for the Psychical Research Society?"

"Yes. Till then I hadn't bothered myself about such matters. I hadn't had time. But the row attracted my attention, and the multitude of letters which poured into the office proved to me how deep was the interest taken in occult matters by men and women in nearly all walks of life. I showed some of these letters to my wife, who, of course, had long ago attended séances, played about with planchette, had her fortune read in her hand, and so forth. She is a Christian Scientist and was a Buddhist, or vice versa; I'm not quite sure. She likes plenty of variety in her life. Anyhow, all these psychic matters were an old tale to her. To me, however, they were not, although, of course, like everyone else, I had heard a good deal about them casually.

"Well, I thought I'd look into them in my off moments, see for myself what I could make of them. First, I put up one of my cleverest young men to make investigations for me—to prepare the ground as it were; and then I came in. I went with this young man, not in my own name of course, to a sitting with a so-called 'psychic' whom he considered to be not the ordinary humbug. I went a second time, a third time. My wife didn't know about it. Unless my young journalist blabbed—and I think I was too valuable to him for him to be such a fool— nobody except himself and the psychic knew about it. And the psychic didn't know who I was. The result of these investigations, although I was thoroughly incredulous when I started them, was that I felt there was, in the common phrase, 'something in it.' We had a lot of messages which seemed to be sheer bunkum. But we had one which was really remarkable. It referred to my wife."

Latimer had by now finished his pipe. He knocked the ashes out of it, and laid it down with a slow and careful gesture.

"This came at the last sitting I attended with my newspaper man. After it I decided not to sit again with him present. It informed me— I tell you this because I've decided to tell you everything—that my wife ceased to love me in a certain month of a certain year. It, moreover, stated that the reason for her change of heart—I believe she had been sincerely attached to me—was the fact that she had come under the influence of an Indian, a Hindu, at the time mentioned. All this was conveyed to us by the medium, who was a man, but when in a trance was apparently controlled by the spirit of a woman called Minnie Harfield. This Minnie Harfield in real life, so the spirit stated, was a woman of but humble class whom the Hindu had taken to be his mistress and had discarded on meeting my wife. Owing to her despair at this desertion, Minnie Harfield had committed suicide. No doubt"— here Latimer shot a self-conscious glance at the doctor—"all this seems to you a farrago of absurdity. So it did to me. But the medium gave the Hindu's name—Nischaya Varman—and certain details of his appearance, position and acquirements. These things, of course, had hitherto been unknown by me."

"And were these statements given fluently by the supposed spirit?" I asked.

"No, with some apparent difficulty, and as it were under cross-examination."

"By you?"

"By me. Yes. I—I became interested."

"Naturally. Go on."

"When the sitting was over I walked away with my journalist. He's an extremely clever and shrewd young man, or he wouldn't be on my staff. Nevertheless, I played a part with him. There seemed nothing else to do. I told him that I was totally unable to verify what the medium had said, and that I absolutely disbelieved in the medium's *bona fides*. The Minnie Harfield spirit I jeered at. I added that I was resolved never to visit the medium again, and that I relied on him—the journalist—never to speak of what had just happened to anybody. He replied that, of course, he would do as I wished, and that no doubt we had both been listening to a series of foolish lies, deliberate inventions of the medium. And there ended my association with him in occult matters."

"Can you tell me his name?"

Latimer looked surprised.

"His name is Maurice Isaacs. Needless to say, he's a Jew."

"Thank you. Well?"

"Well now, doctor, I had told Isaacs that I absolutely disbelieved what the medium had said about my wife and the Hindu. Nevertheless, I determined to find out, if possible, whether there was anything at all in it. You see, I was by way of investigating—eh?"

"Precisely!" I said.

"I knew that my wife was a great admirer of Mrs. Sidon, the Theosophist and lecturer. I also knew, as of course you do, that Mrs. Sidon, who usually lives in India, has a very wide acquaintance among the natives. Certain women of society occasionally gave evening parties to meet Mrs. Sidon when she was in London. My wife had been to these parties. It was quite probable that she had met Easterns in that circle, though I could not remember that she had ever spoken to me of having done so. Had she ever met a Hindu called Nischaya Varman? That was what I wanted to know. Chance favoured my curiosity. The London season was just beginning, and one evening my wife mentioned that Mrs. Sidon had returned from India and was to give a lecture on 'The Mysteries' at Queen's Hall on the following Sunday.

"'Are you going?' I asked.

"'Yes,' she answered.

"'I should like to go with you,' I said.

"'Of course—come. You've never heard her, have you?'

"'Never.'

"'She speaks better than any man I ever listened to.'

"On the Sunday we went. We sat not far from the platform. On it there were several Indians. I saw my wife looking at them directly we had taken our places.

"'Do you know any of those dark fellows?' I asked her.

"'Yes. That'—she indicated a slim boy—'is the boy whom many people in India expect to develop into a world teacher.'

"I knew his name and said it.

"'And who are the others?'

"But at this moment Mrs. Sidon came on to the platform dressed in white, and looking like a Pope, and for the next hour and twenty minutes no voice was heard but hers.

"When the lecture was over I told my wife I wished she would take me behind and introduce me to Mrs. Sidon, by whose speaking powers I had really been impressed. She seemed rather surprised by my request.

"'She must be well worth knowing,' I said.

"'Yes; but she doesn't want to know everybody,' said my wife rather doubtfully.

"'Do you think she'd mind if you took me?'

"'It's nothing to do with the newspapers?'

"'On my word of honour—not.'

"'Then I'll find out if we can see her.'

"She did, and I met Mrs. Sidon. I also met two or three of her Indian adherents, which was what I had intended to do. And with one of these, a Hindu called Satyavan, I managed to become so friendly in a few minutes that it ended by my arranging to meet him again at dinner during the following week. I did not tell my wife about the dinner. She was talking to Mrs. Sidon at the moment and did not hear us fixing up the appointment.

"Satyavan and I dined together at the Indian Restaurant. Have you ever heard of it?"

"No, never," I answered.

"Well, it's not a hundred miles from Piccadilly Circus, a quiet, unpretending little place on a first floor, where you get native cooking that's quite good. We had an excellent meal. We had to send out for wine, which I drank but which was refused by my new friend. I dare say you will have guessed my reason for cultivating the acquaintance of Satyavan. As he was a Hindu, living in London and frequenting the circle of Mrs. Sidon, I thought it probable that he might know Nischaya, if, indeed, such a person really existed. Towards the end of dinner I drew a bow at a venture.

"'By the way,' I said, 'you seem to know most of Mrs. Sidon's followers. What has become of Nischaya Varman?'

"'Did you know him?' said Satyavan, fixing his deep eyes upon me.

"'No; but I have heard of him.'

"'He passed over to the other side three months ago.'

"'Ah! He was rather a remarkable man, wasn't he?'

"'Very. He had great powers, a strong, very strong personality. Mrs. Sidon had a high opinion of him and often consulted him when she was writing. He was in communication with the masters.'

"'But he had a—a rather strong earthly side, too, hadn't he?' I asked.

"Satyavan, who was lighting a cigarette, gazed at me for what seemed a full minute before he said:

"'He was a man like other men in certain ways.'

"'Ah! Poor Minnie Harfield!' I ejaculated.

"Satyavan's face did not change, but his unfathomable and very sad eyes seemed to challenge me.

"'You knew her then?' he said.

"'No; but I know all about her. She killed herself on Nischaya's account.'

"'Well, if she chose to!' said Satyavan. 'A man cannot stay in one place forever. We are travellers. We pass on from one place to another, from one soul to another.'

"'From one body to another?' I hazarded.

"'The body is very little. No doubt Minnie Harfield had to expiate some fault committed in a former existence. She gave Nischaya much trouble, as did other women. A man must not be the prey of women.'

"'No, indeed. There is so much in life besides love. The activities of the brain—'

"I branched off to other topics, doctor. Satyavan's confirmation of the medium's statements about Nischaya and Minnie Harfield made a great impression upon me. Do you wonder?"

"Not altogether," said I, non-committally.

"But I had yet to confirm the most important statement of all, the one which concerned my wife. I—I care for my wife."

There was a moment of complete silence. Then Latimer resumed:

"I resolved to return to the medium. I resolved to try to get into communication through him, not with Minnie Harfield again, but with someone else. By this time I had come to believe in the medium's powers. I made an appointment with him by telephone without giving my name, and went to Fulham—he lived there—alone at night. On this occasion I told the medium I had come with a special purpose, but said nothing as to what it was. The medium, who was a very weak-looking young man, with thin, primrose-coloured hair, flabby white hands, a bending body, and a very genteel Cockney accent, seemed pleased and heartened. I remember he said I was very sympathetic. We sat down in a small, vulgar room on the first floor, with a portrait of H. P. Blavatsky on the wall, and a rep-covered sofa near the window. Before we began the actual sitting, however, I inquired of the medium whether there was any means of summoning a particular spirit through him. He had, he had already informed me, two 'controls,' but was sometimes taken possession of by spirits whom he rather irreverently spoke of as 'outsiders.' I made him understand that I was there that night to communicate with an outsider. How was I to do it?

"My young gentility—he was very ineffective when he was not entranced—seemed puzzled by the question. He advised me, however, as soon as he fell into the trance condition to 'put my mind on' the spirit I wished to communicate with.

"'Do spirits come at call, then?' I asked. 'I have been told you ought never to fix your mind at a sitting, but ought always to try not to force anything.'

"'There are no rules as I know of,' he said weakly. 'They may come or they mayn't. It's just as it happens.'

"He was not illuminating, and I let him alone. Obviously he knew little more about such matters than I did. He was, perhaps, merely an instrument. Indeed, I must say for him that he claimed to be nothing else.

"We sat. He fell presently into a trance. I followed his suggestion. I 'put my mind on' the Hindu. Indeed, that night I could have done nothing else. With all the mental force, the power of will, at my disposal I summoned him to come and to communicate with me. Presently the medium's usual controls, Katey and Johannes, came in turn, or purported to come. They talked a good deal about matters uninteresting to me, and I became very irritated and almost despairing. Then the medium came out of his trance. I was—I confess it—by now in a high state of nervous tension. It may seem ridiculous to you, doctor, but sitting there in that vulgar little room in a Fulham slum, with that ignorant, genteel young man, I was companioned by the feeling that there, and only there, could I arrive at a knowledge of the truth about my wife. It seemed to me—of course I was strung up—that already I felt some influence, which I believed to be the Hindu's, not far from me; that it had been attracted towards me by my mental demand; that, perhaps, only a very slight obstacle stood between me and it. And there, meanwhile, was the medium weakly patting his white forehead with his flabby hands, and murmuring that he must refresh himself with a glass of sherry and water. Sherry and water!

"Well, I controlled myself. I believe I showed no sign of the intense nervous irritation I was feeling. I let him swallow his disgusting refreshment, and then I urged him to try again.

"'Oh, but I'm gone quite flabby with it,' he protested. 'They take it out of me, I do assure you.'

"I said I would double the fee.

"'It isn't only the money,' he said. 'A man must know when to stop.'

"I aimed a blow at his vanity then. Without mentioning my name I told him I had great influence with the newspapers, that already I was much struck by his powers, that I sought a complete proof of them.

"'I feel you can give it to-night,' I said. 'We were on the very verge of something remarkable when you came out of the trance.'

"'How do you know that?' he asked, sipping at the sherry glass with his too flexible lips.

"'I felt it. I feel it now. There is something that wants to communicate, and can't unless you are entranced.'

"He seemed impressed by my earnestness, and glanced round the dingy room with his pale eyes. 'Well, I'll see what I can do,' he said, with the air of one making a concession. 'But, my word, shan't I be poor-spirited after!'

"To cut further detail, doctor, for I don't want to weary you—no, really—the medium did eventually fall once more into a trance, and that night, for the first time, the spirit of Nischaya Varman, the Hindu, purported to control him, to come into connection with mine."

"You say purported!" I observed. "Then you are still not thoroughly convinced?"

As I spoke I turned slightly in my armchair and looked rather sharply at him.

"I want—I want to be unprejudiced. I want to put fancies at a distance."

Latimer suddenly sprang up from his chair, with a movement almost startlingly swift in so heavy a man, and, standing by the fire, he continued:

"You shall be the judge. That's why I am telling you the whole business."

"Give me the material necessary to form a judgment on," I said.

"After the medium had been entranced for a few minutes, perhaps five, a very peculiar voice spoke out of him. Have you ever heard a Hindu speaking?"

"I don't think I have."

"In my opinion it was the voice of a Hindu. The voice stated that it was

Nischaya Varman who was speaking. It seemed very reluctant to communicate. In fact, the whole impression produced on me upon that occasion was one of deep and almost violent reluctance. You know how it is when you, as it is called, force something out of a person."

"Yes."

"The Hindu spoke like one forced to speak and almost malignant under the obligation. I didn't care, I went straight to the point. I spoke at once of the Minnie Harfield communication, and asked for the truth of the matter. There followed a long silence, during which the medium seemed strangely agitated. The impression on me was of a human being rent. It was almost a convulsion, and alarmed me. Nevertheless my curiosity prevented me from interfering. I continued to sit. I continued almost fiercely to demand the truth from the Hindu. I seemed to feel opposed to me in the room a tremendously strong influence which nevertheless my force of will had compelled to draw near to me in despite of its own desire. I believe I have a strong will. I don't like anything to get the better of me. And just then the thought of my wife stiffened my will, doctor. Had she been overcome by this influence when it was in life to my horrible detriment? Then it was surely my part to compel it to my will now. I was resolved. I was hard as steel. All dread, if I had had any, of things occult utterly left me. The convulsions of the medium did not deter me. I insisted. I said, 'You shall not go. I forbid you to go. I brought you here. I forced you to come and I'll force you to remain.' I felt the thing, whatever it was, struggling against me."

"How?" I interjected.

"I can't tell you. These occult things can't always be told of, even when they are known. I say to you that I felt the thing struggling, like moving water, all about me...."

"Yes?"

"... until it broke away, as an enemy might tear himself out of your hands. It was gone. The medium awoke. Poor chap! He was very exhausted that night. He asked me what had happened. He seemed frightened. I did my best to reassure him, for I was resolved to make of him my instrument, at whatever cost to myself or him, until I had got through him the information I wanted. By this time I was convinced that I really was in communication with some other plane, or world, call it whatever you like. I know little of spiritist jargon. I had momentary doubts, of course. But I know my inner conviction must have been as I say because of my intense preoccupation with the medium, my resolute determination to use him. If I had not secretly believed, I could not have been so ruthless. If I had known that the weak young man in Fulham would suffer in health, even would eventually die, because of the efforts to which I urged him, I should not have desisted from them.

"As I said, he was very exhausted that night. When he seemed a little better I paid him double his fee and said I was coming again on the following evening. He said that really he couldn't risk it. I replied I should come. He drank some more sherry and almost piteously protested. I asked him if he had any idea of what was happening when he was entranced. He said that as a rule he was quite unconscious, but that during the last sitting he had been faintly aware of something which had seemed to be tormenting him, doing him harm.

"'And look how it's left me!' he concluded. 'I'm all to pieces, really I am. You've brought something you oughtn't to 'a' brought, something bad, something with too much power. I dunno!'

"His words added to my determination. The end of it was, doctor, that I overcame all the objections of the poor thing by sheer bribery. He found I was rich. He realised that I was influential, and he became my creature. It did him much harm. It practically wrecked his health for a time. I didn't care.

"I won't describe my sittings with him in detail. It isn't necessary. I'll merely give you my general impression of the sum of them.

"During them, so it seemed to me, there began and persisted a relentless struggle between two wills, mine on this plane, and another—the Hindu's, as I supposed—on some other plane. It was almost as if two men were striving on either side of a doorway, one to drag the other through it into the room where he was, the other not to be dragged through. The wretched medium was, as it were, the doorway. The door was opened only by his falling into trance. At other times it was fast shut. My whole being was bent upon overcoming the intense resistance of the Hindu to my desire that he should answer to my summons and hold communication with me.

"In the first sittings—three or four—he came, or purported to come, and spoke a few words. But just as I was beginning to feel that perhaps my power was going to prevail over his, he was gone. It was as if he died out of the medium. I had the impression of a receding wave. My irritation at these escapes was intense, but my will was not weakened by frustration. I am accustomed to carry through things that I undertake. I was resolved to carry this thing through."

"You had come to be absolutely certain, then, that it was really the spirit of the Hindu?" I dropped out.

Strong man though he was Latimer looked shamefaced.

"I suppose I had. Yes, I had."

"Go on!" said I.

"I took to timing the visits of the Hindu to that vulgar room in

Fulham, and I found that with each sitting the period during which I was in communication with him grew slightly longer. This encouraged my persistence. But the creature was horribly alert, was wary as a snake. His communications were fragmentary, and often almost meaningless. By degrees, however, I arrived at a very definite conception of him, a conception of sinuous power, of brooding imaginative thoughtfulness, varied by outbreaks of slippery cunning. And I detected in him fascination."

"In what did the fascination lie?"

"I could scarcely tell you. But—well, now and then there came from the lips of the medium, speaking in the Hindu's voice, a phrase that pierced, or in which there was poetry. And at those moments I knew that a woman might be moved by such phrases spoken in such a way, moved to the trembling that is like the trembling of a violin string. Words catch at women when the voice that speaks them is strange. Women love a strange voice even when it's ugly. Haven't you noticed that in regard to actors?"

He did not wait for me to answer, but continued:

"At last one night I attained my object; I forced the Hindu to come directly the medium was entranced, although till then he had always been preceded by the medium's usual 'controls.' Not only did I force him to come immediately, but I forced him to speak of my wife. Hitherto, when I had mentioned my wife, either I had received evasive or unmeaning replies, or the Hindu had died out of the medium, who had abruptly returned to consciousness. On this occasion, however—why, I don't know—I felt a power as of iron within me, a merciless faculty which seemed to enable me to use my power as never before. The impression I had was of pinning something down, something that struggled to escape but could not. I—sometimes I wish now that it had succeeded in escaping."

Latimer paused. There was a dawning of horror in his eyes.

"Why do you wish that?" said I.

"Do you think it possible—or, let me say, can you imagine it to be possible, for one here on earth, on this plane, so to exercise power over a being on another plane that the being is in some strange way dislodged from his natural sphere, and cannot regain it? Could such a thing be?"

"I have had no experience in such matters," I replied.

"Or another thing might happen," continued Latimer, staring hard at me with eyes that now had an inward look. "If a man forced something to come to him, when it was wholly bent on not responding to his summons, it might afterwards refuse to go when he wanted to get rid of it. It might revenge itself in some such way as that."

"Do I understand then that you made the Hindu come, and that he did not go as on former occasions? Is that what you mean?"

"He came—yes, and he seemed to go. But that may have been his cunning. Anyhow he came, and I asked him about my wife. Briefly, he said he had known her, had subdued her to his power. About physical things nothing was said. I gathered that her mind and nature had undergone the impress of his, that she had been willing to do anything he told her to do, that she had looked to him as her master. That was enough for me."

"You believed it then?" I said.

"That night I did. And I was seized by a sort of mad rage such as I had never thought to experience. I believe I was almost frenzied. I longed to get at the Hindu. I was physically moved. I wanted him, this seducer of women, there before me in the body. It drove me almost mad to think that, having done his vile work, he had tranquilly passed away into some other sphere while I was unconscious even of his existence. Keep this in your mind, doctor; I wanted the Hindu in the body that night that I might punish him in the body. I remember clenching my fists; I remember the perspiration breaking out upon me. I am a very ordinary man, doctor, with plenty of the unregenerate brute in me, and there was something in my peculiar situation calculated to madden such a man. At such moments men go to the animal within them. I did that. I sent up to the Hindu a silent cry—'Come back from the place where you are that I may punish you as you deserve! Come back!' This silent cry persisted in me till I felt absolutely exhausted. I fell back in my chair. My eyes—I remember—closed. My whole body became cold and almost numb."

Latimer had been speaking with unusual intensity, but now his manner changed, turned to an almost frigid dryness. He paused, lit a cigar with slow deliberation, sat down near to me, crossed his legs, leaned forward, and said:

"Now we come to the matter which altered my life, sent me travelling, and at last brought me to your door.

"As on former occasions, the Hindu seemed to die out from the medium, who emerged from his trance. I paid a big fee and got up to go. Looking down on the trembling and white-faced young man, I said:

"'I may not need to come to you again.'

"He stared at me with his pale eyes. He seemed unable to understand what I said.

"'If you are ever in difficulties,' I continued, 'you can always write to this address.'

"And I gave him the name and address of a confidential secretary of mine, and went out."

"And has he ever written to the address?" I asked.

"He has, a good many times," answered Latimer, with a hint of impatience.

"And received help?"

"Of course; liberal help."

"Go on."

"That night, as it happened, I found my wife sitting alone in the drawing room when I got home. She was reading the last pamphlet by Mrs. Sidon. Raising her eyes from it as I came into the room, she said:

"'How ill you look, Johnnie!'

"'I feel just as usual,' I answered.

"I glanced down at what she was reading.

"'More of Mrs. Sidon!' I said. 'Do you think that sort of thing does you much good?'

"She looked at the pamphlet.

"'It's deeply interesting.'

"'Is it? And where does it lead you—into light, or into darkness?'

"'Certainly not into darkness,' she answered.

"She looked at me again with, I thought, a flickering of curiosity.

"'Have you got anything against Mrs. Sidon?' she asked. 'I thought you admired her. You were anxious to know her.'

"I sat down rather deliberately. I was trying hard to control myself, not to show the excitement, the—the—it was almost rage that was boiling up in me.

"'She's a remarkable woman,' I said. 'But don't you think she might easily upset very sensitive people, throw them off their balance?'

"'Sensitive!' she said. 'Do you mean by that weak?'

"'Why should you think so?' I replied.

"At that moment, doctor, I was on the very edge of telling her all I had learnt from the medium. I wanted to tell her. I longed to disturb her equanimity, to attack her ferociously for the silence she had kept. But beneath my anger, my acute sense of wrong, there was something else, something cautious—it's a part of my very nature, I suppose, and I have cultivated it, for I know its value. And this caution lifted its voice. I got up abruptly, and, before she could answer my question, I had left the room.

"It was just ten o'clock. I was gnawed by a horrible restlessness. I took my hat and went out, thinking I would go down to the big building where my papers are produced. I started to walk. It was a damp and foggy winter's night. The fog was not dense, but it added to the mystery and the dreariness of the darkness. I crossed Oxford Street, and when

I came to the farther side of it decided—I don't know exactly why—that I would not go to the office. I think I felt then a necessity to be quite alone. Anyhow, I walked on and soon found myself in Grosvenor Square. It seemed entirely deserted, but I crossed over to the pavement that runs by the railings of the square garden, and there, feeling safe in my loneliness, sheltered by the softly trailing fog, I walked slowly and, I think, very quietly, brooding over the misery that was mine. I had walked round the square more than once, always keeping to the pavement on the garden side, when a man slipped by me in the fog and immediately was gone. I hadn't time to see his face, or even to notice how he was dressed, though it was not so densely dark but that I could have got an impression of him had I known he was coming upon me. His passing disturbed me, indeed it distressed me strangely."

Latimer paused.

"Strangely!" I said. "What do you mean by that?"

"Well, it made me feel uneasy," Latimer answered, with an air of discomfort which almost suggested shame. "I—I found myself suddenly aware of the dark loneliness of the garden on my left, disliking it—imaginatively, I think. And—this will seem very contemptible to you, doctor—"

"Certainly not!" said I.

"Well, I went over at once to the other side of the square, where I had the houses close on my right. This done, I walked on again slowly.

"I was just about to cross the road by the house at the corner of Duke Street opposite to the Japanese Embassy, when I realised that someone was approaching me. I did not hear him—I knew it was not a woman—but I felt him coming; I felt, too, that he was the man who had already once passed me when I was on the opposite pavement. I stopped short. I had a mind to turn sharply to my right down Duke Street, and to get away from the approaching stranger. But the cessation from movement seemed to recall me to my normal self, and I understood at once that—I think for the first time—I was the prey of something very like unreasoning fear. The knowledge came to me like a hard blow. I tingled with shame. And instantly I walked on to meet the man who was approaching me. We met under a lamp. He was an Indian."

"Ah!" I ejaculated.

Latimer looked at me sharply.

"Had you expected that he would prove to be an Indian?" he said.

"Please go on. Don't question me," I replied.

After a rather long silence Latimer resumed:

"This Indian wore a soft black hat and a brown coat, almost buff-coloured, with the collar turned up. He slipped by me, without looking at me, and immediately disappeared into the fog. His height was much less than mine. He seemed to be very thin. I guessed that he had very small bones. I could, I suppose, have picked him up and thrown him into the road without turning a hair. Yet I felt afraid of him."

Almost furtively Latimer glanced at me, and a dull flush of red showed on his powerful face.

"I can honestly say that I had never felt afraid of a man till that moment," he added.

"Why did you feel afraid of this man?" I asked.

"Well, I was startled when I saw he was an Indian. That seemed to me very strange."

"Because at the moment you happened to be thinking deeply about an Indian."

"Yes."

"An odd coincidence—but nothing more."

"That's what I told myself. I battled with myself, with a strong, almost overpowering desire to get away from the square at once. And almost immediately—I had stopped for a moment on the pavement— I went forward. As I did so I knew that in a few minutes I should meet the Indian again. It was inevitable. He had chosen Grosvenor Square for a nocturnal prowl as I had. Perhaps, indeed, he lived, or was staying, in the square. When I met him again I was quite decided not to be disturbed. Well, doctor, not long after I had passed the Italian Embassy and was at the end of the square nearest to Hyde Park, I was aware that the Indian was again drawing near to me. I heard no footfall. He was a silent mover. But I knew that he was close to me. And this time my fear of him increased. Indeed it was only by a strong effort that I checked myself from—well, call it bolting if you like. We met again under a lamp. This time I forced myself to stare hard at the man. He was certainly a Hindu.

"What makes you think that? Did you see him plainly?"

"Fairly well. He was a Hindu. He slipped by me noiselessly without looking at me, and immediately disappeared into the fog. I turned. I gazed after him. I listened. And, doctor, I sweated. My whole body ran with sweat. After standing for two or three minutes I left the square by the nearest turning. It was Upper Grosvenor Street. I reached Park Lane, met a taxi, hailed it and drove straight home. My wife had gone to bed, but I saw her light. (We slept in communicating rooms.) I did not disturb her. I took a cold bath—"

"Very injudicious!" I said.

"Was it? And went to bed. I won't describe the night. It was a bad one. During the following day I attended to business as usual. I had an engagement for the evening, to dine out with my wife at a house in Eaton Square. About four I telephoned to her to say I couldn't go with her, as I should have business to attend to late. I also telephoned to my prospective hostess. I felt in no fit state for society. Besides, I wanted to dine elsewhere. Soon after eight I started on foot for the Indian Restaurant."

"Can you tell me exactly what led you there?"

"I felt a sort of horror of darkness, of what is sometimes called 'colour.' Therefore I went where I knew I should meet colour. That was an act of defiance. But in addition I was driven by an intense, probably morbid, curiosity. I wanted to see the Hindu again, to see him in full light."

"Why should he be at the Indian Restaurant?"

"I thought he might be there. It is a place frequented by Indians."

"I understand."

"I walked rapidly from my house, crossed Piccadilly Circus, and was soon at the restaurant. Mounting the stairs, I entered the first room. I must tell you that the restaurant consists of two rooms, or rather, perhaps, I should say of one large room divided into two compartments by a screen of wood and glass. In the first compartment there are several small tables. In the second there is one long table. I don't know, but I conclude that those who dine in the second compartment pay a regular pension, come to the place habitually. When I got in I found a party of seven people dining at a table close to the window in the first compartment—three Indian men, an Englishman, and three Englishwomen. Four more Indians were dining, each one alone, at separate small tables. In the compartment beyond I saw three or four heads as I stood for a moment. Then one of the three young women who served gave me a smile and indicated a table. I hung up my coat and hat and sat down facing the room and the screen.

"The man I had met in the square was not among the diners."

"But you could not see the faces of those in the farther compartment, could you?" I interposed.

"No; but he wasn't in the farther room. I felt it."

"Go on."

"I ordered my dinner. When it came I began to eat very slowly. On my right hand was the party of seven. They had a couple of bottles of champagne on the table, were half through their dinner, and were talking and laughing in lively fashion. Solemnly the dark men at the little tables ate, and smoked cigarettes while waiting for food. I watched the English girls chattering to their strangely expressive companions and thought about my wife and the dead Hindu. Had she ever dined here with him? I imagined them sitting together at one of the little tables eating dishes of the East, deep in converse, and the blood went to my head, doctor. I had no appetite, but I forced myself to eat. When I had finished one thing I ordered another. I wished to prolong my stay. Presently I asked for a bottle of wine. It had to be sent out for. While I was waiting for it two or three people, all coloured, dropped in and passed into the farther room beyond the screen. At last the wine arrived, and the girl who waited on me came with it to my table smiling. She stood in front of me to uncork it, and I spoke to her. She replied. We talked for a moment, and my mind was taken away from its brooding and expectation. We were both laughing, I remember, and I was looking at her while she drew the cork, when I was aware that a man came in softly and quickly and passed into the room beyond the screen. I saw him, as it were, with the tail of my eye. He had on a soft black hat, a brown, almost buff-coloured coat. I did not see his face. But I knew it was the Hindu of Grosvenor Square.

"'Who is that?' I asked the attendant.

"She put the bottle down on my table.

"'Who d'you mean?' she asked, looking round.

"'The man who has just gone into the other room,' I said. 'In a black hat and brown coat.'

"'One of our regular people, I s'pose,' she said. 'I didn't catch sight of him. Is your wine all right?'

"I sipped it and made some answer. She went away.

"I stared towards the screen. Through the opening in it I saw two or three people sitting at dinner, but not the man who had just passed in. Half an hour went by. My seven neighbours left their table hilariously, gathered together their coats and wraps, and went laughing down the stairs. Other diners finished their meals, paid their bills and departed. Some came from the inner compartment, but not the Hindu. I sat over my wine, pretending to drink, smoking and waiting. Now and then I saw the girls, when they were not attending to customers, glancing at me and whispering among themselves. Evidently they were surprised that I sat so long. I was now the only customer on my side of the screen and I could see no one at the long table in the second compartment; nor did I hear any sound of voices coming to me from the hidden part of the room. Nevertheless I knew that the Hindu was still there. He had gone in and he had never returned. He must be there. I was resolved to wait where I was till he came out. I should then have a full sight of him, a full and definite impression of him. Presently I ordered coffee. The young woman, when she brought it, remarked:

"'You're the last. We're closing in ten minutes from now.'

"'You're glad when closing time comes?'

"'Rather.'

"'But I'm not the last,' I said. 'There's still someone in the farther room.'

"She looked surprised and raised her fair eyebrows.

"'No, there isn't,' she said. 'Everyone's gone.'

"'Not the man with the black hat and the brown coat whose name I asked you.'

"'Well, you are a funny one!' she said archly. 'If you don't believe me come and see for yourself.'

"I took her at her word and went with her to the opening in the screen. The long table was cleared. The compartment was empty. And, doctor, there was no way of leaving it except through the compartment in which I had been sitting.

"'What d'you say now?' said the girl.

"'That I made a mistake,' I answered.

"I gave her a tip, took my hat, and went off down the stairs. But I had not made a mistake. The Hindu had gone into the compartment beyond the screen but he had never come out of it."

"Are you absolutely certain he didn't come out when your attention happened to be distracted from watching for him?"

"It never was distracted. I feel sure of that."

"Well, what did you make of it?"

"I think you know," said Latimer.

"I wish you to tell me," I said firmly.

"Very well."

Latimer paused, then sat forward and closed his hands into fists like a man making a strong effort.

"When I met the Hindu in Grosvenor Square I felt at once that there was something dreadful, something wholly unnatural about him, something which made me want to get away from him. The same feeling came to me in the Indian Restaurant when he passed through the compartment in which I was sitting; it was with me till I looked and found him gone. Then suddenly I knew why his nearness had horrified me. As I made my way down into the humming street I felt like a man condemned. For I was certain that I had seen Nischaya Varman, the man who had taken my wife from me and who was what we call dead. In a wild moment of anger, I had striven to summon him to me that I might punish him. He had obeyed my summons that he might punish me."

"So you considered yourself haunted by the Hindu?" I said calmly.

"Since that night I have seldom known what it is to feel safe."

"Give me the facts. You have seen the Hindu—I mean by that had the impression of seeing him—many times?"

"Many times. But do you believe the whole thing is a delusion on my part?"

"Haven't you come to me in the hope that it is so, and that I may be able to prove that it is by getting rid of it?"

"In my situation one hopes mad things and catches at every straw," said Latimer morosely.

"Now what happened after that night at the Indian Restaurant?"

"I was badly shaken but I made a fight of it. All that night I fought what seemed to be my own knowledge. I told myself that I was ill. If I ceased henceforth to traffic with mediums, if I drove the whole matter out of my mind and gave myself up to the daily work then, I told myself, all would be well.

"A very good programme, though it didn't cover quite everything."

"You mean—my wife?"

"Did you proceed to put it into execution?" I asked, ignoring Latimer's question.

"I tried to. I put my back into it, doctor. I gave myself more than ever to my newspapers, the children I had created—the only children—and I saw scarcely anything of my wife. I did not visit the medium again, of course. By then I had a horror of him, and of all his brethren. Several days passed without any special incident occurring. But I was never free from apprehension; I never even for a moment had the impression that the menace I was so conscious of had been removed from me. I'll go further and tell you the exact truth. I knew it had not been removed.

"One night my wife said:

"'I've got a box to-morrow for the first night at the St. James's Theatre. I've asked'—she mentioned some friends. 'Will you come?'

"I was on the point of refusing when I noticed in her eyes an expression of—I thought—suspicious and intent inquiry. Immediately I decided to go. And I went. You know what a St. James's first night is; a crowd of people one has seen everywhere. The boxes are very large. We had three people with us, and were all able to sit in line. I was in the corner next the stage and could see practically the whole of the stalls. During the first act I happened to notice that one stall, rather far back and well in the middle of the house, was empty. Doctor, directly I saw this empty stall I knew who was presently coming to fill it. I was seized with a sort of horrible panic which made me know, and I did not take my eyes from the little gap in the crowd till the woman next me said:

"'Do you hate the drama, Mr. Latimer?'

"'No,' I answered. 'On the contrary, I'm fond of the theatre. Why d'you ask me?'

"'Well, you never look at the stage.'

"She was gazing at me with an expression of definite surprise which put me at once on my guard. I devoted, or seemed to devote, all my attention to the stage from that moment, but, doctor, I knew—I'll swear it—the exact instant when that empty stall was filled. I felt the arrival of the Hindu."

"You didn't see him come in?" I asked.

"No, because I wouldn't look. But directly the curtain went down I turned. And he was there looking straight at me. For the first time I saw him fully, saw his whole face and his head uncovered. He was in evening dress, doctor."

"Just so," I said casually.

"There was something intense and, I thought, unrelentingly malignant in the gaze of his profound and lambent eyes. They said to me, 'I am here to punish you.' I got up. My wife was lifting an opera glass. She put it to her eyes and looked down upon the stalls. I saw her examining the long rows of seated figures, beginning with those nearest to the stage. What would happen when she saw the Hindu? I was painfully excited. I longed to draw her attention to him, to say to her, 'Look at that man. Do you remember him?' But I pretended carelessness. I talked to our friends. I discussed the play, the people in the house. And all the time furtively I was watching my wife. Presently it seemed to me that she was staring through her glasses straight at the Hindu. Yet her hand did not tremble, her face did not change. I heard her say:

"'What an odd gown Mrs. Lester has on!'

"'Where is she?' I asked, bending to her.

"'Over there, a little to the left, near Sir Charles Digby.'

"She made a gesture towards the stalls. I looked and saw Mrs. Lester, an acquaintance of ours, sitting in the row behind the Hindu, and perhaps three feet to his left. There was a discussion between my wife and one of the women in our box about Mrs. Lester's gown, which I interrupted—I couldn't help it—by saying:

"'What a remarkable-looking Indian that is.'

"'An Indian! Where is there an Indian?' said my wife.

"'Close to Mrs. Lester, the row in front of her to the right.'

"'I don't see him,' said my wife.

"'Nor I,' said the woman next to her.

"'There!' I said, pointing, and leaning forward in my excitement. 'Surely you must see him—a Hindu.'

"'But I don't see him!' said my wife, also leaning forward, and gazing apparently straight at the Hindu.

"'You're looking right at him now!' I exclaimed.

"As I spoke the lights went down and the curtain rose on the last act.

"When the play was over and the actors were being called for, I searched once more for the Hindu. But he had vanished."

"And nobody saw him but yourself, so far as you know?" I observed.

"So far as I know—nobody."

"Now before you go on I want to ask you a few questions," I said.

"Very well," said Latimer, more calmly.

"You've been travelling, I understand?"

"Yes."

"How many times did you see the Hindu before you left England?"

"About eight or nine times in all, I should think."

"Did you ever see him in the daytime?"

"No."

"Did you ever try to speak to him?"

"No. I intended to, but—when the moment came something always held me back."

"Have you ever spoken to your wife about him, except that night at the theatre?"

"No."

"I gather that you suffered so much from these appearances that you decided to leave England?"

"I did."

"In the faint hope, I suppose, of leaving the Hindu behind you in England?"

"It was very ridiculous of me, no doubt," said Latimer painfully.

"It was a very natural thing to do. Change of scene, you know! Where did you go, and did you go alone?"

"You don't want to hear any more about my English experiences?"

"We needn't go into them just now, I think. Well?"

"I took my man, Cradon, with me. We went first to Marseilles and stayed at the Hotel du Louvre."

"I know it. Now go on. Resume your narrative."

"Oh!"

Latimer hesitated, then refilled his pipe, lit it, and said nervously:

"Let's see—where was I?"

"At Marseilles, the Hotel du Louvre."

"To be sure. Yes, Marseilles."

He puffed two or three times at his pipe, staring before him. Evidently he was trying to fix his mind which had wandered away.

"When I had crossed the Channel, had left Paris behind me, and was running down South," he said at length, "I had a sense of relief. A burden seemed to have fallen from my shoulders. The sun shone at Marseilles. The city was full of almost boisterous animation. As I stepped out of the train I remember I felt more optimistic than I had felt for many weeks. This happy sensation persisted during the day. I intended passing a couple of nights at Marseilles to—well, to test a certain matter. If things were satisfactory I thought of going on to the Riviera. I slept well the first night, and the second day was without any unpleasant incident. I began to hope. I looked back on the dreadful persecution—it was most dreadful, doctor—I had suffered in England from the Hindu, and I was able to think that my tortured nerves had conjured up that dark apparition. It was due, perhaps, merely to a morbid condition of mind produced by ill-health; and that ill-health—I now told myself—had been brought about by the shock of the medium's revelation about my wife. In the bright sunshine of Marseilles the blackness of the past began to fade. I was even able to say to myself that out of the mouth of the medium lies had come to me. I could not, of course, doubt the Minnie Harfield statement about the Hindu's existence and her suicide. But I tried to doubt, and almost succeeded in doubting, the statement about my wife. There was, I acknowledge, little reason in such a differentiation between the two statements. Nevertheless, I think I made it. That day I was almost light-hearted. But in the evening all my misery was brought back by a hideous incident. You know the hall of the Hotel du Louvre which fronts the covered courtyard into which carriages can drive?"

"Yes."

"After dinner in the restaurant I was sitting there, smoking and reading a newspaper, when the hotel omnibus drove up from the station with some newly arrived travellers. I realised this, as one may realise a thing when reading, without really attending to it. Travellers got out—I know—went to the bureau, took their rooms, received the tickets with their room numbers, and so forth, and passed by me on the way to the lift which, you'll remember, is in the centre at the bottom of the staircase. I went on with my reading, knowing all this and not attending to it. But suddenly a horrible sensation came upon me. It was the sensation I had had that night in Grosvenor Square, when for the first time I set eyes on the Hindu. I felt that he was coming into the hall, that he was passing me. I did not look up. I tried to deny the assertion of my mind and body—for I felt him with both. With my eyes glued to my paper I said to myself, 'You are a morbid fool. He is not here. Some casual traveller is passing you.' And I strove to read on. But something overcame my resolution. It was like a sort of terrible curiosity, insistent, stronger than my will to defy it. I swung round abruptly in my chair and looked towards the staircase. Doctor, I saw the Hindu with his back to me on the point of entering the lift which had just descended from an upper floor. He wore the black hat, the almost buff-coloured coat. He went into the lift. The lift man, with a click, shut the gate. The Hindu turned and looked full at me. Then the lift shot up, carrying him out of my sight."

Latimer's face was tormented. It was easy to see how even the mere recollection of this incident made him suffer.

"I had almost dared to think myself free," he said with a hoarse note in his voice. "And now I—the—the thing had followed me. I was conscious at that moment of its horrible persistence, of the malignity by which it was driven. At that moment something that was like sheer desperation seized me. I threw down my newspaper and got up from my chair. I saw the manager in the bureau, and I went up to him.

"'Those travellers,' I said, 'who have just arrived. What train did they come by?'

"'The *rapide* from Paris, monsieur.'

"'A traveller from London would be likely to come by that train?'

"'If he had stayed the night in Paris, monsieur, he would.'

"'Have you the names of those who have just come in the omnibus?'

"'Yes, monsieur. They are all in the visitors' book.'

"'May I see it?'

"'Certainly, monsieur.'

"He pushed it towards me. I looked. I scarcely know, but I think I had a wild hope of seeing some Indian name unknown by me, of finding that my fears had betrayed me, and that the Hindu who had just mounted in the lift was some ordinary traveller on his way to the East. There was no Indian name in the book. I saw surprise dawning in the manager's face.

"'I thought I might find the name of—of a friend,' I muttered, turning away.

"'Quite so, monsieur,' said the manager, with detached courtesy.

"As I left the bureau I saw the lift standing empty with the attendant beside it. I went to it and got in. The man followed.

"'Which floor, monsieur?'

"I told him. Directly the lift had started I pressed ten francs into his hand.

"'Who was that Indian gentleman you took up just now?' I said.

"'An Indian gentleman, monsieur?'

"'Yes.'

"'But I took no Indian gentleman.'

"'Do you deny that a moment ago you took the lift up?'

"'Certainly not, monsieur.'

"'Very well. An Indian was with you in the lift.'

"'Pardon, monsieur, but monsieur is mistaken.'

"'But I saw you go up.'

"'There was no one in the lift with me, monsieur, I assure you! I took the lift up because the bell on the fourth floor rang. I have just brought a lady down.'

"'Do you deny that there was an Indian with you when you went up, a man wearing a soft black hat and a light brown coat?'

"'Monsieur is mistaken. I was quite alone in the lift.'

"For over a minute the lift had been stationary at my floor. The expression on the man's face warned me that I was wasting my time and arousing strong suspicions concerning my own sanity. Without another word I got out of the lift and went to my room. Next morning after a sleepless night I left the hotel. I might almost say I fled from it."

"And you went to the Riviera?"

"No. I crossed the sea. I heard there was a ship starting for Philippeville in Algeria. I went on board. I suppose I had a mad idea of escaping from that traveller who had pursued me from England. Of course it was a crazy notion. One may escape from a living man. The sea may be an effectual barrier between you and him. But I was pursued by one who could overpass any barrier at will. I knew this, and yet, when we were out at sea, when Marseilles had disappeared on the horizon, I felt some sense of relief. After a voyage of about thirty-six hours, I landed at Philippeville. I stayed there one night, then took the train and went on to a little place called Hammam Meskoutine, where there are hot water springs impregnated with sulphur."

"What took you there?" said I.

"Hitherto I had always seen the Hindu in the midst of men, either in London or in Marseilles. Hammam Meskoutine I knew to be a tiny place buried in the African solitude, though far from the desert. I thought, 'Perhaps he will not follow me into the solitudes.'

"The hotel at the baths stands quite alone, surrounded by a delicious flowering country, smiling and intimate. The sulphur springs boil up out of the earth at a little distance away. There is a small, but well-arranged, bath establishment just below the hotel, which is of the bungalow type, with all the rooms on the ground floor. Mine opened by a French window on to a paved walk. Beyond was an open space with trees bounded by outbuildings. On the right, and at right angles, was a terrace backed by the public room of the hotel. Few people were staying there, only some four or five Colonial French people. The landlord was cordial; the servants were friendly, cheerful and attentive. And the whole atmosphere of the place was serene and remote, yet eminently happy. Even my man, Cradon, was struck by the sweet tranquillity of this African retreat.

"'I've always liked towns, sir,' he observed, on the evening of our arrival just before dinner. 'But I think a man could forget all about them here.'

"Something in the commonplace words cheered and almost reassured me. Suddenly it occurred to me that perhaps I, for years a colossal worker, untiring in energy and always living in the midst of crowds—for I never took a real holiday—had, without being aware of it, become thoroughly overworked."

"Why not?" I said. "What more likely?"

"You think"—a gleam of hope shone in Latimer's eyes—"you think overwork might—" He stopped. "But madness would be worse than all!" he muttered, as if to himself.

"Madness! Rubbish!" I said. "You're no more mad than I am."

"You are sure?" said Latimer, whose eyes at that moment had an almost imploring expression.

"Positive," said I. "If I thought otherwise I should take you to-morrow to Vernon Mansfield, the specialist in lunacy—if you'd come."

A faint smile flitted over Latimer's face.

"But if I'm not mad then I am really haunted, I am really the victim of a diabolic persecution. There's no other alternative."

"I'm not at all sure of that," I said. "No, no; don't ask me questions. Go on—till I stop you. Did anything happen at Hammam Meskoutine?"

"Yes."

"What was it?"

"Nothing happened the first night. But I felt very uneasy on account of my room being on the ground floor, and opening by the French window on to the paved walk. There were persiennes of wood outside the window, and before going to bed I shut them securely, but, nevertheless, I disliked the idea that anyone could walk, or pause, outside within a few feet of me as I lay in bed."

"But if you were haunted what was to prevent the Hindu from appearing in your room, even with doors and windows locked?" I asked.

"I know, I know," returned Latimer. "But that had never happened, and, as a matter of fact, it never did happen. I always saw him in circumstances which seemed to make it possible that he was an ordinary man. He never appeared and disappeared as so-called ghosts are said to do, though on one or two occasions, as at the Indian Restaurant, it was impossible for me to imagine the means of his exit from the place to which I had seen him go."

"So you were not afraid of seeing him with you when you had locked the door and shut the window?"

"Somehow I was not. But I dreaded his coming along the pavement, and, perhaps, lingering in the night outside my window. Therefore I lay awake. But nothing occurred on that first night, and the dawn broke heralding a day of celestial clearness, such as we never see in England. Insects were humming, I remember, as I came out into the sunshine that morning. Two or three Arabs were dreaming under the eucalyptus trees. There was a marvellous peace, a clear serenity in the atmosphere, which affected my spirits happily. I felt drowsy after my almost sleepless night, but there was nothing to do, and it occurred to me that it would be pleasant to seek some shady place, to lie down among the wild flowers which abound in that region, and, like an Arab, to dream away the shining hours. After breakfast on the terrace and a pipe, therefore, I wandered away from the hotel into the smiling and empty country, which was peopled chiefly, it seemed, by butterflies. First I took my way to the sulphur springs; then I made a detour, and presently came upon a most delicious stream, bordered thickly with aromatic shrubs and bushes. Beside the windings of this stream I strolled on for some time till I came to a place where it made a loop and widened out into a sort of pool. Here there were shade and silence, and I lay down on the bank, pulled my hat down over my eyes, and, presently, fell deliciously into a light sleep. I don't really know how long I slept, but when I woke—I did not open my eyes immediately—I knew at once that I was no longer alone beside the stream. I heard no sound except the wide hum of the insects, and the very faint and sucking murmur of moving water against earth and weeds, but I felt men near me, silent men. And in a moment the faint scent of tobacco was in my nostrils. Then I opened my eyes, and saw not far from me a group of meditative Arabs. Three were squatting on the bank at edge of the stream, shrouded in burnouses, calmly contemplating me, and smoking. A fourth was lying stretched upon the ground entirely muffled up in voluminous clothing. The whole of his head and face was hidden from me. I supposed him to be in a very profound sleep.

"I gazed at the Arabs and the Arabs gazed at me tranquilly. Their presence was really soothing. They were picturesque and immobile. Nevertheless, as soon, I think, as I was absolutely wide awake, I was aware of a feeling of distress. I looked from one to the other. Then my eyes fell on the sleeper and remained fixed on him. He looked just like a long bundle which had been flung down by the waterside. But I divined a body beneath the muddle of garments. And while I looked the bundle stirred and a bare leg was thrust into view. The leg was dark brown and abnormally thin, as thin as a stick.

"Doctor, as soon as I saw it I thought of the Hindu. I stared at the leg; noted the fineness of the ankle, and a sick shudder went through me. I got up. I wanted to get away, and yet I felt I must see the face of that sleeping man. I stood for a moment, trying to collect myself, to consider what to do. Then I forced myself to approach the group. I took out some money and offered it to the Arabs. They held out their hands gravely. As I was giving them the money the bundle stirred. A thin arm came out of the clothes. Then a face and a pair of glittering eyes showed themselves. Again I looked on the Hindu."

Latimer ceased speaking for a moment. He seemed to be profoundly moved.

"Now you had your opportunity," I said. "Of course you took it. Of course you made sure that this man was a comrade of the Arabs, that they were aware of his presence among them. Of course you gave him money, too. Didn't you?"

Latimer shook his head.

"I thought of that as I stood there. I meant to do it. I tried mentally to force myself to do it. But I couldn't, doctor. Horror had seized me. I left them. I plunged into the thick undergrowth. My only idea was to get away."

"While you were there did any of the Arabs appear to take any notice of the huddled figure?"

"No. They were looking at me."

"And when the figure moved?"

"None of them looked at it. Their eyes were always on me."

"If only you could have plucked up courage on that occasion," I said, with intentional brusqueness, "you would have found that you had to deal with some wandering Oriental. You missed your chance."

"Possibly—on that one occasion," said Latimer.

"You told me," I continued, still brusquely, "that during your last sitting with the medium you longed for the Hindu's bodily presence that you might punish him. You told me that you made an intense effort of the will to force him to return to earth. According to your account your effort was successful. Did you never attempt to take advantage of your success?"

"I have thought of that too," said Latimer with a sort of morose shame. "I thought of that many times. But the Hindu seemed to lay upon me a prohibition. I cannot exactly explain its nature to you. His will seemed to come upon me and to prohibit me from playing the man. That fact was, and is, perhaps the most distressing part of my whole experience. The Hindu's will bound me fast in cowardice. Nevertheless I did make one attempt to break the spell. It was while we were at

Tunis."

"Tell me about it," said I. "And then, perhaps, I will not trouble you to give me the whole of the remainder of your adventures."

"Do you—have you formed any opinion?" exclaimed Latimer, with sudden excitement.

"Perhaps I have. But I shall not tell it to you to-night," I answered. "Some time will be needed to confirm or upset it."

"But can't you say at least—"

"Not now," I interrupted. "Tell me what happened at Tunis. Did you go there soon?"

"I left Hammam Meskoutine the day after I saw the Hindu beside the stream, and I went straight to Tunis, where I arrived very late at night. For some reason—I think the Foreign Minister had just disembarked there from Paris to assist at some French national demonstration—the European hotels were crowded. I tried three of them and could not get a room. The last I went to was the Grand. There they recommended me to try what they called a native hotel. It was now the dead of night. The manager sent with me a Maltese man, a sort of tout, I supposed, to show me the way. He carried my hand luggage with the help of my man, Cradon, who was by this time in a somewhat depressed, not to say surly, humour. We walked for about ten minutes, or perhaps more, and came into the native quarter, close to the bazaars. We turned into an alley, which had a sufficiently evil look, and presently arrived at a door above which was a light showing the words, 'Hôtel Taxim.' The guide pushed the door which opened showing a tiled stairway, up which we went and arrived at a sort of large landing where, to my surprise, we found three enormous women, with artificial flowers in their greasy black hair, sitting solemnly on a yellow settee near a cottage piano. The guide spoke in Arabic to one of them, in a low voice and at considerable length. The creature arose heavily, went to a bureau, found some keys, and then, moving lethargically, showed me to a door which she unlocked and opened carefully. Within was a clean bare bedroom, fairly large, with a tiled floor. The luggage was put down, and in a few minutes I was alone with the door locked. Cradon, whose face had been a study in respectable consternation during these proceedings, was, I understood, to be lodged in some other part of the house. I undressed at once and went to bed.

"In the morning rather early I rang the bell, intending to ask for coffee. After a long pause I heard a shuffling sound outside as of someone moving over the tiles in loose slippers. The shuffling ceased at my door, and then there came a light, I might almost say a fragile, knock. I—I felt that a very thin hand had struck that blow, and I hesitated to open the door."

"Did you open it?" I asked, as Latimer was silent.

"No," he said very painfully. "I couldn't. I—I was afraid."

"What did you do?"

"I called out in French that I wanted coffee and a roll. There was no answer, but I heard the footsteps shuffle away."

"A servant of the house, of course; probably a woman."

"I don't know. While I waited for the coffee I tried to pull myself together. I was horribly ashamed of my panic. I realised that my nerves were going absolutely to pieces. It's very unpleasant for a man when he—he's obliged to realise that, doctor."

"Nerves can be put right," said I firmly. "And it's my job to see to that."

A sort of momentary relief came into his face, but it faded away immediately.

"Nerves couldn't play such tricks," he said, in a low voice.

"If you knew as much about them as I do," I said, "you mightn't be so free with your negatives. Did the coffee and roll come?"

He started.

The coffee? Oh—yes, presently it did. I heard a quite different footstep from the shuffling tread, and there came a bang on my door. I opened, and there stood my Maltese guide of the night before with a breakfast tray. He gave me a rough '*Bon jour*,' came into the room and set the tray down. He was about to go away when I stopped him.

"'Who told you I wanted coffee?' I asked.

"'The bell rang,' he replied.

"'You didn't answer it.'

"'But I have answered it, m'sieu!' he said, pointing to the coffee tray.

"'You didn't come to take my order?'

"'No, m'sieu.'

"'Someone did. Someone came and knocked, and I called out. Who was it?'

"'I don't know. There are often people about in this house.' He smiled in a rather peculiar way.

"'Could it have been a native servant? Do they wear loose slippers?'

"'I don't know who it was,' said he brusquely. 'You should have opened the door.'

He smiled again, with a peculiarly knowing look. Then he added:

"'I heard the bell and I knew it was for coffee. And there it is!'

"He pointed again with a dark brown hand, gave me a monkey-like smirk, and hurried away. I noticed that he wore strong boots which made a squeaking noise on the tiles.

"That morning Cradon gave me certain information about the

reputation of the house we were in, and I resolved to sally forth and see if I could bribe the management of the Tunisia Palace Hotel to give me rooms there.

"As I was about to descend the tiled staircase of the 'Taxim,' which led out to the alley through a Moorish archway, I saw in the archway, leaning against the wall, the thin figure of a native wearing a turban. When I put my foot on the first stair he turned and looked up at me. Doctor, it was the Hindu. I stood still for a moment. That prohibition came upon me from him, and I was afraid to go down. While I paused he moved into the alley, crossed slowly a patch of sunlight and disappeared. It was then that I made a determined effort to break the spell which bound me to cowardice. Something rose up in me which defied the will of the Hindu. It was, I think, a sort of panic courage such as comes at moments to the most timid of God's creatures; such courage makes men run upon danger, go out to meet pain. I hurried down the stairs and into the alley. I took the way the Hindu had taken. Before me I saw several native figures strolling along with that sort of indolent nonchalance which is so characteristic of the East. They all looked much alike, and I could not identify one as the Hindu. I followed, came up with them one after the other, and looked narrowly into their faces. But I did not see my man. I hurried on and found myself almost immediately in the slipper bazaar. Here there was already a crowd, and I despaired of coming upon the Hindu, though I seemed to feel all this time that he was near to me."

"What did you intend to do if you came upon him?" I said.

"Lay hands on him," said Latimer. "Find out at once and forever what he was. I mingled with the crowd. Flies were buzzing and men were buzzing like flies. There was a tumult of voices and a silent tumult of gestures. But through the tumult glided many who were silent and who seemed detached. And among these silent ones I sought for the Hindu. But I sought for him in vain, and I grew tired.

"Presently, from a tiny hole where he sat cross-legged in the midst of his wares behind a little counter, a perfume seller leaned out and called to me. I then stopped, sat down on a wooden bench, and tested his perfumes as he rubbed them delicately on my outstretched hand and wrist. And while this happened my sense of the Hindu's nearness left me. The perfumes—amber, lilac, attar of roses, geranium —affected me, seemed to steal upon my will and to lull the fever of my intention. The Hindu had escaped from me. Let him go! However, I felt neither courage nor cowardice. For a brief space I dropped into rest.

"I was buying a diapered bottle of geranium when I realised that a man had stopped close behind me. I looked round and saw an enormous

Tunisian, with gigantic moustaches, and black eyes which shone with cunning, who stared steadily at me.

"'Monsieur is rich!' said he, in French. 'Monsieur wishes to buy beautiful things. I will take him to Babouchi Brothers. There he will see carpets that are worth millions.'

"'Very well,' said I.

"And I paid for the perfume and followed the tout, who looked and moved like an Emperor in some glittering fairy tale. When we reached his patron's bazaar I found that it was really one of the finest in Tunis, if not the finest. On the ground floor there was a large hall lined with splendid carpets, full of embroideries, weapons, ancient lamps, incense burners, screens of exquisite woodwork. Rows and rows of shelves were piled with stuffs of multi-coloured hues. A fountain played in a corner, throwing up scented water. From this hall a staircase led up to a balcony which ran all round a courtyard open to the sky, and from this balcony opened a veritable network of narrow and shadowy rooms, a maze crammed with all sorts of things—furniture, carpets, prayer rugs, bronzes, ivories, tiles, and I know not what. Looking here and there into the shadowy recesses of this maze, I saw figures of dark-hued men moving, squatting, or standing in watchful attitudes, waiting, no doubt, for opportunities to display the treasures by which they were surrounded.

"Doctor, when I mounted to this balcony and stood in the midst of this maze, I was suddenly again aware of the presence of the Hindu. I did not see him, but I felt him; and I was absolutely certain that the figure I had seen leaning against the archway of the Taxim Hotel had escaped from me into this warren full of hiding places, and was somewhere quite near to me. Again I felt fear, but I remembered that I had set forth in pursuit of the Hindu, and I resolved to face the thing out this time. I had suffered so much through yielding to fear that I was driven at last into action. The most intimate part of me tried to rush down the staircase, to be lost in the crowds of Tunis. I defied that part, which seemed me. I had just then the impression of being two persons, and the weaker rose up to do battle with the stronger of the two, and for the moment got the better in the contest.

"'I'll look at all your best things,' I said to the enormous tout, who was always with me. 'But first let me wander about by myself.'

"'I will show monsieur.'

"'No,' I said, 'I wish to go round by myself. I don't mean to steal things.'

"He protested volubly, but showed no inclination to leave me.

"'Very well,' I said. 'Then I won't buy anything.' And I made as though to be off. This brought him promptly to obedience.

"'Go anywhere, monsieur!' he cried. 'You are English. All the English are honest.'

"He paused.

"'And so generous!' he added, showing an upturned palm.

"I crossed it with silver and left him.

"Doctor, then began a hunt through that Oriental maze. I entered the chamber nearest to me and went slowly through it, pretending to examine the treasures it contained, now and then handling a weapon, or holding a fold of silk to the light. The native attendants, I must tell you, left me alone. The tout had somehow managed to convey to them a hint that I was a mad Englishman, whose mania was to be allowed free scope for a time. Later, of course, I was to pay for it.

"From room to room of the maze I went, always conscious of the presence of the Hindu in some remote recess of it. Sometimes he seemed almost close to me, at other times he receded. I had the sensation that he was playing with me, was luring me on like a malignant will-o'-the-wisp. But my resolve did not falter. I had braced myself to the encounter. I was on his track, and I was resolved to come up with him.

"After threading several windings of the maze, I was aware of a strong and drowsy smell of incense. When it first reached my nostrils I was standing in a small room full of prayer rugs. They lay heaped upon shelves, strewn upon the floor, and in piles upon the divans. Seated in the midst of them was a thin black man with mournful eyes, who was twisting a necklace of bright yellow beads through his fingers. As I smelt the incense, which came to me from a dark chamber on my right, not yet visited by me, I knew that the Hindu was close by. It may seem very absurd, but—but the incense seemed to tell me so. I felt as if his personality, his will, floated to me as smoke wreathes and floats from an incense-burner—almost as if they were mingled with that scented smoke of the East which perfumed the maze. I remember I thought of the malignant genius who came out of his prison in smoke.

"Making a great effort to conquer my repulsion and fear, I approached the threshold of the chamber beyond and, without entering it, looked stealthily in. It was very dark. (Afterwards I knew that thin Indian hangings obscured the light from the balcony.) In the gloom I perceived many grotesque idols arranged upon pedestals, and small tables of inlaid work in which fine ivory, ebony, mother-of-pearl and cedar-wood were blended. They looked down, peered down fatuously or maliciously, too, from tall cabinets. Lamps of dingy metal and dark-coloured glass hung from the ceiling, across which carpets were stretched. The scent of the incense here was very strong, almost overpowering. After a pause I ventured into the room. It was long and much larger than I had expected, running back in an almost black vista peopled with curiosities. I could see no one in it. Nor could I see the brazier from which the smoke of the incense came. As I stood there I began to feel like one coming under the influence of a drug, slightly intoxicated, faintly light-headed. There was a divan near me covered with rich embroideries. I sat down on it and leaned back."

"Did you still feel the nearness of the Hindu?" I asked.

"Yes. I felt that he was almost close to me. As I did not move for several minutes the black man in the room I had quitted stole in, I suppose to see what I was doing. He only remained for an instant, but soon returned bringing me Turkish coffee and cigarettes. He set them down on a low table by the divan and vanished without making a sound. I drank two cups of coffee. It had a stimulating effect upon me. The queer light-headed sensation diminished. I stood up and looked all round me.

"On every side I saw the dim faces of the idols smiling or rigid in the gloom. They seemed to me at that moment to be an audience assembled there to witness the encounter between me and the Hindu. I knew now that he was somewhere in that room with me. We were enclosed together at last, and I was resolved to face him.

"All the back part of the room was indistinct from where I stood. He must be hidden there among the rummage of cabinets, carpets, and ornaments. Walking very slowly and warily, and calling all my will power to fight down the unnatural fear which always overtook me when the Hindu was near me, I went towards the back of the room. I walked on till I saw the wall at the end, which was hung with carpets. Rolls of carpet were stacked against it. Some of them, standing on end, looked like dwarfish forms in the twilight. The scent of the incense was here much stronger, and as I stared about me I presently saw a faint spiral of scarcely defined smoke curving quite near me. I stood still by a tall cabinet. On the wall, close to my hand, there was a sword with a Damascene blade. My hand went up to it instinctively, took it down and gripped it. Then I did what I had done in the medium's rooms at Fulham. I sent out to the Hindu the silent cry, 'Come to me from the place where you are that I may punish you!' I exerted the whole strength of all my being. In a moment among the rolls of carpet I saw something stirring low down. It seemed to uncurl, doctor, to stretch itself, to extend itself towards me. I saw thin arms held out for an instant; then a thoroughly defined human body in a long native robe rising from the place where it had been crouched near the incense brazier. Beneath the snow-white folds of a turban I saw a man's dark face and attentive eyes. It was the Hindu. I said something—I don't know what, but I addressed him. There was no reply. He simply stood there looking at me. Then I—I attacked him."

"You laid hands upon him?" I interjected.

"No, I couldn't do that. I struck at him with the blade of the sword. I scarcely know what happened. The light was very dim. But he must have moved with abnormal quickness. For there was a crash. The sword flew out of my hand, and when the black man glided in from the adjoining room a—it's horribly absurd, doctor!"

"Never mind. Tell me."

"A bronze statue of Buddha lay at my feet. The sword was splintered and the Hindu was gone."

"The attendant of the room of the idols, you mean?"

Latimer said nothing, but his face was grimly obstinate, the face of the man under the obsession of the fixed idea.

"And when the black man came?" I asked.

"I paid for the statue and for the sword, and got away quickly."

"And since then?"

"I have seen the Hindu on several occasions, but I have never attempted to speak to, or confront him. On the contrary, I have got away from him. And—and the persecution has increased. I know he follows me. I am certain he is always seeking me."

"That will do for the moment," I said. "Now will you do what I tell you?"

"Yes."

"Very well. To-morrow you will go into a rest cure which will last six weeks. I have an establishment at Hampstead arranged for nervous sufferers, with nurses of my own selection. You will have a first-rate male nurse. For six weeks you will be isolated from the world. You will have no letters, no newspapers, no visitors except myself. The Hindu will not be able to come near you. Do you understand?"

I got up and laid my hand on his forehead.

"You will not see the Hindu for six weeks," I repeated in a firm voice several times.

Latimer looked at me in silence. I took away my hand.

"You will call at my house to-morrow at ten with any luggage you require. The male attendant who will look after you and give you massage will be there to go with you to Hampstead. You will be at my house punctually at ten."

"I will," replied Latimer in a low voice.

"And now," said I, in a brisk and practical tone, "I'll ask you to give me a couple of addresses."

"A couple of addresses?" said Latimer in a surprised voice.

"Yes; the address of the medium you visited at Fulham, and the address of the Jewish journalist who accompanied you on your first visit there."

"But why do you want them? What can—"

"Mr. Latimer," I said, "I am accustomed to have my own way when I take up a nervous case. I have my own methods of working. Nobody need fall in with them. On the other hand, I am perfectly free to refuse to treat you. And I shall refuse unless all my instructions are carried out."

"But what can my giving you those addresses have to do with my cure?"

"Possibly everything," I replied.

Latimer looked at me for a minute in silence. Then he went to his writing table, wrote out a couple of addresses and handed them to me.

"Thank you," said I. "And now I'll wish you good night. Don't sit up. Go straight to bed, look steadily at some shining object—half a crown will do—and say aloud, 'When I have counted ten my eyes will close and I shall fall into a refreshing sleep.' Say this several times, and try to believe it while you're saying it. I tell you now that your eyes will close and that you will sleep. Good night."

He seized my hand and held it fast.

"But do you really believe that—that you can bring this persecution to an end?"

"I have very little doubt of it. I fully expect to get rid of the Hindu."

His grip tightened on my hand.

"I shall do exactly what you tell me to do," he said.

And from that moment I knew that he would.

Next morning punctually at ten Latimer arrived with his luggage, and I handed him over to the nurse I had spoken of. He disappeared from the world for six weeks. Before he left my consulting room he told me that he had followed my directions and had slept well the night before. My last words to him were:

"Remember you will not see the Hindu for six weeks."

"Thank God!" he replied.

He then went away looking almost cheerful.

I had now three things to do in connection with his affairs. I had to see the medium, the journalist, and Mrs. Latimer. I decided first to visit the medium. That same evening I looked his name out in the telephone book. His name, let us say, was Algernon Wigston. I found it and called him up. A very soft and genteel voice answered, and said:

"Yes? Beg pardon! Yes?"

"Mr. Algernon Wigston?" said I.

"Yes, indeed!" said the genteel voice. "I am Mr. Wigston."

"I have heard of your marvellous powers," I said. "Could you give me a sitting? It is very important."

"Oh, reely!" said Algernon.

"Money is no object," I breathed into the telephone.

"Who is it, please?" said Algernon.

"I prefer not to give my name. It's rather well known. But I will pay any reasonable fee you care to name."

After a slight pause the voice said:

"I'm very much sought after. What would you say to three guineas?"

"That it's extremely moderate considering your reputation," said I.

A very pleased voice made an appointment with me for the following evening at nine. I kept it.

When I arrived at the house in which he lived at Fulham, a maid, wearing her cap very much on one side, showed me into the room Latimer had described to me, and in a few minutes I was joined there by Algernon Wigston. At first sight he looked a weak, well-intentioned and rather foolish young man, but I had only been with him for two or three minutes when I noticed that his pale and wandering eyes could look very sly on occasion, and that he was by no means devoid of shrewdness. I paid him a few compliments, which he received with gusto, but avoided answering his questions, which were directed to finding out who had told me about him and his wonderful powers. Finally, when I had made up my mind as to his character, I asked for the promised "sitting." He complied with my request. We sat down at a table, placed our hands upon it, and very soon he seemed to go into a trance. Something of this sort followed.

His "control," Katey, took possession of him and babbled foolishly till I made up my mind to get to business. Then I said:

"I wish to speak with Minnie Harfield."

The medium jumped, and there was a dead silence.

"I am here to-night to speak to Minnie Harfield," I continued. "The woman who committed suicide on account of the Hindu, Nischaya Varman."

Silence prevailed.

"I ask for Minnie Harfield," I said in a sterner, more insistent voice.

The medium writhed in his chair, breathed hard, and then slowly opened his eyes showing the whites.

"They've left me," he said in a weak voice.

"Who has left you?" said I.

"The controls."

"Let us try again," I said.

"I don't feel well," he murmured.

"Take some sherry and water," I said.

Again Algernon jumped.

"Sherry! How did you know—" He stopped.

I could see by his expression that he was debating what line to take with me, whether to "stand up to me" or to try at once to get rid of me. He chose the latter course.

"I'm afraid it's no good to-night," he said. "I don't feel well. There's something wrong. I'm afraid I must ask you to come another evening. As to the fee—"

"There'll be no difficulty about that," I interrupted, "if you answer a few questions which, possibly, the spirits might not understand."

"Questions!" he said. "I'm not here to answer questions."

"But I'm here to get them answered," I said. "And I don't mean to go till you've satisfied my curiosity on certain points."

"Who are you?" he cried.

"I'm acting for Mr. Latimer," I replied.

His natural pallor was accentuated. There seemed to be a touch of green in it at that moment.

"Mr. Latimer!" he said, getting up and pressing his flabby white hands on the table. "Are you a—a lawyer?"

"Never mind what I am. I'm here on Mr. Latimer's behalf. You've had a good deal of money from him recently."

"He told me—"

"I know. And you took him at his word."

"I—I've only had—"

"Half of the money sent by his secretary," I interposed. "Or perhaps less than half. The rest went to Mr. Maurice Isaacs, the journalist who brought him to you."

Algernon sat down.

"Has—has Isaacs blabbed?" he stammered.

"You'd better make a clean breast of it," I said. "Otherwise I'm afraid you'll find yourself in very serious trouble. Mr. Latimer isn't a man who can be tricked, or even defied, with impunity."

"Has Isaacs—"

"Look here, Mr. Wigston," said I. "How could I know about this affair if Isaacs hadn't talked?"

That seemed to decide him. Suddenly he became shrill with anger against Maurice Isaacs.

"He put me up to it!" he exclaimed. "I've never done such a thing before. I'm an honest medium, I am. The spirits use me. I've always lived honest. The greatest people in London have been to me. I've had Royal people in this very room."

"But Isaacs led you astray. You're more sinned against than sinning, eh?"

"That's it!" he cried. "You've got it. Isaacs tempted me. That man's the devil and a Jew rolled in one. He come to me"—Algernon's grammar got shaky at times under the influence of excitement— "and he led me on; said how very wonderful I was with miraculous powers, and how it troubled him to see me living so humble. 'You might be rolling,' he said, 'and here you live, poor in the midst of plenty. Look here,' he said, 'I'll do you a good turn if you like.' And then he goes and tells me one of the greatest and richest men in London, the biggest newspaper owner of the day, was coming with him to test me. 'Convince him of your powers!' says he, 'and your fortune's made. But fail to and he'll ruin you, get his knife into you in every paper in England.' I fell in a sweat. I did indeed. And then he played upon me. 'Suppose when I bring him.' he says, 'the spirits let you down? What then?' I sat and just sweated. 'Don't they ever let you down?' he says. I couldn't but answer they did. 'And then you're ruined,' he says. 'You're down and out.' 'I won't see him,' I says. 'If you don't he'll go for you,' he says. 'Be a man. Take him on and make your fortune out of him.' 'Put me in the way, for God's sake,' I says. And, to cut it short, he put me in the way. He pitched me a tale about Mr. Latimer's wife and a Hindu, and how a woman called Minnie Harfield had killed herself from love of the dark fellow, and a lot more. 'It's all true and he don't know it,' says he. 'Dribble it out to him by degrees. Start in your own way and presently get to Minnie. Act according to how he acts. We'll stand in together with regard to the cash.' Well, I did as he said. I presently got to Minnie, and when he was on the string I dribbled it out to him. Isaacs taught me things to say, made me take things out of a book by some Indian feller, called Tagory."

"Exactly. And you were never in a trance at all."

"Not with him I wasn't, but—"

"I know. And the cash? How much has Isaacs taken?"

Algernon grew scarlet with rage.

"Three-quarters of everything I've had, if you'll believe me!" he almost screamed, lifting his puny little arms. "Day in, day out he's been here. 'Write again to the seketery,' he says. 'You can get what you like. Put it across!' he says. And—"

As I had learnt enough at this point I brought our pleasant little interview to a close. I must confess to an act of weakness. I gave Algernon three guineas. It was quite wrong of me, but— Well, I was pleased with myself that night, and it was my egoism which gave him his fee. He took it with an air of self-respect which did credit to his ingenuity, and I left him to the refreshment of his sherry bottle.

On the following day, again in the evening, I paid a visit to Mr. Isaacs. I had taken the precaution of telephoning to him beforehand, asking for an appointment, giving my name simply as Turnbull, and stating that I wished to see him for a very important reason. I ventured to add that I was a friend of his employer, Mr. Latimer, who had spoken very favourably of his abilities to me. Apparently Isaacs had no suspicion of a trap, for a suave voice replied through the telephone suggesting an appointment at a club. I answered that I would prefer to call at his private address in the Bloomsbury district, if it would not put him to inconvenience. After a perceptible pause Isaacs agreed to the suggestion and appointed the hour of nine for our meeting. I was there to the minute, and rang the bell of a flat on a third floor. The bell was answered almost instantaneously by a quite well-dressed young Jew, with dark, crinkly, and very thick hair, clever dark eyes, good features and an air of unshakable self-possession. I noticed at once that he was the sort of man likely to prove attractive to unrefined women, and to be attracted by them. He was smart, and in a way handsome; he looked sensual; and he knew not the meaning of shyness, a quality which is anathema to the modern young woman.

"Are you Mr. Turnbull?" said Isaacs, looking me over swiftly.

"My name is Turnbull," I said.

He held out a welcoming hand.

"Glad to see you. Do come in."

"This is only a bachelor flat," he remarked, taking my hat and umbrella. "I live here alone."

As he spoke I noticed his forehead wrinkle in a momentary frown, as his eyes noted something in the comfortable sitting room beyond me. I walked in, he followed me closely, and immediately, in a swift but casual way, got rid of a woman's long white glove which was lying on the back of a sofa. At the same time he shot a searching glance at me, but I was looking at some caricatures of public men which hung on the wall, and I don't think my expression at the moment was intelligent.

"Do sit down," he said. "Will you have a drink?"

"Thanks. No; I've just dined."

We sat down, and Isaacs said:

"Very sad about Mr. Latimer, isn't it? We never see him at the office now. He seems gone all to pieces. And he's such a marvellous man."

"He seems to think very well of you," I said.

A gratified smile curved Isaacs's rather thick lips.

"Glad to hear you say so. You're a friend of his?"

"I hope at any rate to prove myself so," I answered.

Isaacs looked at me narrowly.

"But I thought you said through the telephone—" he began.

"I'm attending him as a doctor."

"Oh, you're a doctor! I hope you don't think badly of his condition?"

"I expect to see him all right soon."

"That's good hearing. And now—I think you said there was an important matter you wished to discuss with me?" He looked sharply inquisitive.

"There is. You're a very intelligent man, Mr. Isaacs. Mr. Latimer told me so, and I can see it now for myself. Why d'you allow women to ruin you?"

The change in his face was startling. It grew instantly harder, more common and much more animal. The cheekbones looked more prominent, and the lips stretched showing the large white teeth.

"Women!" he said. "What d'you mean? What d'you know about me and women?"

"I know you've been playing a very dirty game on Mr. Latimer to get money, and that you spend that money on women. Come, come now, Mr. Isaacs, you didn't hide that white glove quite quickly enough."

"What's it to you if I choose to have women friends?" he said fiercely. "And I haven't ever played dirty with Lat—Mr. Latimer. I work hard for him, and he pays me a good screw for it. What d'you mean by coming here to interfere with my private affairs?"

He got up.

"I'll ask you to go at once!"

"If I do, I think you'll be sorry for it," I said quietly. "Do you want to be indicted for conspiracy and obtaining money by false pretences?"

"I haven't. What do you mean?"

His eyes pierced me.

"Simply that Algernon Wigston's given you away," I said.

His jaw dropped.

"Wigston—you—Latimer has—"

He stopped.

"Mr. Latimer has told me of your visits with him to Fulham, and Wigston has informed me of the fraud which you suggested and he carried out; also of the money transactions between you."

"But—but Latimer—does he know that—that?"

"I am going to tell him to-morrow."

Isaacs dropped down into a chair.

"For God's sake, don't. I shall be ruined."

"No doubt."

"It wasn't my fault. It's the women."

"They are an expensive luxury, I know, especially nowadays when they all wear silk stockings."

"They bleed a man white. Don't tell Latimer."

"I shall," I said. "But on one condition I'll undertake, before I tell him, to get from him a promise not to proceed against you and ruin you publicly."

"But he wouldn't do that," said Isaacs, sharply and swiftly.

"Why not? Because of his wife?"

"Well, he wouldn't."

"He will. I'll take care he does, unless you make a clean breast of the whole story of Minnie Harfield and the Hindu. And be careful to stick to the truth. I am going to check your story. Tell me the whole truth and I'll undertake that Mr. Latimer shall let you alone. Of course you'll have to leave his employment. You'll have to resign from his staff."

Isaacs looked very blank.

"If you don't he'll kick you out, of course," I said; "I can't undertake to prevent that. You can choose. Either—"

"Who are you?" he interrupted. "What right have you, a mere ordinary doctor?"

"I'm Sir William Turnbull of Cavendish Square," I interrupted.

"What, the great nerve man!" he was good enough to exclaim.

"Yes. Mr. Latimer has put himself entirely in my hands. He will do exactly what I tell him to do in this matter. That I can promise you. Your future lies with me, Mr. Isaacs, whether you like it or not. I advise you to tell me the truth."

Well, he told it to me. It seems that Minnie Harfield was at one time a friend of his, that he introduced to her Nischaya Varman, whom he had met at one of Mrs. Sidon's lectures, and that she did eventually commit suicide on the Hindu's account. So far the medium had related facts.

"And as to Mrs. Latimer's connection with the story?"

I had to press Isaacs on that point. He was suspicious, and wanted to know whether Mrs. Latimer had been approached by me, whether she knew of her husband's visits to the medium. I declined to satisfy his curiosity, but left him with the impression that possibly I had taken her into my confidence.

"She did know Nischaya," he said.

"I'm aware of that," I said blandly.

"Why d'you ask me then?"

I didn't think it necessary to inform him that I was aware of it because he had just told it to me.

"Mrs. Latimer knew Nischaya, but why did you put such shameful lies about her into the medium's mouth?"

"How d'you know they're lies?"

"Never mind. But I do know."

At that moment I was merely guessing, but my guess, it seemed, was right. For, after a pause, Isaacs answered:

"She tried to do me a bad turn."

"But she didn't know you."

"No; but she knew my work. And she hated it. She thought it beastly vulgar. And she said so more than once."

"To whom?"

"To Latimer. She wanted him to get rid of me. He didn't tell me, but I got to know of it through one of the editors to whom he repeated it."

"That was a very poor reason for trying to ruin her reputation."

"Oh," he said coarsely, "it wasn't so much that. I knew the way to get him on the string was to bring in her name."

That same evening I drove straight to Portman Square, sent in my card, and asked to see Mrs. Latimer. She was at home, and I was shown into the drawing room, where she was reading by a shaded electric lamp. She got up quickly when I entered, and came towards me.

"Sir William Turnbull!" she said. "He isn't worse?"

As the footman went out and shut the door she added:

"He—he's not going mad?"

I took her thin hand.

"Of course not," I said cheerily.

"But what is the matter with him? Sometimes he frightens me."

"His nerves have broken down through long overwork. But I shall get him right. And you can help me!"

"How?" she said eagerly.

"May I sit down?"

"Oh—please do."

I was with her for more than an hour, and I laid the whole matter before her. Latimer hadn't given me leave to do so, but that didn't bother me. I was out to cure him, and knew the best way to do it. She was very indignant at one point of the story, and was evidently deeply hurt by her husband's injurious suspicions.

"How could he believe such a thing, and about a Hindu, a man whom I scarcely knew?" she said. "A man whom I only met two or three times, and always in public?"

She got up. She was naturally a highly strung woman, and she was quivering with nervous excitement.

"Let me tell you a little about the nervous system and about the power of suggestion," I said.

And I gave her a short lecture, which I needn't repeat to you, on the tricks nerves can play on a man, and on the cruel powers of neurasthenia. When I left her that night I think she had almost forgiven her husband. Certainly she loved him very much.

When the six weeks of Latimer's rest cure were just up—it was, in fact, his last night in the house at Hampstead—I sat down beside his bed, and I told him all that had happened while he had been secluded. I never saw a man by turns so indignant, so ashamed, and so relieved. He was furious at having been taken in, bitterly ashamed at having suspected his wife and at having been duped by a couple of rogues, and immensely relieved at realising that he had certainly never been in communication with the denizen of another world. As we talked I saw his fear of the Hindu die away. But presently anxiety again shone in his eyes, and he exclaimed:

"But, doctor, surely I must have been mad. I saw the Hindu again and again. How do you account for that?"

"I believe that in Grosvenor Square you really met an Indian who was out for a stroll like yourself. The encounter was entirely fortuitous. It only made such a deep impression upon you because of what had just happened at the medium's. At the Indian Restaurant I believe you saw the same man, and that he left the place at a moment when your attention was distracted, although you thought that your watchfulness never ceased. No doubt you saw a living Indian, though perhaps not the same one, at the St. James's Theatre."

"But my wife didn't see him!"

"Merely because she had not really turned her glasses upon him, though you fancied she had."

"But at Marseilles!"

"On that occasion I think you were the victim of your nervous system and of auto-suggestion. It is possible that a dark man passed you and went up in the lift."

"But the attendant denied it!"

"Probably he had made two journeys up and down while you were at the bureau, instead of one, as you believed, and on the second of these journeys he had really gone up alone."

"That's possible!" said Latimer.

"At Hammam Meskoutine you saw a native whom you mistook for the Hindu. At Tunis the same thing occurred. But—mind—I do not exclude the possibility of your having sometimes imagined that you saw a figure, an appearance, before you when in fact there was nothing. You have overworked for years. There are heavy penalties attached to such folly."

"But you really don't think I'm mad?"

I smiled.

"I may possibly come to think you are if, when you go out again into the world, you continue to meet with the Hindu," I answered. "But I don't think you will."

As a matter of fact, from that night to this Latimer has never set eyes on the Hindu.

Sir William Turnbull paused.

"What about Isaacs?" I said.

"He cleared out without waiting for Latimer's appearance at the office."

"And—Mrs. Latimer?" I hazarded.

"She and her husband seem quite happy together again. She still reads Mrs. Sidon's pamphlets. Some people say that Latimer is completely dominated by her now, that she rules him in everything."

"And—you? What do you say? "

"Well," said the doctor, smiling. "It's generally very dangerous for a man to be forgiven by a woman. Women forgive and—remember."

The Lighted Candles

I am very fond of moving about and seeing fresh places, but I hate the tedium of railway travelling. On a misty night, therefore, when I stepped into the Paris express to go to Rome, I anticipated a long and weary journey, and was in no very cheerful mood. I had engaged a berth in the sleeping-car, and had stipulated that it must be in a compartment that held only two, and I had some hopes of having the compartment to myself. But when I came into it these hopes were at once dispelled. The beds had not yet been made, and on the long plush-covered seat a traveller was already established, calmly smoking a big cigar. As I came in, he bowed slightly and cast an inquiring glance upon me. I returned his salutation and his glance, arranged my things as conveniently as possible in the small space allotted to us, replaced my hat by a cap, and sat down beside him.

In a few minutes the train glided out of the Gare de Lyon, and the attendant came to ask if he should make our beds. I glanced at my companion and he at me.

"You wish—" he began.

"No," I said; "I'm in no hurry. I couldn't sleep so early."

"Nor I. Shall we say in another hour, then?"

"Certainly."

I told the attendant, and we were left alone.

Then I lit a cigar and looked for something to read. I had with me a book which I had bought at Victoria, called *Real Ghost Stories,* and some papers. The book I lifted up, then laid down again between me and my companion. I thought I would glance through the French papers before I attacked anything else. The papers were full of news of an upheaval in Russia—sad, even horrible, reading. Presently I had had enough, and, turning to get my book, I met my companion's eyes.

"Terrible, this Russian business, isn't it?" I said.

"Frightful. I wonder how it will end."

We fell into a desultory conversation. My companion, a man of about forty, English, but an Englishman of the cosmopolitan species, was agreeable and interesting. Now and then he showed a gleam of imagination which attracted me. I began to be glad that I was not going to be alone on the journey. After some talk about Russia, he said:

"I see you've got a book about ghosts with you."

"Yes," I said. "I haven't read much of it yet. Stead brought it out. Perhaps such a book would bore you."

"Not necessarily."

"In it, I see, he says something to the effect that it is almost impossible to be in a company of people not one of whom has seen a ghost, or had some ghostly experience. I wonder if that is so."

"I don't know. It may be. It would be if I were one of the company—at least, I believe so."

"Then you have had such experience?"

"Well, I think so. And, oddly enough, it had—or so I must believe—some connection with Russia."

"I wish you would tell it to me."

"I will with pleasure. But, if it is to be interesting, my narrative must be rather detailed and long."

"Capital. I must tell you I'm a writer, so perhaps I shall be the better able to appreciate your story."

"Use it, if you think it's worth using. By the way, are you bound for Rome?"

"Yes."

"So am I. And it was in Rome that these circumstances took place."

"So much the better!"

He smiled. Then, as the train rushed on through the night towards the frontier, he told me very quietly this tale of the lighted candles.

"Although I do not claim to be unusually brave," he said, "I have a peculiar dislike, I may almost call it a peculiar dread, of a coward. If I may say so, it amounts to this—I fear fear. Nothing irritates and distresses my nerves so much as the sight of an exhibition of terror. Nothing makes me so uneasy as the proximity of a fearful being.

"Well, three years ago I went to Rome in the autumn with the intention of settling down there for the winter. I wished to be quiet and my own master, so I resolved to take an apartment instead of going to a hotel, and as soon as I arrived I intended to visit an agent and to make inquiries as to where I could find a suitable one.

"I arrived in Rome early in the morning, and scarcely had I got out of the train before a porter came up and asked me if I were going to a hotel or if I wanted an apartment.

"Perhaps you know that a good many of the porters in Rome act as touts for flat owners, and get a commission upon any business done through their means.

"I told the man that I did want a furnished apartment, and he begged me to come at once with him and see the one he had mentioned. He described it as *bellissimo* and *stupendo,* and was so persuasive that I got into a cab with him and went to look at it.

"Before I arrived in Rome I had had some idea of settling in one of the old quarters, of trying to find something in the Via Giulia, perhaps, or the Via delle Botteghe Oscure, something with a touch of romance about it, or a hint of mystery. But when I saw the porter's flat it suited me in many respects so well that I decided to go into it at once.

"It was a modern apartment on the third floor of a good-sized house, looking out upon an open space which was rented by a man who gave lessons in bicycling. As it had no houses opposite to it, and faced south, it got plenty of sun, and was extremely cheerful. It was also well furnished, and contained as many rooms as I required. The rent was remarkably reasonable, and before the morning was over I had taken the flat for three months from its owner, an Italian woman, who kept a tobacconist's shop.

"That very night I was installed in it. Now I must just describe it to you.

"When you entered the flat you found yourself in a hall with chairs and an oaken settle. On the right of this hall were three rooms—my bedroom and dressing room and the dining room. These rooms looked out on to the open space I have already alluded to. Opposite to the dining room, on the other side of the hall, was the drawing room, which was rather dark, and had a window looking on to a small garden surrounded by the backs of houses. Parallel with this drawing room was a narrow passage which led to a kitchen on the left, and which ended in a servant's bedroom. Both of these looked out on to the backs of the houses surrounding the little garden, and from their windows one could see the windows of the staircase of the house in which my flat was. This section of my flat, in fact, jutted out at right angles to that part of the house which contained the staircase, and was commanded by the staircase windows. I hope I make myself clear?"

"Quite," I answered.

"There was also a bathroom at the end of the hall between the drawing room and the dining room.

"I intended to engage a woman to act as my cook and housekeeper and a man to open the door and valet me. But on the first evening I was alone. The *padrona* came in to make my bed and see that I had candles, matches, and the few things absolutely necessary. Then she withdrew with a *buona sera*, and a hope that I should be comfortable. She was a large and oily Neapolitan, and as she uttered her final remark I thought her bulging black eyes rested upon me with a rather peculiar expression, half-searching, half-defiant.

"When she was gone I went again over the flat. In the servant's room, upon a table under the window, stood a candle and a box of matches. The candle was new and had never been lighted. Why I did it I don't know, but I remember putting a match to it idly, holding it up, glancing round the room, then setting it down again upon the table, and—I believe—extinguishing it.

"Night had closed in, and presently I went out, dined at a restaurant, looked in at a theatre, and returned home. It was late when I reached the front door of the house and let myself in with one of my two latchkeys. I was at once confronted by the blackness of the stone staircase. All the lights were out, and I had not taken the precaution of providing myself with a candle end to illuminate my progress to the third storey.

"I struck a match and began to go up as quickly as I could. Before I got to the first floor the match had gone out, and I made some groping steps in the darkness. Then I struck a second match, which lighted me to the second floor. There it sputtered and died down, and I stood still for a moment fumbling for a third match. But there was not one. I had been smoking a good deal during the evening and had exhausted my supply.

"*Diavolo!*" I thought.

"Then I remembered that there was a box full on the little table in the hall, and I moved on cautiously, feeling my way, until I reached the staircase window, which looked out upon the windows of my kitchen and the unoccupied servant's bedroom. In the latter there shone a light.

"I stood still. I was greatly astonished.

"Over the window a thin white blind hung down, through which the light was visible. For some short time—two or three minutes I suppose—I stood on the staircase watching it. Who could be there, in my flat at this time of the night? Had the *padrona* returned to seek something? Or had some malefactor—I drew out my revolver, cocked it, crept up the stairs, and very quietly inserted my key in the door, after some groping, as I was without a light. The door opened, I stepped into the hall and felt for the matches, all the time straining my ears to catch the smallest sound. I found a match, struck it, and set it to the candle. Then, leaving the front door open, I went on tiptoe to the entrance of the passage, at the end of which was the door of the servant's bedroom. It stood open, and I saw the bed and the wall illuminated by the light within. I waited, listening intently. I heard nothing. Then I walked swiftly into the room. It was empty. On the table under the window stood a lighted candle burned down almost to the socket. I took it up and went from room to room. The flat was empty. Nothing had been disturbed.

"When I had finished searching I shut the front door, barred it for the night, and went to bed.

"The explanation of the candle being lighted must be a simple one. That was what I was telling myself. I must have forgotten to extinguish it. I remembered lighting the candle. I remembered extinguishing it. So my mind told me. But my mind must have been playing me false. I must have left the candle burning. And yet I could have sworn—but then we often could, couldn't we?"

I nodded.

"Telling myself this, giving my own memory the lie, as it were, I turned over and soon fell asleep.

"In the morning I went forth early to an agency and engaged a cook, a charming woman called Lucia, a native of Albano. She agreed to begin her duties with me that very day. This done, I paid a visit to my *padrona di casa*. I had a question to ask her.

"'I suppose there is no other latchkey to my flat besides mine?' I said to her. 'You haven't one you could lend me for my servant?'

"'No, signore, I have only the one.'

"'I'll have another made,' I said carelessly.

"I had been thinking of the lighted candle of the preceding night, and had wished to find out whether the *padrona* had means of access to my flat. It seemed not. Evidently, therefore, my memory had been at fault.

"I went to get another latchkey made for my cook, and dismissed the matter of the lighted candle from my mind—for the time.

"Lucia was married, and lived with her husband not far from me, so till I engaged a manservant I was alone in my flat at night.

"I dined at home that evening, and stayed in till Lucia had gone away for the night. When the front door had closed upon her, I went down the passage to the servant's room. The candlestick had been moved, no doubt by Lucia, and placed on a little stand beside the bed, with a fresh candle in it and the box of matches laid nearby. Wooden shutters had been fastened over the windows. I had not noticed them before. I glanced round the room. Then I went out.

"I spent the evening at the Salone Margherita, reading the *Tribuna*, and listening to a variety entertainment. When I got home it was about ten minutes to twelve. This time I had provided myself with a candle end to light me up the staircase, and I reached my door without difficulty, let myself in, lit my candle, barred the door, and went at once into my bedroom. There I began to undress.

"Now, I must tell you that I am not at all a nervous or suspicious man. I have been about the world and slept soundly in many strange places. Yet that night, when I was about to get into bed, I felt an odd uneasiness come over me, as if I had left something undone, something that imperatively ought to be done. I stood for a moment in my pyjamas by the dressing table. What was it that I had forgotten to do?

"After a moment's hesitation I opened my bedroom door and looked out into the hall towards the place where the passage began. A faint light issued from it. Leaving my candle in the bedroom, I went on my stockinged feet to the passage and stared down it. Beside the empty bed the candle was burning, the candle which, to-night, I had left unlighted.

"Again I went into the room and found no one. Again I went over the flat and found everything in its place, no sign of any intruder.

"This time I felt really uncomfortable. It was now obvious to me that someone, some stranger hidden I knew not where in Rome, possessed a key of my door, and, for some reason which I could not divine, visited my flat at night when I was out of the way. What could be this person's purpose? And why should so furtive a creature be so careless as to leave a lighted candle to tell me of his, or her, nocturnal entry? I now felt quite certain that it was not I who had left the candle lit on the previous night. My memory had not betrayed me. For a long time I stood wondering uneasily, and when I at length got into bed I could not sleep.

"I thought again of the *padrona*, that Neapolitan woman with the searching eyes. But she denied having a key of my door. And if she had one, why should she come at night? I wondered who had been my predecessor in the flat. Whoever it was might have carried away a latchkey on leaving, might have it still, or might have lost it. It might have passed into other hands. All my sense of comfort, of being at home in the flat, was rapidly departing.

"Only towards morning did I fall asleep.

"The next day I again called on the *padrona* on some pretext, and in the course of my conversation carelessly asked to whom the flat had been let before I took it. The woman suddenly looked glum.

"'To a Russian,' she answered, after a pause.

"'A man?'

"'No, signore. The Princess Andrakov.'

"'And she has left Rome?'

"'The princess is dead, signore.'

"She shut her loose-lipped mouth with a snap. Somebody came into the shop, and I went away.

"'The Princess Andrakov.' As I went out into the sunshine I was mentally repeating that name and wondering—idly, I thought—what the princess had been like.

"It was a glorious day, and I strolled on till I reached the church of the Sacred Heart, at the top of the steps that lead from the Piazza di Spagna to the Trinita de' Monte. There I paused for a moment and glanced down.

"A peculiar-looking man, young, perhaps twenty-five years old, was coming up from the Piazza. He was tall, fair, with a broad face, a flat nose, very prominent cheekbones, and long frizzly light hair. He was dressed in frayed trousers, an old green overcoat, and a soft and dusty black hat. I thought he looked like a Russian student. When he reached the top of the steps he stopped for an instant beside me, then walked on towards the Pincio. I followed—I don't know why. Simply, I had to go somewhere, and on a fine morning what can one do better than walk towards the Pincio? Just in front of the Villa Medici the young man stopped to look at the view over Rome. I stopped, too, drawn to stillness by the splendour of the city lying beneath the splendour of the clear sky.

"And then—I don't know how—we were talking, I and this young man, talking in French, and soon with a freedom that was almost like intimacy.

"He was, I found, a Russian, and an art student. We spoke of art, of Rome and its wonders, of— I have really forgotten what else. But I know that presently, when we were going to part, the young man handed me his card, in foreign fashion, and I gave him mine, with my Roman address written on it. He glanced at it, then started, and stared at me rather oddly.

"'Have I given you—what is it?' I asked.

"'Nothing, only—you are living in a house in which I had once an—an acquaintance.'

"'The Princess Andrakov?' I asked.

"'Yes. Did you know her, monsieur?'

"'No; but I have the flat she formerly occupied.'

"The young man looked at me, I thought, with great attention.

"'She is dead, I understand,' I continued.

"'Oh, yes, she is dead.'

"'Did she die in Rome?'

"'Yes, monsieur.'

"'Did she die in the flat?'

"'Yes, monsieur.'

"'I wonder'—I was thinking now of the lighted candles—'I wonder whether she was a careless person,' I said, trying to speak carelessly.

"'Careless, monsieur?'

"'Yes.'

"'Have you any particular reason for asking me that question, monsieur?'

"I hesitated. This young man was an absolute stranger to me, and I am not, as a rule, accustomed to take strangers into my confidence. But there was something in the look of his large, light eyes which told me I might go on. And I did. I related to him what I have related to you—the episode of the lighted candles.

"When I had finished, I said:

"'What I am wondering is this: whether my predecessor in the flat lost her latchkey, or gave it to one of the servants.'

"'The princess had no servants,' he said.

"'No servants?'

"'No, she was a very peculiar person.'

"'Indeed?'

"'Yes, a very suspicious nature. She was afraid to have servants in Rome.'

"'Why?'

"'She was afraid they might be got at.'

"He used a French expression equivalent to that phrase of ours.

"'By thieves?' I asked.

"'Well—no. It is a disagreeable story, but the princess is dead, and—'

"He hesitated.

"'I knew her in Russia,' he said at last. 'Her husband was an important man, a general, at one time a governor of a province in Southern Russia. There had been some trouble there, and he was sent to stamp it out. His methods of stamping out trouble were not appreciated either by the peasants or by the revolutionaries. He was hated, but the princess was more than hated; she was execrated.'

"'Why?'

"'She was an aristocrat of the hardest, most reactionary type. She egged her husband on to excesses. There is no doubt of that. She openly boasted of it. He would not have done half of what he did if it had not been for her. He was the governor of a province, but she was his governor. Everybody knew it. The end of it was that one day at a railway station he was assassinated by a young girl.'

"'Horrible.'

"'The girl disappeared, perhaps to Siberia. The princess disappeared—to Rome.'

"'Was she afraid?'

"'Terrified. I must tell you that she was an old woman, a skinny, coquettish old woman, years older than her husband. And, as I believe sometimes happens with people of advanced age, her nerves, which had seemed to be of iron, suddenly snapped. In one day she was changed from a cruel tyrant into a cringing, terror-stricken coward. That day was the day of her husband's murder. For she, too, had been condemned, and she knew it.'

"'That was why she left Russia?'

"'Yes, she fled. She came to Rome and took your flat under an assumed name. For though she was a princess, her real name was not Andrakov. In Rome her fear grew upon her. She believed she had been dogged. She ceased to go out. She kept no servants for fear they might be bribed by those who had vowed to destroy her. The porter's wife brought up her food, and she received it at the front door. She lived in a room at the back of the house, for fear she might be seen and recognised from the street if she went near to the front windows. And finally she died of sheer terror in that back room. A warning had been thrust into her letter box telling her that her place of retreat was known.'

"'Then she died in the room where the candles are lighted?' I said.

"'A back bedroom, the only one.'

"'Yes; but, excuse me, monsieur, how do you know all this?'

"'Oddly enough, the princess had shown me and my family kindness, monsieur. She was fond of my mother, who had been reader to her. (She was a very intellectual woman.) And she partly paid for my studies in Rome. I ought to be grateful to her, and so I am. But even my gratitude could never make me feel any affection for her. Three or four times I was admitted to see her in the flat. But towards the end she became afraid even of me. She was found dead in that back bedroom, with an expression of abject terror on her face and a guttering candle beside her. They broke into the flat as she did not answer the door when the porter's wife brought her food. It seems she had only just died. But for more than twenty-four hours she had not answered the door.'

"Such was the young Russian's story of my predecessor in the flat.

"I must confess that it scarcely made my new home seem more home-like to me. When I was back again in it my imagination set to work. I called up mentally the 'skinny, coquettish old woman,' barred in alone there, a prey to perpetual terror, living in solitude in the little room that looked out upon the garden, finally finding her sentence of death in the letter box, and succumbing to an access of senile fear, with a guttering candle to light her into eternity.

"A guttering candle beside her. The young Russian was not without an appreciation of detail. Why had he happened to mention that one? Probably because I had told him of the lighted candles. The mind goes back sometimes without being aware of it. Do we not know this from our dreams?

"My friend of the morning had not offered any suggestion for the elucidation of my mystery. I remembered that only after I had left him. His narrative of the princess had drawn him away, and me with him, into another channel of thought. But, if it had not been so, what explanation could he have suggested? Somebody had means of access to my flat, and had used these means two nights running. That was all I knew. What more could this young man know? My having thus entered into conversation with the only person admitted to the flat while the princess occupied it was one of those strange coincidences which occur continually in life.

"All that day my mind dwelt upon the Russian's narrative and the lighted candles, trying, I think now, to find a link between this dead old woman of an evil nature and the person who came to the flat from which her corpse had been carried out. Those Russians who had plotted her death, could they? But at this point I had the sense to realise that I was allowing myself to be carried away into absurdity. The person, whoever it was, who visited my rooms, must, of course, know that they were no longer occupied by the princess.

"That night I dined at home, and when Lucia left me and I had been over the flat I settled down in the drawing room with a cigar and a book. I had extinguished the gas in the hall and left the door of the drawing room open, for, to tell the truth, I had little inclination for reading. I knew that I was going to listen for the sound of a key inserted in my front door, for a step in the hall. If the visitor of the two previous nights came a third time—well, he or she would find the host who had been lacking before. I said to myself that, of course, no one would come since I was at home. My going out must have been seen. To-night the fact that I did not go out would doubtless be known. No one would come.

"Nevertheless, I waited and listened with the door open into the dark hall.

"In the distance I heard the muffled roar of Rome. Somewhere out there was the person who came to my flat by night, unless, indeed, the intruder dwelt within this building full of apartments. The time wore on. I read some pages of my book, but scarcely knew what I read, so attentive was my ear to catch the smallest near sound.

"If anyone came he should not enter without my knowledge.

"But at last the distant sounds began to die down. It was deep in the night and weariness overtook me. I resolved to go to bed, and got up to do so, at the same time looking at my watch. A quarter to one. I had had no idea that the hour was so late, and realised for the first time how intently I had been listening, with what anxiety I had been waiting.

"Having lit my bedroom candle, which was on the writing table, I turned out the gas and stepped into the hall. Owing to the situation of the drawing room I was at once opposite to the passage. It was dark, and the door of the servant's bedroom was shut. Had I shut it? I could not remember. I waited a moment, looking at the door. Instantly I was aware of a pale, small ray of light issuing from the darkness directly before me. It came through the keyhole of the door. Within the room the candle was lighted.

"By whom?

"This time I held my breath. I was conscious of a feeling of extraordinary disquietude, almost of fear, of a strong repugnance against going into the chamber of the lighted candle.

"It seemed to me that, if I did so, I should find within a skinny, coquettish old woman; that as I opened the door all the coquetry would die out of her; that my entrance would be greeted with a harsh, strangled cry of fear.

"At that moment, for the first time, I seemed to be conscious of the nearness to me of terror. And the thought of this terror near me made my hair bristle up on my head.

"What I really wanted to do just then was to go straight out of the flat, down the stairs, and into the open street, to find myself under the stars, to see the lights in the cafés, to hear the hum of happy people. What I did, after a pause, was to relight my candle, walk quickly, with a firm step, down the passage, and brusquely fling open the door of the bedroom.

"Silence, emptiness, and beside the bed, burning steadily, the lighted candle.

"I stood looking round.

"It was a small, uninteresting room, containing a bed, a chair, a table, a washhand-stand, and a stand for a candle by the bed. The wooden shutters were closed. From the wall an oleograph of the Madonna and Child regarded me with lacklustre eyes. In that bed the old princess had died of terror. Upon that stand had been the guttering candle, lighted as a protection against the trooping terrors of the night.

"And now—who lighted the candles in this room?

"I sat down on the only chair the room contained, sat down resolutely—for I did it against my will— and tried to reason the matter out. On the previous two nights I had supposed, I had felt quite sure, that someone who possessed a key of the door had come in for some purpose I could not divine, had lighted the candle in order to see to accomplish that purpose, and had gone away, carelessly forgetting to extinguish the candle. But to-night no one had entered the flat. I had been alone in it. And yet the candle had been lighted. By what? And why?

"By what? I had got to this point in my thinking. Was it extraordinary? There are certain things one can say one knows. That night I knew that no one could have come into the flat without my knowledge. It was impossible to open the front door without noise with a key. Without a key the front door could not be opened at all. I knew that the door had not been opened. The windows of the kitchen and the back bedroom were securely closed and were shuttered. No one could have got in by them. Nevertheless the candle had been lighted.

"Therefore, I asked myself the question: by what had it been lighted?

"In the passage, when I first saw the ray of light, I had felt as if the old princess were secluded within the room; as if I caught the infection of her fear. But now my terror—for I suppose it must have been the touch of terror that made my hair rise—was abated. I felt calmer, and I tried deliberately to be receptive; to make myself, as it were, an empty vessel into which might be poured the truth of that room.

"I should tell you that, at the time of which I speak, I was neither a believer nor an unbeliever in another world, in spirit agencies. I kept an open mind, capable, I trust, of conviction. Nevertheless, I was not prepared, at a moment's notice, to swallow marvels without investigation. I cannot, however, deny that since my meeting with the Russian student I looked upon this dull little room with altered eyes. And now as I sat in it, I felt about it strangely.

"As I told you, I was now calm; at least, I believe so. I let my mind alone. I sat, if I may use the expression, with all my mental muscles relaxed. The vessel was empty. It seemed to me that something flowed into it and filled it like a fluid; some influence, some personality that was inhabiting the room. It seemed to me that I was conscious of the shivering touch of fear; that I heard far, far off, faint and yet horrible, the shuddering cry of fear; that I knew—because somehow I was told— why that candle had been lighted; and that it had been lighted by something that dwelt in that room and was abjectly afraid of being killed in the dark.

"Ridiculous, you will say. The story of the Russian student peopling an excited mind with imaginations. I tried to say the same thing to myself. I left the room presently (I took with me the candle that had been so mysteriously lighted, and carefully shut and locked the door), saying the same thing to myself. I lay awake saying it.

"You must not think I yielded feebly to crazy ideas unworthy of a full-grown man. I did not. I combated them as you would. And when the morning came I resolved that if I had peopled the back bedroom with figments of the imagination, I would people it now with something very different.

"By lunchtime I had engaged a manservant. He was not a Roman, but a Sicilian, who had only just come to Rome in the hope of earning some money. He was about twenty-four, pleasant, and active-looking, and had excellent references from a well-known Sicilian family in Palermo. Like the cook, he was ready to come to me at once, and as I was in a hurry to have him, the bargain was promptly made.

"That afternoon he entered my service.

"Now, at about four the same day I was again at the Pincio, strolling near the parapet of the terrace, and listening to the music, when I encountered the Russian student. He took off his hat and looked inclined to join me. And I was nothing loath. We presently sat down together on two chairs in the sunshine, and I told him of the episode of the previous night. When I had finished I added that I had now engaged a Sicilian manservant, who would sleep in the back bedroom, and that he entered my service that day.

"The young Russian, who had listened to me with deep attention, shook his shoulders with a movement that looked like a shiver.

"'I would not be your servant, monsieur,' he said. 'I would not sleep in the bed where the old princess—ooh.'

"'But this man knows nothing and will feel nothing.'

"'What if the candle is lighted?'

"'Then you—?'

"I paused.

"'Monsieur,' he said, 'in Russia we are superstitious. I am glad you have engaged this young man. You say he is of the people of Sicily. The Sicilians are bold, but they are sensitive. This man knows nothing about your flat, about the little room, about the lighted candles. Let him be a touchstone. Can I say that? If he feels nothing, if he sees nothing—very well, there is nothing, and there is some simple explanation of the lighted candles. If not—if he is affected, if he fears, then there is something.'

"He added, after a moment of thought:

"'They say, those who are superstitious, that three lighted candles are a sign of death.'

"'Many English people think that too.'

"'Do you, monsieur?'

"'I have never bothered about such things. The strange—by that I mean the abnormal, using the word in the sense in which it is generally used—has not entered my life until now.'

"Giovanni, the Sicilian servant, settled in very comfortably, and seemed pleased with his room. He was a gay-looking youth, and that evening, when I heard him laughing and talking with Lucia in the kitchen, I felt as if a cloud, which had been lowering over me, were lifting.

"I did not go out that night, and went to bed early, and slept well."

My travelling companion stopped speaking at this point.

"What is it?" I asked. "Is anything the matter?"

"Well," he answered, "I never can recall the next day without a feeling of horror."

"Why? What happened?"

"Simply this. In the morning when Lucia arrived, Giovanni did not come out of his room. When I got up and asked for him, she said that he had not opened his door. I thought he had overslept himself, went to his room, and found the poor fellow dead."

"Good heaven! Why? What had he died of?"

"There was an expression of terror on his face. I went at once for a doctor, who examined him, and said that his death was caused by heart failure. Although he had looked strong, he had had a very weak heart. The same day Lucia gave me warning. She said that the Evil Eye had looked upon my flat."

"And you?"

"I removed to a hotel. Do you wonder?"

"Not at all."

"Unfortunately I had taken the flat for three months, and was obliged to pay the rent. I did so, and, of course, it continued to be my flat, although I did not live in it. Giovanni was buried and the flat remained empty, I keeping the keys and able to go in and out whenever I liked."

"And did you ever go there?"

"I did with the Russian student. I must tell you that my acquaintance with him developed into a sort of intimacy. His knowledge of the old princess, I think, attracted me to him. For I must confess that I could never think of the lighted candles and of Giovanni's death without thinking of her. But I soon grew to like him for his own sake. There was something unconventional, enthusiastic, about him that pleased me. But I also had other reasons for seeking him. He puzzled me. Despite his enthusiasm, his frankness, even his apparent carelessness, he was reserved. I was always conscious that there were depths in this young man which I had not sounded, that there were mysteries in his character which I had not explored.

"It was as if one always saw a door wide open, yet could never go into the room beyond, a room that was dimly lit.

"I had told him about the fate of my servant and my departure from the flat. He said, 'You did wisely. Death is there.'

"One day, perhaps three weeks after Giovanni's death, we were dining together at the Café Berardi, near the Piazza di Spagna, when— I scarcely know why—I was moved to tell the Russian that, though I had left the flat, I was often tormented by an itching desire to go back to it, if only for an hour now and then; that something seemed to draw me to the door, yet that, when I was there, I felt a reluctance to enter.

"'Have you ever gone in again?' he inquired.

"'Not since the day I left. Can you understand my sensation?'

"'Yes. Where mystery or fear abide there is always fascination. Why, they say that even murderers find it difficult to keep away from the places where their crimes have been committed.'

"'I suppose—' I hesitated.

"'Yes, monsieur?'

"'I suppose you wouldn't come into the flat with me one night—say to-night—and spend an hour and smoke a cigar?'

"He darted at me a swift look that, I fancied, was suspicious.

"'I?' he said. 'Why should I go there?'

"I was surprised by his emphasis.

"'Merely to keep me company.'

"'Oh, I see.' His voice was changed. 'Well, why not?'

"'Perhaps you dislike the idea?'

"With a sort of sudden gush of frankness, eminently characteristic of him, he said:

"'I both dislike and am attracted by it. Why shouldn't I speak the truth, monsieur? I connect your apartment with horror—the death from fear of the princess my patroness—therefore I am drawn to it. I have long wanted to go there. Yet in all Rome there is no place I dread so much. That is the truth. Make of it what you can.'

"'Let us go,' I said with sudden decision, getting up from my chair.

"He seemed startled by my abruptness, but after an instant's hesitation he got up too.

"'Very well,' he said.

"And again he cast at me a glance that seemed a glance of suspicion. I wondered what it meant. We went out, got into an open cab, and drove to the house in which my deserted apartment was.

"'You've got the key, then, monsieur?' said the Russian, when I gave the cabman the address.

"'Yes.'

"He said nothing more during the drive. When we reached the house it was not yet ten; the porter was still up and the lamps were still burning on the staircase. The porter looked much surprised to see me.

"'You have come back, signore!' he exclaimed.

"'Only for a little while. I'm not going to stay.'

"'Better not,' the old man muttered. 'Better not.'

"He glanced at my companion.

"'But perhaps the signore is thinking of taking the apartment. I have seen him here before, when the—'

"'*Basta*,' said the Russian rather roughly.

"And he began to mount the stairs.

"'This signore is a friend of mine,' I said to the porter. 'He has not come after the apartment.'

"And I followed the Russian to the third floor, leaving the old man mumbling to himself.

"I found my friend—I will call him Drovinsky—standing on the third landing, with his hand on the balustrade of the staircase. As I came up he said in a low voice:

"'Now, what are we here for?'

"'Why, to—"

"'No, but what are we going to do? Doesn't it seem rather absurd for two grown men?'

"'You want to cry off,' I said, rather bluntly, I fear.

"Again that glance of suspicion.

"'No, monsieur. Only let us know why we are doing this.'

"'Inside I'll tell you.'

"I inserted the key in the door and we stepped into the hall. In a moment I had lit the gas.

"'There is gas in the drawing room, too,' I said. 'Let us sit there.'

"Drovinsky was standing by the hall door, which he had shut.

"'Very well,' he said.

"He followed me closely as I went to the drawing room.

"'How deserted it looks already,' I said, lighting the gas.

"'Yes. Now, are we to sit down and smoke?'

"'I wonder if I can find a candle. I left some candles.'

"'Why do you want a candle?'

"'Merely to look into the rooms. Wait a moment.'

"I found a candle in the kitchen, lit it and went over the flat. Meanwhile Drovinsky remained in the drawing room. When I came back I said:

"'It is just as I left it.'

"'Naturally.'

"'Yes. Well, shall we light our cigars?'

"'And you will tell me why we are doing this?'

"'But you know already,' I said, taking out my cigar case. 'You yourself have told me. Where mystery and fear abide—'

"And I lit my cigar and sat down. He laughed and followed my example.

"'But, after all, do they, can they, abide here?'

"He glanced round at the very small modern furniture of the small modern room, and laughed again. And his own laugh seemed to answer 'Yes' to his question.

"'I think they can abide wherever tragedy has been. And tragedy has been here.'

"'You mean that poor fellow?'

"'And the Princess Andrakov.'

"'Oh, the princess—'

"'Could anything be more tragic than to die of terror alone, at night?'

"'She had brought terror to others.'

"His voice was suddenly hard. He had sat down near me and had begun to smoke. I confess that, knowing the princess had been kind to him, I was sometimes rather surprised by the way in which Drovinsky spoke of her. I was surprised now.

"'But you were a friend of hers,' I said.

"'Scarcely that. Because she had liked my mother the princess certainly did something for me. Still, I cannot be blind to her character.'

"He looked at me searchingly.

"'What is it?' I said.

"'I wonder—I wonder what your view of me would be if I were to tell you something. It is very strange that here, in this place where she died, I feel a strong, an almost overpowering inclination to speak.'

"He stopped, still looking at me with deeply inquiring eyes.

"'Speak then,' I said.

"'Do you remember my saying at Berardi's that I believed murderers often were compelled to come back to the places of their crimes?'

"'Yes.'

"'Well—I have done that.'

"'You?' I cried, startled.

"'I killed the Princess Andrakov.'

"I sprang from my seat in horror.

"'Wait, monsieur,' said the Russian. 'My weapon was a letter.'

"'What do you mean?'

"'It was I who put into her letter box the paper which told the princess that her place of concealment was known, and it was the terror caused by that communication that killed her.'

"I sat down again.

"'You meant to warn the princess so that she might escape?'

"'Monsieur, I wished her to die.'

"'Why?'

"'If she had not died, I should have killed her.'

"'Your patroness? The woman who had been kind to you?'

"'I was not a free agent. I belonged to a secret society whose orders I had to obey. The assassination of the princess fell to my lot.'

"'And you would have?'

"'If she had not died—yes.'

"He spoke calmly, fatalistically, but, as he finished, he glanced towards the door almost as if he expected someone to come in.

"'You were in Rome for that?' I asked.

"'No, monsieur. It was advisable for me to get out of Russia, so I came here. Because I was here I was chosen to kill the princess when it was known that she was in Rome.'

"'And you—?'

"'No,' he interrupted. 'I did not tell them. What do you think of me?'

"'I think you have a great deal of nerve.'

"'Why?'"

"'To come into this apartment after what I have told you.'

"'But I am not alone.'

"The devil prompted me to say:

"'Would you pass a night here alone?'

"'Why should I?'

"'Would you for a bet?'

"I knew the man was very poor. The devil certainly was at my elbow.

"'I will bet you a thousand lire to one,' I said, 'that you won't do it.'

"'You are joking?'

"'No; a thousand lire to one. *Parola d'onore.*'

"I saw that he was tempted.

"'To-morrow morning I will come here. We will breakfast together, and you shall have a thousand lire.'

"'If I do it,' he said, with obvious hesitation. 'I make one proviso.'

"'What is it?'

"'I will not go into the back bedroom.'

"'You need not.'

"'Very well, then, monsieur, I accept your wager.'

"Oddly enough, directly my proposition was accepted I began to regret having made it.

"'But if you feel—' I began.

"'Monsieur, I accept your wager. *Parola d'onore!*'

"'Certainly,' I replied hastily, seeing that he thought I was jibbing at the idea of losing my money. '*Parola d'onore.*'

"There was a short uneasy silence between us, during which neither looked at the other. Then I said:

"'Well, I think I'll be off now. What time shall I come to-morrow morning?'

"'When you please, monsieur.'

"'Shall we say eight o'clock?'

"'Certainly—eight o'clock.'

"'All right. There's the candle if you want to use the front bedroom. There isn't any gas there.'

"'Thank you, monsieur.'

"A constraint had certainly come between us since the Russian's confession and my suggestion of the wager.

"I went out into the hall. He followed me.

"'You know the front rooms?' I asked.

"'No, monsieur.'

"'This is the dining room.'

"We went into it. The shutters were not closed, and I went to the window to close them. Before doing so I felt the window to see if it was fastened. It flew open, and, by a faint moonlight, I saw the open space opposite, used by bicyclists for their lessons. A dark figure was standing there motionless as if looking up at the house. I stared at it for a minute. Then I shut the window and closed the shutters. We went together through the two remaining rooms and came to the hall door.

"'Good night,' I said.

"'Good night, monsieur.'

"Again reluctance overtook me—reluctance to leave him there alone.

"'You are really going to stay?'

"'Really.'

"'You don't think—'

"'I am going to stay.'

"His voice was strange as he said those last words. I began to believe that, apart from the money, he now wished to remain, that he had a more personal reason for his desire. And I thought of his words about the fascination of fear.

"'Good night, then,' I said.

"I held out my hand. He took it for a moment. His hand was very cold.

"'Good night, monsieur.'

"His high cheekbones, light eyes, frizzly hair, disappeared as he softly closed the door.

"I walked home to my hotel which was at some short distance off, asking myself almost angrily what had prompted me to make the suggestion of the bet. Why should I wish the Russian to spend the night alone in the flat? There could only be one reason and that condemned me. I thought there was some danger there. This bet had forced me to face a fact. I knew now that I believed the flat to be still occupied by all that was left of the old princess—all that was left above ground. The body was hidden in the grave, but the essence of that formerly terrible, and latterly terrified, human being had been released from the body and remained where the body had died."

At this moment the attendant put in his head.

"It is twelve o'clock, messieurs. Shall I make the beds?"

"I've just finished," said my companion.

"Another five minutes," I said, putting five francs into his hand.

He disappeared yawning into the rocking corridor.

"There really is little more to tell," said my companion. "In the morning, at eight o'clock, I was at the flat door. I let myself in with my key and before I had shut the door, called out in a voice which was deliberately cheery and commonplace:

"'Monsieur Drovinsky!'

"There was no reply. I opened the bedroom door on the right. It was unoccupied.

"'Monsieur Drovinsky! Drovinsky!' I called again.

"Silence.

"With an effort I shut the front door, and, walking softly, went to the dressing room, then to the dining room. Both were empty. So was the drawing room, into which I next looked. I began to think that I had won my bet, that Drovinsky had not remained in the flat for the night. But there were still three rooms to be examined, the bathroom, the kitchen, and—but I knew Drovinsky would not have entered the back bedroom. When taking my bet he had made it a proviso that he need not go into it.

"No one in the bathroom. No one in the kitchen.

"The door of the back bedroom was shut. I confess I hesitated to open it. Of course, Drovinsky had gone away. It was useless to look into this room. He had told me that he would not enter it. My task was over. I turned away from the door. I even walked a few steps down the passage. Then I stopped. I knew I was playing the coward. I was afraid to go into that room. I remembered Giovanni's death, and—I threw open the door.

"Drovinsky lay on the bed, his face turned towards the door, the light, frizzly hair falling across his cheeks. His eyes were open. The flickering flame of a candle, burned down to the socket, wavered across them, the semblance of the inner flame of life.

"But they were dead eyes in a dead man's face."

My companion stopped.

"But," I said, "that's not all?"

"Remember," he answered, "this is a true story. Life is not an adroit novelist who gathers up all the threads."

"Why should the Russian have gone into that room?"

"I imagine—I feel sure—that the fascination of fear led him there."

"And you think he—he was visited?"

"As Giovanni was? What else can I think?"

"To me," I said, "the strangest part of the whole story is the lighted candles."

"The corpse candles. And to me. The first, it is true, I may possibly have lighted myself. My memory may have betrayed me. It is just conceivable. The second may have been lighted by someone who gained access to the flat while I was out."

"But the third?"

"To me the third is entirely inexplicable. I once told this story to a man, however, who explained it in this way. He said that Lucia, my cook, must have lighted it and left it lighted by accident when she went home. I told him that after her departure I had looked into the room and found it in darkness. He asked me if I had looked in with a lighted candle in my hand. I acknowledged that I had. Then, he said he was not convinced. I myself had carried light into the room and might not have observed a light already burning in it. This irritated me, and I said, 'Then my eyes can absolutely deceive me?' 'All eyes deceive at times,' he replied. And then he told me of an odd fact bearing upon his statement. It was this:

"He was in perfect health, and was staying in a country house. He went in the middle of the day into a small room to write a letter. This room had only one door, from which you saw at once the whole of the room. There was no dazzling sunshine, just ordinary diffused daylight. He opened the door and saw that the room was empty. This pleased him, as he did not wish to be disturbed while writing. He shut the door, and, walking quickly forward to the writing table, encountered a solid body. There was a man in the room, a fellow guest standing directly before him. For some reason, quite inexplicable, he had looked hard at this person and had not seen him—had not seen that anyone was there. He told me that when he came up against this invisible man his blood ran cold with surprise, and his bones seemed to turn to wax.

"So the eyes can trick. Well, it may be so with me. How can I, how dare I, swear it was not so?"

"And the Russian's death?"

"Heart failure, like Giovanni's. Since then I have not entered that flat, and I believe it has not been let. Before I took it, it had got a bad name. That must have been why the *padrona* looked at me so strangely. She was wondering if I had heard anything, wondering whether I was brave or merely ignorant."

"No doubt. And one thing more. That dark figure you saw apparently watching the house from the bicycling ground?"

"Ah! I have sometimes wondered whether that dark figure held any key to the mystery. Could Drovinsky have earned the wrath of any of his brothers in crime? Could any enemy have known he was in the flat that night—have gained entrance? Could there have been a scene and could Drovinsky have died in a fit of passion? *Non lo so*, as the Italians say. Perhaps the whole thing has a natural explanation."

"But you believe the contrary?"

"And possibly I am a fool."

He threw his cigar end out of the window into the darkness. As he did so the attendant came in once more to make the beds.

And this time we let him make them.

Sea Change

Part I

THE RAINBOW

"Nothing of him that doth fade,
But doth suffer a sea change,
Into something rich and strange."
SHAKESPEARE.

In London nightfall is a delirium of bustle, in the country the coming of a dream. The town scatters a dust of city men over its long and lighted streets, powders its crying thoroughfares with gaily dressed creatures who are hidden, like bats, during the hours of day, opens a thousand defiant yellow eyes that have been sealed in sleep, throws off its wrapper and shows its elaborate toilet. The country grows demure and brown, most modest in the shadows. Labourers go home along the damp and silent lanes with heavy weariness. The parish clergyman flits like a blackbird through the twinkling village. Dogs bark from solitary farms. A beautiful and soft depression fills all the air like incense or like evening bells. But whether night reveals or hides the activities of men it changes them most curiously. The difference between man in day, man in night, is acute.

The arrival of darkness always meant something to the Rev. Peter Uniacke, whose cure of souls now held him far from the swarming alleys and the docks in which his early work had been done. He seldom failed to give this visitor, so strange and soft-footed, some slight greeting. Sometimes his welcome was a sigh, sometimes a prayer, sometimes a clenching of the hands, a smile, a pause in his onward walk. Looking backward along his past he could see his tall figure in many different places, aware of the first footfalls of the night, now alone and thinking of night's allegory of man's end, now in company, when the talk insensibly changed its character, flowing into deeper, more mysterious or confidential channels. Peter Uniacke had listened to informal confessions, too, as the night fell, confessions of sin that at first surprised him, that at last could no longer surprise him. And he had confessed himself, before the altar of the twilight, and had wondered why it is that sometimes Nature seems to have the power of absolution, even as God has it.

Now, at the age of thirty-two, he heard the footsteps of night on a windy evening of November. They drew near to the wall of the churchyard in which stood the sturdy and rugged building where now he ministered, on a little isle set lonely in a harsh and dangerous northern sea. He listened to them, leaning his arms along this wall, by which the grey and sleepless waves sang loudly. In the churchyard, growing gradually dim and ethereal, were laid many bodies from which the white vampires of the main had sucked out the souls. Here mouldered fisher lads, who had whistled over the nets, and dreamed rough dreams of winning island girls and breeding hardy children. Here reposed old limbs of salty mariners, who had for so long defied the ocean that when they knew themselves taken at the last, they turned their rugged faces down to their enemy with a stony and an ironic wonder. And here, too, among these cast-up bodies of the drowned, lay many women who had loved the prey of the sea, and kissed the cheeks turned acrid by its winds and waters. Some of them had died from heart-sickness, cursing the sea. Some had faded, withering like the pale sand roses beside the sea. Some had lived to old age by empty hearths, in the sound of the sea.

Inscriptions faded upon the stones that lay above them. Texts of comfort in which the fine, salt films crept, faint verses of sweet hymns defiled by the perching seabirds, old rhymes like homely ejaculations of very simple hearts, sank into the gathering darkness on every hand. The graves seemed murmuring to the night: "Look on me, I hold a lover;" "And I—I keep fast a maiden;" "And within my arms crumbles a little child caught by the sea;" "And I fold a mother, whose son is in the hideous water foliage of the depths of the sea;" "And I embrace an old captain whom the sea loved even in his hollow age." The last inscription that stood clear to Peter Uniacke's eyes in the dying light ran thus:

"Here lies the body of Jack Pringle, cast up by the sea on December 4th, 1896. He was boy on the schooner *Flying Fish*. His age seventeen. 'Lead kindly Light.'"

Uniacke watched this history go into the maw of the darkness, and when it was gone he found himself environed by the cool sea noises which seemed to grow louder in the night, wondering whether the "Kindly Light" was indeed leading on Jack Pringle, no longer boy on the schooner *Flying Fish,* but—what? The soul of a fisher lad, who had kissed his girl, and drunk his glass, and told many a brave and unfitting tale, and sworn many a lusty oath, following some torch along the radiant ways of Heaven! Was that it? Uniacke had, possibly, preached now and then that so indeed it was. Or, perhaps, was the light-hearted and careless living lad caught fast, like sunk wreckage, in the undersea of Hell, where pain is like a living fire in the moving dimness? "His age seventeen." Could that be true and God merciful? With such thoughts, Uniacke greeted the falling of night. In the broad daylight, full of the songs and of the moving figures of his brawny fisher folk, he had felt less poetically uncertain. He had said like men at sea, "All's well!" More, he had been able to feel it. But now he leaned on the churchyard wall and it was cold to his arms. And the song of the sea was cold in his ears. And the night lay cold upon his heart. And his mind—in the grim, and apparently unmeaning way of minds set to sad music in a sad atmosphere—crept round and round about the gravestone of this boy; bereft of boyhood so early, of manhood ere he won to it, and carried so swiftly into mystery beyond the learning of all philosophy. Ignorance, in jersey and dripping sea-boots, set face to face with all knowledge, and that called a tragedy!

Yet now to Peter Uniacke it was tragedy, and his own situation, left in the safety of ignorance preaching to the ignorant, tragedy too, because of the night, and the winds and the sea noises, and the bareness of this Isle.

Beyond the church a light shone out, and a bearded shadow towered and dwindled upon a white blind. Uniacke, a bachelor, and now almost of necessity a recluse, entertained for the present a visitor. Remembering the substance of the shadow he opened the churchyard gate, threaded his way among the gravestones, and was quickly at the Vicarage door. As he passed within, a yellow glow of lamplight and of firelight streamed into the narrow passage from a chamber on the left hand, and he heard his piano, surprised to learn that it could be taught to deliver passionately long winding melodies from *Tristan and Isolde*. Uniacke laid down his hat and stick and entered his sitting room, still companioned by the shadowy thought-form of the boy of the schooner *Flying Fish*, who seemed to tramp at his side noiselessly, in long sea-boots that streamed with the salt water.

The man at the piano turned round, showing a handsome and melancholy face, and eyes that looked as if they were tired, having seen too many men and deeds and cities.

"I make myself at home, you see," he said, "as I hope you will some day in my studio, when you visit me at Kensington."

Uniacke smiled, and laid his hand on a bell which tinkled shrewishly.

"It is a great treat for me to hear music and a voice not my own in this room," he answered. "Are you ready for tea?"

"Thank you, I painted till it was dark. I was able to paint."

"I'm glad of that."

"When it was too dim to see, and too cold to feel the brush between my fingers, I came back in the twilight to my new roof tree. I am thankful to be out of the inn, yet I've stayed in worse places in Italy and Greece. But they were gilded by the climate."

He sat down by the fire and stretched his limbs. Uniacke looked at him rather curiously. To the lonely clergyman it was a novel experience to play host to a man of distinction, to a stranger who had filled the world with his fame years ago. Three days before, in one of his island walks, Uniacke had come upon a handsome bearded man in a lane full of mud, between bleak walls of stone. The man stopped him courteously, asked if he were not the clergyman of the Isle, and, receiving an affirmative reply, began to make some enquiries as to lodging accommodation.

"My name is Sir Graham Hamilton," he said presently.

Uniacke started with surprise and looked at the stranger curiously. He had read much of the great sea painter, of his lonely wanderings, of his melancholy, of his extraordinary house in Kensington, and, just recently, of his wretched condition of health, which, it was said, had driven him suddenly from London, the papers knew not whither.

"I thought you were ill," he blurted out.

"I am not very well," the painter said simply, "and the inn here is exceedingly uncomfortable. But I want to stay. This is the very home of the sea. Here I find not merely the body of the sea but also its soul."

"There are no good lodgings, I am afraid," said the clergyman. "Nobody ever wants to lodge here, it seems."

"I do. Well, then, I must keep on at the inn."

"Come to stay with me, will you?" Uniacke suddenly said. "I have a spare room. It is scarcely ever occupied. My friends find this island a far cry, except in the height of summer. I shall be glad of your company and glad to make you as comfortable as I can."

"You are very kind," said the painter, hesitating. "But I scarcely—"

"Come as my guest," said the clergyman, reddening slightly.

"Thank you, I will. And some day you must come to me in London."

Now the painter was installed at the Vicarage, and blessed, each hour, his happy escape from the inn, whose walls seemed expanded by the forcible and athletic smell of stale fish.

Uniacke's servant girl brought in the tea. The two men had it by the fire. Presently Hamilton said:

"Nightfall is very interesting and curious here."

"I find it so almost everywhere," Uniacke said.

"Yes. It can never be dull. But here, in winter at least, it is extraordinarily—" he paused for the exactly right word, in a calm way that was peculiar to him and that seemed to emphasise his fine self-possession—"pathetic, and suggestive of calamity."

"I have noticed that, indeed," Uniacke answered, "and never, I think, more than to-night."

Hamilton looked across at him in the firelight.

"Where did you see it fall?" he asked.

"I was by the wall of the churchyard."

"It was you, then, whom I saw from the window. It seemed to be a mourner looking at the graves."

"I was looking at them. But nobody I care for deeply is buried there. The night, however, in such an island as this, makes every grave seem like the grave of a person one has known. It is the sea, I daresay."

"So close on every hand. Why, this house of yours might be a ship afloat a hundred miles from land, judging by the sounds of the waves."

He sighed heavily.

"I hope the air will do you good," Uniacke remarked, with a sudden relapse into conversational lameness.

"Thank you. But sea air is no novelty to me. Half of my life, at least, has been spent in it. I have devoted all the best of my life, my powers, my very soul to the service of the sea. And now, when I am growing old, I sometimes think that I shall hate it before I go."

"Hate it!"

"Yes."

"Well—but it has brought you fame."

"H'm. And wealth and a thousand acquaintances. Yes, that's quite true. Sometimes, nevertheless, we learn in the end to hate those who have brought us most. Perhaps, because they have educated us in the understanding of disappointment. You love the sea?"

"Yes."

"You wouldn't be here otherwise."

"I did not come here exactly because of that," Uniacke said slowly.

"No," said the painter.

"Rather to forget something."

"I doubt if this is a place which could teach one to forget. I find it quite otherwise."

The two men looked at each other, the elderly painter on his height of fame, the young clergyman in his depth of obscurity, and each felt that there was a likeness between them.

"I came here to forget a woman," Uniacke said at last, moved by a strange impulse to speak out.

"Yes, I see. It is the old idea of sorrowful men, a hermitage. I have often wondered in London, in Rome, in Athens, whether a hermitage is of any avail. Men went out into the desert in old days. Legend has it that holiness alone guided them there. All their disciples believed that. Reading about them I have often doubted it."

He smiled rather coldly and cynically.

"You don't know what a hermitage can mean. You have only been here three days. Besides, you come in search of—"

"Search!" Hamilton interrupted, with an unusual quickness.

"Of work and health."

"Oh, yes. Do you care, since we are on intimate topics, to tell me any more about yourself and—and—"

"That woman?"

"Yes."

"I loved her. She disappeared out of my life. I don't know at all where she is, with whom, how she lives, anything at all about her. I don't suppose I ever shall. She may be dead."

"You don't think you would know it if she were?"

"How could I? Who would tell me?"

"Not something within you? Not yourself?"

Uniacke was surprised by this remark. It did not fit in precisely with his conception of his guest's mind, so far as he had formed one.

"Such an idea never occurred to me," he said. "Do you believe that such an absolute certainty could be put into a man's mind then, without a reason, a scrap of evidence, a hint to eye, or ear?"

"I don't know. I—I want to know."

"That someone's dead?"

"That someone is not dead. How loud the sea is getting!"

"It always sounds much like that at night in winter."

"Does the winter not seem very long to you up here quite alone?"

"Oh, yes."

"And monotonous?"

"Often. But we have times of keen excitement, of violent, even of exhausting activity. I have had to rush from the pulpit up to my shoulders in the sea."

"A wreck?"

"Yes, there have been many. There was the schooner *Flying Fish*. She broke up when I was holding service one December morning. Only the skipper was saved alive. And he—"

"What of him?"

"He went what the people here call 'silly' from the shock—not directly.

It came on him gradually. He would not leave the island. He would never trust the sea again."

"So he's here still?"

"Yes."

Just then the two plaintive bells of the church began to ring on the wind.

"There he is!" Uniacke said.

"Where?"

"He's our bellringer. It's the only thing he takes any pleasure in, ringing the bells for church and at nightfall. I let him do it, poor fellow. He's got a queer idea into his brain that his drowned mates will hear the bells some night and make the land, guided by the sound. When the darkness falls he always rings for a full hour."

"How strange! How terrible!"

They sat by the fire listening to the pathetic chime of the two bells, whose voices were almost hidden in the loud sea voices that enveloped the little island with their cries. Presently the painter shifted in his armchair.

"There is something—I—there is something very eerie to me in the sound of those two bells now I know why they are ringing, and who is ringing them," he said, with a slight irritation. "Don't you find they affect your nerves at all?"

"No. I like to hear them. They tell me that one poor creature is happy. The Skipper—all we Island folk call him so—believes he will bring his mates safe to shore someday. And each time he sets those bells going he thinks the happy hour is perhaps close at hand."

"Poor fellow! And he is summoning the drowned to come up out of their world."

They sat silent again for three or four minutes. Then Sir Graham said:

"Uniacke, you have finished your tea?"

"Yes, Sir Graham."

"Has your day's work tired you very much?"

"No."

"Then I wish you would do me a favour. I want to see your skipper. Can I get into the church?"

"Yes. He always leaves the door wide open while he rings the bells— so that his mates can come in from the sea to him."

"Poor fellow! Poor fellow!"

He got up.

"I shall go across to the church now," he said.

"I'll take you there. Wrap yourself up. It's cold to-night."

"It is very cold."

The painter pulled a great cloak over his shoulders and a cap down over his glittering and melancholy eyes, that had watched for many years all the subtle changes of the colour and the movement of the sea. Uniacke opened the Vicarage door and they stood in the wind. The night was not dark, but one of those wan and light grey nights that seemed painted with the very hues of wind and of cloud. It was like a fluid round about them, and surely flowed hither and thither, now swaying quietly, now spreading away, shredded out as water that is split by hard substances. It was full of noise as is a whirlpool, in which melancholy cries resound forever. Above this noise the notes of the two bells alternated like the voices of stars in a stormy sky.

"Even living men at sea to-night would not hear those bells," said the painter. "And the drowned—how can they hear?"

"Who knows?" said the clergyman. "Perhaps they are allowed to hear them and to offer up prayers for their faithful comrade. I think faithfulness is heaven in a human heart."

They moved across the churchyard, and all the graves of the drowned flickered round their feet in the gusty greyness. They passed Jack Pringle's grave, where the "Kindly Light" lay in the stone. When they gained the church Sir Graham saw that the door was set wide open to the night. He stood still.

"And so those dead mariners are to pass in here," he said, "under this porch. Uniacke, cannot you imagine the scene if they came? Those dead men, with their white, sea-washed faces, their dripping bodies, their wild eyes that had looked on the depths of the sea, their hanging hands round which the fishes had nibbled with their oval lips! The procession of the drowned to their faithful captain. If I stood here long enough alone my imagination would hear them, would hear their ghostly boat grate its keel upon the Island beach, and the tramp of their sodden sea-boots. How many were there?"

"I never heard. Only one body was cast up, and that is buried by the churchyard wall. Shall we go in?"

"Yes."

They entered through the black doorway. The church was very dim and smelt musty and venerable, rather as the cover of an old and worn Bible smells. And now that they were within it, the bells sounded different, less magical, more full of human music; their office—the summoning of men to pray, the benediction of the marriage tie, the speeding of the departed on the eternal road—became apparent and evoked accustomed thoughts.

"Where is the belfry?" said Sir Graham in a whisper.

"This way. We have to pass the vestry and go up a stone staircase."

Uniacke moved forward along the uncarpeted pavement, on which his feet, in their big nailed boots, rang harshly. The painter followed him through a low and narrow door which gave on to a tiny stairway, each step of which was dented and crumbled at the uneven edge. They ascended in the dark, not without frequent stumbling, and heard always the bells which seemed sinking down to them from the sky. Presently a turn brought them to a pale ray of light which lay like a thread upon the stone. At the same moment the bells ceased to sound. Both Uniacke and Sir Graham paused simultaneously, the vision of the light and the cessation of the chimes holding them still for an instant almost without their knowledge. There was a silence that was nearly complete, for the tower walls were thick, and kept the sea voices and the blowing winds at bay. And while they waited, involuntarily holding their breath, a hoarse and uneven voice cried out, anxiously and hopefully from above:

"Are ye comin', mates? Are ye comin'? Heave along, boys! D'ye hear me! I'm your skipper. Heave along!"

Uniacke half turned to the painter, whose face was very white.

"What are ye waitin' for?" continued the voice. "I heard ye comin'. I heard ye at the door. Come up, I say, and welcome to ye! Welcome to ye all, mates. Ye've been a damned long time comin'."

"He thinks—he thinks—" whispered Uniacke to his companion.

"I know. It's cruel. What shall we—"

"Ye've made the land just in time, mates," continued the voice. "For there's a great gale comin' up to-night. The *Flying Fish* couldn't live in her under bare poles, I reckon. I'm glad ye've got ashore. Where are ye, I say? Where are ye?"

The sound of the voice approached the two men on the stairs. The thread of light broadened and danced on the stone. High up there appeared the great figure of a man in a seaman's jersey with a peaked cap on his head. In his broad rough hands he held a candle, which he shaded with his fingers while he peered anxiously and expectantly down the dark and narrow funnel of the stairway.

"Hulloh!" he cried. "Hulloh, there!"

The hail rang down in the night. Sir Graham was trembling.

"I see ye," cried the Skipper. "It's Jack, eh? Isn't it little Jack, boys? Young monkey! Up to his damned larks that I've reckoned up these many nights while I've stood ringin' here! I'll strike the life out of ye, Jack, I will. Wait till I come down, lads, wait till I come down!"

And he sprang forward, his huge limbs shaking with glad excitement. His feet missed a stair in his hurry of approach, and throwing abroad his hands to the stone walls of the belfry in an effort to save himself, he let fall the candlestick. It dropped on the stones with a dull clatter as the darkness closed in. The Skipper, who had recovered his footing, swore a round oath. Sir Graham and Uniacke heard his heavy tread descending until his breath was warm on their faces.

"Where are ye, lads?" he cried out. "Where are ye? Can't ye throw a word of welcome to a mate?"

He laid his hands heavily on Uniacke's shoulders in the dark, and felt him over with an uncertain touch.

"Is it Jack?" he said. "Why, what 'a ye got on, lad? Is it Jack, I say?"

"Skipper," Uniacke said, in a low voice, "it's not Jack." As he spoke he struck a match. The tiny light flared up unevenly right in the Skipper's eyes. They were sea-blue and blazing with eagerness and with the pitiful glare of madness. Over the clergyman's shoulder the pale painter with his keen eyes swept the bearded face of the Skipper with a rapid and greedy glance. By the time the match dwindled and the blackness closed in again the face was a possession of his memory. He saw it even though it was actually invisible; the rugged features dignified by madness, the clear, blue eyes full of a saddening fire, and—ere the match faded—of a horror of disappointment, the curling brown beard that flowed down on the blue jersey. But he had no time to dwell on it now, for a dreary noise rose up in that confined space. It was the great seaman whimpering pitifully in the dark.

"It isn't Jack," he blubbered, and they could hear his huge limbs shaking. "Ye haven't come back, mates, ye haven't come back. And the great gale comin' up, the great gale comin'."

As the words died away, a gust of wind caught the belfry and tore at its rough-hewn and weather-worn stones.

"Let us go down," said Sir Graham, turning to feel his way into the church.

"Come, Skipper," said Uniacke, "come with us."

He laid hold of the seaman's mighty arm and led him down the stairs. He said nothing. On a sudden all the life and hope had died out of him. When they gained the grey churchyard and could see his face again in the pale and stormy light, it looked shrunken, peaked and childish, and the curious elevation of madness was replaced by the uncertainty and weakness of idiocy. He shifted on his feet and would not meet the pitiful glances of the two men. Uniacke touched him on the shoulder.

"Come to the Vicarage, Skipper," he said kindly. "Come in and warm yourself by the fire and have some food. It's so cold to-night."

But the seaman suddenly broke away and stumbled off among the gravestones, whimpering foolishly like a dog that cannot fight grief with thought.

"The sea—ah, the hatefulness of the sea!" said the painter, "will it ever have to answer for its crimes before God?"

Uniacke and his guest sat at supper that night, and all the windows of the Vicarage rattled in the storm. The great guns of the wind roared in the sky. The great guns of the surf roared on the island beaches. And the two men were very silent at first. Sir Graham ate little. He had no appetite, for he seemed to hear continually in the noises of the elements the shrill whimpering of a dog. Surely it came from the graves outside, from those stone breasts of the dead.

"I can't eat to-night," he said presently. "Do you think that man is lingering about the church still?"

They got up from the table and went over to the fire. The painter lit a pipe.

"I hope not," Uniacke said, "but it is useless attempting to govern him. He is harmless, but he must be left alone. He cannot endure being watched or followed."

"I wish we hadn't gone to the church. I can't get over our cruelty."

"It was inadvertent."

"Cruelty so often is, Uniacke. But we ought to look forward and foresee consequences. I feel that most especially to-night. Remorse is the wage of inadvertence."

As he spoke, he looked gloomily into the fire. The young clergyman felt oddly certain that the great man had more to say, and did not interrupt his pause, but filled it in for himself by priestly considerations on the useless illumination worldly success seems generally to afford to the searchers after happiness. His reverie was broken by the painter's voice saying:

"I myself, Uniacke, am curiously persecuted by remorse. It is that, or partly that, which has affected my health so gravely, and led me away from my home, my usual habits of life, at this season of the year."

"Yes?" the clergyman said, with sympathy, without curiosity.

"And yet, I suppose it would seem a little matter to most people. The odd thing is that it assumes such paramount importance in my life; for I'm not what is called specially conscientious, except as regards my art, of course, and the ordinary honourable dealings one decent man naturally has with his fellows."

"Your conscience, in fact, limits its operations a good deal, I know."

"Precisely. But if it will not bore you, I will tell you something of all this."

"Thank you, Sir Graham."

"How the wind shakes those curtains!"

"Nothing will keep it out of these island houses. You aren't cold?"

"Not in body, not a bit. Well, Uniacke, do you ever go to see pictures?"

"Whenever I can. That's not often now. But when my work lay in cities I had chances which are denied me at present."

"Did you ever see a picture of mine called *A Sea Urchin*?"

"Yes, indeed—that boy looking at the waves rolling in! —who could forget him? The soul of the sea was in his eyes. He was a human being, and yet he seemed made of all sea things."

"He had never set eyes upon the sea."

"What?" cried Uniacke, in sheer astonishment, "the boy who sat for that picture? Impossible! When I saw it I felt that you had by some happy chance lit on the one human being who contained the very soul of an element. No merman could so belong of right to the sea as that boy."

"Who was a London model, and had never heard the roar of waves or seen the surf break in the wind."

"Genius!" the clergyman exclaimed.

"Uniacke," continued the painter, "I got £1,000 for that picture. And I call the money now blood-money to myself."

"Blood-money! But why?"

"I had made studies of the sea for that picture. I had indicated the wind by the shapes of the flying foam journeying inland to sink on the fields. I wanted my figure, I could not find him. Yet I was in a sea village among sea folk. The children's legs there were browned with the salt water. They had clear blue eyes, sea eyes; that curious light hair which one associates with the sea and with spun glass sometimes. But they wouldn't do for my purpose. They were unimaginative. As a fact, Uniacke, they knew the sea too well. That was it. They were familiar with it, as the little London clerk is familiar with Fleet Street or Chancery Lane. The twin brother of a prophet thinks prophecy boring table-talk—not revelation. These children chucked the sea under the chin. That didn't do for me, and for what I wanted."

"I understand."

"After a great deal of search and worry I came to this conclusion: that my purpose required of me this—the discovery of an exceptionally imaginative child, who was unfamiliar with the sea, but into whose heart and brain I could pour its narrated wonders, whose soul I could fill to the brim with its awe, its majesty, its murmuring sweetness, its wild romance and its inexhaustible cruelty. I must make this child see and know, but through the medium of words alone, of mental vision. If I took it to the sea the imagination would be stricken down—well, by such banalities as paddling and catching shrimps."

Uniacke smiled.

"But on the contrary, in London, far from the sea, I could give to the child only those impressions of the sea that would wake in it the sort of sea-soul I desired to print. I should have it in my power. And a child's soul cannot be governed by a mere painter, when a conflict arises between him and sandcastles and crabs and prawns and the various magicians of the kind that obsess the child so easily and so entirely."

"Yes, children are conquered by trifles."

"And that, too, is part of their beauty. Under this strong impression, I packed up my traps and came back to London with the studies for my picture. I placed them on an easel in my studio and began my search for the child. At first I sought this child among my cultivated friends; married artists, musicians, highly-strung people, whose lives were passed in an atmosphere vibrating with quick impressions. But I went unrewarded. The children of such people are apt to be peevishly receptive, but their moods are often cloudy, and I wished for a pellucid nature. After a time I went lower down, and I began to look about the streets for my wonder-child."

"What a curious quest!" said Uniacke, leaning forward till the firelight danced on his thin face and was reflected in his thoughtful hazel eyes.

"Yes, it was," rejoined the painter, who was gradually sinking into his own narrative, dropping down in the soft realm of old thoughts revived. "It was curious, and to me, highly romantic. I sometimes thought it was like seeking for a hidden sea far inland, watching for the white face of a little wave in the hard and iron city thoroughfares. Sometimes I stopped near Victoria Station, put my foot upon a block, and had a boot half ruined while I watched the bootblack. Sometimes I bought a variety of evening papers from a ragged gnome who might be a wonder-child, and made mistakes over the payment to prolong the interview. I leaned against gaunt houses and saw the dancing waifs yield their poor lives to ugly, hag-ridden music. I endured the wailing hymns of voiceless women on winter days in order that I might observe the wretched ragamuffins squalling round their knees the praise of a Creator who had denied them everything. Ah! forgive me!"

"For some purpose that we shall all know at last," said Uniacke gently.

"Possibly. In all these prospectings I was unlucky. By chance at length I found the wonder-child when I was not seeking him."

"How was that?"

"One day the weather, which had been cold, changed and became warm, springlike, and alive with showers. When it was not raining, you felt the rain was watching you from hidden places. You smelt it in the air. The atmosphere was very sweet and depressing, and London was full of faint undercurrents of romance, and of soft and rapidly changing effects of light. I went out in the afternoon and spent an hour in the National Gallery. When I came out my mind was so full of painted canvas that I never looked at the unpainted sky, or at the vaporous Square through which streamed the World, opening and shutting umbrellas. I believe I was thinking over some new work of my own, arranged for the future. Now the rain ceased, I went down the steps and walked across the road into the stone garden of the lions. Round their feet played pigmy children. I heard their cries mingling with the splash of the fountains, but I took no notice of them. Sitting down on a bench, I went on planning a picture—the legendary masterpiece, no doubt. I was certainly very deep in thought and lost to my surroundings, for when a hand suddenly grasped my knee I was startled. I looked up. In front of me stood a very dirty and atrociously-dressed boy, whose head was decorated with a tall, muddy paper cap, funnel-shaped and bending feebly in the breeze. This boy was clutching my knee tightly with one filthy hand, while with the other he pointed to the sky on which his eyes were intently fixed.

"'Look at that there rainbow!' he said. 'Look at that there rainbow!'

"I glanced up and saw that the clouds had partially broken and that London lay under a huge and perfect coloured arch.

"'I never did!' continued the boy.

"He stared at me for an instant with the solemn expression of one who reveals to the ignorant a miracle. Then he took his hand from my knee, hurried to an adjoining seat, woke up a sleeping and partially intoxicated tramp, requested him to observe closely the superb proceedings of Nature, took no heed of his flooding oaths, and passed on in the waving paper cap from seat to seat, rousing from their dreams, and sorrows, and newspapers, the astounded habitués of the Square, that they might share his awe and happiness. Before he had finished teaching a heavy policeman the lessons of the sky, I knew that I had found my wonder-child."

"You followed him?"

"I captured him in the midst of a group of emaciated little girls in the shadow of Lord Nelson. All the childish crowd was looking upward, and every eye was completely round over each widely-opened mouth, while paper-cap repeated his formula. Poor children, looking at the sky! Ah, Uniacke, what do you think of that for a sermon?"

The young clergyman cleared his throat. The red curtains by the narrow window blew outward towards the fire, and sank in again, alternately forcible and weak. The painter looked towards the window and a sadness deepened in his eyes.

"Where is my wonder-child now?" he said.

"You have lost sight of him?"

"Yes—though the blood-money lies at my bank and the paper-cap is in my studio."

"Is he not in London?"

"No, no; I learnt his history, the history of a gamin of fifteen or thereabouts. It was much the same as a history of a London pavement, with this exception, that the gamin had a mother to whom he presented me without undue formality. The impression made upon me by that lady at first was unfavourable, since she was slatternly, drank, and was apparently given to cuffing and kicking the boy—her only child. I considered her an abandoned and unfeeling female. She dwelt in Drury Lane and sold something that most of us have never heard of."

"I can see her."

"I wish to heaven I could not," the painter said, with a sudden outburst of fire.

He was silent a moment and then continued: "I had no difficulty in persuading her to let me paint the boy. I don't think she rightly understood what I meant, except that for some foolish reason I was prepared to give her money, apparently in return for nothing, that I meant to have little Jack decently dressed—"

"Jack—was that his name?"

"Yes, and that he was to spend certain hours—snatched from Trafalgar Square—in my house in Kensington."

"I see."

"The boy turned up in the jersey and cap and boots I had bought him. And then his education began. On first entering my studio he was numb with surprise, a moving and speechless stare—more overcome than by rainbows."

"Poor little chap!"

"I let him stray about examining everything. He did so completely oblivious of my presence, and of the fact that all the things in the place were mine. By his demeanour one might have supposed him engaged in an examination of works of God never before brought to his notice. While I smoked and pretended to read, he crept about like a little animal, penetrating into corners where statues stood, smelling—so it seemed—the angles of painted walls, touching the petals of flowers, smoothing rugs the wrong—but soon the right—way. I can hear his new boots creaking still. He was a very muscular little chap, but small. When he was able to speak I questioned him. He had never seen the sea. He had never been out of London for a day or slept away from Drury Lane for a night. The flask was empty; now to pour the wine into it. I told him to sit down by the open hearth. He obeyed, staring hard at me before he sat, hard at the chair when he was sitting. I interested him much less than old brocade and lighted wax candles, which inspired him with a solemnity that widened his eyes and narrowed his features. He looked on a new, and never-before-imagined, life. And he was grave to excess, though, later, I found plenty of the London child's impish nature in him."

"That impish quality hides in nearly all street-bred children," said Uniacke. "I have seen larkiness dawn in them for an instant at some recollection, even when they were dying."

"I daresay. I can believe it. But Jack was solemn at first, his brow thunderous with thought, as he examined his chair and the rug under his new boots. Then in the firelight I began my task. I wrought to bring about in this Trafalgar Square soul a sea change. For a time I did not attempt to paint. I merely let the boy come to me day by day, get accustomed to the studio, and listen to my talk—which was often of the sea. I very soon found that my intention had led me to the right mind for my purpose; for the starved gaze that had been fixed on the rainbow could turn itself, with equal wonder, similar rapture, on other things. And the mind also could be brought to see what was not visible to the eye. My studio—you must see it someday—is full of recollections of sea days and nights. Jack explored them. I eliminated from the studio important objects of art which might lead him to think of towns, of villages inland, of wonderful foreign interiors. I fixed all his nature upon this marvellous element which had never murmured round his life before. I played to him music in which the sea could be heard. I described to him the onward gallop of the white horses, racing over impenetrable depths. I painted for him in words the varying colours of waves in different seas, the black purple of tropical waters, the bottle-green turmoil of a Cornish sea on a choppy day, the brown channel waves near shore, the jewelled smoothness of the Mediterranean in early morning sunshine, its silver in moonrise, melting into white and black. I told him of the crowd of voices that cry in the sea, expressing all the emotions which are uttered on land by the voices of men; of the childish voices that may be heard on August evenings in fiords, of the solemn sobbing that fills an autumn night on the Northumbrian coast, of the passionate roaring in mid Atlantic, of the peculiar and frigid whisper of waters struggling to break from the tightening embrace of ice in extreme northern latitudes, of the level moan of the lagoons. I explained to him how this element is so much alive that it is never for a moment absolutely still, even when it seems so to the eyes, as it sleeps within the charmed embrace of a coral reef, extended, like an arm, by some Pacific island far away. I drew for him the thoughts of the sea, its intentions, its desires, its regrets, its griefs, its savage and its quiet joys. I narrated the lives in it, of fishes, of monsters; its wonders of half human lives, too, the mermaids who lie on the rocks at night to see the twinkling lights on land, the mermen who swim round them, wondering what those lights may mean. I made him walk with me on the land under the sea, where go the divers through the wrecks, and ascend the rocky mountains and penetrate the weedy valleys, and glide across the slippery, oozy plains. In fine, Uniacke, I drowned little Jack—I drowned him in the sea, I drowned him in the sea."

The painter spoke the last words in a voice of profound, even of morbid, melancholy, as if he were indeed confessing a secret crime, driven by some wayward and irresistible impulse. Uniacke looked at him in growing surprise.

"And why not?" Uniacke asked.

But the painter did not reply. He continued:

"I made him see the rainbows of the sea and he looked no more at the rainbows of the sky. For at length I had his imagination fast in my net as a salmon that fishermen entice within the stakes. His town mind seemed to fade under my fostering, and, Uniacke, 'nothing of him that did fade but did suffer a sea change into something rich and strange.'"

The painter got up from his chair and walked over to the blowing wind that crept in at the window fastenings. The red curtains flew out towards him. He pushed them back with his hands.

"Into something rich and strange," he repeated, as if to himself. "And strange."

"Ah, but that was said, surely, of one who was actually drowned in the sea," said the clergyman. "It might be suitably placed on many of the memorial slabs in the church yonder," he continued, waving his hand towards the casement that looked on the churchyard. "But your sea urchin—"

"Oh, I speak only of the fading of the town nature into the sea nature," rejoined the painter quickly, "only of that. The soil of the childish mind was enriched; his eyes shone as if touched with a glow from the sun, swaying in the blue sea. The Trafalgar Square gamin disappeared, and at last my sea urchin stood before me. As the little Raleigh may have looked he looked at me, and I saw in the face then rather the wonder of the sea itself than the crude dancing desire of the little adventurer who would sail it. And it was the wonder of the sea embodied in a child that I desired to paint, not the wakening of a human spirit of gay seamanship and love of peril. That's for a Christmas number—but that came at last."

He stopped abruptly and faced the clergyman.

"Why does the second best succeed so often and so closely the best, I wonder," he said. "It is very often so in the art life of a man, even of a great man. And it is so sometimes—perhaps you know this better than I—in the soul life of a nature. Must we always sink again after we have soared? Must we do that? Is it an immutable law?"

"Perhaps for a time. Surely, surely, not forever," said Uniacke.

His guest's conversation and personality began to stir him more and more powerfully. It seemed so new and vital an experience to be helped to think, to have suggestion poured into him now, after his many lonely island evenings.

"Ah, well, who can say?" said the painter. "I had the best for a time— long enough for my immediate purpose; for now I painted, and I felt that I was enabled by little Jack to do fine work. It seems he told his drinking mother in Drury Lane, in his lingo, of the wonders of the sea. This I learnt later. And, in his occasional, and now somewhat fleeting visits to Trafalgar Square, he explained to the emaciated little girls, in the shadow of Nelson, the fact that there was to be found, and seen, somewhere, water of a very different kind from that splashing and churning in the dingy basins guarded by the lions. Meanwhile I painted little Jack, all the time keeping alive in his nature the sea change, which was, in the end, to bring into my pocket £1,000 in hard cash."

Sir Graham said this with an indescribable cold irony and bitterness.

"I can hear that money jingling in the wind, upon my soul, Uniacke," he added, frowning heavily.

The young clergyman was touched by a passing thought of the painter's notorious ill health.

"Before the picture was finished—quite completed—the impish child began to waken in the wonder-child, and I had to comply with the demands of this new-born youngster. Our conversation—little Jack's and mine—drifted from the sea itself to the men and ships that travel it, to the deeds of men that are done upon it; raidings of Moorish pirates, expeditions to the Spanish Main in old days, to the whaling grounds in new, and so forth. When we got to this sort of thing my work was nearly done and could not be spoiled. So I let myself go, and talked several boys' books in those afternoons. I was satisfied, damnably satisfied—your pardon, Uniacke—with my work, and I was heedless of all else. That is the cursed, selfish instinct of the artist; that is the inadvertence of which we spoke formerly. You remember?"

Uniacke nodded.

"My picture was before me and a child's budding soul, and I thought of nothing at all but my picture. That's sin, if you like. Little Jack, in his jersey and squeaky boots, with his pale face and great eyes, was my prey on canvas and my £1,000. I hugged myself and told him wild stories of bold men on the sea. Uniacke, do you believe in a personal devil?"

"I do," replied the young clergyman, simply.

"Well, if there is one, depend upon it he sometimes requires an introduction before he can make a soul's acquaintance. I effected the introduction between him and my wonder-child when I sat in the twilight and told Jack those tales of the sea. The devil came to the boy in my studio, and I opened the door and bowed him in. And once he knew the boy, he stayed with him, Uniacke, and whispered in his ear— 'Desert your duty. Life calls you. The sea calls you. Go to it. Desert your duty!' Even a dirty little London boy can have a duty and be aware of it, I suppose. Eh?"

"Yes. I think that. But—"

"Wait a moment. I've nearly finished my tale, though I'm living the sequel to it at this moment. One day I completed my picture; the last touch was given. I stood back, I looked at my canvas. I felt I had done well; my sea urchin was actually what I had imagined. I had succeeded in that curious effort—to accomplish which many of us give our lives— in the effort to project perfectly my thought, to give the exactly right form to my imagination. I exulted. Yes, I had one grand overwhelming moment of exultation. Then I turned from my completed picture. 'Jack,' I cried out, 'little Jack, I've made you famous. D'you know what that means?'

"I took the little chap by the shoulders and placed him before the picture. 'See yourself,' I added. The boy stared at the sea urchin, at those painted eyes full of the sea wonder, at those parted lips, that mouth whispering to the sea. His nose twisted slightly.

"'That ain't me,' he said. 'That ain't me.'

"I looked down at him, and knew that he spoke the truth; for already the wonder-child was fading, even had faded. And a little adventurer, a true boy, stood before me, a boy to pull ropes, lend a hand at an oar, whistle in the rigging, gaze with keen dancing eyes through a cold dawn to catch the first sight of a distant land. I looked, understood, didn't care; although the poetry of wonder had faded into the prose of mere desire.

"'It isn't you, Jack?' I answered. 'Well, perhaps not. But it is what you were, what you may be again someday.'

"He shook his head.

"'No, it ain't me. Go on tellin' about them pirits.'

"And, full of gladness, a glory I had never known before, I went on till it was dark. I said good-by to little Jack on the doorstep. When he had gone, I stood for a moment listening to the sound of his footsteps dying away down the road. I did not know that I should never hear them again. For, although I did not want Jack anymore as a model, I was resolved not to lose sight of him. To him I owed much. I would pay my debt by making the child's future very different from his past. I had vague thoughts of educating him carefully for some reasonable life. I believe, Uniacke, yes, on my soul, I believe that I had bland visions of the sea urchin being happy and prosperous on a high stool in an office, at home with ledgers, a contented little clerk, whose horizon was bounded by an ABC shop, and whose summer pastime was fly-killing. My big work finished, a sort of eager idiocy seized me. I was as a man drugged. My faculties must have been besotted, I was in a dream. Three days afterwards I woke from it and learnt that there may be grandeur, yes, grandeur, dramatic in its force, tragic in its height and depth, in a tipsy old woman of Drury Lane."

"Jack's mother?"

The painter nodded. All the time he had been talking the wind had steadily increased, and the uproar of the embracing sea had been growing louder. The windows rattled like musketry, the red curtains shook as if in fear. Now there came a knock at the door.

"Come in," said the clergyman.

The maid appeared.

"Do you want anything more to-night, sir?"

"No, thank you, Kate. Good-night."

"Good-night, sir."

The door shut.

"Is it late?" said the painter.

"Nearly eleven. That is all."

"Are you tired, Uniacke? perhaps you are accustomed to go to bed early?"

"Not very. Besides to-night the gale would keep me awake; and I want to hear the end of your story."

"Then—Drury Lane invaded me one evening, smelling of gin, with black bonnet cocked over one eye, an impossible umbrella, broken boots, straying hair, a mouth full of objurgation, and oaths, and crying between times, 'Where's Jack? Where's my boy? What 'a yer done with my boy,—yer!' I received Drury Lane with astonishment but, I hope, with courtesy, and explained that my picture was finished, that Jack had left me to go home, that I meant to take care of his future.

"My remarks were received with oaths, and the repeated demand to know where Jack was. 'Isn't he at home?' I asked. 'No, nor he ain't been 'ome.' After a while I gathered that Jack had disappeared in darkness from my house on the night when I put the last touch to my picture, and had not been seen by his mother since. She now began to soften and to cry, and I observed that maternity was in her as well as cheap gin. I endeavoured to comfort her and promised that little Jack should be found.

"'If he ain't found,' she sobbed, 'I'm done for, I am; 'e's my hall.'

"There was something horribly genuine in the sound of this cry. I began to see beyond the gin in which this poor woman was soaked; I began to see her half-drowned soul that yet had life, had breath.

"'We'll find him,' I said.

"'Never, never,' she wailed, rocking her thin body to and fro, 'I know 'e's gone to sea, 'e 'as. Jack's run away fur a sailor.'

"At these words I turned cold, for I felt as if they were true. I saw in a flash the result of my experiment. I had shown the boy the way that led to the great sea. Perhaps that night, even as he left my door, he had seen in fancy the white waves playing before him in the distance, the ships go sailing by. He had heard siren voices calling his youth and he had heeded them. His old mother kept on cursing me at intervals. Instinct, rather than actual knowledge, led her to attribute this disappearance to my initiative. I did not attempt to reason her out of the belief, for alas! I began to hold it myself, Uniacke."

"You thought Jack had run away to sea, prompted by all that you had told him of the sea?"

"Yes. And I think it still."

"Think—then you don't—"

"I don't know it, you'd say? Do I not? Uniacke, a little while ago, when you told me of that—that woman for whom you cared much, you remember my saying to you, was there not something within you that would tell you if she were dead?"

"Yes, I remember."

"That something which makes a man know a thing without what is generally called knowledge of it. Well, that something within me makes me know that little Jack did run away to sea. I searched for him, I strove, as far as one can do such a thing, to sift all the innumerable grains of London through my fingers to find that one little grain I wanted. I spared no pains in my search. Conceive, even, that I escorted Drury Lane in the black bonnet to the Docks, to ships lying in the Thames, to a thousand places! It was all in vain; the wonder-child was swallowed up. I had indeed drowned little Jack in the sea. I have never set eyes on him since he left me on the evening of the day when I completed my ʹ picture. Shall I ever set eyes on him again? Shall I, Uniacke? Shall I?"

Sir Graham put this strange question with a sort of morose fierceness, getting up from his chair as he spoke. The young clergyman could think of no reply.

"Why not?" he said at last. "He may be well, happy, active in a life that he loves, that he glories in."

"No, Uniacke, no, for he's far away from his duty. That hideous old woman, in her degradation, in her cruelty, in her drunkenness, loved that boy, loves him still, with an intensity, a passion, a hunger, a feverish anxiety that are noble, that are great. Her hatred of me proves it. I honour her for her hatred. I respect her for it! She shows the beauty of her soul in her curses. She almost teaches me that there is indeed immortality—at least for women—by her sleepless horror of me. Her hatred, I say, is glorious, because her love shines through it. I feed her. She doesn't know it. She'd starve rather than eat my bread. She would kill me, I believe, if she didn't fancy in her vague mind, obscured by drink, that the man who had sent her boy from her might bring him back to her. For weeks she came every day—walking all the way from Drury Lane, mind you—to ask if the boy had returned. Then she endured the nightmare of my company, as I told you, while we searched in likely places for the vanished sea urchin. Jack did nothing for the support of his mother. It was she who kept him. She beat him. She cursed him. She fed him. She loved him; like an animal, perhaps, like a mother, certainly. That says all, Uniacke. It was I who sent that boy away. I must give him back to that old woman. Till I do so I can never find peace. This thing preys upon my life, eats into my heart. It's the little worm gnawing, always gnawing at me. The doctors tell me I am morbid because I am in bad health, that my bad health makes the malady in my mind. On the contrary, it is my mind that makes the malady in my body. Ah! you are wondering! You are wondering, too, whether it's not the other way! I see you are!"

"I cannot deny it," Uniacke said gently.

"You are wrong. You are wrong, I assure you. And surely you, a clergyman, ought to be the very man to understand me, to know how what seems a slight thing, a small selfishness, well, the inadvertence we spoke of lately, may punish the soul, may have a long and evil train of consequences. I was careless of that child, careful only of my ambition. I ground the child in the mortar of my ambition; is it not natural that I should suffer now? Does not your religion tell you that it is right? Answer me that?"

Uniacke hesitated. A conviction had been growing up in him all the evening that his guest was suffering severely under some nervous affliction; one of those obscure diseases which change the whole colour of life to the sufferer, which distort all actions however simple and ordinary, which render diminutive trials monstrous, and small evils immense and ineffably tragic. It seemed to Uniacke to be his duty to combat Sir Graham's increasing melancholy, which actually bordered upon despair. At the same time, the young clergyman could not hide from his mind—a mind flooded with conscience—that the painter was slightly to blame for the action which had been followed by so strange a result.

"I see you hesitate, Uniacke," said Sir Graham. "Ah, you agree with me!"

"No; I think you may have been careless. But you magnify a slight error into a grievous sin; and I do indeed believe that it must be your present bad state of health which acts as the magnifying glass. That is my honest opinion."

"No, no," said the painter, almost with anger, "my illness is all from the mind. If I could find that boy, if I could give him back to his mother, I should recover my peace, I should recover my health—I should no longer be haunted, driven as I am now. But, Uniacke, do you know what it is that I fear most of all, what it is that dogs me, night and day; though I strive to put it from me, to tell myself that it is a chimera?"

"What?"

"The belief that little Jack is dead; that he has been drowned at sea, perhaps lately, perhaps long ago."

"Why should you think that? You do not even know for certain that he ran away to sea."

"I am sure of it. If he is dead! If he is dead!"

The painter, as if in an access of grief, turned abruptly from the fire, walked over to the window, pulled one of the blowing curtains aside and approached his face to the glass.

"In spite of the storm it is still so light that I can see those graves," he said in a low voice.

"Don't look at them, Sir Graham. Let us talk of other things."

"And—and—yes, Uniacke, that poor, mad Skipper is still out there, lingering among them. He is by the churchyard wall, where you were standing this evening in the twilight: one would say he was watching."

The clergyman had also risen from his seat. He moved a step or two across the little room, then stood still, looking at Sir Graham, who was half concealed by the fluttering curtains.

"He is just where I stood?" Uniacke asked.

"Yes."

"Then he is watching."

"By a grave?"

"Yes. Only one of his crew ever gained the land. He gained it—a corpse. He is buried by that wall. I was reading the inscription upon his tombstone, and wondering—"

"Wondering? Yes?"

"Where he is, how he is now, far away from the voice of the sea which took his life, the wind which roared his requiem."

"Poor man! You were here when he was washed up on the beach?"

"Yes. I buried him. The Skipper—sane then, though in terrible grief—was able to identify him, to follow the drowned body as chief mourner, to choose the inscription for the stone."

"What was it?" asked Sir Graham, without curiosity, idly, almost absently.

"'Lead, kindly light.' He would have that put. I think he had heard the boy sing it, or whistle the tune of it, at sea one day."

"The boy? It was a boy then?"

"Yes."

The clergyman spoke with a certain hesitation, a sudden diffidence. He looked at the painter, and an abrupt awkwardness, almost a shamefacedness, crept into his manner, even showed itself in his attitude. The painter did not seem to be aware of it. He was still engrossed in his own sorrow, his own morbid reflections. He looked out again in the night.

"Poor faithful watchdog," he murmured.

Then he turned away from the window.

"The Skipper does not wait for that boy," he said. "He knows at least that he never come to him from the sea."

"Strangely—no. Indeed, he always looks for the boy first."

"First, do you say? Was it so to-night?"

Again Uniacke hesitated. He was on the verge of telling a lie, but conscience intervened.

"Yes," he said.

"Didn't he speak of little Jack?" said Sir Graham slowly, and with a sudden nervous spasm of the face.

"Yes, Sir Graham."

"That's curious."

"Why?"

"The same name—my wonder-child's name."

"And the name of a thousand children."

"Of course, of course. And—and, Uniacke, the other name, the other name upon that tomb?"

"What other name?"

"Why—why the surname. What is that?"

The painter was standing close to the clergyman and staring straight into his eyes. For a moment Uniacke made no reply. Then he answered slowly:

"There is no other name."

"Why not?"

"Why—the—the Skipper would only have Jack put, that was all. Jack—he was the boy on the schooner *Flying Fish*—'Lead, kindly light.'"

"Ah!"

The exclamation came in a sigh, that might have been a murmur of relief or of disappointment. Then there was a silence. The painter went over again to the fire. Uniacke stood still where he was and looked on the ground. He had told a deliberate lie. It seemed to grow as he thought of it. And why had he told it? A sudden impulse, a sudden fear, had led him into sin. A strange fancy had whispered to him, "What if that boy buried by the wall yonder should be the wonder-child, the ragamuffin who looked at the rainbow, the sea urchin, the spectre haunting your guest?" How unlikely that was! And yet ships go far, and the human fate is often mysteriously sad. It might be that the wonder-child was born to be wrecked, to be cast up, streaming with seawater on the strand of this lonely isle. It might be that the eyes which worshipped the rainbow were sightless beneath that stone yonder; that the hands which pointed to it were folded in the eternal sleep. And, if so, was not the lie justified? If so, could Peter Uniacke regret it? He saw this man who had come into his lonely life treading along the verge of a world that made him tremble in horror. Dared he lead him across the verge into the darkness? And yet his lie troubled him, and he saw a stain spreading slowly out upon the whiteness of his ardent soul. The painter turned from the fire. His face was haggard and weary.

"I will go to bed," he said. "I must try to get some sleep even in the storm."

He held out his thin hand. Uniacke took it.

"Good-night," he said.

"Good-night. I am sorry I have troubled you with my foolish history."

"It interested me deeply. By the way—what did you say your wonder-child's name was, his full name?"

"Jack—Jack Pringle. What is it?"

"Nothing. That gust of wind startled me. Good-night."

The painter looked at Uniacke narrowly, then left the room.

The clergyman went over to the fire, leaned his arms on the mantelpiece, and rested his head on them.

Presently he lifted his head, went softly to the door, opened it and listened. He heard the tread of his guest above stairs, moving to and fro about the spare room. He waited. After a while there was silence in the house. Only the wind and the sea roared outside. Then Uniacke went into the kitchen, pulled out a drawer in a dresser that stood by the window, and took from it a chisel and a hammer. He carried them into the passage, furtively put on his coat and hat, and, with all the precaution of a thief, unlocked the front door and stole out into the storm.

Part II

THE GRAVE

In the morning the storm was still fierce. Clouds streamed across a sky that bent lower and lower towards the aspiring sea blanched with foam. There was little light, and the Rectory parlour looked grim and wintry when Sir Graham and Uniacke met there at breakfast time. The clergyman was pale and seemed strangely discomforted and at first unable to be natural. He greeted his guest with a forcible, and yet flickering, note of cheerfulness, abrupt and unsympathetic, as he sat down behind the steaming coffee pot. The painter scarcely responded. He was still attentive to the storm. He ate very little.

"You slept?" asked Uniacke presently.

"Only for a short time towards dawn. I sat at my window most of the night."

"At your window?" Uniacke said uneasily.

"Yes. Somebody—a man—I suppose it must have been the Skipper—came out from the shadow of this house soon after I went to my bedroom, and stole to that grave by the churchyard wall."

"Really," said Uniacke. "Did he stay there?"

"For some time, bending down. It seemed to me as if he were at some work, some task—or perhaps he was only praying in his mad way, poor fellow!"

"Praying—yes, yes, very likely. A little more coffee?"

"No, thank you. The odd thing was that after a while he ceased and returned to this house. One might have thought it was his home."

"You could not see if it was the Skipper?"

"No, the figure was too vague in the faint stormy light. But it must have been he. Who else would be out at such a time in such a night?"

"He never heeds the weather," said Uniacke.

His pale face had suddenly flushed scarlet, and he felt a pricking as of needles in his body. It seemed to him that he was transparent like a thing of glass, and that his guest must be able to see not merely the trouble of his soul, but the fact that was its cause. And the painter did now begin to observe his host's unusual agitation.

"And you—your night?" he asked.

"I did not sleep at all," said Uniacke quickly, telling the truth with a childish sense of relief, "I was excited."

"Excited!" said Sir Graham.

"The unwonted exercise of conversation. You forget that I am generally a lonely man," said the clergyman, once more drawn into the sin of subterfuge, and scorching in it almost like a soul in hell.

He got up from the breakfast table, feeling strangely unhappy and weighed down with guilt. Yet, as he looked at the painter's worn face and hollow eyes, his heart murmured, perhaps deceitfully, "You are justified."

"I must go out. I must go into the village," he said.

"In this weather?"

"We islanders think nothing of it. We pursue our business though the heavens crack and the sea touches the clouds."

He went out hurriedly and with the air of a man painfully abashed. Once beyond the churchyard, in the plough-land of the island road, he continued his tormented reverie of the night. Never before had he done evil that good might come. He had never supposed that good could come out of evil, but had deemed the supposition a monstrous and a deadly fallacy, to be combated, to be struck down to the dust. Even now he was chiefly conscious of a mental weakness in himself which had caused him to act as he had acted. He saw himself as one of those puny creatures whose so-called kind hearts lead them into follies, into crimes. Like many young men of virtuous life and ascetic habit, Uniacke was disposed to worship that which was uncompromising in human nature, the slight hardness which sometimes lurks, like a kernel, in the saint. But he was emotional. He was full of pity. He desired to bandage the wounded world, to hush its cries of pain, to rock it to rest, even though he believed that suffering was its desert. And to the individual, more especially, he was very tender. Like a foolish woman, perhaps, he told himself to-day as he walked on heavily in the wild wind, debating his deed of the night and its consequences.

He had erased the name of Pringle from the stone that covered little Jack, the wonder-child. And he felt like a criminal. Yet he dreaded the sequel of a discovery by the painter, that his fears were well founded, that his sea urchin had indeed been claimed by the hunger of the sea. Uniacke had worked in cities and had seen much of sad men. He had learnt to read them truly for the most part, and to foresee clearly in many instances the end of their journeys. And his ministrations had taught him to comprehend the tragedies that arise from the terrible intimacy which exists between the body and its occupant the soul. He could not tell, as a doctor might have been able to tell, whether the morbid condition into which Sir Graham had come was primarily due to ill-health of the mind acting upon the body or the reverse. But he felt nearly sure that if the painter's fears were proved suddenly to him to be well founded, he might not improbably fall into a condition of permanent melancholia, or even of active despair. Despite his apparent hopelessness, he was at present sustained by ignorance of the fate of little Jack. He did not actually know him dead. The knowledge would knock a prop from under him. He would fall into some dreadful abyss. The young clergyman's deceit alone held him back. But it might be discovered at any moment. One of the islanders might chance to observe the defacement of the tomb. A gossiping woman might mention to Sir Graham the name that had vanished. Yet these chances were remote. A drowned stranger boy is naught to such folk as these, bred up in familiarity with violent death. Long ago they had ceased to talk of the schooner *Flying Fish,* despite the presence of the mad Skipper, despite the sound of church bells in the night. Fresh joys, or tragedies, absorbed them. For even the island world has its record. Time plants his footsteps upon the loneliest land. And the dwellers note his onward tour.

Uniacke reckoned the chances for and against the discovery of his furtive act of mercy and its revelation to his guest. The latter outnumbered the former. Yet Uniacke walked nervously as one on the verge of disaster. In the Island cottages that morning he bore himself uneasily in the presence of his simple-minded parishioners. Sitting beside an invalid, whose transparent mind was dimly, but with ardent faith, set on Heaven, he felt hideously unfitted to point the way to that place into which no liar shall ever come. He was troubled, and prayed at random for the dying—thinking of the dead. At the same time he felt himself the chief of sinners and knew that there was a devil in him capable of repeating his nocturnal act. Never before had he gathered so vital a knowledge of the complexity of man. He saw the threads of him all ravelled up. When he finished his prayers at the bedside, the invalid watched him with the critical amazement of illness.

He went out trembling and conscience-stricken. When he reached the churchyard on his way homewards, he saw Sir Graham moving among the graves. He had apparently just come out from the Rectory and was making his way to the low stone wall, over which shreds of foam were being blown by the wind. Uniacke hastened his steps, and hailed Sir Graham in a loud and harsh voice. He paused, and shading his eyes with his arched hands, gazed towards the road.

Uniacke hurried through the narrow gate and joined his guest, who looked like a man startled out of some heavy reverie.

"Oh, it is you," he said. "Well, I—"

"You were going to watch the sea, I know. It is worth watching to-day. Come with me. I'll take you to the point—to the nigger."

"The nigger?"

"The fishermen call the great black rock at the north end of the Island by that name. The sea must be breaking magnificently."

Uniacke took Sir Graham's arm and led him away, compelling him almost as if he were a child. They left the churchyard behind them, and were soon in solitary country alone with the roar of wind and sea. Branching presently from the road they came into a narrow, scarcely perceptible, track, winding downward over short grass drenched with moisture. The dull sheep scattered slowly from them on either side of the way. Presently the grass ceased at the edge of an immense blunt rock, like a disfigured head, that contemplated fixedly the white turmoil of the sea.

"A place for shipwreck," said Sir Graham. "A place of death."

Uniacke nodded. The painter swept an arm towards the sea.

"What a graveyard! One would say the time had come for it to give up its dead and it was passionately fighting against the immutable decree. Is Jack somewhere out there?"

He turned and fixed his eyes upon Uniacke's face. Uniacke's eyes fell.

"Is he?" repeated Sir Graham.

"How can I tell?" exclaimed Uniacke, almost with a sudden anger. "Let us go back."

Towards evening the storm suddenly abated. A pale yellow light broke along the horizon, almost as the primroses break out along the horizon of winter. The thin black spars of a hurrying vessel pointed to the illumination and vanished, leaving the memory of a tortured gesture from some sea-thing. And as the yellow deepened to gold, the Skipper set the church bells ringing. Sir Graham opened the parlour window wide and listened, leaning out towards the graves. Uniacke was behind him in the room. Vapour streamed up from the buffeted earth, which seemed panting for a repose it had no strength to gain. Ding dong! Ding dong! The wild and far-away light grew to flame and faded to darkness. In the darkness the bells seemed clearer, for light deafens the imagination. Uniacke felt a strange irritability coming upon him. He moved uneasily in his chair, watching the motionless, stretched figure of his guest. Presently he said:

"Sir Graham!"

There was no reply.

"Sir Graham!"

He got up, crossed the little room and touched the shoulder of the dreamer. Sir Graham started sharply and turned a frowning face.

"What is it?"

"The atmosphere is very cold and damp after the storm."

"You wish me to shut the window? I beg your pardon."

He drew in and shut it, then moved to the door.

"You are going out?" said Uniacke uneasily.

"Yes."

"I—I would not speak to the Skipper, if I were you. He is happier when he is let quite alone."

"I want to see him. I want him to sit for me."

"To sit!" Uniacke repeated, with an accent almost of horror.

"Yes," said Sir Graham doggedly. "I have a great picture in my mind."

"But—"

"The Skipper's meeting with his drowned comrades, in that belfry tower. He will stand with the ropes dropping from his hands, triumph in his eyes. They will be seen coming up out of the darkness, grey men and dripping from the sea, with dead eyes and hanging lips. And first among them will be my wonder-child, on whom will fall a ray of light from a wild moon, half seen through the narrow slit of the deep-set window."

"No, no!"

"What do you say?"

"Your wonder-child must not be there. Why should he? He is alive."

"You think so?"

Uniacke made no reply.

"I say, do you think so?"

"How can I know? It is impossible. But—yes, I think so."

The clergyman turned away. A sickness of the conscience overtook him like physical pain. Sir Graham was by the door with his hand upon it.

"And yet," he said, "you do not believe in intuitions. Nothing tells you whether that woman you loved is dead or living. You said that."

"Nothing."

"Then what should tell you whether Jack is dead or living?"

He turned and went out. Presently Uniacke saw his dark figure pass, like a shadow, across the square of the window. The night grew more quiet by slow degrees. The hush after the storm increased. And to the young clergyman's unquiet nerves it seemed like a crescendo in music instead of like a diminuendo, as sometimes seems the falling to sleep of a man to a man who cannot sleep. The noise of the storm had been softer than the sound of this increasing silence in which the church bells presently died away. Uniacke was consumed by an apprehension that was almost like the keen tooth of jealousy. For he knew that the Skipper had ceased from his patient task and Sir Graham did not return. He imagined a colloquy. But the Skipper's madness would preserve the secret which he no longer knew, and, therefore, could not reveal. He made the bells call Jack Pringle. He would never point to the defaced grave and say, "Jack Pringle lies beneath this stone." And yet sanity might, perhaps, return, a rush of knowledge of the past and recognition of its tragedy.

Uniacke took his hat and went to the door. He stood out on the step. Seabirds were crying. The sound of the sea withdrew moment by moment, as if it were stealing furtively away. Behind, in the rectory passage, the servant clattered as she brought in the supper.

"Sir Graham!" Uniacke called suddenly. "Sir Graham!"

"Yes."

The voice came from somewhere in the shadow of the church.

"Will you not come in? Supper is ready."

In a moment the painter came out of the gloom.

"That churchyard draws me," he said, mounting the step.

"You saw the Skipper?"

"Yes, leaving."

"Did he speak to you?"

"Not a word."

The clergyman breathed a sigh of relief.

In the evening Uniacke turned his pipe two or three times in his fingers and said, looking down:

"That picture of yours—"

"Yes. What of it?"

"You will paint it in London, I suppose?"

"How can I do that? The imagination of it came to me here, is sustained and quickened by these surroundings."

"You mean to paint it here?" the clergyman faltered.

Sir Graham was evidently struck by his host's air of painful discomfiture.

"I beg your pardon," he said hastily. "Of course I do not mean to inflict myself upon your kind hospitality while I am working. I shall return to the inn."

Uniacke flushed red at being so misunderstood.

"I cannot let you do that. No, no! Honestly, my question was only prompted by—by—a thought—"

"Yes?"

"Do not think me impertinent. But, really, a regard for you has grown up in me since you have allowed me to know you—a great regard indeed."

"Thank you, thank you, Uniacke," said the painter, obviously moved.

"And it has struck me that in your present condition of health, and seeing that your mind is pursued by these—these melancholy sea thoughts and imaginings, it might be safer, better for you to be in a place less desolate, less preyed upon by the sea. That is all. Believe me, that is all."

He spoke the last words with the peculiar insistence and almost declamatory fervour of the liar. But he was now embarked upon deceit and must crowd all sail. And with the utterance of his lie he took an abrupt resolution.

"Let us go away together somewhere," he exclaimed, with a brightening face. "I need a holiday. I will get a brother clergyman to come over from the mainland and take my services. You asked me some day to return your visit. I accept your invitation here and now. Let me come with you to London."

Sir Graham shook his head.

"You put me in the position of an inhospitable man," he said. "In the future you must come to me. I look forward to that. I depend upon it. But I cannot go to London at present. My house, my studio are become loathsome to me. The very street in which I live echoes with childish footsteps. I cannot be there."

"Sir Graham, you must learn to look upon your past act in a different light. If you do not, your power of usefulness in the world will be crushed."

The clergyman spoke with an intense earnestness. His sense of his own increasing unworthiness, the fighting sense of the necessity laid upon him to be unworthy for this sick man's sake, tormented him, set his heart in a sea of trouble. He strove to escape out of it by mental exertion. His eyes shone with unnatural fervour as he went on:

"When you first told me your story, I thought this thing weighed upon you unnecessarily. Now I see more and more clearly that your unnatural misery over a very natural act springs from ill-health. It is your body which you confuse with your conscience. Your remorse is a disease removable by medicine, by a particular kind of air or scene, by waters even it may be, or by hard exercise, or by a voyage."

"A voyage!" cried Sir Graham bitterly.

"Well, well—by such means, I would say, as come to a doctor's mind. You labour under the yoke of the body."

"Do you think that whenever your conscience says, 'You have done wrong'? Tell me!"

Uniacke, who had got up in his excitement, recoiled at these words which struck him hard.

"I—I!" he almost stammered. "What have I got to do with it?"

"I ask you to judge yourself, to put yourself in my place. That is all. Do you tell me that all workings of conscience are due to obscure bodily causes?"

"How could I? No, but yours—"

"Are not. They hurt my body. They do not come from my body's hurt. And they increase upon me in this place, yes, they increase upon me."

"I knew it," cried Uniacke.

"Why is that?" said Sir Graham, with a melancholy accent. "I feel, I begin to feel that there must be some powerful reason—yes, in this island."

"There cannot be. Leave it! Leave it!"

"I am held here."

"By what?"

"Something intangible, invisible—"

"Nothing, then."

"All-powerful. I cannot go. If I would go, I cannot. Perhaps—perhaps Jack is coming here."

The painter's eyes were blazing. Uniacke felt himself turn cold.

"Jack coming here!" he said harshly. "Nonsense, Sir Graham. Nobody ever comes here."

"Dead bodies come on the breast of the sea."

The painter looked towards the window, putting himself into an attitude of horrible expectation.

"Is it not so?" he asked, in a voice that quivered slightly as if with an agitation he was trying to suppress.

Uniacke made no reply. He was seized with a horror he had not known before. He recognised that the island influence mysteriously held his guest. After an interval he said abruptly:

"What is your doctor's name, did you say?"

"Did I ever say whom I had consulted?" said Sir Graham, almost with an invalid's ready suspicion, and peering at the clergyman under his thick eyebrows.

"Surely. But I forget things so easily," said Uniacke calmly.

"Braybrooke is the man—Cavendish Square. An interesting fellow. You may have heard of his book on the use of colour as a sort of physic in certain forms of illness."

"I have. What sort of man is he?"

"Very small, very grey, very indecisive in manner."

"Indecisive?"

"In manner. In reality a man of infinite conviction."

"May I ask if you told him your story?"

"The story of my body—naturally. One goes to a doctor to do that."

"And did that narrative satisfy him?"

"Not at all. Not a bit."

"Well—and so?"

"I did not tell him my mental story. I explained to him that I suffered greatly from melancholy. That was all. I called it unreasoning melancholy. Why not? I knew he could do no more than put my body a little straight. He did his best."

"I see," said Uniacke, slowly.

That night, after Sir Graham had gone to bed, Uniacke came to a resolution. He decided to write to Doctor Braybrooke, betray, for his guest's sake, his guest's confidence, and ask the great man's advice in the matter, revealing to him the strange fact that fate had led the painter of the sea urchin to the very edge of the grave in which he slept so quietly. No longer did Uniacke hesitate, or pause to ask himself why he permitted the sorrow of a stranger thus to control, to upset, his life. And, indeed, is the man who tells us his sorrow a stranger to us? Uniacke's creed taught him to be unselfish, taught him to concern himself in the afflictions of others. Already he had sinned, he had lied for this stricken man. He, a clergyman, had gone out in the night and had defaced a grave. All this lay heavy on his heart. His conscience smote him. And yet, when he saw before him in the night the vision of this tortured man, he knew that he would repeat his sin if necessary.

The next day was Sunday. He sat down and tried to think of the two sermons he had to preach. The sea lay very still on the Sabbath morning, still under a smooth and pathetic grey sky. The atmosphere seemed that of a winter fairyland. All the seabirds were in hiding. Small waves licked the land like furtive tongues seeking some dainty food with sly desire. Across the short seagrass the island children wound from school to church, and the island lads gathered in knots to say nothing. The whistling of a naughty fisherman attending to his nets unsabbatically pierced the still and magically cruel air with a painful sharpness. People walked in silence without knowing why they did not care to speak. And even the girls, discreet in ribbons and shining boots, thought less of kisses than they generally did on Sunday. The older people, sober by temperament, became sombre under the influence of sad, breathless sky, and breathless waters. The coldness that lay in the bosom of nature soon found its way to the responsive bosom of humanity. It chilled Uniacke in the pulpit, Sir Graham in the pew below. The one preached without heart. The other listened without emotion. All this was in the morning. But at evening nature stirred in her repose and turned, with the abruptness of a born coquette, to pageantry. A light wind got up. The waves were curved and threw up thin showers of ivory spray playfully along the rocks. The sense of fairyland, wrapped in ethereal silences, quivered and broke like disturbed water. And the grey womb of the sky swelled in the west to give up a sunset that became tragic in its crescendo of glory. Bursting forth in flame—a narrow line of fire along the sea—it pushed its way slowly up the sky. Against the tattered clouds a hidden host thrust forth their spears of gold. And a wild-rose colour descended upon the gentle sea and floated to the island, bathing the rocks, the grim and weather-beaten houses, the stones of the churchyard, with a radiance so delicate, and yet so elfish, that enchantment walked there till the night came down, and in the darkness the islanders moved on their way to church. The pageant was over. But it had stirred two imaginations. It blazed yet in two hearts. The shock of its coming, after long hours of storm, had stirred Uniacke and his guest strangely. And the former, leaving in the rectory parlour the sermon he had composed, preached extempore on the text, "In the evening there shall be light."

He began radiantly and with fervour. But some spirit of contradiction entered his soul as he spoke, impelling him to a more sombre mood that was yet never cold, but rather impassioned full of imaginative despair. He was driven on to discourse of the men who will not see light, of the men who draw thick blinds to shut out light. And then he was led, by the egoism that so subtly guides even the best among men, to speak of those fools who, by fostering darkness, think to compel sunshine, as a man may mix dangerous chemicals in a laboratory, seeking to advance some cause of science and die in the poisonous fumes of his own devilish brew. Can good, impulsive and radiant, come out of deliberate evil? Must not a man care first for his own soul if he would heal the soul of even one other? Uniacke spoke with a strange and powerful despair on this subject. He ended in a profound sadness and with the words of one scourged by doubts.

There was a pause, the shuffle of moving feet. Then the voice of the clerk announced the closing hymn. It was "Lead, Kindly Light," chosen by the harmonium player and submitted to Uniacke, who, however, had failed to notice that it was included in the list of hymns for the day. The clerk's voice struck on him like a blow. He stared down from the pulpit and met the upward gaze of his guest. Then he laid his cold hands on the wooden ledge of the pulpit and turned away his eyes. For he felt as if Sir Graham must understand the secret that lay in them. The islanders sang the hymn lustily, bending their heads over their books beneath the dull oil lamps that filled the church with a dingy yellow twilight. Alone, at the back of the building, the mad Skipper stood up by the belfry door and stared straight before him as if he watched. And Uniacke's trouble increased, seeming to walk in the familiar music which had been whistled by Jack Pringle as he swarmed to the masthead, or turned into his bunk at night far out at sea. Sir Graham had spoken of intuitions. Surely, the clergyman thought, to-night he will feel the truth and my lie. To-night he will understand that it is useless to wait, that the wonder-child can never come to this island, for he came on the breast of the sea long ago. And if he does know, now, at this moment, while the islanders are singing,

"And with the morn those angel faces smile—"

how will he regard me, who have lied to him and who have preached to him, coward and hypocrite? For still the egoism was in Uniacke's heart. There is no greater egoist than the good man who has sinned against his nature. He sits down eternally to contemplate his own soul. When the hymn was over Uniacke mechanically gave the blessing and knelt down. But he did not pray. His mind stood quite still all the time he was on his knees. He got up wearily, and as he made his way into the little vestry, he fancied that he heard behind him a sound as of someone tramping in sea-boots upon the rough church pavement. He looked round and saw the bland face of the clerk, who wore perpetually a little smile, like that of a successful public entertainer. That evening he wrote to Doctor Braybrooke.

On the morrow Sir Graham began the first sketch for his picture, "*The Procession of the Drowned to their faithful Captain.*"

Three mornings later, when Uniacke came to the breakfast table, Sir Graham, who was down before him, handed to him a letter, the envelope of which was half torn open.

"It was put among mine," he said in apology, "and as the handwriting was perfectly familiar to me, I began to open it."

"Familiar?" said Uniacke, taking the letter.

"Yes. It bears an exact resemblance to Doctor Braybrooke's writing."

"Oh!" said Uniacke, laying the letter aside rather hastily.

They sat down on either side of the table.

"You don't read your letter," Sir Graham said, after two or three minutes had passed.

"After breakfast. I don't suppose it is anything important," said the clergyman hastily.

Sir Graham said nothing more, but drank his coffee and soon afterwards went off to his work. Then Uniacke opened the letter.

"Cavendish Square,
London, Dec.—

"Dear Sir:

"I read your letter about my former patient, Sir Graham Hamilton, with great interest. When he consulted me I was fully aware that he was concealing from me some mental trouble, which reacted upon his bodily condition and tended to retard his complete recovery of health. However, a doctor cannot force the confidence of a patient even in that patient's own interest, and I was, therefore, compelled to work in the dark, and to work without satisfaction to myself and lasting benefit to Sir Graham. You now let in a strange light upon the case, and I have little doubt what course would be the best to pursue in regard to the future. Sir Graham's nervous system has broken down so completely that, as often happens in nervous cases, his very nature seems to have changed. The energy, the remarkable self-confidence, the hopefulness and power of looking forward, and of working for the future, which have placed him where he is—these have vanished. He is possessed by a fixed idea, and imagines that it is this fixed idea which has preyed upon him and broken him down. But my knowledge of nerve-complaints teaches me that the fixed idea follows on the weakening of the nervous system, and seldom or never precedes it. I find it is an effect and not a cause. But it is a fact that the fixed idea which possesses a man under such circumstances is often connected, and closely, with the actual cause of his illness. Sir Graham Hamilton is suffering from long and habitual overwork in connection with the sea; overwork of the imagination, of the perceptive faculty, and in the mere mechanical labour of putting on canvas what he imagines and what he perceives. In consequence of this overstrain and subsequent breakdown, he has become possessed by a fixed sea-idea, and traces all his wretchedness to this episode of the boy and the picture. You will say I did not succeed in curing him because I did not discover what this fixed idea was. How can that be, if the idea comes from the illness and not the illness from the idea. In reply I must inform you that a tragic idea, once it is fixed in the mind of a man, can, and often does, become in itself at last a more remote, but effective, cause of the prolonged continuance of the ill-health already started by some other agent. It keeps the wound, which it has not made, open. It is most important, therefore, that it should, if possible, be banished, in the case of Sir Graham as in other cases. Your amiable deception has quite possibly averted a tragedy. *Continue in it, I counsel you.* The knowledge that his fears are well founded, that the boy—for whose fate he morbidly considers himself entirely responsible—has in very truth been lost at sea, and lies buried in the ground beneath his feet, might, in his present condition of invalidism, be attended by most evil results. Someday it is quite possible that he may be able to learn all the facts with equanimity. But this can only be later when long rest and change have accomplished their beneficent work. It cannot certainly be now. Endeavour, therefore, to dissuade him from any sort of creative labour. Endeavour to persuade him to leave the island. Above all things, do not let him know the truth. It is a sad thing that a strong man of genius should be brought so low that he has to be treated with precautions almost suitable to a child. But to a doctor there are many more children in the world than a statistician might be able to number. I wish I could take a holiday and come to your assistance. Unfortunately, my duties tie me closely to town at the present. And, in any case, my presence might merely irritate and alarm our friend.

"Believe me,

Faithfully yours,
John Braybrooke."

Uniacke read this letter, and laid it down with a strange mingled feeling of relief and apprehension. The relief was a salve that touched his wounded conscience gently. If he had sinned, at least this physician's letter told him that by his sin he had accomplished something beneficent. And for the moment self-condemnation ceased to scourge him. The apprehension that quickly beset him rose from the knowledge that Sir Graham was in danger so long as he was in the Island. But how could he be persuaded to leave it? That was the problem.

Uniacke's reverie over the letter was interrupted by the appearance of the painter. As he came into the room, the clergyman rather awkwardly thrust the doctor's letter into his pocket and turned to his guest.

"In already, Sir Graham?" he said, with a strained attempt at ease of manner. "Ah! work tires you. Indeed you should take a long holiday."

He spoke, thinking of the doctor's words.

"I have not started work," the painter said. "I've—I've been looking at that grave by the church wall—the boy's grave."

"Oh!" said Uniacke, with sudden coldness.

"Do you know, Uniacke, it seems—it seems to me that the gravestone has been defaced."

"Defaced! Why, what could make such an idea come to you?" exclaimed the clergyman. "Defaced! But—"

"There is a gap in the inscription after the word 'Jack,'" the painter said slowly, fixing a piercing and morose glance on his companion. "And it seems to me that some blunt instrument has been at work there."

"Oh, there was always a gap there," said Uniacke hastily, touching the letter that lay in his pocket, and feeling, strangely, as if the contact fortified that staggering pilgrim on the path of lies—his conscience. "There was always a gap. It was a whim of the Skipper's—a mad whim."

"But I understood he was sane when his shipmate was buried? You said so."

"Sane? Yes, in comparison with what he is now. But one could not argue with him. He was distraught with grief."

Sir Graham looked at Uniacke with the heavy suspicion of a sick man, but he said nothing more on the subject. He turned as if to go out. Uniacke stopped him.

"You are going to paint?"

"Yes."

Again Uniacke thought of the doctor's advice.

"Sir Graham," he said, speaking with obvious hesitation, "I—I would not work."

"Why?"

"You are not fit to bear any fatigue at present. Creation will inevitably retard your recovery."

"I am not ill in body, and work is the only panacea for a burdened mind. If it cannot bring me happiness, at least—"

"Happiness!" Uniacke interrupted. "And what may not bring that! Why, Sir Graham, even death—should that be regarded as a curse? May not death bring the greatest happiness of all?"

The painter's forehead contracted, but the clergyman continued with gathering eagerness and fervour:

"Often when I pray beside a little dead child, or—or a young lad, and hear the mother weeping, I feel more keenly than at any other time the fact that blessings descend upon the earth. The child is taken in innocence. The lad is bereft of the power to sin. And their souls are surely at peace."

"At peace," said the painter heavily. "Yes, that is something. But the mother—the mother weeps, you say."

"Human love, the most beautiful thing in the world must still be earth-bound, must still be selfish."

"But—"

"Sir Graham, I'll confess to you even this, that on Sunday evening, when, after the service, we sang that hymn, 'Lead, Kindly Light,' I thought would it not be a very beautiful thing if the body mouldering beneath that stone in the churchyard yonder were indeed the body of— of your wonder-child."

"Uniacke!"

"Yes, yes. Don't you remember how he looked up from his sordid misery to the rainbow?"

"How can I ever forget it?"

"Does that teach you nothing?"

There was a silence. Then the painter said:

"Death may be beautiful, but only after life has been beautiful. For it is beautiful to live as Jack would have lived."

"Is living—somewhere," interposed Uniacke quickly.

"Perhaps. I can't tell. But I hear the mother weeping. I hear the mother weeping."

That night Uniacke lay long awake. He heard the sea faintly. Was it not weeping too? It seemed to him in that dark hour as if one power alone was common to all people and to all things—the power to mourn.

Next day, despite Uniacke's renewed protests, Sir Graham began to paint steadily. The clergyman dared not object too strongly. He had no right. And brain-sick men are bad to deal with. He could only watch over Sir Graham craftily and be with him as much as possible, always hoping that the painting frenzy would desert him, and that he would find out for himself that his health was too poor to endure any strain of labour.

The moon was now past its second quarter, and the weather continued cold and clear. Sir Graham and Uniacke went out several times by night to the belfry of the church, and the painter observed the light effects through the narrow window. In the daytime he made various studies from memory of these effects. And presently Uniacke began to grow more reconciled to this labour of which—prompted by the doctor's letter—he had at first been so much afraid. For it really seemed that toil could be a tonic to this man as to many other men. Sir Graham spoke less of little Jack. He was devoured by the fever of creation. In the evenings he mused on his picture, puffing at his pipe. He no longer continually displayed his morbid sorrow, or sought to discuss at length the powers of despair. Uniacke was beginning to feel happier about him, even to doubt the doctor's wisdom in denouncing work as a danger, when something happened which filled him with a vague apprehension.

The mad Skipper, whom nothing attracted, wandering vacantly, according to his sad custom, about the graveyard and in the church, one day ascended to the belfry, in which Sir Graham sat at work on a study for the background of his picture. Uniacke was with his friend at the time, and heard the Skipper's heavy and stumbling footsteps ascending the narrow stone stairs.

"Who's that coming?" the painter asked.

"The Skipper," Uniacke answered, almost under his breath.

In another minute the huge seaman appeared, clad as usual in jersey and peaked cap, his large blue eyes full of an animal expression of vacant plaintiveness and staring lack of thought. He showed no astonishment at finding intruders established in his domain, and for a moment Uniacke thought he would quietly turn about and make his way down again. For, after a short pause, he half swung round, still keeping his eyes vaguely fixed on the artist, who continued to paint as if quite alone. But apparently some chord of curiosity had been struck in this poor and benumbed mind. For the big man wavered, then stole rather furtively forward, and fixed his sea-blue eyes on the canvas, upon which appeared the rough wall of the belfry, the narrow window, with a section of wild sky in which a weary moon gleamed faintly, and the dark arch of the stairway up which the drowned mariners would come to their faithful captain. The Skipper stared at all this inexpressively, turned to move away, paused, waited. Sir Graham went on painting; and the Skipper stayed. He made no sound. Uniacke could scarcely hear him breathing. He seemed wrapped in dull and wide-eyed contemplation. Only when at last Sir Graham paused, did he move away slowly down the stairs with his loose-limbed, shuffling gait, which expressed so plainly the illness of his mind.

In the rectory parlour, a few minutes later, Uniacke and Sir Graham discussed this apparently trifling incident. A feeling of unreasonable alarm besieged Uniacke's soul, but he strove to fight against and to expel it.

"How quietly he stood," said the painter. "He seemed strangely interested."

"Yes, strangely. And yet his eyes were quite vague and dull. I noticed that."

"For all that, Uniacke, his mind may be waking from its sleep."

"Waking from its sleep!" said Uniacke, with a sudden sharpness. "No— impossible!"

"One would almost think you desired that it should not," rejoined Sir Graham, with obvious surprise.

Uniacke saw that he had been foolishly unguarded.

"Oh, no," he said, more quietly, "I only fear that the poor fellow can never recover."

"Why not? From what feeling, from what root of intelligence does his interest in my work spring? May it not be that he vaguely feels as if my picture were connected with his sorrow?"

Uniacke shook his head.

"I am not sure that it is impossible," continued Sir Graham. "Tomorrow I begin to make studies for the figures. If he comes to me again, I shall sketch him in."

Uniacke's uneasiness increased. Something within him revolted from the association of his guest and the Skipper. The hidden link between them was a tragedy, a tragedy that had wrecked the reason of the one, the peace of the other. They did not know of this link, yet there seemed horror in such a companionship as theirs, and the clergyman was seized with fear.

"You are going to draw your figures from models?" he said, slowly, speaking to cover his anxiety, and speaking idly enough.

The painter's reply struck away his uncertainty, and set him face to face with a most definite dread.

"I shall have models," said Sir Graham, "for all the figures except for little Jack. I can draw him from memory. I can reproduce his face. It never leaves me."

"What!" said Uniacke. "You will paint an exactly truthful portrait of him then?"

"I shall; only idealised by death, dignified, weird, washed by the sad sea."

"The Skipper watched you while you were painting. He saw all you were doing."

"Yes. And I think he'll come again."

"But then—he'll—he'll see—"

The clergyman stopped short.

"See—see what?" Sir Graham asked.

"Himself," Uniacke replied, evasively. "When you paint him with the ropes dropping from his hands. May it not agitate, upset him, to see himself as he stands ringing those bells each night? Ah! there they are!"

It was twilight now, cold, and yellow, and grim; twilight of winter. And the pathetic, cheerless appeal of the two bells stole out over the darkening sea.

"Perhaps it may agitate him," Sir Graham said. "What then? To strike a sharp blow on the gates of his mind might be to do him a good service. A shock expelled his reason. Might not a shock recall it?"

"I can't tell," Uniacke said. "Such an experiment might be dangerous, it seems to me, very dangerous."

"Dangerous?"

Uniacke turned away rather abruptly. He could not tell the painter what was in his mind, his fear that the mad Skipper might recognise the painted face of the dead boy, for whom he waited, for whom, even at that moment, the bells were ringing. And if the Skipper did recognise this face that he knew so well—what then? What would be the sequel? Uniacke thought of the doctor's letter. He felt as if a net were closing round him, as if there could be no escape from some tragic finale. And he felt too, painfully, as if a tragic finale were all that he—he, clergyman, liar, trickster—deserved. His conscience, in presence of a shadow, woke again, and found a voice, and told him that evil could not prevail for good, that a lie could not twist the course of things from paths of sorrow to paths of joy. Did not each lie call aloud to danger, saying, "Approach! approach!" Did not each subterfuge stretch out arms beckoning on some nameless end? He seemed to hear soft footsteps. He was horribly afraid and wished that, in the beginning of his acquaintance with Sir Graham, he had dared consequence and spoken truth. Now he felt like a man feebly fighting that conqueror, the Inevitable, and he went in fear. Yet he struggled still.

"Sir Graham," he said, on the following day, "forgive me, but I feel it my duty to urge you not to let that poor fellow watch you at work. It is not safe. I do not think it is safe. I have a strong feeling that—that the shock of seeing—"

"Himself?"

"Exactly! —might be dangerous."

"To him?"

"Or to you. That is my feeling. Possibly to you. He is not sane, and though he seems harmless enough—"

"I'm fully prepared to take the risk," said Sir Graham abruptly, and with a return of his old suspicious expression. "I'm not afraid of the man."

He got up and went out. The mere thought of danger, in his condition, warmed and excited him. He had resolved before actually starting upon his picture to make some *plein air* studies of the islanders. Therefore he now made his way into the village, engaged a fisher-lad to stand to him, returned to the rectory for his easel and set it up just beyond the churchyard wall. He posed the shamefaced and giggling boy and set to work. Uniacke was writing in the small bow window, or pretending to write. Often he looked out, watching the painter, waiting, with a keen anxiety, to know whether the interest shown in his work by the Skipper was only the passing whim of insanity, or whether it was something more permanent, more threatening perhaps.

The painter worked. The sailor posed, distending his rough cheeks with self-conscious laughter. Uniacke watched. It seemed that the Skipper was not coming. Uniacke felt a sense of relief. He got up from his writing table at last, intending to go into the village. As he did so, the tall form of the Skipper came into view in the distance. Dark, bulky, as yet far off, it shambled forward slowly, hesitatingly, over the short grass towards the painter. While Uniacke observed it, he thought it looked definitely animal. It approached, making detours, like a dog, furtive and intent, that desires to draw near to some object without seeming to do so. Slowly it came, tacking this way and that, pausing frequently as if uncertain or alarmed. And Uniacke, standing in the shadow of the red curtain, watched its movements, fascinated. He did not know why, but he had a sensation that Fate, loose-limbed, big-boned, furtive, was shambling over the grass towards his guest. Sir Graham went on quietly painting. The Skipper made a last detour, got behind the painter, stole up and peered over his shoulder. Once there, he seemed spellbound. For he stood perfectly still and never took his large blue eyes from the canvas. Uniacke went into the little passage, got his hat and hastened out, impelled yet without purpose. As he crossed the churchyard he saw Sir Graham put something into the sailor's hand. The sailor touched his cap awkwardly and rolled off. Uniacke hurried forward.

"You've finished your work?" he said, coming up.

Sir Graham turned and made him a hasty sign to be silent.

"Don't alarm him," he whispered, with a slight gesture towards the Skipper, who stood as if in a vacant reverie, looking at the painted sailor boy.

"But—" Uniacke began.

"Hush!" the painter murmured, almost angrily. "Leave us alone together."

The clergyman moved away with a sinking heart. Indefinable dread seized him. The association between these two men was fraught with unknown peril. He felt that, and so strongly, that he was almost tempted to defy convention and violently interfere to put an end to it. But he restrained himself and returned to the rectory, watching the two motionless figures beyond the churchyard wall from the parlour window as from an ambush, with an intensity of expectation that gave him the bodily sensation of a man clothed in mail.

In the late afternoon Sir Graham showed him an admirable study of the Skipper, standing with upraised arms as if ringing the church bells, his blue eyes fixed as if he scanned a distant horizon, or searched the endless plains of the sea for his lost companions.

"Forgive my abruptness this morning," the painter said. "I was afraid your presence would scare the Skipper."

Uniacke murmured a word in admiration of the painting.

"And to-morrow," he added.

"To-morrow I shall start on the picture," Sir Graham replied.

After supper he drew aside the blind and looked forth.

"The moon is rising," he said. "I shall go out for a little while. I want to observe light effects, and to think over what I am going to do. My mind is full of it, Uniacke; I think it should be a great picture."

His eyes were shining with excitement. He went out. He was away a long time. The clock in the rectory parlour struck eleven, half-past eleven, he did not return. Beginning to feel anxious, Uniacke went to the window and looked out. The night was quiet and clear, bathed in the radiance of the moon, which defined objects sharply. The dark figure of the painter was approaching the house from the church. Uniacke, who did not wish to be thought curious, drew hastily back from the window and dropped the blind. In a moment Sir Graham entered. He was extremely pale and looked scared. He shut the door very hastily, almost as if he wished to prevent someone from entering after him. Then he came up to the fire without a word.

"You are late," Uniacke said, unpleasantly affected, but trying to speak indifferently.

"Late, am I? Why—what time is it?"

"Nearly midnight."

"Indeed. I forgot the hour. I was engrossed. I—" He looked up hastily and looked down again. "A most strange, most unaccountable, thing has happened."

"What?" said Uniacke. "Surely the Skipper hasn't—"

"No, no. It's nothing to do with him. I haven't seen him. No, no—but the most unaccountable—how long have I been out there?"

"You went out at nine. It's a quarter to twelve now."

"Two hours and three-quarters! I should have said ten minutes. But then—how long was I with it?"

"With it?" repeated Uniacke, turning cold.

"Yes, yes—how long? It seemed no time—and yet an eternity, too."

He got up and went to and fro uneasily about the room.

"Horrible!" he muttered, as if to himself. "Horrible!"

He stopped suddenly in front of Uniacke.

"Do you believe," he said, "that when we think very steadily and intensely of a thing we may, perhaps, project—give life, as it were, for the moment to our thought?"

"Why do you ask me?" said Uniacke. "It has never happened to me to do such a thing."

"Why do I ask? Well, I'll—"

He hesitated, keeping his eyes fixed on Uniacke's face.

"Yes, I'll tell you what took place. I went out thinking of my picture, of its composition, of the light effect, of the faces of the drowned men, especially of the face of little Jack. I seemed to see him coming into that belfry tower—yes, to greet the Skipper, all dripping from the sea. But—but—no, Uniacke, I'll swear that, in my mind, I saw his face as it used to be. That was natural, wasn't it? I imagined it white, with wide, staring eyes, the skin wet and roughened with the salt water. But that was all. So it couldn't have been my thought projected, because I had never imagined—"

He was evidently engrossed by his own reflections. His eyes had an inward expression. His voice died in a murmur, almost like the murmur of one who babbles in sleep.

"Never had imagined what?" said Uniacke, sharply.

"Oh, forgive me. I cannot understand it. As I paced in the churchyard, thinking of my picture, and watching the moon and the shadows cast by the church and by the stones of the tombs, I came to that grave by the wall."

"The grave of the boy I told you about?" said Uniacke with an elaborate indifference.

"Yes, the boy."

"Well?"

"I suppose I stood there for a few minutes, or it may have been longer. I can't tell at all. I don't think I was even aware that I was no longer walking. I was entirely wrapped up in my meditations, I believe. I saw my picture before me, the Skipper, the dripping sailors—Jack first. I saw them quite distinctly with my mental vision. And then, by degrees, somehow those figures in the picture all faded into darkness, softly, gradually, till only one was left—Jack. He was still there in the picture. The moonlight through the narrow belfry window fell on him. It seemed to make the salt drops sparkle, almost like jewels, in his hair, on his clothes. I looked at him—mentally, still. And, while I looked, the moonlight, I thought, grew stronger. The belfry seemed to fade away. The figure of Jack stood out in the light. It grew larger—larger. It reached the size of life. And then, as I stared upon it, the face altered before my eyes. It became older, less childish, more firm and manly—but oh, Uniacke! a thousand times more horrible."

"How? How?"

"Why, it became puffy, bloated, dropsical. The eyes were glazed and bloodshot. On the lips there was foam. The fingers of the hands were twisted and distorted. The teeth grinned hideously. The romance of death dropped away. The filthy reality of death stood before me, upon the grave of that boy."

"You imagined it," muttered Uniacke.

He spoke without conviction.

"I did not. I saw it. For now I knew that I was no longer thinking of my picture. I looked around me and saw the small clouds and the night, the moon in the pale sky, the black church, this house, the graves like creatures lying side by side asleep. I saw them all. I heard the dull wash of the sea. And then I looked again at that grave, and on it stood Jack, the dead thing I sent to death, bloated and silent, staring upon me. Silent—and yet I seemed to feel that it said, 'This is what I am. Paint me like this. Look at what the sea has done to me! Look—look at what the sea has done!'—Uniacke! Uniacke!"

He sank down into a chair and stared before him with terrible eyes. A shudder ran over the clergyman, but he said, in a voice that he tried to make calm and consolatory,

"Of course it was your fancy, Sir Graham. You had conjured up the figures in your picture. There was nothing unnatural in your seeing one—the one you had known in life—more distinctly than the others."

"I had not known it like that. I had never imagined anything so distorted, so horrible, tragic and yet almost grotesque, a thing for the foolish to—to laugh at, ugh! Besides, it stood there. It was actually there on that grave, as if it had risen out of that grave, Uniacke."

"Your fancy."

Uniacke spoke with no conviction, and his lips were pale.

"I say it is not. The thing—Jack, come to that! —was there. Had you been with me, you must have seen it as I did."

Uniacke shook his head.

"Believe me, Sir Graham," he exclaimed, "you ought to go from here. The everlasting sound of the sea—the presence of the Skipper—your idea for this terrible picture—"

"Terrible! Yes, I see it must be terrible. My conception—how wrong it was! I meant to make death romantic, almost beautiful. And it is like that. To-morrow—to-morrow—ah, Jack! I can paint you now!"

He sprang up and hurried from the room. Uniacke heard him pacing up and down above stairs till far into the night.

The clergyman was deeply and sincerely religious, but he was in nowise a superstitious man. Association with Sir Graham, however, and the circumstances attendant upon that association, had gradually unnerved him. He was now a prey to fear, almost to horror. Was it possible, he thought, as he sat listening to that eternal footfall overhead, that Providence permitted a spirit to rise from the very grave to proclaim his lie, and to show the truth in a most hideous form? He could almost believe so. It seemed that the dead boy resented the defacement of his tomb, resented the deliberate untruth which concealed from the painter his dreary destiny, and came up out of the other world to proclaim the clergyman's deception. It seemed as if God himself fought with a miraculous means the battle of truth and tore aside the veil in which Uniacke had sought to shroud the actuality of death. Uniacke could not bring himself to speak to the painter, to acknowledge the trickery resorted to for a sick man's sake. But this vision of the night paralysed his power to make any further effort in deception. He felt benumbed and impotent. A Power invisible to him fought against him. He could only lay down his weapons—despicable, unworthy, as they were—and let things take their course, while he looked on as one in a sad dream, apprehensive of the ending of that dream.

Sir Graham began his picture on the morrow. His first excitement in the conception of it, which had been almost joyous, was now become feverish and terrible. He was seized by the dreary passion of the gifted man who means to use his gifts to add new and vital horrors to the horrors of life. He no longer felt the pathos, the almost exquisite romance, of his subject. He felt only its tragic, its disgusting terror. While he painted feverishly the mad Skipper hovered about him, with eyes still vacant but a manner of increasing unrest. It seemed as if something whispered to him that this work of a stranger had some connection with his life, some deep, though as yet undiscovered, meaning for him. The first figure in the picture was the Skipper himself. When it was painted the likeness was striking. But the poor mad seaman stared upon it with an ignorant vagueness. It was evident that he looked without seeing, that he observed without comprehending.

"Surely he will not know Jack," Uniacke thought, "since he does not know his own face."

And he felt a faint sense of relief. But this passed away, for the unrest of the Skipper seemed continually to grow more marked and seething. Uniacke noticed it with gathering anxiety. Sir Graham did not observe it. He thought of nothing but his work.

"I shall paint Jack last of all," he said grimly, to Uniacke. "I mean to make a crescendo of horror, and in Jack's figure the loathsomeness of death shall reach a climax. Yes, I will paint him last of all. Perhaps he will come again and pose for me upon that grave." And he laughed as he sat before his easel.

"What painter ever before had such a model?" he said to Uniacke.

And that night after supper, he got up from the table saying:

"I must go and see if Jack will give me a sitting to-night."

Uniacke rose also.

"Let me come with you," he said.

Sir Graham stopped with his hand on the door. There was a smile on his lips, but his eyes were full of foreboding.

"Do you want to see Jack, then?" he asked, with a dreadful feigning of jocularity. "But you are not a painter. You require no model, living or dead." He burst again into a laugh.

"Let me come with you," the clergyman repeated doggedly.

Sir Graham made no objection, and they went out together.

The moon was now growing towards the full, but it was yet low in the sky, and the night was but faintly lit, as a room is lit by a heavily shaded lamp. Sir Graham's manner lost its almost piteous bluster as he stood on the doorstep and felt the cold wind that blew from the wintry sea. He set his lips, and his face twitched with nervous agitation as he stole a furtive glance at the clergyman, whose soft hat was pulled down low over his eyes as if to conceal their expression.

The two men walked forward slowly into the churchyard. Uniacke's heart was beating with violence and his mind was full of acute anticipation. Yet he would scarcely acknowledge even to himself the possibility of such an appearance as that affirmed by Sir Graham. They drew near to the grave of little Jack, round which the chill winds of night blew gently and the dull voices of the waves sang hushed and murmurous nocturnes. Uniacke was taken by an almost insurmountable inclination to pause, even to turn back. Their progress to this grave seemed attended by some hidden and ghastly danger. He laid his hand upon the painter's arm, as if to withhold him from further advance.

"What is it?" Sir Graham asked, speaking almost in a whisper.

"Nothing," said Uniacke, dropping his hand.

Sir Graham's eyes were full of sombre questioning as they met his. Moving slowly on, the two men stood at length by Jack's grave. The moon rose languidly, and shed a curious and ethereal twilight upon the stone at its head. The blurred place from which Uniacke had struck the name was plainly visible. Instinctively the clergyman's eyes sought the spot and stared upon it.

"Does it not bear all the appearance of having been defaced?" said Sir Graham in his ear.

Uniacke shook his head.

"The Skipper would have it so," he murmured, full of a heavy sense of useless contest against the determination of something hidden that all should be known to his companion, perhaps even that very night. They waited, as mourners wait beside a tomb. As the moon rose, the churchyard grew more distinct. The surrounding graves came into view, the crude bulk of the rectory, the outline of the church tower, and the long wall of the churchyard. On the white faces of the two men the light fell pitilessly, revealing the strained and anxious expression of Uniacke, the staring watchfulness of the painter. The minutes ran by. Uniacke shivered slightly in the wind. By degrees he began to lose the expectation of seeing any apparition. Presently he even sneered silently at himself for his folly in having ever entertained it. Nevertheless he was strongly affected by the nearness of the wonder-child's grave, from which seemed to emanate an influence definite and searching, and— so he felt—increasingly hostile, either to himself or to the artist. It came up like a thing that threatened. It crept near like a thing that would destroy. Uniacke wondered whether Sir Graham was conscious of it. But the painter said nothing, and the clergyman dared not ask him. At length, however, his fanciful sense of this dead power, speaking as it were from the ground under his feet, became so intolerable to him that he was resolved to go; and he was about to tell Sir Graham of his intention when the painter suddenly caught his arm in a tight grip.

"There it is," he whispered.

He was staring before him over the grave. Uniacke followed his eyes. He saw the short grass stirring faintly in the night wind. He thought it looked like hair bristling, and his hair moved on his head. He saw the churchyard in a maze of moon-rays. And with the moonlight had come many shadows. But not one of them was deceptive. Not one took the form of any spectre. Nevertheless Uniacke recoiled from this little grave at his feet, for it seemed to him as if the power that had been sleeping there stirred, forsook its recumbent position, rose up warily, intent on coming forth to confront him.

"You see it?" whispered Sir Graham, still keeping hold of his arm.

"No, no I see nothing; there is nothing. It's your fancy, your imagination that plays tricks on you."

"No, it's Jack. Oh, Uniacke, see—see how he poses! He knows that I shall paint him to-morrow. How horrible he is! Do the drowned always look like that?"

"Come away, Sir Graham. This is a hideous hallucination. Come away."

"How he is altered. All his features are coarsened, bloated. My wonder-child! He is tragic now, and he is disgusting. How loathsomely he twists his fingers! Must I paint him like that—with that grinning, ghastly mouth—little Jack? Ah! ah! He poses—he poses always. He would have me paint him now—here in the moonlight—here—here—standing on this grave!"

"Sir Graham, come with me!" exclaimed Uniacke.

And this time he forcibly drew his companion with him from the grave. The painter seemed inclined to resist for a moment. He turned his head and looked long and eagerly behind him. Then suddenly he acquiesced.

"It has gone," he said. "You have driven it away."

Uniacke hurried forward to the Rectory. That night he implored the painter for the last time to leave the island.

"Can't you feel," he said, almost passionately, "the danger you are running here, the terrible danger to yourself? The sea preys upon your mind. You ought not to be near it. Every murmur of the waves is suggestive to your ears. The voices of those bells recall to your mind the drowning of men. The sigh of that poor maniac depresses you perpetually. Leave the sea. Try to forget it. I tell you, Sir Graham, that your mind is becoming actually diseased from incessant brooding. It begins even to trick your eyes in this abominable way."

"You swear you saw nothing?"

"I do. There was nothing. You have thought of that boy until you actually see him before you."

"As he is?"

"As he is not, as he will never be."

The painter got up from his chair, came over to Uniacke, and looked piercingly into his eyes.

"Then you declare—on your honour as a priest," he said slowly, "that you do not know that my wonder-child is the boy who is buried beneath that stone?"

"I buried that boy, and I declare on my honour as a priest that I do not know it," Uniacke answered, desperately but unflinchingly.

It was his last throw for this man's salvation.

"I believe you," the painter said.

He returned to the fireplace, and leaned his face on his arm against the mantelpiece.

"I believe you," he repeated presently. "I have been mistaken."

"Mistaken—how?"

"Sometimes I have thought that you have lied to me."

Uniacke's heart grew heavier at the words.

In the morning Sir Graham said to him, with a curious calmness:

"I think perhaps you are right, Uniacke. I have been considering your words, your advice."

THE BLACK SPANIEL & OTHER STRANGE STORIES

"And you will take it?" Uniacke said, with a sudden enormous sense of gratefulness.

"I think I shall."

"Think—Sir Graham!"

"I'll decide to-night. I must have the day to consider. But—yes, you are right. That—that horrible appearance. I suppose it must be evoked by the trickery of my own brain."

"Undoubtedly."

"There can be no other reason for it?"

"None—none."

"Then—then, yes, I had better go from here. But you will come with me?"

"To London?"

"Anywhere—it does not matter."

He looked round him wistfully.

"If I am to leave the island," he said sorrowfully, "it does not matter where I go."

"To London then," Uniacke said, almost joyously. "I will make my arrangements."

"To-morrow?"

"To-morrow. Yes. Excuse me for the present. I must run over to the mainland to settle about the Sunday services. I shall be back in a few hours."

He went out, feeling as if a weight had been lifted from brain and heart. So good could come out of evil. Had he not done right to lie? He began to believe that he had. As he crossed to the mainland he wrapped himself in warm and comfortable sophistries. The wickedness of subterfuge vanished now that subterfuge was found to be successful in attaining a desired end. For that which is successful seldom appears wholly evil. To-day Uniacke glowed in the fires of his sinfulness.

He transacted his business on the mainland and set out on his return home, driving through the shallow sea in a high cart. The day, which had opened in sunshine, was now become grey, very still and depressing. An intense and brooding silence reigned, broken by the splashing of the horse's hoofs in the scarcely ruffled water, and by the occasional peevish cackle of a gull hovering, on purposeless wings, between the waters and the mists. The low island lay in the dull distance ahead, wan and deprecatory of aspect, like a thing desiring to be left alone in the morose embrace of solitude. Uniacke, gazing towards it out of the midst of the sea, longed ardently for the morrow when Sir Graham would be caught away from this pale land of terror. He no longer blamed himself for what he had done. Conscience was asleep. He exulted, and had a strange feeling that God smiled on him with approval of his sin.

As he reached the island, the grey pall slightly lifted and light broke through the mist. He came up out of the sea, and, whipping the wet and weary horse, drove along the narrow lanes towards the Rectory. But when he came within hail of the churchyard all his abnormal exultation was suddenly quenched, and the oppressive sense of threatening danger which had for so long a time persecuted him, returned with painful force. He saw ahead of him Sir Graham seated before his easel painting. Behind the artist, bending down, his eyes fixed intently on the canvas, his huge hands gripping one another across his chest, stood the mad Skipper. As the wheels of the cart ground the rough road by the churchyard wall, Sir Graham looked up and smiled.

"I'm doing a last day's work," he called.

Uniacke stopped the cart and jumped out. The Skipper never moved. His eyes never left the canvas. He seemed utterly absorbed.

"You are not working on the picture?" said Uniacke hastily.

"No."

"Thank God."

"Why d'you say that?"

"I—the subject was so horrible."

"This is only a study. I shall leave the picture as I am leaving the Island. Perhaps someday—" He paused. Then he said: "I call this 'Sea Change.' Go indoors. In about half an hour I will come and fetch you to see it. Where will you be?"

"In my little room at the back of the house. I have some letters to write."

"I'll come there. Don't disturb me, till then. I think the picture will be strange—and I hope beautiful."

And again he smiled. Reassured, Uniacke made his way into the Rectory. He sat down at his writing table, took up his pen and wrote a few words of a letter. But his mind wandered. The pen dropped on the table and he fell into thought. It was strangely still weather, and there was a strange stillness in his heart and conscience, a calm that was sweet to him. He felt the relief of coming to an end after a journey that had not been without dangers. For, during his intercourse with Sir Graham, he had often walked upon the edge of tragedy. Now he no longer looked down from that precipice. He leaned his arm on the table, among the litter of papers connected with parish affairs, and rested his head in his hand. Almost unconsciously, at that moment he began to rejoice at his own boldness in deviating from the strict path of uncompromising rectitude. For he thought of it as boldness, and of his former unyielding adherence to the principles he believed to be right, as timidity. After all, he said to himself, it is easy to be too rigid, too strict. In all human dealings we must consider not only ourselves, but also the individuals with whom we have to do. Have we the right to injure them by our determination to take care of the welfare of our own souls? It seemed to him just then as if virtue was often merely selfishness and implied a lack of sympathy with others. He might have refused to lie and destroyed his friend. Would not that have been selfishness? Would not that have been sheer cowardice? He told himself that it would.

Calm flowed upon him. He was lost in the daydream of the complacent man whose load of care has fallen away into the abyss from which he has fortunately escaped. The silence of the Island was intense to-day. His conscience slept with the winds. And the sea slept too with all its sorrow. He sat there like a carven figure with his face in his hand. And, by degrees, he ceased to feel, to think actively. Conscious, not asleep, with open eyes he remained in a placid attitude, lulled in the arms of a quiet happiness.

He was distracted at length by some sound at a distance. It broke through his daydream. At first he could not tell what it was, but presently he became aware that a hoarse voice was ejaculating some word outside, probably in the churchyard. He took his hand from his face, sat up straight by the writing table and began to listen, at first with some slight irritation. For he had been happy in his daydream. The voice outside repeated the word. Uniacke thought of the street cries of London to which he was going, and that this cry was like one of them. He heard it again. Now it was nearer. Short and sharp, it sounded both angry and—something else—what? Dolorous, he fancied, keen with a horror of wonder and of despair. He remembered where he was, and that he had never before heard such a cry on the Island. But he still sat by the table. He was listening intently, trying to hear what was the word the voice kept perpetually calling.

"Jack! Jack!"

Uniacke sprang up, pushing back his chair violently. It caught in a rug that lay on the bare wooden floor and fell with a crash to the ground.

"Jack! Jack!"

The word came to his ears now in a sort of strident howl that was hardly human. He began to tremble. But still he did not recognise the voice.

"Jack!"

It was cried under the window of the parlour, fiercely, frantically. Uniacke knew the voice for the mad Skipper's. He delayed no longer, but hastened to the front room and stared out across the churchyard.

The Skipper, with his huge hands uplifted, his fingers working as if they strove to strangle something invisible in the air, was stumbling among the graves. His face was red and convulsed with excitement.

"Jack!" he shouted hoarsely, "Jack!"

And he went on desperately towards the sea, pursuing—nothing.

Uniacke looked away from him towards the place where Sir Graham had been painting. The easel stood there with the canvas resting upon the wooden pins. On the ground before it was huddled a dark thing.

Uniacke went out from his house. Although he did not know it he walked very slowly as if he dragged a weight. His feet trod upon the graves. As he walked he could hear the hoarse shout of the skipper dying away in the distance towards the sea.

"Jack!"

The voice faded as he gained the churchyard wall.

The dark thing huddled at the foot of the easel was the painter's dead body. On his discoloured throat there were the marks of fingers. Mechanically, Uniacke turned his eyes from those purple and red marks to the picture the dead man had been painting. He saw the figure of a boy in a seaman's jersey and long sea-boots dripping with water. The face of the boy was pale and swollen. The mouth hung down hideously. The hair was matted with moisture. Only the eyes were beautiful, for they looked upward with a rapt and childlike expression.

"He sees the rainbow!" murmured the clergyman.

And he fell forward against the churchyard wall with his face buried in his arms. The voice of the grey sea was very loud in his ears. Darkness seemed to close in on him. He had done evil to do good, and the evil he had done had been in vain. His heart beat hard, and seemed to be in his throat choking him. And in the darkness he saw a vision of a dirty child, dressed in rags and a tall paper cap, and pointing upwards.

And he heard a voice, that sounded far off and unearthly, say:

"Look at that there rainbow! Look at that there rainbow!"

He wondered, as a man wonders in a dream, whether the dead painter heard the voice too, but more clearly—and elsewhere.

THE END

Robert Hichens Bibliography
(1864-1950)

Novels

The Coast Guard's Secret (1886)
The Green Carnation (published
  anonymously, 1894; republished as
  by Hitchens, 1948)
An Imaginative Man (1895)
Flames (1897)
The Londoners (1898)
The Daughters of Babylon (1899;
  with Wilson Barrett)
The Slave (1899)
The Prophet of Berkeley Square
  (1901)
Felix (1902)
The Garden of Allah (1904)
The Woman With the Fan (1904)
Call of the Blood (1905)
Barbary Sheep (1907)
A Spirit in Prison (1908)
Bella Donna (1909; reprinted as
  Temptation, 1946)
The Dweller on the Threshold (1911)
The Fruitful Vine (1911)
The Way of Ambition (1913)
In the Wilderness (1917)
Mrs. Marden (1919)
The Spirit of the Time (1921)
December Love (1922)
After The Verdict (1924)
The Unearthly (1925; UK as *The
  God Within Him*)
The Bacchante and the Nun (1926;
  US as *The Bacchante*)
The First Lady Brendon (1927)
Dr. Artz (1928)
On the Screen (1929)
The Bracelet (1930)
The Gates of Paradise (1930)
The First Lady Brendon (1931)
Mortimer Brice (1932)
The Paradine Case (1933)
The Power to Kill (1934)
Susie's Career (1935)
The Pyramid (1936)

The Sixth of October (1936)
Daniel Airlie (1937)
Secret Information (1938)
The Journey Up (1938)
That Which Is Hidden (1939)
The Million (1940)
Married or Unmarried (1941)
A New Way of Life (1941)
Veils (1943)
Young Mrs. Brand (1944)
Harps in the Wind (1945; U.S. as *The
  Woman in the House*)
Incognito (1945; Hutchinson)
Too Much Love of Living (1947)
Beneath the Magic (1950; U.S. as
  Strange Lady)
The Mask (1951)
Night Bound (1951)

Collections

After To-Morrow, and the New Love
  (1895)
The Folly of Eustace and Other
  Stories (1896)
Bye-Ways (1897)
Tongues of Conscience (1898, 1900)
The Black Spaniel and Other Stories
  (1905)
Snake-Bite and Other Stories (1919)
The Last Time (1924)
The Streets and Other Stories (1928)
The Gates of Paradise and Other
  Stories (1930)
My Desert Friend and Other Stories
  (1931)
The Gardenia, and Other Stories
  (1934)
The Afterglow and Other Stories
  (1935)
The Man in the Mirror and Other
  Stories (1950)
The Return of the Soul and Other
  Stories (2001; ed. S. T. Joshi)

Nonfiction
Old Cairo (1908; article)
Egypt and Its Monuments (1908)
The Holy Land (1910)
The Spell of Egypt (1910; orig.
  published as *Egypt and Its
  Monuments*, 1908)
The Near East (1913)
Yesterday (1947)

Plays
The Medicine Man (1898; with H. D.
  Traill)
Becky Sharp (1901; with C. G.
  Lennox; U.S. title: *Vanity Fair*)
The Real Woman (1909)
The Garden of Allah (1911; with
  Mary Anderson)
The Law of the Sands (1916)
Black Magic (1917)
Press the Button! (1918)
The Voice from the Minaret (1919)

Filmography [based on the novel
  unless otherwise noted]

Bella Donna (directed by Edwin S.
  Porter and Hugh Ford;1915)
The Garden of Allah (directed by
  Colin Campbell; 1916)
Barbary Sheep (directed by Maurice
  Tourneur; 1917)
Flames (directed by Maurice Elvey;
  UK, 1917)
The Slave (directed by Arrigo Bocchi;
  UK, 1918)

Hidden Lives (directed by Maurits
  Binger and B. E. Doxat-Pratt;
  Netherlands, 1920, based on a
  play by Robert Hichens and John
  Knittel)
The Call of the Blood (directed by
  Louis Mercanton; France, 1920)
The Woman with the Fan (directed
  by René Plaissetty; UK, 1921)
The Fruitful Vine (directed by
  Maurice Elvey; UK, 1921)
The Voice from the Minaret (directed
  by Frank Lloyd; 1923, based on
  the play)
Bella Donna (directed by George
  Fitzmaurice; 1923)
The Lady Who Lied (directed by
  Edwin Carewe; 1925, based on the
  story)
The Garden of Allah (directed by
  Rex Ingram; 1927)
After the Verdict (directed by Henrik
  Galeen; UK, 1929)
Bella Donna (directed by Robert
  Milton; UK, 1934)
The Garden of Allah (directed by
  Richard Boleslawski; 1936)
Temptation (directed by Irving
  Pichel; 1946, based on the novel
  Bella Donna)
The Paradine Case (directed by
  Alfred Hitchcock; 1947)
Call of the Blood (directed by John
  Clements and Ladislao Vajda; UK,
  1948)

Made in the USA
Middletown, DE
03 November 2023